"Tholian vessel, this is Captain Ro Laren of starbase Deep Space 9."

Ro circled the sit table and mounted the steps closest to the command chair. On the outer ring, she sat down and focused on the overhead display facing her. "Your presence in this system is a violation of sovereign Federation territory and could be considered an act of war. If you do not deactivate your weapons and lower your shields at once, we will have no choice but to open fire on you."

After a beat, Viss said, "Still no response."

"They *are* responding," Slaine said. "They've increased speed to full impulse and are heading directly for the station."

"Fire phasers, two banks," Ro ordered without hesitation. "Target their forward shields."

Slaine's hands darted across the tactical console, and Blackmer heard the auditory signals—like the squawks of a hydraulic pump, he'd always thought—that accompanied the actual triggering of the weapons. On his own panel, the security chief watched on a display as the red-tinged golden streaks found their mark. "Direct hits," Slaine said. "They're still coming. No change in course."

Blackmer saw a pair of energy spikes on the Tholian interloper. "They're returning fire," he said. On one of his screens, twin lightning-white beams leaped from the bow of the juggernaut. An instant later, Blackmer's panel erupted in a profusion of data, detailing the phaser strikes on Deep Space 9.

STAR TREK®
THE FALL

REVELATION AND DUST

DAVID R. GEORGE III

Based upon *Star Trek* and
Star Trek: The Next Generation®
created by Gene Roddenberry
and
Star Trek: Deep Space Nine®
created by Rick Berman & Michael Piller

POCKET BOOKS
New York London Toronto Sydney New Delhi Shavalla

Pocket Books
A Division of Simon & Schuster, Inc.
1230 Avenue of the Americas
New York, NY 10020

This book is a work of fiction. Any references to historical events, real people, or real places are used fictitiously. Other names, characters, places, and events are products of the author's imagination, and any resemblance to actual events or places or persons, living or dead, is entirely coincidental.

First Pocket Books paperback edition September 2013

POCKET and colophon are registered trademarks of Simon & Schuster, Inc.

For information about special discounts for bulk purchases, please contact Simon & Schuster Special Sales at 1-866-506-1949 or business@simonandschuster.com.

The Simon & Schuster Speakers Bureau can bring authors to your live event. For more information or to book an event, contact the Simon & Schuster Speakers Bureau at 1-866-248-3049 or visit our website at www.simonspeakers.com.

Manufactured in the United States of America

10 9 8 7 6 5 4 3 2

ISBN 978-1-4767-2217-7
ISBN 978-1-4767-2230-6 (ebook)

Historian's Note

The primary events in this tale take place two years after the destruction of Deep Space 9 by rogue forces of the Typhon Pact (in the *Star Trek: Typhon Pact* novels *Plagues of Night* and *Raise the Dawn*). The main story begins on 22 August 2385 CE, just prior to the dedication of the new DS9, and ends on 1 September 2385 CE.

And all of us sail the seas of our lives,
Each guiding the tiller by our own hand,
Sometimes slipping far into unknown climes,
Leaving us on some darkling shore to land.

We live as we can in that foreign realm,
We hide as needed, or settle, or roam,
Riding time's currents, struggling to helm
Our years, always seeking a return home.

When finally we find the course to brave,
We set out on turbulent ocean flows,
Staring down each trough, cresting every wave,
Yet still we remain adrift in shadows.

—Akorem Laan,
Revelation and Dust, "The Path to Ascendance"

Prologue

The Darkling Shore

She flew through the air, anticipating the hard impact of her body against the unforgiving deck.

Only moments before, Vedek Kira Nerys had pointed the bow of the purloined runabout she piloted toward a Romulan warbird trespassing within the Celestial Temple. When Kira first entered the wormhole, the alien starship had been engaged against a Starfleet vessel, the *Galaxy*-class *U.S.S. Robinson*, commanded by Captain Benjamin Sisko—the Emissary of the Prophets. Beyond the two ships, a great red wound gaped in the wall of the Celestial Temple, a misshapen circular rupture through which another wormhole attached. Peering into the ragged-edged lesion, Kira experienced a *pagh'tem' far*—a sacred vision—after which the vedek knew what she must do.

At once, Kira had turned her runabout, *Rubicon*, into a projectile, aiming it at the Romulan starship in a bid both to aid the Emissary and his crew, and to safeguard the very realm of the Prophets. As she raced for the rear of the runabout's main compartment to take cover, the bow of her smaller vessel tore through the long neck that connected the forward, beaked hull of the warbird to the ship's main body. Amid the din of the collision and the unnatural sounds of rending metal, Kira pitched to her hands and knees, her head snapping back painfully. As she steadied herself and gazed through *Rubicon*'s lateral viewports, she saw the tremendous damage that the runabout had wrought to the warbird, severing the forward section from the rest of the starship. At the same time, she witnessed *Robinson* freed from its confrontation and dashing toward the Alpha Quadrant terminus of the wormhole.

The cockpit had turned cold as its internal heat and atmosphere rushed out through a breach in the runabout's hull. Kira looked toward the bow to see how badly *Rubicon* had been compromised. Instead, she saw Elias Vaughn.

Or perhaps she'd seen merely a simulacrum of her friend and former first officer, or perhaps she'd only imagined him aboard the runabout. Certainly the figure she saw—or thought she saw—did not resemble the man she'd visited earlier that day at a hospice on Bajor. After suffering a traumatic brain injury during the Borg invasion two and a half years prior, Vaughn had never regained consciousness, surviving only by means of various life-sustaining medical equipment. His daughter, Prynn Tenmei, had over time ordered all but his feeding and hydration tubes removed, and then, within the previous few weeks, she'd directed that even those be disconnected.

When Kira had seen Vaughn before appropriating *Rubicon*, his frail body had seemed destined for an imminent death, a fate long ago experienced by his mind. What remained of Vaughn bore only the barest likeness to the hale man Kira had once known. The tall, strapping officer, with his head of thick salt-and-pepper hair and matching mustache and beard, had given way to an emaciated, balding ghost.

Aboard *Rubicon*, though, Vaughn had appeared reinvigorated. He stood over Kira no longer withered and dying but looking as he had when first he'd arrived on

Deep Space 9—on the erstwhile Terok Nor, the Cardassian monstrosity of an ore-processing facility that Starfleet had taken over and run as a dedicated space station, but which had lately come to the end of its days, much like Vaughn himself. Or so Kira had thought.

"How did you get here, Elias?" she had asked, although she'd barely heard her words over the squall of air discharging out into space. Kira thought to ask more than that—she wanted to know how Vaughn had grown healthy again, and why he'd suddenly appeared aboard *Rubicon*—but before she could, he moved toward her. Without answering her question or even uttering a word, he reached forward and hoisted Kira into his arms, cradling her in a way that made her think he intended to carry her away, as though he could simply exit the runabout and bear her through space to safety, an act that seemed manifestly impossible. Vaughn took no steps, though; rather, he bent at the knees, twisted his torso, then unwound himself, whirling around and tossing Kira into the air.

The vedek faced upward as she sailed across the compartment, the lighting panels in the overhead passing before her eyes. She waited to crash to the deck. Expecting to strike it hard, she attempted to brace herself for the impact.

But then Kira landed on her back, and although the force knocked the air from her lungs, she knew that she had not come down inside *Rubicon*. The surface beneath her felt firm but offered more give than the inflexible metal of a runabout deck. Further, where the air about her had only a moment before gusted noisily in the cabin as it blustered through a break in the hull, it had all at once settled into an eerie stillness.

Even as Kira gasped in great gulps of air, she worked to

push herself up. She bent at the waist, propping herself up on her hands. She wanted to examine her surroundings, but a brilliant white light suddenly rose all about her, with no apparent source. She squinted against it, but it continued to intensify, effectively blinding her.

It occurred to Kira that perhaps the loss of the runabout's atmosphere had brought on hypoxia and an altering of her perceptions. Perhaps she'd hallucinated Vaughn's presence aboard *Rubicon*. She might even have lost consciousness, her awareness and observations relegated to the netherworld of her dreams. Or maybe her potentially lethal circumstances had led her to experience a near-death delirium.

Or maybe I'm actually *dying,* Kira thought. *Or already dead.*

Kira felt no fear at the thought, but melancholy washed over her for the potential loss of a life she hadn't finished living. She had spent so much of her existence—a quarter of a century—captive to the brutal yoke of Cardassian occupation, fighting daily, year upon year, to liberate her people. When that had finally happened, she'd gone to Deep Space 9 for nearly a decade, first as the station's executive officer and then as its commander, vigorously protecting Bajor's newfound freedom. It had been only in the five and a half years that followed that Kira had finally been able to find her way forward past the violence that had so permeated her life in both thought and deed.

Just a little more than a month ahead, her fortieth birthday beckoned—an objectively meaningless marker, she knew, a mere arithmetic trifle, but she nevertheless regarded it as a milestone. For most of Kira's life, she'd assumed that she wouldn't reach forty, and so she thought that it would serve as an indicator of the progress she'd made and the peace she'd found within herself. She viewed the date both as a measure of her emotional and spiritual growth, and as a way station along her journey of devotional service. It had taken only three years for Kira to progress through the ranks of the Bajoran clergy up to the position of vedek, but she understood that she still had much to learn—about herself, about her people, and about their shared creed. Though she had already traveled far on her personal and religious trek, she envisioned the road ahead of her widening and climbing to greater heights. More than anything, she wanted to continue walking the path that the Prophets had laid out for her.

The Prophets, Kira thought. She squinted into the gleaming light, striving to make out any detail but seeing nothing at all. Her breathing had eased back almost to its normal pace, and so she felt the need to take action, but she still could not discern anything about her surroundings.

It doesn't matter, she avowed, employing the force of her will to beat back her despondency, and turning to her faith as a source of strength. *I was in the Celestial Temple,* Kira thought, reminding herself that she had flown *Rubicon* into the wormhole. *I must still be within its confines.*

The bright light evoked memories of the two times in Kira's life when she had communed with the Prophets. During her convalescence from the terrible injuries she'd suffered at the hands of Taran'atar, her mind had soared into the Celestial Temple. There, the Prophets designated her Their hand, explaining—in Their abstruse way—that she must take action on Their behalf with respect to the Eav'oq and the Ascendants. The Prophets later reinforced that message when Kira ended up falling into the wormhole alongside Iliana Ghemor and the Cardassian spy's alternate-universe counterpart, the three of them floating through space, bereft of either ship or space suit.

Ultimately, Kira *had* acted, although it seemed to her that others—Benjamin, the Eav'oq named Itu, the Ascendant Raiq, even Taran'atar—had achieved so much more than she. Several times since those events had played out, Kira had wondered whether she'd truly fulfilled the Prophets' designs for her. It pained her to consider that she might have disappointed Them, but she took solace in knowing that she had honestly tried her best; given the outcome of the Ascendants situation, perhaps she had accomplished precisely what They had wanted of her. No matter the measure of her performance in those matters, though, Kira never in any way doubted the Prophets.

About Kira, the brightness of the light still left her unable to see. She closed her eyes and focused on her location within the Celestial Temple. She trusted the Prophets wholly, and she would readily accept whatever new path They wished her to follow.

A sense of calm filled Kira, and almost as though her emotions controlled it, the light shining on her eyelids dimmed. She waited several seconds, wanting to ensure that it did not brighten again. Finally, she opened her eyes.

A night sky extended across Kira's field of vision like no other she had ever seen. A panoply of stars adorned the heavens almost as densely as the grains of sand on a beach. Even out in the countryside, away from the light pollution of cities, even out in space, removed from the dulling effects of an atmosphere, she had never beheld such a rich stellar tapestry.

As she gazed up at the magnificent starscape, Kira became aware of a gritty coolness beneath her hands. She peered down to see that she sat atop a patch of simple earth, made visible by the faint glow of starlight. She dug her fingers into the ground, then brought her hand up to her face to see granules of dirt.

Kira reached down and pushed herself up. When she did, she saw that the land appeared to fall away not too far ahead of her. She walked forward, and the horizon quickly drew near. Kira expected to look down on a valley or canyon, but instead she stood on the edge of space. Beyond the end of the terrain, she glimpsed the great sweep of stars stretching down as far as she could see.

The view caused Kira to swoon. She quickly took two steps back and waited for the sensation to pass. Once it did, she dropped to her hands and knees and crawled forward, until she could see straight down past the rim of the land. The ground plummeted vertically away from her in striated runs of earth, and beyond, more stars shined back at her. Kira perched not on a planet, she realized, but more like on a surface section of a world that had somehow been scooped up and set adrift in space—yet managed to maintain an atmosphere and gravity.

Kira backed away from the edge, stood up, and turned to survey the rest of her surroundings. A coarse, rocky plain marched away from her, with sheer cliffs rising up on either side. Above, the sparkling sea of stars disappeared from view behind a roiling mass of unbroken gray clouds. Flashes of lightning illuminated the scene in staccato bursts.

Several hundred paces ahead, a wide chasm split the land, extending from one ridged rock face to the other. Unlike with the drop-off into space behind her, though, Kira could see more territory beyond the canyon. What lay on the other side could not have provided more of a contrast to the stark reality of Kira's immediate environs.

Across the chasm, clear blue skies replaced the churning cloud cover. A rolling, sun-bathed grassland put Kira in mind of Alavanu Green, the largest park in Bajor's capital city of Ashalla. Trees of various shapes and sizes dotted the landscape, interspersed with low-lying foliage. Flowers of assorted hues lent color to the verdant setting.

Kira stared across the dichotomous vista, trying to fathom what it meant. She did not entirely believe in the physical reality of what she saw, but she also suspected that even if it existed only in her mind, she would still have to interact with it. She simply did not understand how.

Once more as though summoned by her thoughts, a change occurred to the scene before her. On the far side of the canyon, a sparkling hourglass shape appeared. It hovered just above the grass, spinning slowly in place and emitting an otherworldly green-white glow. The vedek recognized it immediately as an Orb of the Prophets.

Just the sight of the hallowed artifact delighted Kira. She wondered about its identity and whether or not it was one of the nine extant such objects known to the Bajoran people. Even the possibility of a new Orb thrilled the vedek.

I have to go to it, Kira thought. *I have to learn what it has to tell me.*

Just before departing Bajor aboard *Rubicon,* she had consulted the Orb of Destiny at the Vanadwan Monastery. She had not completely understood the experience—nobody ever did—but it had left her with a new awareness and the knowledge of what she next needed to do. It only made sense that she should approach the Orb that had appeared before her in order to learn whatever information or intuition it could impart to her.

Kira started forward. She didn't know how she would

cross the canyon that separated her from the parkland opposite and the Orb that hovered just above it, but she continued onward. She believed that if the Prophets meant her to reach the Orb, she would find a way.

Above Kira, the dark clouds flared with lightning, rinsing the rocky ground and the steep cliff walls in a silvery, spectral radiance. The land quaked beneath her feet. She hastened her step.

Suddenly, the land to Kira's left fractured in jagged streaks. Intense white light emerged from the fissures and shot up to the swirling sky. The vedek veered right, but then the ground there broke open. More brilliant rays burst upward. Kira adjusted her course, hoping to thread herself between the newly formed crevices, but then they came together in front of her. She quickly turned so that she could backtrack and wend her away around the shattered terrain, but she found herself surrounded by it.

Kira spun again to look toward the chasm. She considered attempting to leap the ruptures and through the light, but before she could, the earth jolted again, knocking her from her feet. She landed once more on her back. Around Kira, the fissures widened and lengthened, the eruptions of white light sewing together and enveloping her in their unfeeling luster.

At first, her body seemed to float, but then she lost all sense of her position, location, and even orientation. By degrees, Kira became aware of her own heartbeat, slow and steady, like the rhythmic pounding of a drum. She listened to it, concentrated on it, then raised a hand to cover her eyes. She flexed her fingers in the whiteout, trying to evaluate the quality of her sensations.

Abruptly, a series of images sped across her mind: a recumbent woman; a figure catching a white ball in a leather mitt; a second woman, wearing a red headdress; and a Borg. It took a moment for Kira's thoughts to catch up to her visualizations, but then she realized that she knew all the faces she saw, even as she grasped that the people represented something beyond themselves: the Prophets. Kira opened her mouth to speak with Them, but before she could say anything at all, she heard somebody ask a question, seemingly from somewhere nearby.

"Who are you?"

Kira gathered that the query had not been meant for her. As though in response, another quartet of likenesses rose in her mind: a man kissing a woman, a newborn baby, a teenage boy, and then another woman. Kira could still hear the pulse of her own heart.

"Who are you?" the voice asked again, louder and more insistent.

Kira lowered her hand from before her face to discover that the all-encompassing white light had retreated. To her surprise, she no longer lay on a splintering fragment of land, but stood on a sun-drenched beach of golden sand, the waves of a dark-blue ocean rolling onshore. A woman—the first person whose image had played across Kira's consciousness—rested on a blanket and gazed up at a man who stood above her. The vedek knew him at once.

It was Benjamin Sisko.

Revelation

One

Captain Ro Laren waited uneasily atop a bluff that overlooked the rolling parkland below. She glanced down at the lush vista, at the walking paths that rose and fell throughout, at the stands of trees and arrays of colorful flowers. A gentle breeze wisped past, carrying with it fresh scents, including the crisp hint of water.

Ro peered down briefly at the small lake off to her right, then cast her gaze in the opposite direction. Atop the highest point in sight, Prynn Tenmei stepped toward the edge of a promontory. The lieutenant wore not her Starfleet uniform, but a formfitting lavender flight suit that contrasted dramatically with her porcelain complexion. Her jet hair—which, though not long, typically rose in wild kinks from her scalp—had been pulled back and gathered into a small bun.

Anxiety mounted in Ro as she watched Tenmei. The lieutenant stood ramrod straight, her arms tucked behind her back. With a quick motion, Tenmei suddenly took one more pace forward, to the brink of the stony outcropping, and then flung herself headlong into the open air.

Tenmei fell in a graceful arc, but at a rate noticeably slower than normal. Even so, she descended fast enough to injure herself—seriously, even fatally—if she struck the ground. Ro knew that couldn't happen, that local sensors would detect an impending accident and trigger an automatic transport to safety, but she still tensed watching Tenmei plunge toward the park.

Seconds seemed to elongate, and the captain consciously stopped herself from clenching her hands into fists as Tenmei drew uncomfortably close to the ground. When the lieutenant reached a height of perhaps ten meters— surely close to the sensors' safety limit—Ro expected her to vanish in a blur of white transporter light. At that instant, though, Tenmei thrust her arms out to her sides and waved them downward. The gossamer wings she wore swelled as they caught the air. Her descent slowed, and when she flapped her arms once, twice, her course curved upward. She banked to one side and described a fluid turn, fluttering her wings to gain altitude.

The susurrus of distant applause reached Ro. Satisfied that Tenmei controlled her flight, the captain looked away from *Defiant*'s primary conn officer and about the park. Around the tree-lined base of the half-dome–shaped enclosure, and interspersed along the footpaths and up and down the knolls, hundreds of her crew had congregated. Although still five days away from the station's formal dedication and its transition to full operational status, Ro had made the decision to conduct a small celebration ahead of time, exclusively for the complement of the new Deep Space 9.

A grand amalgam of engineering and nature, of technology and beauty, the park occupied an arc of the station's primary section, a central sphere. In addition to its use as a place for the crew's recreation, it served as a functioning part of DS9's life-support systems. Soil and stone and flora had been imported from Bajor to create the undulating, grass-covered hills, with rocky elevations rising up along about a quarter of the perimeter. Above, a simulated blue sky crowned the locale, although as the internal environment of the station progressed into the nighttime portion of its virtual twenty-six-hour day, the holographic morning and subsequent afternoon would fade, and the stars would become visible through the transparent hull overhead. The park had been intentionally positioned away from the three perpendicularly intersecting rings that encircled DS9's main sphere, thereby affording evening visitors to the picturesque setting an unimpeded view of the nocturnal sky.

Ro wondered what that view would look like if the wormhole ever sprung back to life. The station had been oriented in such a way that the spectacle would be visible from the park. It had been nearly two years, though, since the events that had collapsed the wormhole, and although the official Bajoran position maintained that the Celestial Temple endured and would one day reappear, Federation scientists had so far been unable to detect any indication of its continued existence. The captain also knew that the design and construction of DS9 allowed for the capability to move the station safely from the Denorios Belt to the orbit of Bajor, should that become politically acceptable to the first minister and her people.

Lieutenant Tenmei completed three circuits above the park, occasionally flapping her wings as she glided easily through the elevated, low-gravity envelope that facilitated her flight. Finally, she alit opposite the location from where she'd begun, setting down in one of four designated landing zones, where the field of reduced gravity situated above the park reached all the way to the ground. Once more, a round of applause went up.

The captain saw several crew members approach

Tenmei, while others disbursed throughout the park. The lieutenant's flight—the first on the station, outside of testing—concluded the brief ceremony, which Ro had begun with a few words via her communicator to those assembled. She'd congratulated and thanked them for all their efforts during the previous twenty-three months. After the destruction of the original Deep Space 9, most of the surviving crew had stayed on, some on Bajor, some on the various starships that had patrolled the system, and some alternating between the two. Starfleet had quickly renovated an abandoned planetside transportation center, converting it into a place dubbed Bajoran Space Central, which helped substitute for some of DS9's lost services while awaiting completion of the new station. Other services had required the use of orbital tenders, while still others had been undertaken by the crews of several Starfleet vessels.

In Ro's remarks, she had chosen not to mention those who had perished with the first Deep Space 9. When rogue elements of the Typhon Pact—along with an Andorian Starfleet officer dispirited both by his people's ongoing reproductive crisis and by their secession from the United Federation of Planets—had attacked and demolished the station, eleven hundred UFP citizens had died, a majority of them Starfleet personnel, and *all* of them Ro's responsibility. The captain had not forgotten any of that, nor did she think she ever could, but in addressing her crew that morning, she'd wanted to focus on the positive as the Corps of Engineers released the final section of the new DS9—its park—for use. She intended to repeat her comments thirteen hours later, at the other end of the day, to ensure that, no matter the shift on which they served, every member of her crew—nearly twenty-five hundred strong on the massive station—would have the opportunity to attend. Ro also planned to host a memorial for her crew on the day before the dedication. Moreover, she would honor the fallen at the dedication ceremony, and felt sure that she would not be the only one of the speakers to do so.

"Impressive," said one of the two people standing beside Ro. The captain turned toward Rakena Garan, castellan of the Cardassian Union. The woman owned a delicate figure, not much taller than a meter and a half, but she bore her status as the elected leader of her people with power and intensity.

Although noteworthy for Ro to be in the presence of an important political leader, it pleased the captain that it no longer discomfited her to stand beside a Cardassian. It had been more than a decade and a half since the end of the Occupation, and nearly three years since the Union had joined the Federation, the Klingon Empire, and the Ferengi Alliance in the Khitomer Accords, and it seemed as though the old hatreds had begun to fade, perhaps even replaced with a ration of forgiveness. It also helped that for the previous two years, a member of the Cardassian Guard, Zivan Slaine, had served as a member of Ro's crew, and that she had done so admirably well. Holding the Guard's rank of *dalin*, roughly equivalent to a lieutenant commander in Starfleet, Slaine served DS9 as a tactical officer.

"That was indeed impressive," agreed Asarem Wadeen, the first minister of Bajor. "I've always wanted to fly." Although only a dozen or so centimeters taller than the castellan, Asarem had a toned, almost muscular physique, and so seemed even more imposing than her Cardassian counterpart. Like Garan, the first minister exuded charisma, a quality that, if not a definite prerequisite for elective office, Ro figured must certainly prove useful for politicians pursuing leadership posts. Though the captain stood taller than both women and had earned her own position of authority, she held no illusions about their relative bearings; Ro commanded the loyalty and respect of her crew, but that hardly equated to having hundreds of millions of people willfully select her as their head of state.

"If you'd like," Ro told Asarem, "it wouldn't take long for the replicator to fit you for a pair of wings."

Asarem lifted her eyebrows in an expression of interest, but then glanced over her shoulder. Ro followed her gaze. Past Asarem's chief of staff, a woman named Enkar Sirsy, and Garan's aide, a man named Onar Throk, two sets of attentive, stone-faced men and women—one pair Cardassian, the other Bajoran—stood like coiled springs, tensed and ready to leap forward. *If there's one thing that all sentient species have in common,* Ro thought, *it's the steely look of their security personnel.*

"I don't think my protective detail would appreciate me leaping from high places into midair," Asarem said, "no matter what tricks you play with gravity."

"I'm sure you're right," Ro said. "Should we continue your tour of the station, then?"

Both the first minister and the castellan agreed, and Ro led them down the gentle slope leading from the bluff. The aides and the security detachments fell in around them, both clusters of personnel already aware of the day's schedule. The group reached the tree line, which masked the bulkhead enclosing the park at "ground" level. A pair of large, thick metal doors opened at their approach, revealing the corridor beyond—a corridor that, although wider and taller, put Ro in mind of those aboard the starships on which she'd served. She appreciated DS9's spacious, brightly illuminated passages, which she considered substantial upgrades over those of its Cardassian-constructed predecessor, with their narrow, low-ceilinged dimensions and murky lighting. Where the previous station had reflected the oppressive sensibilities of its slavedriving builders, lending the entire facility a claustrophobic air, the new structure had clearly been designed as a comfortable place for people to live, work, and visit.

Ro crossed to a turbolift, its doors parting in front of her. Two of the security officers, one Bajoran and one Cardassian, entered the cab ahead of First Minister Asarem, Castellan Garan, their aides, and Captain Ro, and the other two escorts trailed the group inside. As with the corridors on the new station, the lifts improved upon those they replaced: well lighted, very roomy, and quiet. Ro specified their destination, and the cab immediately began to descend.

"The station looks very different from the last time I saw it," said Asarem. "It's amazing how much work has been done since then." The first minister had previously visited Deep Space 9 a year into its construction, by which time the installation of its first two fusion reactors had rendered almost half of its interior habitable, and after some members of Ro's crew had relocated there; the captain herself had divided her time between DS9 and Bajoran Space Central.

In the intervening eleven months, while Chief O'Brien and Lieutenant Commander Nog led the Starfleet Corps of Engineers in completing the station, Ro and her staff had begun familiarizing themselves with their new home. Eventually, even as construction continued, they initiated partial operations, mostly as a staging area for the routing of aid and other goods to Cardassia. The DS9 crew also started processing some imports and exports to and from Bajor, as well as handling some travelers headed for the planet. All that work and more continued to be supplemented by the efforts of the personnel at Bajoran Space Central and aboard the remaining Starfleet vessels—*Defiant* and *Robinson*—assigned to patrol the system. Upon becoming fully operational, the station crew would undertake all of those duties in their entirety, as well as assuming increased freight and passenger services, not just for Bajor, but for the greater region.

Deep Space 9 would also function as a full-fledged starbase. It would provide maintenance, repair, and support for starships in the sector and beyond, and its advanced scientific and medical laboratories would help sustain research. Starfleet Command also intended to utilize the station as a platform from which to stage exploratory missions out beyond the Bajoran system. Despite the absence of the wormhole and the corresponding lack of ready access to the Gamma Quadrant, Bajor still floated on the outer reaches of known space. With respect to matériel, Starfleet had almost completely recovered from the Borg invasion four and a half years earlier. Although the ranks of the Federation's space service had been depleted of legions of experienced officers, five Academy classes had graduated since then, and the number of fresh recruits continued to swell. With new allies in the Cardassian Union and the Ferengi Alliance, and with two years of relative peace among the nations of the Khitomer Accords and the Typhon Pact, Starfleet had recently renewed its commitment to voyages of discovery. It pleased Ro to know that her Deep Space 9 crew would constitute a major supporting component of those efforts.

"It also seems considerably larger than any Cardassian stations I've been to," Garan noted.

"At the moment, it's the largest deep-space starbase Starfleet has ever built," Ro confirmed, revealing nothing not observable to anybody with even a rudimentary knowledge of Starfleet's remote stations, which surely the castellan possessed. "At normal capacity, we can support a total population of thirteen thousand, not including the crews and passengers present on any ships docked at the station."

"How many vessels can you accommodate at one time?" Asarem asked.

"Each of the station's rings is composed primarily of docking facilities, cargo holds, and repair bays," Ro said. "Depending on the size of the ships, we can directly support dozens at a time." Again, she related only obvious information. The captain did not mention the sensor arrays, shield generators, or weapons ports also housed in the rings, though DS9's sphere also boasted defensive and offensive systems. The starbase, she knew, had been conceived not only to replace and improve upon its antecedent in terms of its basic functions, but also to stand as a veritable fortress in the Bajoran system.

"Even though a number of the crew have been here for almost a year," Ro added, "we're still getting to know the station." Those efforts had grown increasingly hectic of late, since the Starfleet Corps of Engineers had finished the starbase an entire month ahead of schedule. Among other repercussions of that early delivery, the dedication ceremony had been moved up to coincide with the two-year anniversary of the original DS9's destruction.

I have to remember to thank and *dress down Chief O'Brien for that,* Ro thought archly. After the loss of the first DS9, the engineer had been transferred to the Bajoran system to lead the design and construction of its replacement. Going forward, he would serve as the station's chief engineer, with Lieutenant Commander Nog as his right hand.

The turbolift slowed to a halt, and its doors opened to reveal another large compartment, though not quite so considerable as the station's park. Ro led the group out of the cab, into a large atrium, one of four evenly laid out around that level. Public benches lined the space, and artwork of varying origin decorated the bulkheads. In the center of the area stood a black pyramidal base, above which hung a translucent holographic image of Deep Space 9, projected in three dimensions. Ro crossed the atrium toward the outer surface of the sphere.

"Welcome to the Plaza," she said, spreading her arms wide to take in the broad, three-story-tall concourses that stretched away from the atrium to the left and right, hugging the curvature of the hull. Along the outer side, a transparent bulkhead bowed out around the Plaza and the residential deck below, offering views not only of surrounding space, but also of DS9's x-axis ring, which swept past in a horizontal arc. Ro saw two ships moored there: the *Galor*-class Cardassian starship—*Trager*—that had brought the castellan to the station, and the much smaller transport that had ferried the first minister from Bajor.

The captain also spied a runabout towing a work platform. She could not see the name on the ship's hull, but the registration number, NCC-77543, identified it as *Glyrhond*, one of a score of the auxiliary craft assigned to the station. A trio of figures in space suits occupied the platform, their tools flashing as they labored over equipment clearly extracted from an open hatch on the top of the ring. Ro knew that the active defense monitors had detected a failing power junction in one of the shield emitters, and that Chief O'Brien had sent out a repair team to replace it. In the meantime, a secondary emitter had been shunted into use with the primary system.

"This is the station?" Garan said—more statement than question—as she walked over to the spherical hologram. "I didn't have the opportunity to see it from the outside when we arrived."

"This is it," Ro said, striding back toward the castellan, with the first minister joining them. The captain regarded the representation of DS9. The first of the new Frontier-class starbases, it contained enough details—the curves and proportions of its individual elements, its gray-white hull, the lettering and symbols that embellished it—to mark it as a Starfleet facility. Several instances of the space service's skewed-chevron emblem emblazoned the *x*-ring, each occurrence marking the intersections with the vertical rings. The words Deep Space 9 read down the upper arcs of the *y*-ring on either side of the sphere, as did United Federation of Planets on the upper arcs of the *z*-ring. The placement of the identification reflected the gravitational orientation of the station's interior.

"And this is where we are," Ro continued. She reached to the top of the pyramidal base and pressed a control surface marked by a red circle enclosing a crosshair. In the hologram, an outer section of the station began to glow red just above its equator. Ro tapped the highlighted area and it expanded outward, revealing the atrium in which they stood. The replica of the space also included representations of their entire group: the first minister, the castellan, their aides and security officers, and Ro herself.

The captain touched the projection again and it shrank

back into its place in the diagram. Then she activated another control and said, "Show the entire Plaza." On the map of DS9, a bright red curve illuminated, extending out from the atrium and wrapping all the way around the circumference of the sphere. Ro tapped a fingertip to extract the indicated area from the station and magnify it, revealing it in greater detail. "We have an eclectic mix of establishments here to support our population—civilian and Starfleet—as well as visitors and transients. There are restaurants, cafés, taverns, game rooms, sports fields, a library, computer and communications facilities . . . a large number of different venues." Again, she pressed a control. "Show the names of the different sites on the Plaza, using Bajoran and Cardassian labels." Small informational tags appeared in the hologram and hovered over the various storefronts. Ro saw that she'd neglected to mention a number of them, including the Bajoran temple and a non-denominational place of worship, the valuation and auction house, the theater, and a music and dance hall.

"You are a veritable city in space," Garan said.

"We have to be," Ro said. "While Bajor isn't far, it still requires a journey to get there. As a Federation starbase, we need to be self-contained—not just for the sake of our crew and residents, but for all the visitors who'll pass through here."

Asarem looked away from the hologram and toward the outer ring of the Plaza. Ro peered in that direction as well and saw only a handful of people about, most of them clad in Starfleet uniforms. "For a city," the first minister said, "you don't seem very crowded."

"We've recently reduced the amount of traffic to the station so that we can better prepare for the dedication ceremony and our elevation to full operational status,"

Ro explained. The captain and her crew needed to ensure both the safety and the comfort of the numerous dignitaries who would attend the upcoming event. Invited guests included Federation President Nanietta Bacco, the leaders of allied nations—Klingon Chancellor Martok, Ferengi Grand Nagus Rom, in addition to Castellan Garan—as well as those of *prospective* allies—Gorn Imperator Sozzerozs and Romulan Praetor Gell Kamemor. "We've also restricted movement along the route of your tour today."

Ro had been informed that Garan would arrive at DS9 several days ahead of the ceremony so that she could meet one-on-one with the first minister. Although the Bajorans had been providing aid to the battered people of Cardassia almost since the very end of the Dominion War, and although Bajor, as a member of the United Federation of Planets, found itself a de jure ally of the Cardassian Union within the framework of the Khitomer Accords, the relationship between the two governments and the two populations remained essentially at a remove. Even with nearly a decade of peace between them, enmity still existed on both worlds. The captain didn't know with certainty the motives of the castellan and first minister in meeting with each other, but their plans called for two days of talks on DS9, then two more on Bajor, before Asarem and Garan returned to the station for the dedication. The castellan's visit to Bajor would mark the first time that a Cardassian head of state visited the planet during peacetime.

"I'd be interested to see Deep Space Nine when it's busy," Garan said. "I'm sure it will have a very . . . interstellar . . . flavor to it."

"It absolutely will," Ro said. "And that'll become more and more apparent over the next few days, but if you want to see the Plaza then, you'll have to convince your security teams." Ro peered over at the Bajoran and Cardassian officers charged with protecting the two leaders. "Before then, though, we can continue on," Ro said, gesturing toward the wide concourse that led away from the atrium.

As Asarem and Garan voiced their desire to see more of the station, Ro heard the turbolift doors whisper open, and she looked over to see Colonel Cenn Desca emerge onto the Plaza. He immediately made eye contact with Ro as he approached the group. "Please excuse the interruption, Captain," Cenn said, "but you wanted to be informed when Lieutenant Commander Blackmer was ready to execute his drills." With the imminent arrival of additional dignitaries and the inauguration of the station to full operation, DS9's chief of security had crafted a comprehensive plan for him and his staff to rigorously test their integrated security systems. Ro wanted to observe those drills herself.

"Yes, thank you," the captain told Cenn. Turning to Asarem and Garan, she said, "I'm afraid my duties require my presence elsewhere."

"Of course, Captain," Asarem said.

"Completely understandable, considering the circumstances," Garan said.

Ro held a hand out toward Cenn. "This is Colonel Cenn Desca, my first officer and the Bajoran liaison to the station," she said. Asarem knew Ro's exec, but Garan didn't. "I will leave you in his capable hands."

Asarem and Garan thanked the captain, and Ro headed for the turbolift. As its doors closed, she said, "The Hub." The command complex of Deep Space 9 had been dubbed *operations,* or simply *ops,* by its designers, but because of its disc shape and its location at the upper intersection of the two vertical rings, the crew at some point had begun calling it *the Hub*. Eventually, Ro had ordered the turbolifts programmed to accept the added nomenclature.

As the lift glided down and then forward, Ro thought about what lay ahead. She strongly hoped that the security testing proved out, since the crew would have only five days in which to correct any shortcomings. The captain trusted the expertise of Blackmer and his staff, and the last year had demonstrated the high quality of the Corps of Engineers' work in constructing the new DS9. That construction had only just been fully realized, though, and so the possibility of uncovering flaws remained. The station had been planned and built as a stronghold, but like any fortification, it would prove only as strong as its weakest defect. Fortunately, the assessments the crew had performed to that point, along with their partial operation of the station over the previous year, had revealed only minor problems, reparable with relative ease and, in any event, not compromising the safety of those aboard. For those reasons, the captain felt confident about hosting the dedication ceremony for so many important leaders.

Later, though, after everything that happened, Ro would think back to that moment in the turbolift, back to all the successful testing subsequently accomplished by Blackmer and his staff, and she would realize that it had already been too late: by the time she left First Minister Asarem and Castellan Garan with Colonel Cenn on the Plaza, Deep Space 9's security had already been breached.

Two

The beating of Kira's heart drummed unrelentingly in her ears. She stood awkwardly on the beach, her footing on the sand uneven, her presence there disconcerting. She peered from where the Emissary stood in a swimsuit and a sleeveless pullover shirt to the woman lying on a purple blanket. The woman's straight, dark hair hung down to the tops of her shoulder blades, and she wore a two-piece bathing suit that exposed much of her caramel-colored skin. Kira recognized her, partly from having seen photographs of her in Benjamin's quarters aboard Deep Space 9, but also from some inner sense that corroborated her identity: Jennifer Sisko. It didn't matter that Benjamin's first wife had died more than fifteen years earlier aboard the starship on which he served, a casualty of an attack by the Borg. It didn't matter because even though the image of the woman belonged to Jennifer, her substance did not; she was a Prophet.

"It is corporeal," Jennifer said. "A physical entity."

"What?" Benjamin said, visibly puzzled. The captain did not seem to embody a Prophet, but only himself. He stared directly ahead, as though he saw neither Jennifer nor Kira—nor even the beach itself. "What did you say?"

Benjamin's apparent confusion left Kira herself uncertain. When she had first entered the Celestial Temple years earlier, she had encountered the Emissary—or at least some fragment of him that still existed with the Prophets—but his questions at the current moment belied that interpretation of the man she saw before her. Nor did it seem as though she stood on the beach with the Ben Sisko who had resided for a time in the Celestial Temple and then returned to Bajor.

Unsure of what she could conclude about the version of the Emissary she saw, Kira studied him. She noticed that he did not wear the casual beach attire she'd first seen him in, but a Starfleet uniform, and in the next moment, she realized that they no longer stood on a long stretch of oceanfront sand, but in a conference room aboard a Federation starship. Kira staggered, then caught herself. She focused on her new environs, which no longer included Jennifer. Instead, she watched Captain Jean-Luc Picard—no doubt a representation employed by another Prophet—pace in front of Benjamin and come to a stop. "It is responding to visual and auditory stimuli," Picard said. "Linguistic communication."

"Yes, linguistic communication," Benjamin said, his eyes tracking with the *Enterprise* captain, evidently at last aware of his own surroundings. "Are you capable of communicating with me?"

What? Kira thought. *But Benjamin has spoken with the Prophets. He is Their Emissary.* Kira wondered if perhaps he did not recognize Them in Their human guises.

A hand reached between the two men and up to Benjamin's cheek, where it gently guided his head so that he looked in another direction. Kira turned her head as well and somehow peered not at another part of the *Enterprise* conference room, but into a section of a Bajoran monastery. The unexpected change in location once more caused a wave of dizziness to spill over her, but she fought to maintain her balance, and she quickly righted herself.

The guiding hand, Kira saw, belonged to Opaka Sulan. It seemed perfectly appropriate for a Prophet to assume the likeness of the Bajoran spiritual leader, a former kai and a woman whom Kira revered. Captain Picard had gone, leaving only the Emissary and the kai facing each other. Numerous candles flickered around the tableau, sending patterns of orange light wavering across Opaka's sallow features and Benjamin's rich brown flesh.

"What . . . are you?" the kai asked. The question made no sense to Kira. The Prophets *knew* Benjamin, had *selected* him as Their Emissary, had *ensured* his birth so that he could fulfill that role. Surely They must know his origin.

"My species is known as human," Benjamin said. "I come from a planet called Earth."

"Earth?" asked another Prophet in the form of Benjamin's son, Jake. The boy—for the Jake Sisko before Kira had yet to grow into a man—sat in a pastoral setting, above a pond, his legs dangling from the edge of a covered plank bridge. Kira had anticipated more transitions to new locations, and so the latest felt less jarring to her. She could still hear the pulse of her heart.

"This is what my planet looks like," Benjamin said, sitting beside Jake with his back to one of the bridge's support posts. Opaka had gone; apparently only Kira and Benjamin conveyed from one scene to the next. "You and I are very different species. It will take time for us to understand one another."

The exchange continued to perplex Kira. She opened her mouth to speak with Benjamin, as she had the first time she'd visited the Celestial Temple, but then she realized that he did not wear the current uniform of

Starfleet—gray shoulders on a black shirt—but an older pattern, with red shoulders. She also saw only three rank pips at his neck rather than four, distinguishing him not as a captain but as a commander. It all seemed consistent with Jake's recaptured youth.

And does Benjamin also look younger? Kira asked herself. She hadn't thought so, perhaps because his close-cropped hair and clean-shaven face matched his appearance when she'd most recently seen him just fifteen days earlier. As she studied his aspect, though, she discerned that he hadn't yet accrued all the years since last he'd worn a red-shouldered uniform.

Kira looked down and took stock of her own apparel. She expected to find herself in old Bajoran Militia regalia, but instead did not see a uniform at all—not anything she'd worn while serving in the Militia or in Starfleet—or even the vestments of a vedek, but simple civilian clothing. She wore brown slacks and a textured crimson blouse, with a yellowish-green knit vest—precisely the outfit she'd dressed in that morning, although the memory of that time seemed very distant.

"What is this . . . time?" Jake asked. He could have been responding to Kira's thoughts, but he still peered at Benjamin, who had just said that it would take time for him and the Prophets to understand each other. Clearly the Prophet did not question the word but rather the concept. However Kira perceived the dialogue unspooling before her, the reality of the interaction between Benjamin and the Prophets must be transpiring on a deeper level.

And what about *time?* Kira thought. According to the Emissary, the Prophets did not live a linear existence. They had no past and no future, only a present that encompassed the totality of Their lives. They transcended time.

But if Their past and future are one and the same as Their present, Kira pondered, *then how can They not know the Emissary? How could there ever have been a time when They didn't know him?*

Kira didn't understand, but that didn't trouble her. She accepted her incomprehension with equanimity. Throughout her life, she'd read the sacred texts, but she hadn't always gleaned their meaning. She'd consulted the Orbs of the Prophets and had been swept away by the visions that they sometimes imparted to her, but almost always without her divining just how those experiences related to her own life. Even in the face of not knowing, though, Kira's faith in the Prophets sustained her.

The vedek noticed Benjamin wearing a bewildered expression. She didn't know if she could communicate with him—she didn't even know if he could see her, and if he could, whether he recognized her for herself—but she decided again to try. Before she could say a word, though, Benjamin jerked his head around to one side. When Kira looked where he did, she saw Captain Picard in the *Enterprise* conference room again.

"The creature must be destroyed before it destroys us," Picard said, urgency clearly driving his words. Kira trusted in the Prophets, but it did not sound right to her ear for Them to refer to Benjamin as a *creature*, much less for Them to assert that he should be destroyed, or that he would—or even *could*—destroy Them. It occurred to her that the Pah-wraiths might be attempting to deceive her, but she dismissed the idea: Kira knew, she could *feel*, the presence of the Prophets.

Again without warning, the location shifted. On the crowded bridge of a starship—*U.S.S. Saratoga*, Kira somehow knew—she beheld on the main viewscreen the image of Jean-Luc Picard transformed into a Borg drone. *"It is malevolent,"* announced the altered captain, continuing to sound the Prophets' alarm against Benjamin.

On a baseball diamond, players uniformed in white prepared to play. One man stood at home plate and swung a wooden bat at a pitched ball. "Aggressive," he declared. "Adversarial."

Back on *Enterprise*, in the conference room, Captain Picard said, "It must be destroyed."

"I am not your enemy," Benjamin contended. "I was sent here by the people *you* contacted."

Picard circled around Benjamin. "Contacted?"

"With your devices. Your Orbs." The Bajoran faith held that the Orbs provided indirect physical links to the Prophets.

"We seek contact with other life-forms," said Picard, "not corporeal creatures who annihilate us." The fearful words gave Kira pause.

"I have not come to annihilate anyone," Benjamin insisted.

On the main viewscreen on the *Saratoga* bridge, the Borg-modified Picard said, *"Destroy it now."*

From among the crew, Benjamin walked out from behind a freestanding control console and into the center of the compartment. "My species respects life above all else," he said, addressing the Borg-altered Picard on the main screen. "Can you say the same?" When he received no reply, he turned and regarded the other personnel on the bridge. "I do not understand the threat I bring to you—"

Neither do I, Kira thought.

"—but I am not your enemy," Benjamin finished. *Saratoga*'s Vulcan captain—another Prophet—looked to the other officers, but their attention remained on Benjamin. "Allow me to prove it."

"Prove it?" asked Opaka in the monastery.

"It can be argued that a human is ultimately the sum of his experiences," Benjamin told the kai.

"Experiences?" asked Jake from where he sat on the covered bridge that crossed the pond. "What is this?"

"Memories," Benjamin said. "Events from my past, like this one." He gestured to take in the setting.

"Past?" Jake asked.

"Things that happened before now," Benjamin said. Jake responded with only a look of bafflement. "You have absolutely no idea what I'm talking about."

"What comes before now is no different than what is now, or what is to come," averred Jake. "It is one's existence."

"Then for you," Benjamin reckoned, "there is no linear time."

Walking along the beach beside Benjamin, Jennifer asked, "Linear time . . . what is this?"

"My species lives in one point in time," Benjamin said, "and once we move beyond that point, it becomes the past. The future, all that is still to come, does not exist yet for us."

"Does not exist yet?" Jennifer asked.

"That is the nature of our linear existence," Benjamin asserted, "and if you examine it more closely, you will see that you do not need to fear me."

Look at who I've been, at what I've done, and You'll see who I will *be, the types of actions I* will *take,* Kira thought, following Benjamin's reasoning, though she could not fathom why he would need to make such an argument to the Prophets. *He is Their Emissary,* she thought. *Why would They—*

And then Kira understood. She didn't know the true location of her body, whether she actually moved from place to place with each apparent change of scene, or whether she physically remained in the Celestial Temple and only her mind traveled. Nor did she know whether all that she saw and heard simply comprised images and sounds playing across her consciousness, but regardless, she realized that what she observed had already occurred fourteen years earlier. *I'm seeing the first meeting of the Emissary with the Prophets,* she thought, feeling a deep reverence. *I'm witnessing history.*

All at once, Kira stood in a field of wild grass, surrounded by trees and hills, with children playing in the distance. Dressed in olive-drab pants and a vertically striped shirt of muted purple and green and yellow and red, Benjamin lay on a blanket with his long-dead first wife.

"Jennifer," she said, motioning to herself as though making a discovery. She wore a salmon-colored dress that sent a wide strap across her left shoulder.

Benjamin examined their new locale and rose to a sitting position. Jennifer sat up as well. "Yes, that was her name," he confirmed.

"She is part of your existence."

"She is part of my past," Benjamin clarified. "She's no longer alive." Kira believed that the statement must have been difficult for him to speak aloud, no matter how much time had passed since her death.

"But she is part of your existence," Jennifer persisted.

"She *was* a most important part of my existence, but I lost her some time ago."

"Lost?" Jennifer asked. "What is this?"

"In a linear existence," Benjamin told her, "we can't go back to the past to get something we left behind, so . . . it's lost." The reality that the word described plainly impacted him. Kira empathized with his pain. While she had never suffered the death of a spouse, she had lost lovers, as well as many family members and friends who had very much formed important parts of *her* existence.

"It is inconceivable that any species could exist in such a manner," Jennifer said, the expression on her face exposing her aversion to such a notion. A moment later, though, her eyes widened in sudden understanding: "You are deceiving us."

"No," Sisko said. "This is the truth. This day, this . . . this park . . . it was almost . . . fifteen years ago—far in the past. It was a day that was very important to me . . . a day that shaped every day that followed. That is the essence of a linear existence. Each day affects the next." Benjamin appeared satisfied with his explanation, but also as though he had never himself considered the nature of humanoid life in exactly that way. Kira had never done so either.

Not far away, children ran through the grass, their voices joining with the chirps of birds to fill the air like the music of a summer's day. Benjamin and Jennifer peered in that direction, and when Kira also looked, it surprised her to see another incarnation of the couple lying on a blanket in the park, wearing the same clothes and seeming for all the world like the same people. When the vedek glanced back, she saw the first Benjamin and Jennifer watching their doppelgängers.

Kira's heart still beat loudly in her ears as a strange sensation flowed over her. She felt somehow doubled in her own person, as though time had wrinkled and trapped different versions of her in its folds. She glanced around, expecting to espy another manifestation of herself, but she spotted none.

"Listen to it," the second Benjamin said, sitting up on the blanket.

"To what?" the second Jennifer asked with a smile as she also pushed herself up.

The second Benjamin lifted his hand and covered the eyes of the second Jennifer. "The sound of children playing," he said. As he lowered his hand, he asked, "What could be more beautiful?"

"So you like children?" Consistent with Benjamin's comment about that day taking place fifteen years prior, it seemed to Kira that the conversation developing before her antedated the couple's marriage, if not their entire romantic relationship.

"That almost sounds like a domestic inquiry," the second Benjamin said lightly.

The second Jennifer shrugged a shoulder. "I've heard that Starfleet officers don't want families because they complicate their lives."

"Starfleet officers don't often find mates who want to raise families on a starship," the second Benjamin replied.

"*That* almost sounds like a domestic inquiry," said the second Jennifer mischievously.

"I think it was."

A memory, Kira thought. *One of Benjamin's memories.* Within the historical event she beheld nestled another, older event, a story within a story. To Kira, the moment felt rife with possibilities—as it surely must have to the original participants. The couple leaned in toward each other until their lips met. They each raised a hand to caress the other's cheek.

Kira looked back toward the first Benjamin and Jennifer to see them still watching their doubles. The tension visible in Benjamin's face—his rutted brow, clenched jaw, and trembling lower lip—laid bare his anguish. Kira's friend and former commanding officer had rarely spoken to her of his first wife, but clearly the pain of losing her had run deep within him.

Beside Benjamin, the Prophet manifesting as Jennifer raised a hand to her lips and deliberately kissed the tips of her fingers. The sensation seemed to startle her, and she turned to Benjamin with a quizzical mien. It took him a moment to respond.

"As corporeal entities," he explained, "humans find physical touch to cause pleasure." Despite his words, he continued to look tortured.

"Pleasure?" Jennifer asked. "What is this?" One detail after another, the Prophets wanted to know about worldly beings, about what it meant to have a body.

"Good feelings," Benjamin said quietly. "Happiness." And yet he appeared anything but happy.

"But this—" said another voice, one Kira did not recognize, and before the speaker completed his sentence, Benjamin turned to look at him. When he did, the venue slipped once more, from the calm and open park, bathed in sunlight and fresh air, to a frenzied and enclosed corridor, dense with shadows and smoke. People ran, some wearing Starfleet uniforms, some not. A red alert klaxon blared out its pulsating call above the cacophony of raised voices. The air tasted acrid. Amid the turmoil, Benjamin, once again in uniform, walked slowly forward beside a Bolian officer Kira had previously seen on the *Saratoga* bridge. "—is your existence," the man concluded.

"It's difficult to be here," Benjamin said, his tone

quiet, his manner defeated. "More difficult than any other memory."

These are *Benjamin's memories,* Kira realized. She traversed not through the real world nor through time, nor even through some mental construct created for her benefit, but through the recollections of the Emissary. She did not know the how or why of the process, or the propriety of it—it seemed to Kira like a violation of Benjamin's privacy—but she believed that the Prophets had brought her there, and she had confidence in Their reasons and Their moral justifications for what took place.

"Why?" the Bolian lieutenant asked Benjamin, wanting to know why he found that particular memory the most difficult of all. The two men walked past damaged equipment, jets of escaping gas, loose and hanging cables. Around them, Kira saw disheveled and wounded men and women. Benjamin plodded down the corridor past all of them, seeming to take almost no notice of the chaos around him.

"Because . . ." Benjamin began. He walked as though in a trance. "Because this was the day . . ." He arrived at a door set into the side of the corridor, propped partially open. Smoke billowed out of the cabin beyond, which flickered with the hot orange glow of fire. ". . . that I lost Jennifer." Benjamin stared into the cabin but made no attempt to enter it. Farther down the corridor, Kira saw other individuals watching him—*Prophets observing Their Emissary,* she thought.

"I don't want to be here," Benjamin proclaimed. He turned and paced away from the door, but then he stopped, as though anticipating something. Past him, the corridor erupted in a rolling ball of flame. Inside it, a figure appeared: Jennifer Sisko, incongruously clad in her two-piece bathing suit. She emerged from the blaze and walked up to Benjamin.

"Then why do you exist here?" she asked him.

Confusion replaced the heartache showing on Benjamin's face. "I don't understand."

"You exist *here*," Jennifer reiterated.

Benjamin looked at her, clearly struggling to comprehend what she said. He glanced over his shoulder at the half-open door, then back at Jennifer. Suddenly, a great white light rose in the corridor. It grew in intensity until it engulfed her, until it overwhelmed the surroundings, leaving Benjamin and Kira standing alone in a field of emptiness. He did not appear to see her.

"What's wrong?" he asked. "What's happening?" He stared ahead into the luminous void.

Kira's stomach lurched as the weight of her body abruptly abandoned her. She floated in space as the white light faded, replaced by the shining blue streamers of energy that flowed through the Celestial Temple. She wore no environmental suit but did not suffer for it. She felt small in the great subspace tunnel, dwarfed by the radiant structures she'd seen so many times from the safety of a runabout or a starship.

The vedek did not see Benjamin. She looked about in search of him and spotted an indistinguishable shape in the distance. As she attempted to identify it, it quickly grew into a massive form, resolving into a Cardassian warship. Kira gaped at the vessel as it soared past her. She watched it continue along the wormhole until a circular maw swirled into existence ahead of it, revealing a spread of distant stars. Kira immediately recognized a constellation in the Gamma Quadrant.

The Cardassian ship surged out of the Celestial Temple. Instantly, the contours of the wormhole collapsed, pulling in on themselves until they flashed in a brilliant spark—and then nothing. Back in the immeasurable, empty whiteness, Kira once more saw Benjamin, though he still did not seem to see her.

"Are you still there?" he asked, sounding concerned. "What just happened?"

Back on the beach, Jennifer Sisko walked alongside Benjamin. "More of your kind," she told him.

"Another ship?" Benjamin asked. "In the wormhole?"

"Wormhole?" Jennifer asked, and followed with a familiar refrain: "What is this?"

"It is how we describe the passage that brought me here," Benjamin said.

In the *Enterprise* conference room, Captain Picard declared, "It is terminated."

"Terminated?" said Benjamin.

"Our existence is disrupted whenever one of you enters the passage," Picard said. The declaration would have concerned Kira had she not known that the Prophets would subsequently alter the Celestial Temple to allow the benign transit of starships through it.

On the *Saratoga* bridge, a dark-haired female officer rose from her seat at the conn. "Your linear nature is inherently destructive," she said.

Another dark-haired woman, shorter, with Asian features, stood from her position at the operations station. "You have no regard for the consequences of your actions."

"That's not true," Benjamin protested. Kira saw that behind him, on the main viewscreen, the Borg-enhanced figure of Captain Picard looked on. "We're aware that every choice we make has a consequence."

The Vulcan captain bounded up from the command chair and strode to the middle of the bridge. "But you claim you do not know what it will be."

"We don't," Benjamin admitted.

"Then how can you take responsibility for your actions?" Jake asked from where he sat above the pond, a fishing pole in his hands.

"We use past experience to help guide us," Benjamin said. "For Jennifer and me, all the experiences in our lives prepared us for the day we met on the beach, helped us recognize that we had a future together. When we married, we accepted all the consequences of that act, whatever they might be, including the consequences of you."

"Me?"

"My son, Jake," Benjamin said.

Jennifer peered up from where she lay atop a bio-bed in Starfleet's Potrero Hill Medical Center on Earth—a facility Kira didn't think she'd ever even heard of, but that she nevertheless recognized. On one side of the bed, a nurse gathered readings with a tricorder, while on the other, Benjamin held a newborn baby swaddled in a blanket: Jake. "The child with Jennifer," said the Prophet posing as Benjamin's first wife.

"Yes," Benjamin said.

"Linear . . . procreation?" Jennifer asked.

"Yes," Benjamin said. "Jake is the continuation of our family."

"'The sound of children playing,'" Jennifer quoted Benjamin, as though making an intellectual connection.

On the baseball field, the man at home plate again swung his bat; he missed the ball, which stuck in the catcher's mitt with a smack. "Aggressive," the batter said, just as he had earlier. "Adversarial." His words seemed to Kira more a comment on his own physical actions, as though drawing a clear distinction between the nature of corporeal beings and that of the Prophets. The vedek couldn't disagree, but she worried about the tone of the terms used.

Benjamin stood in the middle of the diamond, on a raised circle of dirt—the pitcher's mound, she recalled—surrounded by grass. Though he wore his old Starfleet uniform, a black cap with a white letter *G* topped his head. "Competition, for fun," he said with a wide smile that Kira had seen many times before—particularly in the holosuites, when he'd played or watched games at similar fields. She didn't much care for the sport—or really even understand it—but she could not deny its ability to transport Benjamin. "It's a game that Jake and I play on the holodeck," he said. "It's called baseball."

Jake removed the padded catcher's mask he wore and stepped forward past the batter. Behind the chain-link fence of the backstop, other players turned to follow the conversation. Like them, Jake wore a white athletic uniform, though protective gear also wrapped his shins and torso. "Baseball," he said. "What is this?"

"I was afraid you'd ask that," Benjamin said. Kira agreed. Although she had eventually learned the rules of the sport, she had never really understood it.

The Emissary plucked a baseball out of a standing wire basket and held it up for Jake and the batter to see. "I throw this ball to you," he said, walking from the mound toward Jake, "and this other player—" He pointed at the batter. "—stands between us with a bat . . . a stick . . . and he . . . and he tries to hit the ball in between these two white lines." Benjamin stopped before home plate and gestured at the foul lines. Jake and the batter gazed at where he pointed, then stared back at him questioningly. "Oh," Benjamin said, perhaps realizing the futility of attempting to explain baseball to the Prophets. "The rules aren't important," he went on. "What's important is—" He seemed to experience a moment of inspiration. He tossed the ball up before him and then snatched it triumphantly out of the air. "—it's linear. Every time I throw this ball, a hundred different things can happen in a game. He might swing and miss. He might hit it. The point is, you never know. You try to anticipate, set a strategy for all the possibilities as best you can, but in the end it comes down to throwing one pitch after another and seeing what happens. With each new consequence, the game begins to take shape."

"And you have no idea what that shape is until it is completed," the batter said, evidently following the metaphor.

"That's right," Benjamin said. "In fact, the game wouldn't be worth playing if we knew what was going to happen."

"You value your ignorance of what is to come?" Jake asked, incredulous.

"That may be the most important thing to understand about humans," Benjamin said. "It is the unknown that defines our existence. We are constantly searching, not just for answers to our questions, but for new questions. We are explorers. We explore our lives, day by day, and we explore the galaxy, trying to expand the boundaries of our knowledge. And *that* is why I am here: not to conquer you with weapons or with ideas, but to coexist and learn." The description of humanoid curiosity sounded to Kira both eloquent and compelling.

"If all you say is true," said the Bolian Starfleet officer, "then why do you exist here?" He crouched amid the wreckage of a smoke-filled cabin, the shrieking call to battle stations and the crash of weapons fire against the hull punctuating the scene. Across from him, on his hands and knees, Benjamin quickly took it all in, awareness dawning on his face. Kira saw with dismay that the inert body of Jennifer Sisko lay between the men, trapped beneath fallen metal girders and other debris.

Benjamin hurriedly backed away, scuttling from under a collapsed beam until he could stand up. Kira could read the horror in his desperate movements, could see the torment in his expression. She had always understood that the loss of his first wife had overwhelmed Benjamin, but she had never truly considered the depth of his despair. Benjamin had been so busy commanding Deep Space 9, and he had spoken so little about the death of Jake's mother . . . and then he'd met Kasidy . . .

And I counseled him against marrying Kas, Kira thought, distraught at the memory. When the Prophets had told Benjamin that if he spent his life with her, he would know nothing but sorrow, Kira had told him that he shouldn't go against the word of the Prophets, and that he was doing the right thing in choosing *not* to wed Kasidy. Even though their eventual marriage had been followed by numerous terrible events, the advice Kira had given disturbed her. *Who was I to speak for the Prophets?* she asked herself. *Who was I to infringe on a chance for the Emissary to lead a happy life?*

Like Kasidy and Jake, like his friends and former crewmates, like the people of Bajor, Kira had celebrated the Emissary's return from the Celestial Temple for the birth of his daughter, Rebecca, but a series of troubling events had followed. The massacre at the village of Sidau had distressed Benjamin, and that mass killing had ultimately led to the confrontation with the Ascendants, led by the deranged Iliana Ghemor. The awful episode on Endalla had taxed Benjamin, but there had also been a number of incidents that impacted him even more personally: the deaths of two close friends in a house fire; the abduction of Rebecca; the loss of nineteen of his crew when he captained *U.S.S. New York* during the Borg invasion; the irrecoverable and finally fatal brain injury suffered by Elias Vaughn; the death of his father; his separation from his wife and daughter; and the destruction of Deep Space 9. Kira didn't understand how all of it fit together, or what she could or should have done differently to help mitigate either individual circumstances or the overall situation. She could not credit the idea that the Prophets had caused the many struggles that Benjamin had endured, but she did not doubt that They had foreseen them.

Kira regarded her friend, standing in mute devastation across the cabin from where his first wife had just perished. And then, with no observable transition, Benjamin crouched again beneath the fallen beam, looking down at the lifeless form of Jennifer. He immediately rushed backward again, as though retreating from a ticking bomb.

"What is the point of bringing me back again to *this*?" he yelled, not masking either his pain or his anger.

"We do not bring you here," said Jake, no longer sitting on the bridge above the pond, but standing in the cabin aboard *Saratoga*, across from Benjamin. Beside him stood Jennifer, dressed as she had been in the park, and even as she lay dead on the deck.

"*You* bring *us* here," she said.

"You exist here," said the Bolian officer, whose name

and position—Hranok Zar, tactical officer—arose in Kira's mind, though she should not have known either piece of information. Zar spoke in a way that made it sound as though he believed his statement not merely accurate, but a truism.

"Then give me the power to lead you somewhere else," Benjamin fired back, moving toward the trio. "*Anywhere else.*"

To Benjamin's right, in front of a pillar of flame, Opaka spoke up. "We cannot give you what you deny yourself," she said. "Look for solutions within, Commander."

Benjamin stopped and looked at Opaka. Kira waited, wondering what the Prophets wanted of him—and what They wanted of *her*. *Why are They showing all of this to me?*

Benjamin looked down at his wife's corpse, then back to Opaka. "I was ready to die with her," he offered quietly.

"Die?" Zar asked, and then, almost predictably, added, "What is this?"

The living Jennifer Sisko stepped forward. "The termination of their linear existence," she said. She walked over to Benjamin and regarded him with an expression that seemed born of both wonder and pity. She raised a hand to his cheek and gently pressed her fingers and palm against his face.

Weapons fire rocked the starship, and the living Jennifer looked down at the still body of Benjamin's wife. "We've got to go now, sir," called another version of Zar—not a Prophet, Kira understood, but a character replaying one of the Emissary's memories.

Beside the body of Jennifer Sisko, Lieutenant Zar threw his hands beneath another iteration of Benjamin and hauled him backward. "We can't just leave her here," yelled Benjamin in his unfolding memory. His words devolved into agonized cries as Zar pulled him across the cabin and out into the corridor.

Benjamin watched himself as he had been on *Saratoga* during that battle against a Borg ship, then slowly turned back toward the Prophet animating the other version of Jennifer. "I never left this ship," he told her, and Kira's heart broke. She knew what it meant to live with death, with loss, holding on to the grief and anger and regret, not moving forward. During her life in the Resistance, she'd learned to channel her emotions, to funnel her rage at the occupiers of her world, the enslavers of her people. It had taken many more years than that, though, and a great deal of effort for her to fully deal with those emotions and put them to rest. After his tragic loss, Benjamin had gone on raising his son, but clearly, by the time he'd arrived in the Bajoran system, he still hadn't understood and processed what he felt.

"You exist here," the living Jennifer told him.

Benjamin's facial muscles tensed. He stared back at the Prophet who wore the form of the woman he had loved and lost. "I . . . exist here," he said, slowly and painfully admitting what he had obviously never confessed to himself.

After a moment, Benjamin made his way past Opaka, through the wrecked cabin, back to the pile of rubble, and kneeled beside his dead wife. The living Jennifer followed and sat down behind him. "I don't know if you can understand," he told the Prophet. "I see her like this." He began to weep. "Every time I close my eyes. In the darkness . . . in the blink of an eye . . . I see her like this."

"None of your past experiences helped prepare you for this consequence," said the living Jennifer.

"And I have never figured out how to live without her," Benjamin said.

"So you choose to exist here," the living Jennifer said. "It is not linear."

"No," Benjamin said, his face contorted by misery. Tears spilled from his eyes. "It is not linear." He began to sob uncontrollably. Kira's temples throbbed, and her vision wavered as her own eyes filled. She lamented not only Benjamin's loss, but his having to relive it so vividly.

Still crying, he looked over at Opaka. She peered back at him without saying anything, the wisdom in her countenance more than a passing re-creation of that possessed by the real Opaka. The former kai returned Benjamin's look as though willing him to find his own answers.

Benjamin then gazed over at Jake, who nodded slowly in response. He too seemed to encourage the Emissary. The gesture seemed very much like a son telling a father that the time had come to move on, to return to living, even if that meant letting go of the son's mother and the father's wife—letting go of the painful memories of Jennifer, shedding the harrowing emotions still invested in her loss.

Still crying, Benjamin nodded back at Jake, indicating that he understood what next must happen. Benjamin physically deflated, falling on the deck a bit, but Kira also saw that, as traumatic as the replayed experience had been for him, the Prophets had still given him a gift: what They had done would allow Benjamin to confront the demons that haunted him so that he could finally move past them.

Kira watched him weep for a long time.

Three

Lieutenant Commander Jefferson Blackmer sat at the security console in the Hub. The panel, canted upward for better viewing, stretched in an arc before him, all of its control surfaces laid out within easy reach, with perfect visibility to all of its displays. Blackmer loved the reconfigurable design, which, after several months of trial and error, he'd finally arranged to his satisfaction, and which he called up for use every time he relieved his delta-shift subordinate.

The security chief also appreciated having a dedicated console in Deep Space 9's operations center. On the old station, he'd been relegated to discharging his responsibilities from his office on the Promenade, a problematic situation when it came to dealing with issues affected by, or affecting, other departments and the chain of command. The new DS9 provided Blackmer with three permanent full-function control panels at which he and his staff could manage the starbase's security needs: in the Hub, in the office adjoining the detention cells on the Plaza, and within the stockade complex. Of course, he could adapt any console on any deck for his use, but working in such circumstances could not compare to doing so in the Hub, alongside the rest of the command crew.

Blackmer swept his gaze across his readouts, verifying the integrity of DS9's internal and external security. His console stood on the raised, outer ring of the operations center. To him, the Hub resembled a starship bridge that had been partially inverted. The primary workstations lined the periphery of the circular space, but marched along the inner edge of the ring rather than along the outer bulkhead. In that way, every major panel faced inward, toward the lower, central area called the Well, which housed a large, round situation table. Spacious and bright, the Hub also contrasted favorably with the confining, shadowy atmosphere of ops on the old station.

Blackmer saw a hologram projected above the sit table, depicting the starbase in real time. He saw the two ships currently docked at the station, both along the *x*-ring: the Cardassian vessel *Trager* and an unnamed Bajoran transport that bore the registry BMV-1. He also saw *Rio Grande*, a runabout on standard patrol, streak past on the outskirts of the three-dimensional image. Everything appeared relatively serene, but the security chief knew that the placid scene represented the calm before the storm. With just three days until DS9's dedication and its evolution to full operation, the station would see a flurry of activity as several more heads of state descended upon it, and the bustle would only increase as Starfleet's newest starbase opened its docking bays to the entire Bajor Sector and beyond.

In the space over the sit table projection, a loop joining four separate but identical viewscreens hung suspended from the overhead, allowing visibility to one of the displays from anywhere in the Hub. An empty starscape showed at present, although the security chief easily picked out the green-white speck of Bajor in the black depths of space. Above, a circular port crowned the Hub.

The turbolift doors to Blackmer's left whispered open.

A quartet of lifts served the Hub, discharging into the operations center at each compass point, all of them carried there via an arc of the starbase's vertical rings. Between each pair stood another door, collectively allowing access to the captain's office, a transporter platform, a conference room, and a refresher facility. Various supplemental panels lined the outer bulkhead between the doors, crewed by supernumerary personnel.

Blackmer glanced over to see Captain Ro enter. Rather than head for the command chair—which sat to her left on the outer ring, across from the doors to her office—she paced directly forward and descended the three steps to the inner deck. She did not take one of the seats at the sit table, but stood and studied the holographic representation of the starbase. Ro then peered up at one of the viewscreens overhead. "Where are we at, Desca?" she asked the first officer, who sat down at his position in the chair beside the captain's.

Before Colonel Cenn could respond, all the displays on Blackmer's console flashed calls for attention. At the same time, the red alert klaxon began to clamor. Messages and sensor measurements filled the central display on the security panel, while an adjoining screen showed an exterior view: a wavering field of stars, as though seen through a pool of choppy water. "Vessel decloaking," he announced, interpreting all of the information presented to him before reading off the numbers posted on his console. "Bearing: thirty-seven degrees, mark eighty-one. Distance: one point eight million kilometers. Velocity: one-quarter impulse." Despite the circumstances and the passage of two years' time, Blackmer experienced déjà vu; he remembered all too well—he knew that all the survivors did—the starships that had decloaked in the Denorios Belt and opened fire on the old Deep Space 9 and its support vessels: first a Romulan warbird, followed by a Tzenkethi marauder, and finally a Breen battle cruiser. The result had been more than a thousand Federation dead and a demolished space station. For that reason, a tachyon detection grid had been erected about the new DS9, far enough away to allow the starbase crew time to react should it uncover the passage of a hidden vessel. The intruding ship decloaked outside that network.

From the tactical console, which abutted Blackmer's to the right, Zivan Slaine spoke up. "Shields automatically raised," she said. "Phasers have been brought online, quantum torpedoes are loading."

Over the past several months, Captain Ro and her senior staff had debated the efficacy of enabling automated responses to potential threats. Deep Space 9 would occupy a major nexus of travel and trade routes in the sector, hosting an ever-changing roster of vessels and crews, meaning that red alerts could end up squalling through the station every five minutes. Because of DS9's large number of residents and its sizable transient population, though, the captain and her entire crew felt more than ever the solemn obligation of safeguarding all those lives as best they could. Adding in the strategic importance of the starbase, as well as the harsh reality of its predecessor's demise, and Captain Ro had chosen to err on the side of caution.

Chief Engineer Miles O'Brien, who had helped design and construct the new station, had worked with the security and tactical staffs to calibrate the automatic defenses. The captain and her command crew retained full control over the starbase's shield and weapon systems, but the few seconds—or even fractions of seconds—saved by allowing the computer to initially react to specific sensor readings could make the difference in any attack on the station. Thinking of O'Brien, Blackmer glanced to his right, past the steps on the other side of Dalin Slaine, to where the chief crewed one of the Hub's two engineering consoles. Ensign Amélie d'Arnaud sat beside him at the second.

Looking back at the sit table, Blackmer saw that the hologram of DS9 had vanished, replaced by the volume of shimmering space. "Get me an identification," Ro said, "and open hailing frequencies."

Directly across the Hub from Blackmer, Lieutenant Ren Kalanent Viss crewed the communications console. "Hailing frequencies," she said, the helmet of her body-hugging environmental suit translating the aquatic clicks and chirps of her native Alonis language into passably feminine Federation Standard.

On one of Blackmer's displays, the fluctuating image resolved into the recognizable form of a starship. Essentially wedge shaped, its hull a collection of straight lines and angles, the vessel carried its warp engines in a pair of equally sharp-edged nacelles. The ship-recognition routine immediately posted a label below it. Slaine announced the class and type of starship from her console, which had clearly provided her the same information. Blackmer and the dalin understood the overlap of their two positions— security and tactical—and they had developed an excellent working rapport that allowed them to function together efficiently. "*Emerald*-class Tholian juggernaut," Slaine said. Blackmer saw that a holographic view of the massive vessel had appeared above the sit table. The ring of displays depending from the overhead also showed the encroaching Tholian ship.

"There's no response to our hails," said Viss.

"They're running with weapons hot and shields raised," Slaine said.

Blackmer quickly surveyed his console. He looked for any red or yellow indicators that would signal either a gap in the starbase's internal security grid or some other possible threat. He had not forgotten that the destruction of the old station two years earlier had been accomplished not just by the attack of the three Typhon Pact vessels, but also by way of explosive devices planted on DS9 itself.

The security panel showed green.

"Open a channel on the standard Tholian frequency," said Ro.

"I have a channel open for you, Captain," Viss said, so quickly that she must have anticipated the order.

"Tholian vessel, this is Captain Ro Laren of starbase Deep Space 9." Ro circled the sit table and mounted the steps closest to the command chair. On the outer ring, she sat down and focused on the overhead display facing her. "Your presence in this system is a violation of sovereign Federation territory and could be considered an act of war. If you do not deactivate your weapons and lower your shields at once, we will have no choice but to open fire on you."

After a beat, Viss said, "Still no response."

"They *are* responding," Slaine said. "They've increased speed to full impulse and are heading directly for the station."

"Fire phasers, two banks," Ro ordered without hesitation. "Target their forward shields."

Slaine's hands darted across the tactical console, and Blackmer heard the auditory signals—like the squawks of a hydraulic pump, he'd always thought—that accompanied the actual triggering of the weapons. On his own panel, the security chief watched on a display as the red-tinged golden streaks found their mark. "Direct hits," Slaine said. "They're still coming. No change in course."

Blackmer saw a pair of energy spikes on the Tholian interloper. "They're returning fire," he said. On one of his screens, twin lightning-white beams leaped from the bow of the juggernaut. An instant later, Blackmer's panel erupted in a profusion of data, detailing the phaser strikes on Deep Space 9. "We've taken direct hits on the north-west quadrant, near the y-ring," he reported. "Shields down to ninety-three percent there." After a twenty-year career in Starfleet, Blackmer felt peculiar reading and repeating information about taking fire without actually hearing the punch of weapons against the station, without sensing the resultant vibrations through the deck, without the inertial dampers destabilizing and allowing the entire structure to quake.

"They're firing again," Slaine said.

"Fire phasers, *all* applicable banks. Concentrate on their forward shields," Ro said. "Launch quantum torpedoes, full spread."

"Firing phasers and torpedoes," Slaine said. Again Blackmer heard the feedback of the weapon systems as Deep Space 9 unleashed its considerable armaments. He peered down to the sit table to see the Tholian ship continue toward the station, firing its own lethal beams. Blackmer watched DS9's phaser bolts streak into the juggernaut, pounding into its forward shields and causing them to flare brightly. When a quantum torpedo exploded on impact, a brilliant blue flash encompassed the entire vessel for a few seconds, but still the juggernaut discharged its weapons at DS9.

"More strikes on the northwest quadrant of the station," Blackmer said. "Shields down to ninety-one percent . . . down to eighty-seven percent."

"Continuous fire," Ro ordered. "I want that ship turned away." Blackmer knew that the captain would first choose to end the confrontation before it escalated, but if she could not avoid a prolonged battle, she would do what she had to do in order to protect the people aboard DS9.

"They're beginning evasive maneuvers," Slaine said, even as Blackmer saw on one of his readouts that the Tholian vessel had deviated from its straight-line path. The juggernaut made a series of rapid course changes, effectively dodging and then outrunning most of the quantum torpedoes, though not all of them: two more crashed into the shields protecting it, and great jags of energy twisted across its hull. Though under assault, the ship still fired its phasers.

"They're concentrating their weapons on the northwest quadrant," Blackmer said. Again, it seemed odd not to physically experience the effects of the attack.

"Two torpedo hits on the Tholian ship," Slaine said. "Their forward shield is showing signs of stress. They're pursuing an irregular course, but they're still headed toward Deep Space Nine."

"Keep firing," Ro instructed, peering across the Hub toward the tactical station. "Seed a wide field of torpedoes in their path."

"Yes, Captain," Slaine said, operating her panel to translate Ro's words into action.

The captain looked toward the security console. "Ready the thoron shield," she said.

"Thoron shield generators are already online and standing by," Blackmer said. A new innovation theorized by Starfleet Research and Development and brought to fruition by Tactical Operations, the thoron shield represented a next step in defensive capabilities—not exactly a step forward, but more like a significant lateral move. The generators provided a seamless energy casing around the starbase, on the inner sides of the rings, with a separate shell around the Hub. The thoron-based screen interfered with DS9's long-range communications and sensors, but functioned as a protective envelope far stronger than typical shields, defending against not only energy weapons and transporter beams, but also actual material objects. While it would not render Deep Space 9 impregnable, it could allow the starbase to withstand some attacks better and longer than traditional shields. Starfleet hoped to eventually install it on its starships, but had yet to find a means of erecting a stable such field around any space that contained a warp core.

"If the Tholians violate our established perimeter, raise the thoron shield," Ro said.

"Yes, sir," Blackmer said. Normally, the captain would have ordered *Defiant*—the bantam starship assigned as a support vessel to the starbase—away from the station and onto the field of battle, but the security chief knew that the current situation would not permit that. He checked his console and monitored the juggernaut's proximity to DS9.

"The Tholian vessel is having to alter course to avoid our torpedoes," Slaine said.

"They're still firing phasers, though," Blackmer said. "Two more hits on the northwest quadrant. Shields at seventy-two percent there."

A vibrant flash momentarily lighted the Hub, followed by another. "Two more quantum torpedo strikes," Slaine said. "Their forward shield is dangerously close to collapse, and one of their phaser emitters appears damaged."

"Continue planting torpedoes along their path," Ro said. "I want—"

"Captain," Lieutenant Viss spoke up from where she sat in her antigrav chair at the communications console. "We're being hailed by the Tholians . . . they say they've shut down their weapons, and they'll agree to lower their shields if we stop firing."

"Confirmed," Slaine said. "The juggernaut has powered down its phaser banks."

Ro stood up from the command chair and gazed at the viewscreen. "Cease fire," she said.

"Yes, Captain," Slaine said, and the sounds of Deep Space 9's weapons faded.

"Maintain sensor contact," Ro said. "If their phasers come back online, resume firing at once."

"Acknowledged," Slaine said.

"What's the course and speed of the juggernaut?" asked Colonel Cenn, standing from his own chair.

"They've come to a stop and are holding their position," Slaine said.

For a moment, silence fell across the Hub. Blackmer studied his console, once more confirming the lack of security breaches on the station. He checked the sensor readings of the Tholian vessel and saw that the ship remained motionless, with its phaser banks off-line.

Finally, from his position at the sciences station, beside Viss at communications, Lieutenant Commander John Candlewood broke the quiet. "I guess they don't want to be destroyed this time," he said.

Ro looked to the communications console. "Kalanent," she said, "see if they're offering up their surrender."

"Right away, Captain," Viss said. Blackmer didn't know if she smiled, but he thought he heard a lilt in the comm officer's voice—noteworthy because of the level of computerized translation involved in interpreting her speech.

"If I know Lieutenant Commander Stinson, he doesn't much like to lose," O'Brien said. "Even in war games."

"Even in war games, Chief, it's better to surrender than be destroyed," Ro offered.

"Our attackers have surrendered," Viss confirmed.

Ro looked toward the security console. "Jeff, you can release the simulation routines."

"Yes, sir," Blackmer said, and he worked his controls to terminate the program that Candlewood and his staff had engineered for the latest test of the starbase's defenses. The code read *Defiant*'s transponder signal and randomly assigned the starship a different identity, then sent corresponding readings and images to the consoles and displays in the Hub. Although the DS9 crew had sent real phasers and quantum torpedoes at the masquerading *Defiant*, the former had been set to one one-hundredth power, while the latter had been equipped with a similarly reduced yield. Because of the presence aboard the starbase of two heads of state—the Bajoran first minister and the Cardassian castellan—Captain Ro had not wanted even diminished weaponry leveled at DS9. Candlewood and his staff had therefore modified their software to read particular transmissions from *Defiant* as weapons fire, and then to detail on the readouts the severity of the damage that would have been done by such attacks. The red alert klaxon did not call out across the entire starbase, but only through active and relevant crew spaces: the Hub, the reactor ring and engineering complex, and weapons control.

Blackmer finished tapping out commands on his panel. "I've shut down the simulator routines," he said. In the center of the Hub, above the situation table, the imposing image of the Tholian juggernaut blinked once more, but it neither cloaked nor decloaked; instead, it transformed into the smaller but still formidable *Defiant*.

"Open a channel," Ro said.

"I've got Commander Stinson for you," Viss said immediately, as though she'd simply been waiting for Ro's order. Deep Space 9's second officer appeared on the screens hanging above the sit table. He'd recently cut short his dark, wavy hair, which had the effect of extending his already long face. A capable, serious officer who did not hide his ambition to rise to starship command, he wore a natural frown, though at the moment he appeared even more dour than usual. He sat in the command chair on the bridge of *Defiant*, which he captained in Ro's absence. In front of him, at the combined conn and ops console, sat Lieutenant Tenmei.

"I believe you're infringing on my starbase, Commander," Ro said with a wry half smile.

"Not for long, apparently," replied Stinson, his words and tone light despite his stern visage.

"No complaints, Wheeler," Ro said. "Remember, you live here most of the time, so it's good to know that we're capable of defending ourselves."

"Agreed," Stinson said, but Blackmer thought there had been at least a nugget of truth to O'Brien's observation: the second officer didn't seem especially pleased that his counterfeit attack on the starbase had been so quickly thwarted.

"Disarm and retrieve the undetonated torpedoes we fired," Ro told Stinson, "then bring the *Defiant* back home."

"Aye, sir."

"Once you're back aboard, report to the conference room for a full analysis of your attack," Ro said. "After that, we'll have our regular status meeting at eleven hundred hours." The command staff—and all the crew, both on DS9 and back at Bajoran Space Central—had been attending weekly and sometimes daily meetings as they prepared to bring the station fully online.

"Understood, sir," Stinson said.

"Ro out." Viss touched a control, and the second officer disappeared from the viewscreens, replaced by a view of *Defiant.* Ro then looked toward the security station. "Jeff, are you ready for *our* meeting?"

"I am," Blackmer said. For the previous two months, he and the captain had met numerous times to discuss security procedures for the starbase in general and for the upcoming dedication in particular. Not everything had gone smoothly—some of the emergency bulkheads around the reactor ring failed their closure tests; the force fields in the stockade overloaded at maximum power; and the energy-weapon inhibitors throughout the station worked too well, preventing even authorized security personnel from firing their phasers—but they had successfully performed all needed repairs in the days leading up to the arrival of the first dignitaries in advance of the dedication ceremony. Ro and Blackmer had spent the past few weeks reviewing the procedures that the security chief had put in place, and he in turn had drilled his staff.

"My office, then," the captain said. Then, to her first officer: "Desca, you have the Hub."

"Yes, Captain," Cenn said, sitting back down. He took the command chair rather than the one reserved for the second-in-command.

The captain circled her chair and headed for the doors to her office. Blackmer reached forward and secured his console, then started around the disc of the Hub to follow. Crewwoman Jan Collins, a junior member of his staff, strode from where she'd been working at a secondary station to take over at the security panel.

As Blackmer trailed the captain into her office, he recalled what she'd said to Stinson: "Bring the *Defiant* back home." The last word sounded a false note to him— not on the captain's lips but in his ears. Blackmer had been among a segment of the crew who had resided on the partially completed starbase for close to a year, and so he'd certainly become accustomed to living there. He realized, though, that he had yet to come to think of Deep Space 9 in the way Ro had characterized it: as *home*.

It must be because the station's been under construction until just recently, he thought. The bulk of the crew had begun relocating to DS9 only within the previous month, and a few more civilian residents just in the prior two weeks. The Plaza and the park had been open for a matter of days.

But that's not all of it, Blackmer thought as he entered the captain's office. Something nagged at him, though he couldn't quite determine what.

The captain crossed the length of her office, passing her desk, which stood to the left in the center of a long bulkhead. A wide, rounded rectangular port filled the far section of hull, offering a view out into space. A door in the far right corner led to a private refresher, Blackmer knew, while another beside it, in the right-side bulkhead, led out into a corridor. Behind the desk hung a large metal-frame sculpture, a stylish, essentially two-dimensional representation of the new Deep Space 9. The piece of art made

Blackmer think of the painting that had adorned Ro's office on the old station, a gold-framed starscape showing Bajor and its five moons suspended in the firmament. The canvas, like so many other things—like so many *people*—had been lost.

"Would you like something to drink?" the captain asked from where she stood in the corner opposite the 'fresher, in front of a replicator alcove.

"No, thank you," Blackmer said. As Ro ordered something for herself, he looked to his right, across from the captain's desk, to where a large viewscreen dominated the bulkhead, set above a long sofa. A detailed grid showed on the display, crosshatching dates and departments in intersections of responsibility. Most of the listed tasks glowed in green characters, with just a few in yellow, and only one—the assignment of permanent quarters to arriving civilian residents—in red. Blackmer followed the column that identified his security staff and saw all of its entries in green, except for the last one, in the row corresponding to the next day; it read ADDITIONAL VIP SECURITY in yellow letters.

As Blackmer waited for the captain, his mind drifted from the tasks before him that day, back to the notion of DS9 as home. He'd served for a full year aboard the old station before its destruction, and although he felt its loss keenly, he had never grown completely comfortable there. He ascribed that to his difficult working relationship with Captain Ro, who for a long time had disliked and distrusted him. They had eventually overcome that, but just two months later, the station had been destroyed, allowing him little time to adjust to the improved situation.

It's more than just that, Blackmer admitted, seeking out what he sensed might be a hard truth about himself.

He thought about the other positions to which he'd been assigned during his Starfleet career—not about the starships, where he'd never felt at ease, but about the space stations. Fresh out of Starfleet Academy, he'd spent five years on Starbase 189, and after that, he'd served another five-year tour on Helaspont Station.

And what did I feel in those places? he asked himself. He always thought that his awkwardness aboard Starbase 189 stemmed from his youth and inexperience, while he believed that nobody serving on Helaspont Station, located so close to the Tzenkethi border, truly settled in to life on the edge of a hostile power.

It was more than that, Blackmer realized. *It's still more than that.*

Captain Ro joined him in front of the viewscreen, a tall glass of a reddish-orange beverage in one hand. "It seems like we'll get there," she said, gesturing up toward the display and the information it contained. She tapped at the square labeled ADDITIONAL VIP SECURITY, and it expanded to fill the screen with a comprehensive register of security crew assignments over the coming days. Blackmer saw that his own name featured prominently on the list, in several locations. "It's hard to believe we're finally on the verge of opening for business," Ro said. Her phrasing struck the security chief as odd, but then so did her relationship with Quark, from whom she had no doubt learned the expression.

But it's not business, Blackmer thought. *It's* life. Even as the thought flew through his mind, though, another joined it. In life, people found homes, places where they felt they belonged, refuges to which they could retreat in times of trouble, sanctums where they could celebrate successes. Blackmer wondered if he would ever find that—not just on Deep Space 9, but anywhere in the universe.

Castellan Rakena Garan paced anxiously in front of the ports that lined the meeting room on the Federation starbase, her fist rapping against the backs of the chairs along the conference table as she passed them. She did not look out into the everlasting night of space, but down at the deck—and even that she did not see. Vaguely, as though from a distance, the clocklike cadence of her heels reached her ears.

Energy coursed through Garan's diminutive body, filling her up—filling the entire room up, it seemed, even though she had no company in the large compartment. Her security detail waited outside in the corridor, along with one of her aides. She had informed her coterie of her change in plans, but she wanted privacy for what she needed to do next.

While she waited, the castellan felt as though she might explode. She moved in an attempt to alleviate the force she felt within her, to calm her rising tide of discontent. Really, she wanted not to stride forward and back, but to take to her heels and run.

But I am *running*, she thought, taking herself to task for the decision she'd made—for the decision she'd been forced to make. She should have been enjoying a series of high-profile political successes, attending the Deep Space 9 dedication ceremony and meeting not only with allied leaders—the Federation president, the Klingon chancellor, and the Ferengi grand nagus—but also with leaders of rival powers—the Romulan praetor and the Gorn imperator. Garan's scheduled trip to Bajor, marking the first visit to that world by a sitting Cardassian head of state, would have brought her the approbation of both her supporters back home and her peers in the Khitomer Accords; ideally, it also would have impressed her detractors, and even helped convince some of her own people to reconsider their petty prejudices and juvenile jingoism.

At the end of the conference table, the castellan stopped and brought her hand down on the back of the last chair, tightly squeezing its headrest. She drew her other hand, fingers tightened into a fist, up behind the small of her back. She stood that way for several moments, trying to will the tension from her body.

Finally, Garan turned and peered through the ports, out into space. One of the great rings that encircled the Federation starbase climbed past the conference room off to the right. She followed its curve upward, then let her gaze drift to the backdrop of stars beyond it. She thought to find Cardassia among them, but she quickly lost sight of all the distant suns, seeing instead the remembered face, the penetrating glare, of the Union's longtime ambassador to the Federation: Elim Garak.

Moments earlier, the castellan had been sitting at a secure companel in her quarters aboard *Trager*, a protected channel open to the Tarlak Sector in Cardassia City. For the second time since she'd departed on her trip to the Bajoran system, she had spoken with Garak. Their first conversation, shortly after the ambassador had returned home from Earth, had allowed him to update her about the negotiations with the Federation, confirming that the castellan's agenda proceeded apace ahead of her upcoming bid for reelection. Their second and most recent discussion, though, had provided her with information that threatened to undermine all of that.

He can't be right, the castellan tried to persuade herself,

still picturing Garak's face as she stood before the ports in
the conference room. It shouldn't have surprised her that
the text of the withdrawal agreement had been leaked,
much less so that her political enemies attempted to use
the content of the document against her. It did come as
a shock, though, to learn the identities of some of those
whom Garak considered possible sources of the leak.

The castellan drew in a deep breath, then exhaled
slowly. The voices of Cardassia First, led by Evek Temet
in the Assembly, had grown louder than they'd ever been,
all the more so because they hadn't had to contend with
the countervailing first-person viewpoint of the castellan.
Garak believed that her administration could ably defend
their record—*her* record—in the media, but she understood
that would not suffice when Temet debated the withdrawal
agreement on a newscast the following morning—even with
Garak going up against him. Cardassia First claimed that
the castellan had become more concerned about her alliance with the Federation and the Klingons and the Ferengi,
about her own standing within the greater interstellar community, than about her own people. They pointed to her
trip to Deep Space 9 and branded it as appeasement and
poor judgment, conveniently neglecting that the Union no
longer counted the UFP as an enemy, but as an ally; they
maintained that Garan should have been at home, dealing
with the clashes in the city of Cemet between the nationalists and the radical progressives.

Cardassia First also mocked the castellan's upcoming
visit to Bajor as prostrating herself before a lesser species
that had brought irreparable harm to the Union. They
alleged that Garan would demean her own people by publicly apologizing for Cardassia's occupation of that world,
a military action that the movement characterized as an

attempt to elevate the backward Bajorans. *The seizure of resources, the implementation of slavery, the sowing of death and destruction, all as means of "helping" the inferior,* the castellan thought. *That was the Cardassian way for so long, and how could it be any other way with the military controlling our society?*

But the Cardassian Guard had done more than simply rule the Union: its leaders had fostered the natural egotism of her people. As a girl, even as a young woman, Garan had subscribed to the idea of Cardassian preeminence. That position seemed much harder to defend after nearly a billion of their people had perished in a war that the Union had helped instigate.

Garan actually did not intend to offer contrition for Cardassia's past sins against the Bajorans; if there had ever been a time for that, it had gone, leaving only the events of the present to pave the way for the future. But the castellan knew that the truth of all that wouldn't matter. The spectacle of discord in the streets of Cemet would matter. The din of the strident nationalists denouncing Garan would matter. The withdrawal agreement with the Federation, no matter its benefits to Cardassia, would matter. And more than all that, the unthinking patriotism and narrow-minded bigotry of small minds would matter.

Cardassia does have a way forward, Garan thought. They had already come so far in the decade since the end of the Dominion War. Alon Ghemor had heroically formed a democratic government, and although he had not endured, his legacy so far had. Great strides had been made in reconstructing Cardassia, from its infrastructure and cities to its population—yes, with the help of the Federation, with the help of Bajor, but that did not diminish those accomplishments.

What would damage that progress would be a resumption of military rule, the castellan thought. The ultranationalist Cardassia First demanded "a return of the Union to its former glory," a goal they believed predicated upon the renewal of government leadership by the Guard. Garan knew that she could prevent that from happening, but only if she remained in power as castellan.

Behind her, one of the two sets of doors in the interior bulkhead opened with a hiss of air. Garan turned to see the Bajoran first minister enter the room alone, which bespoke her perspicacity. Seeing the castellan's security team and aide waiting out in the corridor, Asarem had clearly understood that Garan wished to speak with her one-on-one. Of course, the castellan's request for the unscheduled meeting likely played a role in suggesting its importance and sensitive nature.

The doors slid shut behind Asarem as she walked over to Garan, who met her halfway. "First Minister, thank you for agreeing to meet with me on such short notice," Garan said.

"I'd thought we would next be seeing each other when I welcomed you to Bajor later today," Asarem said. Both *Trager* and the first minister's transport had been scheduled to depart Deep Space 9 in just a short while.

"I thought so as well," Garan said. "But I'm sorry to say that I won't be able to visit Bajor on this trip."

The first minister gave no outward reaction to the statement, though Garan suspected that Asarem did not welcome the news. So far, their first face-to-face summit had yielded positive results. The two women had gotten along well, quickly establishing a deeper rapport than they'd been able to during their several subspace communications over the prior few years. In their two days together at the starbase, Garan and Asarem had discussed numerous topics important to their respective peoples, and they'd even reached nominal agreements on some trade and social-exchange issues. They had also spoken of the castellan's impending visit to Bajor, which both leaders viewed as important to the still-improving relationship between the two worlds. Asarem had neither requested an apology for the Cardassian occupation of her world, nor even intimated that she thought one appropriate at that point.

"I am understandably disappointed," the first minister said, her expression unchanging. "With respect, may I ask why you will not be making the journey to Bajor?"

"It's not a decision I've made lightly," Garan said. "There is a . . . situation . . . on Cardassia that requires my immediate attention."

"Your *immediate* attention?" Asarem said. "I hope it is nothing too serious."

Garan sighed. "There is unrest on Cardassia," she said, not really wanting to discuss her political life, but feeling that she owed the first minister an explanation.

"Such is the price of democracy, is it not?" Asarem said.

"Indeed it is," Garan concurred. "But there is a threat of damage to my government by militant nationalists within it. My return to Cardassia will help put an end to that."

Finally, Asarem's expression melted, if only slightly. "I do understand the responsibilities of leadership," she said. "It's particularly troubling when you have to deal with threats that come from within."

"Troubling," Garan agreed, "and exhausting." The castellan typically relished the field of political battle, but she found it difficult to deal with Cardassia First. They did not argue either honestly or logically, instead brandishing their contentions with religious fervor. *Because it is a religion to them*, she thought. The zealots put their faith not in a god, but in their own inherent superiority. They found anathema anybody or anything not Cardassian, as well as anybody or anything that did not exalt the Union. It wore Garan out to stand up to them, but if she wanted to continue leading her people, she had little choice. She told the first minister as much.

"I understand," Asarem said. "When will you leave?"

"I'll be departing at once," Garan said. "Make no mistake, though: I would not leave if circumstances did not demand it of me. I would like to attend the dedication ceremony for this starbase and meet our fellow leaders. More than all of that, though, I am anxious to continue our dialogue, Wadeen." She hoped that calling the first minister by her given name did not overstep the bounds of propriety, but Garan wanted to express the genuine connection she felt with Asarem. "I am anxious to continue our dialogue, preferably in person, both on Bajor and on Cardassia."

The first minister did not reply immediately, once more showing virtually no reaction to Garan's words other than with her silence. As the pause distended, the castellan began to think she had blundered. She realized that she would have to ask forgiveness for her breach of diplomacy, but then Asarem said, "I would rather that we meet in person as well."

Garan nodded, relieved and pleased with the first minister's response. "Until then, I do not intend for there to be no Cardassian presence either here on the starbase or on Bajor," the castellan said. "I have already sent for

Lustrate Enevek Vorat." In his position as lustrate, Vorat served just beneath Garan in the Union government. "If you have no objection, he will travel directly to Bajor to meet with you in my stead, before arriving at Deep Space Nine for the dedication."

"No, I have no objection; I welcome the lustrate's participation," Asarem said. "I appreciate your effort to avert an interruption in the talks between our governments. I truly believe that we can improve the relations between our two worlds, to the mutual benefit of both."

"As do I," Garan said. "One of my aides, Onar Throk, will be staying behind to assist the lustrate. Throk will coordinate with your staff on Vorat's arrival and his visit to Bajor."

"I will let my aides know at once," Asarem said. "Thank you for your personal attention in this matter." For an instant, Garan thought that the first minister meant to reciprocate her earlier gesture by employing her given name, but then she simply went on without doing so. "Safe travels back to Cardassia, Castellan," she said. "I wish you success."

"Thank you, First Minister," Garan said. Asarem offered a polite bow of her head, then exited the meeting room. The castellan waited, and after a few moments, one of her aides entered. Small in stature, his hair dusted white by age—*By his several decades in Cardassian civil service,* Garan thought, *which would ripen anybody*—Throk quickly crossed the room to stand before her.

"Castellan," he said, "Gul Macet reports that the *Trager* is prepared to depart as soon as you are aboard."

"And what about Lustrate Vorat?" Garan wanted to know.

"He is already on his way to Bajor on the *Jorrene.*"

"Very good," Garan said. "I appreciate your volunteering to stay behind to brief the lustrate on my meetings with the first minister."

"And I appreciate the opportunity to serve, Castellan," Throk said, professional without lapsing into obsequiousness.

"I've already informed Captain Ro of my departure," Garan said. "Coordinate with Colonel Cenn regarding the details of the lustrate's visit to Deep Space Nine, and with Minister Asarem's staff about his trip to Bajor."

"I will see to it at once, Castellan," Throk said.

"I'll be on my way, then," Garan said. She felt confident of Throk's ability to oversee Vorat's stay in the Bajoran system. But as she headed out of the meeting room on her way to *Trager*, she wondered just what she would find when she returned to Cardassia.

Four

With the sound of her heartbeat still enveloping her, Kira watched as Benjamin's tears at last stopped. He looked so miserably sad to her, and yet somehow not defeated, as he had earlier. Around him, flames consumed *Saratoga,* sending skeins of noxious smoke coiling through the air. He sat amid the wreckage of his cabin aboard the ship, the still form of his dead wife lying on the deck before him. "Jennifer," he said, so quietly that Kira did not know if he actually spoke, or if she only read the name on his lips.

After that, Benjamin seemed to gather himself. He closed his eyes, raised his head, and then looked up, away from the lifeless body of the woman he had loved. He rose slowly, with care, and then peered in turn at each of the Prophets with him, who had taken on the forms of his wife and son, the former kai, and *Saratoga*'s tactical officer.

"What do we do now?" Benjamin asked. Kira wondered the same thing.

"The creature must be destroyed," announced the Borg-modified figure of Captain Picard from the viewscreen on the *Saratoga* bridge. The setting still changed so quickly and seamlessly that Kira could not follow the transition, but she had at least grown accustomed to it.

"Corporeal creatures annihilate us," said Picard in the

Enterprise conference room, the captain devoid of Borg alterations.

"They *do* destroy us," agreed Kai Opaka in the Bajoran monastery. "And they do *not.*"

"What does that mean?" Benjamin asked, candlelight quivering across his features. "I told you that I have no interest in destroying you."

"Aggressive," said the batter on the baseball diamond. "Adversarial."

"I do not want to be your adversary," Benjamin said, a baseball cap once more perched on his head. "I want only to communicate with you, to establish a relationship. But to demonstrate that I am not aggressive, I will withdraw from the wormhole if that is what you wish."

"When one of you enters the passage," said Picard, "our existence is disrupted."

"I don't want to disrupt your existence," Benjamin said.

"It is disrupted," said Jennifer, walking along the beach. "And it is not."

"I don't understand," Benjamin said, walking beside her, the trail of their path left as depressions in the sand behind them. Kira didn't understand, either.

"When a corporeal entity travels through the passage, our existence is disrupted," said Opaka in the monastery. "We therefore take steps so that our existence is not disrupted."

Benjamin hesitated, apparently trying to parse the meaning of the Prophet's words. "Does that mean that we can contact you again?" he finally asked.

"You are here now," Opaka told him.

"Yes, but we'd like to continue communicating with

you, to learn about you, to learn *from* you," Benjamin said. "Not just now, but in the future."

"Now *is* what is to come," Opaka said. "There is no difference."

"No," Benjamin said. "There is no difference for you, but there is for us."

"You travel through the passage," said Captain Picard. He peered out through a port in the *Enterprise* conference room. Benjamin followed his gaze, as did Kira. Rather than the stars, she saw the streaming blues and whites and purples of the Celestial Temple.

"We travel through the passage," Benjamin repeated. "Now, and in the future? And we will not disturb your existence?"

On the beach, Jennifer stopped and looked into Benjamin's eyes. "You travel through the passage," she said. "You do so safely."

"I'm glad to hear that," Benjamin said. "I am eager for my people to get to know your people."

Jennifer tilted her head slightly to one side, as though understanding that what she had said and what Benjamin had said did not tally. "You travel through the passage," she said again. "But *we* contact *you*."

Hearing Jennifer's assertion, Benjamin looked askance at her. "So we can use the wormhole, but we're not to attempt to communicate with you?"

"You understand," Jennifer said, a note of finality in her voice.

Behind Benjamin, the sun glinted off the dark-blue water of the ocean, flaring a bright white. Kira narrowed her eyes against it, but it grew brighter still. She turned away, but the brilliant glare surrounded her on all sides.

In just seconds, she found herself once more standing in a featureless field of white.

Kira looked back in the direction of the ocean, which had vanished along with the sand and the sky. Jennifer had disappeared as well, leaving Benjamin standing alone again in a white emptiness. Although she saw him clearly, Kira could tell that he could not see her. She expected him to speak, to call out to the Prophets, but then the all-encompassing whiteness fractured: the unbroken vacuity became intersecting planes of light, with patches of darkness visible between them.

Kira's footing faltered, and she looked down to see a patch of rocky ground beneath her. The earth around her quaked, its surface split into fissures from which the dazzling light emanated. As she peered around, though, the beams actually decreased in strength. Kira saw more of the dark landscape about her. The broken ground seemed to swallow up the light that had burst forth from it, the jagged slits in the earth knitting together like flesh beneath a dermal regenerator.

Suddenly, the light faded completely, leaving Kira on the barren terrain where she had first landed. Before her, Benjamin stood in his Starfleet uniform, his back to her, a runabout sitting with its hatch opened beyond him. He didn't move.

"Benjamin," Kira said. Her voice barely registered in her ears, although the sound of her beating heart no longer overwhelmed her sense of hearing. "Benjamin," she said again, louder, but the name still seemed to leave her mouth and fall to the ground.

Benjamin did not turn around, giving no sign at all that he'd heard Kira. Instead, he began walking forward, slowly at first, but then with more purpose. When he reached the runabout—*Rio Grande*, Kira saw—he climbed aboard and disappeared from view. Kira took a step forward, not really sure if she intended to follow Benjamin, but then the main hatch slid closed.

A moment later, *Rio Grande* lifted off.

The vessel sped off into the night sky. Kira followed it until it became a point of light indistinguishable from the stars. She looked after it anyway, immobile, unsure of all that had happened since Elias had appeared aboard *Rubicon*, picked her up, and hurled her to safety.

If I even am safe, Kira thought. While not entirely certain about her circumstances, though, she did not feel threatened. In the hands of the Prophets, she felt protected.

In her peripheral vision, Kira saw another flare of light—not white, but an ethereal green. She whirled in place, knowing what she would see. In the distance, on the other side of the canyon that divided the land before her, beneath sunlight and blue skies, spread the lush parklike vista she'd seen earlier, so vastly different from her immediate surroundings. The source of the singular green light hovered above the grass: an Orb of the Prophets.

Kira recalled at once her determination that she must get to it. She didn't know why, and she didn't know how she would cross the open chasm separating her from her goal, but she put her faith in the Prophets to guide her. She took one step forward, and then another. She walked purposefully toward the great gap in the land, and beyond it, the Orb.

By degrees as she approached it, the chasm began to glow, emitting another gleaming white light. Kira squinted against it. As before, it began to overwhelm the setting.

Undeterred, Kira began to run.

Five

The doors parted before him, and Captain Benjamin Sisko walked into the quarters he shared on Deck 8 with his wife and daughter. He clutched a personal access display device in one hand. Across from him, he saw the bespeckled sprawl of space through the ports that lined the outer bulkhead of the compartment. "I'm home," he called as the door panels eased shut behind him. "Where are my girls?"

"Well, one of them's right here," Kasidy said.

To Sisko's left, in the near corner of the large living area, Kasidy leaned over their dining table, setting down napkins and utensils. She wore a fetching outfit of a dark ankle-length skirt and a sleeveless cinnamon-red blouse. Sisko quickly sidled in the other direction, to where his desk sat against the inner bulkhead, and tossed down his padd. The device skittered to a stop beside the computer interface, where an indicator light flashed, signaling that he'd received an incoming transmission. The ship's security chief, Lieutenant Commander Uteln, had informed him of the message a few minutes before, when Sisko had been down in engineering, conducting an inspection.

Ignoring the communication for the moment, Sisko headed over to the dining table and cozied up behind Kasidy. He curled his arms around her midsection, pulled her toward him, and nuzzled his face against her neck. Kasidy softened her body and pressed back against him, offering a small purr of approval.

"Here's my old girl," Sisko said, breathing warmly against his wife's flesh.

Kasidy stiffened. "Excuse me, Captain?" she said, her tone playful despite the challenge in her words. "Would you like a second chance to deliver that line?"

Sisko realized his faux pas and tried to explain. "I meant *old* only in comparison to our eight-, soon to be nine-year-old daughter," he said. In just a couple of weeks, they would celebrate Rebecca's birthday.

"Uh huh," Kasidy said, obviously unconvinced. "I don't really care what you meant." She began to turn, and Sisko loosened his arms about her so that she could move freely. When she faced him, she threw her arms over his shoulders. "You might try *woman* and *girl*, or even *girl* and *baby girl*, but I'd stay away from the word *old* if I were you."

"Message received," Sisko said. "But for the record, even though it's been almost fourteen years, you look younger than the day I met you."

"Better," Kasidy said.

Sisko lowered his head and pressed his lips against Kasidy's. They shared a soft, slow kiss. When they parted, he said, "My favorite part of completing my duty shift."

"Mine too," Kasidy said. They kissed again. When they gazed at each other once more, Kasidy reached up and ran her hand across Sisko's bare pate. "Very nice," she said. "You've got that sleek, sexy look again."

"I'm glad you like it." Just a few days prior, Sisko had decided to shave his head for the first time in several years—for the first time since he'd left Kasidy. He'd also thought about regrowing his goatee, though he'd chosen not to, at least for the time being.

Sisko glanced over Kasidy's shoulder at the table. "Only two place settings?"

"Rebecca spent the afternoon after school over at the Dorsons' cabin, and they invited her to stay for dinner." Kasidy stepped away from Sisko, circled the table, and headed toward the replicator. "Rebecca's class has been assigned a report on any domesticated animal in the Federation, and she and Elent are working together on theirs." In the year that Sisko's wife and daughter had lived full time aboard *Robinson*, Rebecca had made only a few friends, none of them closer than Elent Dorson. The child of two unjoined Trill who served in the crew, Elent had already turned ten. Though sweet and adorable in her own way, she had a boisterous and even forceful disposition, and so seemed to Sisko an unlikely companion for his daughter. Even back on Bajor, Rebecca had kept only a small circle of friends, and she'd typically gravitated to a leadership role among them, which seemed incompatible with Elent's inflated personality. In addition, Rebecca, small even for her own age, had been promoted from second grade to fourth, making her a full year younger than her classmates; as a result, Elent, a tall girl, towered over her. Still, the two had become fast friends when they'd attended fourth grade together aboard *Robinson*, and that evidently continued as they began the fifth.

"What animal are they doing their report on?" Sisko asked.

"The last I heard, they'd narrowed it down to a *pylchyk* and a Denebian slime devil."

"A Denebian slime devil?" Sisko said. "Since when are they domesticated?"

"Elent apparently found an example of somebody, somewhere, keeping one as a pet," Kasidy said. "I don't think it's going to matter, though. I think Rebecca has them leaning toward studying the pylchyk."

"Of course she does," Sisko said. Rebecca had first encountered the Bajoran draft animals a few years earlier. She'd taken an immediate liking to them, and she'd never lost that affinity.

Kasidy opened the cabinet beside the replicator and retrieved a tall, slender bottle of curved, translucent glass. It contained a pale blue liquid. "Since it's just us for dinner tonight," she said, holding up the bottle, "I thought we could open this."

"Springwine?" Sisko said. "Is that one of *ours*?" When he and Kasidy had made a home with their daughter on Bajor upon his return from the Celestial Temple, they'd talked about harvesting the *kava* fruit they grew on their land, fermenting its juices, and bottling their own springwine. They never actually got around to doing that, though, but they did find a small local winery—Adarak Cellars—whose vintage they thoroughly enjoyed. The vintner never produced much, but Sisko and Kasidy acquired what they could. Between the amount the couple gave away as gifts and what they consumed themselves, a single year's procurement never lasted them even as long as the subsequent year's press. After Sisko reenlisted in Starfleet and left Kendra Province to serve as captain of *Robinson*, Kasidy stopped getting the wine. As far as he knew, they had no bottles of it left.

"It's not exactly one of ours, but it is from Adarak Cellars," Kasidy said. "Remember the last time I was on Bajor, I ate lunch with Jasmine?" When Rebecca had been abducted at the age of three by an Ohalu extremist, Jasmine Tey, a former member of the first minister's security team, had played a pivotal role in rescuing her and bringing her safely back home. Afterward, Sisko and Kasidy had retained the highly skilled operative. Rebecca loved "Auntie" Jasmine, who had ostensibly helped around the house a few times per week, but who'd actually served as a bodyguard.

"I remember," Sisko said. The assignment of the *Robinson* crew to take on some of the tasks of the destroyed Deep Space 9 during the construction of the replacement station had allowed their family to continue visiting Bajor regularly, which they did mostly to see friends; Jake and his wife, Azeni Korena, remained on Earth, in New Zealand, while he studied writing at the Pennington School. Kasidy had been on Bajor herself a couple of weeks earlier, though, meeting with an agent of the Diplomatic Corps regarding her relatively new position as a Federation envoy.

"We've given Jasmine quite a few bottles over the years, and she still had a few left," Kasidy said. "She knew we didn't have any ourselves anymore, so she thought we'd appreciate getting one back as a going-away present."

Kasidy walked back over to Sisko and handed him the bottle. He read the date carved into the top of its cork: 2377, one of the very best vintages. "That was very thoughtful of Jasmine," he said.

"I know." Kasidy took the bottle back and set it down on the table. "I've got the replicator programmed. We can have dinner whenever you're ready."

"I want to get out of my uniform, and I've got an incoming transmission I need to look at," Sisko said. "Five minutes, maybe ten, depending on the message."

"Great," Kasidy said. "I'll uncork the wine and finish getting ready."

Sisko leaned in and gave her a quick peck on the lips, then padded around the table and through the single-paneled door in the side bulkhead. He quickly ducked right, through another door and into his and Kasidy's refresher, where he washed up. He then crossed the width of the short corridor into their closet, where he picked out dark brown slacks and a red-and-yellow dashiki. He carried the clothes down the hall to their bedroom.

Sisko tossed his civilian togs onto the bed, then turned to the companel set into the inner bulkhead. As he pulled off his uniform shirt, he said, "Computer, play my incoming message." Uteln had told him that the transmission had originated on *U.S.S. Aventine*—Dax's ship—and so he anticipated that it had been sent by his old friend. He'd known Dax for more than thirty years, through three permanent hosts: Curzon Antrani, Jadzia Idaris, and Ezri Tigan. All of them had surprised him many times during their friendships, but perhaps none more so than Ezri, whose petite frame, gentle nature, and chosen profession as a counselor had ultimately transformed into a strong and capable woman taking on the responsibilities of a starship captain. He wondered why she'd sent him a message, and whether she'd done so on a personal level or as a matter of Starfleet business.

When the companel activated, though, the image of the person that appeared in place of the Starfleet emblem did not belong to Ezri Dax. Still, Sisko recognized the face immediately. He had picked up his dashiki and begun to pull it on, but he stopped at once, freezing in place. The woman on the display wore her white hair pulled back behind her head, and deep lines creased her features, particularly around her eyes and mouth. He thought she looked much older than when last he'd had personal contact with her, adding credence to the common notion that her position rapidly aged whoever held it.

"*Captain Sisko,*" she said, "*this is Nan Bacco.*" The voice of the Federation president had a husky quality to it, whether from fatigue or her advanced years—she had to be closing in on a hundred—or some other cause, Sisko didn't know. "*I am currently aboard the Starfleet vessel* Aventine, *on my way to Deep Space Nine for the dedication ceremony. I will be arriving tomorrow, a day ahead of the festivities. In that time, I would like to meet with Odo. Since you are better acquainted with Mister Odo than any other Starfleet officer, I would like you to arrange this meeting aboard the new starbase. I'd like you to attend the meeting as well.*"

The request—or order, really—surprised Sisko. When Odo had first arrived back in the Alpha Quadrant, coincident with the collapse of the Bajoran wormhole, members of both Starfleet Command and the Federation government had arranged to speak with him on several occasions. Sisko had learned from Odo himself, as well as from Admiral Akaar—Starfleet's commander in chief—that the UFP had sought information about the current state of the Dominion and the Founders. Odo had declined to provide any such information, other than to state categorically that his people and their empire posed no threat to the Federation.

"*Please convey to Mister Odo that I would like only a few minutes of his time, but that I believe he will find it of import to him,*" Bacco continued. "*Also, please inform him that I will be asking nothing about his people or the Dominion. This is not an intelligence or a defense matter.*"

Sisko had no idea what President Bacco wanted to discuss with Odo, but he thought her shrewd. She had characterized her request for a meeting in just about the only way he believed Odo would ever agree to meet with her. For Odo's sake, Sisko hoped that the president, in doing so, did not dissemble.

"Please contact me aboard the Aventine *when you have made the arrangements, Captain,"* Bacco concluded. She reached forward to the companel at which she sat and tapped a control, ending the transmission. The Starfleet insignia appeared on the display. Sisko pulled his dashiki over his head, then deactivated his own companel with a touch.

"Captain to bridge," he said.

"Bridge," came the immediate response. *"Lieutenant Radickey here."*

"Lieutenant, I need you to attempt to contact Odo," Sisko said.

"On Bajor, sir?" Radickey asked.

"Yes," Sisko said. "You know where he stays when he's on the planet. If he's there, I'd like to speak with him. If not, leave word that I'd like him to contact me as soon as he's able."

"Aye, sir."

"Sisko out." The captain hadn't spoken to Odo for perhaps two months, just as the Changeling had been preparing to depart Bajor again. Sisko knew that, back then, Captain Ro had asked Odo to the DS9 dedication, and he thought that the first minister had also extended an invitation to him. Before leaving Bajor, Odo had indicated that he would return in time to attend the ceremony.

The captain finished changing out of his uniform, then headed back out into the living area. The door to Rebecca's bedroom stood closed on the other side of the compartment. Sisko saw a glowpane hanging on the panel, but he couldn't read the words on it from that distance. "Did Rebecca put up a new sign?"

"She did," Kasidy replied. "It says, *Authorized Personnel Prohibited*."

Sisko barked out a laugh at the oxymoronic statement. Rebecca had first put up a glowpane on her door half a year or so earlier, after mounting an argument about having to clean her room. Her first pane had read, in her curiously meticulous hand, *Parents Stay Out!* When she'd soon discovered that her parents approved of neither the sign nor the sentiment, she'd changed it to, *Who's There?* which had the peculiar effect of causing Sisko and Kasidy to announce themselves at Rebecca's door even before touching the signal or knocking. Shortly after that, Rebecca had altered the pane to read, *When is a door not a door?* Disappointed that her parents knew the answer to the riddle at once—Rebecca revealed that, once Sisko and Kasidy had read but couldn't answer the question, she planned to leave her door half open—she began rewriting the panel frequently. Her next had asserted, *You are what you read.* That had elicited high marks from her parents, which had pleased Rebecca. It seemed as though she sought a reaction—any reaction—to what she posted. She'd alternately attempted humor, wisdom, provocation, even mere silliness. Sisko and Kasidy enjoyed her creativity.

"Your daughter's too clever by half," the captain told Kasidy with a smile.

"*My* daughter?" Kasidy said. "You're the one who's in charge of the personnel on this ship."

"Yes, but we all know who's in charge in these quarters," Sisko pointed out, still smiling.

Kasidy walked over and placed the tip of one finger in the middle of Sisko's chest. "And don't you forget it," she said. "Are you ready for dinner?"

"Yes, and I'm hungry." He noticed that Kasidy had

placed candles on the table and lighted them. "Everything looks lovely."

"Since we don't often get to enjoy dinner alone, I thought I'd take advantage of the opportunity. Why don't you pour and I'll get our food?"

"All right." As Kasidy went to the replicator, Sisko picked up the bottle of springwine. The cork had already been removed, and so he filled a pair of fluted glasses with the light blue liquid.

Kasidy touched a control on the replicator, and two plates appeared, one of them larger and one smaller. She carried them to the table. "We've got a spinach salad with strawberries and toasted almonds," she said, setting the smaller dish down. "And grilled seitan with smoky paprika, roasted potatoes, and Argelian sweet corn."

"Sounds delicious," Sisko said. He loved seitan, particularly the way Kasidy prepared it—or when she used a replicator, the way she had it prepared. She placed the larger dish beside the first, then went back to the replicator and summoned up a second meal. Once she'd set those two plates on the table, Sisko pulled out a chair for her.

"My, aren't we gallant this evening?" Kasidy said, smiling widely.

Sisko leaned in close to her ear and whispered, "Since we don't get to enjoy dinner alone that often, I thought I'd take advantage of the opportunity," repeating the words she'd used a moment earlier.

Kasidy looked up at him over her shoulder. "I like the way you think, Captain," she said. He kissed her again, gently and easily, but not without passion. It amazed Sisko how far back they had come from the precipice.

When they ended the kiss, Sisko sat down opposite Kasidy. "Computer, lights down one-half," he said, and the room immediately dimmed, giving more life to the candles. "Play some light jazz," he added. "Something romantic." The slow, tuneful notes of a horn began to float through their cabin.

"Well done, Ben."

"And to you, Kas," Sisko said, gesturing toward their dinner. He lifted his glass and tilted it in Kasidy's direction. "To my beautiful, talented, and *young* wife."

Kasidy raised her own glass. "And to my handsome, talented, and *wise* husband," she said. They touched their glasses together with a clink.

"To *us*," Sisko added, and as they both sampled the springwine they had acquired together eight years prior, he marveled again at the journey they'd taken—at the fact that they'd ended up back in each other's arms after all of the terrible events through which they'd suffered.

It's not just the journey that awes me, Sisko thought. *It's Kasidy.* More than four years ago, he'd essentially abandoned her. That he'd done so for the best of reasons—to ensure the safety of their family—did not detract from the pain he had caused her. It had taken a shared vision of Kira Nerys releasing Sisko from his obligations to the Prophets for him to return to Kasidy, and for her to accept him back.

The two years since they'd resumed their relationship hadn't always been easy. Sisko had lost his wife's trust—had mangled it and thrown it away—and he could only hope that he would, through his renewed commitment to her, earn it back one day. As much as he loved and respected Kasidy, though, he had underestimated her capacity for forgiveness. While she felt it vital that Sisko understand precisely how his actions had impacted her and Rebecca, she also sought to comprehend, on an emotional level, just what he had gone through. Her willingness and ability to do that, the depth of her compassion, had given them both a solid foundation on which to rebuild their marriage.

In addition, Kasidy had been willing to examine and change a belief she had held for a long time. She'd always felt strongly that parents needed to provide their children with a safe, consistent, suitable environment in which to grow up, and that a list of such places did not include the inside of a starship. In his time away from Kasidy and Rebecca, though, Sisko had returned to Starfleet as the commander of *U.S.S. Robinson*. When he and Kasidy reunited, he offered to resign his commission. To his surprise, Kasidy didn't immediately accept his proposal.

When they'd come back into each other's lives, Kasidy and Rebecca had been residing on Bajor, but she had been seriously considering relocating—possibly back to Earth, or to Cestus III, where her youngest brother lived. She'd even thought about the colony on Allamegras, with its "rainbow moon" effect. When she and Sisko reconciled, though, she wanted them both to think through what would be best for all of them, as a family. They'd been fortunate that *Robinson* had been assigned to the Bajoran system during the construction of the new Deep Space 9; as they decided the most propitious course to take, that had allowed Kasidy and Rebecca to stay in the house in Kendra Province, and for Sisko to spend a great deal of time with them, even as he continued as a starship captain.

That also helped ease the awkwardness for Kas and me, Sisko thought. They'd been able to resume their relationship at their own pace, and in a way that permitted Rebecca to become accustomed to having her father around much more often. It took a year, but Kasidy eventually told Sisko that if he truly wanted to continue his career in Starfleet, she and Rebecca would join him aboard *Robinson*. They chose to keep the house and land on Bajor, possibly for Jake and Korena once they returned from New Zealand, and maybe even for themselves at some point. For the time being, Jasmine Tey stayed there.

Sisko also knew that it helped both of them that, since recommitting to Kasidy, he'd had no contact of any kind with the Prophets—no visits to the Celestial Temple, no visions, not even any intuitions. And even though he'd had no such contact in the years prior to his leaving Kasidy, their absence since his reunion with her felt convincingly permanent. He'd had dreams of the Prophets during that time—filled with confused, impenetrable images—but he believed them nothing more than the normal imaginings of a sleeping mind. He had struggled with whether or not he should tell Kasidy about them, mindful of the need to be completely open with her, but also concerned about worrying her for no reason. In the end, he'd kept his dreams to himself. Fortunately, over time, even those had stopped.

Once Sisko's family had moved to *Robinson*, Kasidy had become interested in finding a new career for herself. With her wealth of experience dealing with members of myriad alien species during her many years as a freighter captain, she chose to apply for service in the Federation Diplomatic Corps. She underwent training both aboard ship and on Bajor.

"Are you excited about the dedication ceremony?" Sisko asked as they ate. With so many dignitaries from so many different worlds visiting the starbase for its "launch," the Federation would be sending a swarm of diplomats to deal with them all. Officially assigned to *Robinson* as an envoy, Kasidy would mark her first mission in that role with her service around the DS9 dedication.

"I'm excited about it," Kasidy said, "but I'm also a little nervous."

"I'm sure you'll do a wonderful job," Sisko said, and he meant it. "You might be new to the diplomatic service, but you spent years taking your freighter all over the quadrant. You know how to deal with people from a lot of different species. I can't really think of better preparation for your new position."

"Oh, I'm not really worried about doing the job," Kasidy said. "I think it's more that I haven't been doing much of anything lately other than training. It's going to take an effort to get used to reporting for duty."

"Speaking of duty, do you know what you'll be doing yet?" Sisko asked.

"Actually, I received my marching orders this afternoon," Kasidy said. "I meant to tell you. I've been assigned to accompany the Gorn delegation."

Sisko nodded. "Because of your time on Cestus Three." Because her brother lived there, Kasidy had spent a considerable amount of time on the planet. Cestus III bordered the Gorn Hegemony, and so she'd had her share of interactions with its citizens.

"I'm sure that's why," Kasidy said. "Actually, I'm more excited about what comes after that."

Sisko smiled. "So am I." After Deep Space 9 became fully operational, with *Defiant* still assigned there, it would no longer be necessary for other starships to patrol around Bajor to compensate for the lack of a space station in the system. The next assignment for *Robinson*'s crew would be to take the ship into uncharted territory for an extended mission of exploration.

Throughout much of his career in Starfleet—as an occasional intelligence operative, as a shipboard engineer and then exec, as an officer at the Utopia Planitia Fleet Yards, and finally as the commander of a space station—Sisko had never been drawn toward the unknown. But while serving aboard Deep Space 9, he had built a replica of an ancient solar sail and had taken Jake on a voyage intended only to prove the design spaceworthy. Instead, they discovered unknown tachyon eddies that accelerated the vessel to warp speed and swept it all the way to Cardassia. Looking back, Sisko thought that he could trace the first real embers of wanderlust within him to that experience—embers that had surely been stoked by his friendship with Elias Vaughn.

When Sisko had initially taken command of *Robinson*, he had been running from his fear that something awful would happen to Kasidy and Rebecca if he stayed with them. Even if he hadn't been, though, he and his crew had for some time been assigned to patrol duty. Later, after he resumed his parental relationship with Rebecca and accepted his situation with Kasidy, Starfleet Command sent the *Robinson* crew on a six-month journey to explore the Gamma Quadrant. He found that experience remarkably compelling, and since then, he longed to return to a mission of discovery. He couldn't wait until after Deep Space 9's dedication, when he would take his ship and crew back out into the unknown—and he would get to share that experience with his wife and daughter.

Sisko and Kasidy talked about the upcoming mission as they continued their dinner, and about how exciting they both found the prospect of being explorers, traveling into the unknown in the simple pursuit of knowledge. They discussed Rebecca, how smart she was and how happy she seemed, and how well and how quickly she'd adjusted to life aboard a starship. Sisko poured them each a second glass of springwine partway through their meal.

Afterward, they carried their dishes to the replicator and recycled them. Once the plates had vanished, Sisko asked, "So what do we want for dessert?"

Kasidy looked at him for a moment as though he'd suddenly revealed himself to be a Tzenkethi agent. "The Dorsons are bringing Rebecca back at twenty-one hundred hours," she said, a seeming non sequitur. "I don't know what you want for dessert, Ben . . ." She left her sentence hanging as she picked up one of the lighted candles from the table and walked over to the near door in the side bulkhead. The panel glided open and Kasidy glanced back at Sisko over her shoulder. "I don't know what you want for dessert," she said again, "but I was thinking I'd like something sweet." She headed toward their bedroom.

Sisko smiled, and then followed.

He spun his ridged, conical body and curled lithely down toward the orbiting sensor platform. His two long, parallel tentacles trailed out behind him and rippled in the gravitational eddies about the planet, his flanged tail undulating as he propelled himself through the void. The dual barbed antennae that emerged like pincers from the forward part of his elongated body measured the forces of gravity influencing the points around him, allowing him to adjust his mass and dimensions so that he could ride the curvature of space-time.

The sensor platform—a runabout-size cube inset in the center of each side with a pyramid—floated in geosynchronous orbit above the green-and-blue planet. As prescribed, he circled the satellite quickly, once, twice, a third time. He could not see the platform in the traditional way that humanoids did, but he detected the pressure of the light reflecting or emanating from its surfaces. He "felt" the dark circle on one section, and when it glowed brightly three times in succession, those flashes pushed against his senses. He had arranged for the signal himself, confirmation that the people in charge of defending the population below recognized him and would allow him safe passage to the surface along a preset path.

Breaking away from the sensor platform, he swung briefly upward before lunging toward the atmosphere. The upper reaches of the gaseous planetary envelope slowed him, but only minutely. Each moment brought him closer to the world below, and deeper into its gravity well. His body withstood the increasingly strong pull but could not do so indefinitely. Still, he hurtled down, waiting for the proper moment to change. He could not feel friction heating his body, but he knew that it did.

At the appropriate altitude and velocity, the time came. He peered into himself, into the writhing currents, not of gravity, but of possibility. He saw how he existed in his purest form, as a sea of infinite realities always in motion. Whorls of potential spun within him, promised all that he had ever known, and more: imagination offered yet more channels through which his life could flow. He saw what he wanted to become, what he could become, and his body melted within, broke in tides of alteration, deconstructing one form in favor of no form at all—but only for an instant. For in the next, he joined his intention with his elemental being, transforming himself from what he could be into what he would be.

In almost no time, his body had gone, and his tentacles and tail, his gravity-sensing organs, the flesh that covered him. One side of his outer physical self swirled into a spherical, blunt-nosed metal cone, while he thrust wings out from his new frame, then crooked them partway along their length at right angles. He no longer flew, but fell, plummeting through the thickening atmosphere. The shield portion of his new reality heated, but his bent wings sent him into a stable spin, the higher drag limiting his acceleration and thus the temperature of his forward surface.

Down he plunged, through the layers of gases surrounding the planet. When finally he neared the surface, change once more beckoned him. Again he envisioned his metamorphosis, his mind burrowing into the essence of his pliable nature. His wings drew inward, and then his entire body expanded and thinned. Metal became fabric. Closer to the world below, the denser air caught him, filled him, slowed him. He sailed lower.

When he had come far enough down from space, through layers of various gases, bands of radiation, temperature zones, and the broken cover of clouds, he willed his air-filled expanse to fold in on itself. Compact fibers rushed together, liquefied, surged to and fro, and solidified into muscle and bone, flesh and feathers. He stopped falling: as a Tarkalean hawk, he flew.

Exhausted, not just from his descent but also from the long journey that had preceded it, he rode the currents of wind. He glided over a rich, green landscape suffused with the orange hues of sunset. He headed toward a familiar range of mountains and the serpentine river that wound past them. When a small clearing appeared among the trees, Odo at last alit on the surface of Bajor.

He had not yet arrived at his ultimate destination, but the Changeling chose to transform again. From the figure of a Tarkalean hawk, Odo rose into the humanoid appearance he had long ago cultivated, with a brown outfit reminiscent of his old Militia uniform, and his strangely smooth, unfinished face. Although not his natural, amorphous form, the faux Bajoran constable into which Odo made himself felt comfortably authentic; Odo had shaped himself into that physical persona regularly for decades—and for a short time, when the Great Link had deprived him of his shape-shifting abilities, it had become a hard, unchangeable reality.

Odo spied a fallen tree at the edge of the clearing, and he took a seat on its downed trunk. He could not tell whether he did so in order to rest, or simply in service to his long-practiced impersonation of humanoid life. For so long after he had begun to live among the Bajorans, he had sought to emulate their appearance and behavior. At some point, the ways he taught himself to move, the mannerisms he affected, all became second nature to him.

But it's literally my second *nature,* Odo thought. *My* first *nature, my* true *nature, is really something quite different.*

Long ago, before Odo had ever known anything about his origin, he had yearned to discover where he'd come from, to locate his people, to live as he'd been meant to live. Once he did find the Founders, though, it hardly proved the panacea for which he'd hoped. War and attempted genocide rocked the Alpha, Beta, and Gamma Quadrants. Only after years of widespread destruction and death did he finally join his people in the Great Link.

But that didn't last long, did it? he asked himself. He scoffed aloud. Even after returning to link with the Founders, Odo had remained interested in the rest of the Dominion—the Vorta, the Jem'Hadar, and all the other species the empire comprised. Often enough, he parted from his fellow Changelings and assumed his humanoid form so that he could interact with Weyoun and Rotan'talag and others. His goal had been difficult and far-reaching: he wanted to bring a just existence to all the denizens of the Dominion, whether shape-shifter or humanoid. He worked hard to set those changes in motion, but even though he spent considerable amounts of time away from the Founders, he had no wish to desert them.

Instead, they had deserted him. The dissolution of the Great Link shocked and saddened Odo, but it also left him rededicated to re-forming the subsequently leaderless Dominion. He spent years working toward that goal, and even met with some degree of success.

Yet the loss of the Great Link had continued to haunt him. Laas stayed behind with him, and some other Founders eventually returned, but the greater population of their community remained apart. Odo blamed himself, at least in part: he knew that he had never fully given himself over to the Great Link. He wanted to believe that, given another opportunity to do so, he would, but he also didn't want to lie to himself. Yes, he craved the vital oneness of his people when they joined together, but something within him clearly clung to his individuality.

Something within me? Odo thought. It vexed him that, even in his own mind, he did not always confess the truth. Whether or not he could consciously admit it, he knew that he had never stopped loving Kira Nerys. He understood that his reasons for not utterly surrendering himself to the Great Link involved more than that, but it would not help to continue denying his emotions.

As Odo sat on the fallen tree trunk in the clearing, the strong scent of *nerak* blossoms reached him. Although he neither liked nor disliked the smell, he felt grateful that he had learned to cultivate an olfactory sense, since the aroma of the native Bajoran flower—of any Bajoran flower—always put him in mind of Nerys. He wondered if the fragrance had led his thoughts to her, or if his thoughts of her had made him aware of the fragrance.

When the Bajoran wormhole had collapsed and Odo had ended up in the Alpha Quadrant, it had been a bitter irony for him that Nerys had been lost within the great subspace bridge. The news devastated him. Never more had he needed the comfort of communing with his people, of slipping into the Great Link and losing himself within its unique coalescence. Even if he had traveled back to the Dominion, though, most of the Founders remained dispersed.

After the closure of the wormhole, Odo had at first believed himself stranded seventy thousand light-years from the Dominion. He soon discovered, though, that Starfleet's quantum slipstream drive would allow a starship so equipped to deliver him back into the Gamma Quadrant in a matter of days. Eventually, during meetings with Starfleet and the Federation in which they had sought information about the Dominion, they had offered to bring him home.

But what would have I gone back to? Odo asked himself. The Great Link had scattered. He could continue attempting to lead the Vorta and the Jem'Hadar and the others to find their own truths, to seek new purposes and new lives, but could he really accomplish that alone? Might it not be better simply to leave the citizens of the Dominion to find their own ways?

Odo had finally decided to remain in the Alpha Quadrant, at least for a short while. Captain Sisko offered him a position aboard *Robinson*, but that did not appeal to him. Instead, Odo opted to return to his roots.

Early in his existence, he had been one of a hundred Changelings separated from the Great Link and sent out into the universe. He had never attempted to locate another of the Hundred, but another Founder who numbered among them had: Laas had set out to find other shape-shifters, and had succeeded when he'd encountered Odo. With the Great Link no longer extant, and with Kira Nerys lost and probably dead, such a quest seemed to Odo like the best possible use of his time—as well as an apposite outlet for the emotions roiling within him.

And so he had gone to space, though not immediately. First he spoke with Captain Sisko to learn all he could about Nerys's life since last Odo had seen her. After that, with the permission of First Minister Asarem and Kai Pralon, he visited her modest quarters at the Vanadwan Monastery, an act that served as both memorial and pilgrimage. Unexpectedly, he also found a place to reside while on Bajor, and he stayed there for a time. Looking back, he realized that, like the majority of Bajorans, he'd been waiting for the wormhole to reopen; more than that, he understood that he'd still hoped, unrealistic though it might have been, that Nerys would ultimately emerge unharmed from what she thought of as the Celestial Temple.

When finally he had gone into space, he'd cleared his departure and eventual return with the Bajoran Planetary Operations Center. He hoped to find more of the Hundred, or even some of the Founders who had forsaken the Great Link. He reasoned that if both he and Laas had ended up in the Alpha Quadrant, then other Changelings might have as well. Though such a search seemed to him onerous and unlikely to yield positive results, he reminded himself that Laas had once successfully mounted a similar pursuit.

Feeling rested enough, Odo stood from the toppled tree, ready to complete the final leg of his journey. He paced toward the center of the clearing, throwing his arms out to his sides as he did so. Without halting his stride, he turned his mind toward his malleable body. His legs and torso contracted, and his nose lengthened and hardened into a beak. His arms became wings, his flesh covered with feathers. Once more a Tarkalean hawk, he took to the air.

He rose high enough that he could see the Senha River as it traced its way southward along the Releketh Range. With the Bajoran sun dropping toward the horizon at Odo's back, the river meandered darkly along. He spotted a number of vessels floating along the stretch of water visible to him, most of them barges.

When Odo neared the river, he angled south. He followed the lazy course of the Senha until at last he reached the point where the Elestan River branched off from it. Odo swept to his left, putting the tributary below him and tracking it through a break in the mountains to where it carved out a fertile valley along the base of the tallest peak in the range. Odo found a thermal column and used it to gain altitude, then executed a series of switchbacks in order to climb toward the mountain's crest. Once high enough, he soared across the ridge there, past the circular structure standing on the summit, awash in the last, colorful remnants of daylight. Though officially called the Inner Sanctuary, the nine spires atop its outer walls had earned it the appellation "the Crown of Bajor."

About the Inner Sanctuary and down the slope below, an intricate network of long walkways and ranging staircases bound together a complex of ancient buildings. The setting sun pushed long shadows across the Vanadwan Monastery. Odo coasted over it, observing little movement within its confines. At that time of day, he knew, many of the residents would either be sharing their evening meal or participating in vespers. The mostly vacant outdoor spaces would serve him well; he had little taste at the moment even for salutations, much less for conversation.

Odo drifted down along the slope to one of the lower courtyards, an empty cobbled platform encircled by a parapet. He dipped his wings and flew toward it. As his claws set down on its stone surface, he again morphed into his alternate, humanoid self.

Hoping to avoid meeting anybody, he walked quickly through an opening in the low wall bordering the eastern side of the courtyard. He followed a path that declined at a low angle, until he arrived at a divide. There, a set of stone steps led up to the left, while another descended to the right.

Odo hesitated. He would reach his destination by taking the lower walkway, but Nerys's shanty stood along the upper path. Although she had been gone for two years, the leadership at the monastery had focused on her official status of missing. Since she had last been seen within the Celestial Temple, they designated her as missing and presumed to be in the hands of the Prophets. As a result, they had chosen not to assign her quarters to another adherent.

She's not there, Odo told himself. Just because he'd been away from Bajor for the previous two months did not mean that the wormhole had churned back into existence in that time and deposited Nerys back in the Bajoran system. *But it's at least possible,* he thought, even against his better judgment.

Odo hied up the steps to the left. On the upper path, moving through thickening shadows, he counted the dwellings as he passed them. Basic in design and execution, the small wooden structures provided shelter and a place for sleep and private meditation, but little else. Near the end of the hutment, Odo reached the ninth shanty. He braced himself before reading the sign hanging beside the door, preparing to read a name other than Nerys's, which would have been testament to a declaration of her death having been made during his time away.

In Bajoran characters, the sign read: KIRA.

Though he knew the sign proved nothing, Odo felt relieved anyway. He raised his arm, paused, then rapped his knuckles on the door. He received no response. Odo waited a moment, then reached for the latch and released it. He pushed open the door—the monastery equipped none of the rooms with locks—and stepped inside. An overhead light automatically came on, rinsing the small space in dim illumination.

Nerys's living quarters, like the rest of those at the monastery, consisted of only a single room and an attached refresher. It contained little more than a basic sleeping plat- form and mattress, a small desk and chair, a low dresser, and a few floor mats. It looked untouched since the last time he'd visited.

Odo moved over to the dresser, where a large tome sat, along with several framed photographs. He recognized the book, even though its gold-inlay title had been almost completely worn away from its deep-red cover. One of the Bajoran religion's canonical texts, *When the Prophets Cried* had been one of Nerys's favorites, and the only material possession she retained from her early childhood.

Odo gazed from the book to the photographs. Among them, he saw Captain Sisko and his family in one picture, and Bajor's former kai, Opaka Sulan, in another. Odo also saw his own image staring back at him.

I shouldn't have come here, he thought. He had been there before, had looked around Nerys's empty quarters, had seen the photograph of him that she'd kept. It never helped.

Odo made his way back outside, tapping the control for the overhead lighting panel as he left. He retraced his route along the upper path, descended the steps, then went down the next set of stairs and followed the lower walkway. He confirmed the name on the fifth shanty and then knocked. When he received no reply, he unfastened the door and opened it. Inside, a lighting panel activated, revealing living quarters that matched Nerys's almost exactly, but for the lack of padding on the sleeping platform, the dearth of photographs—or anything—sitting atop the dresser, and a padd lying on the desk.

Leaving the door open, Odo moved to the desk, where he pulled out the chair and sat down. Despite his respite in the clearing, he still felt tired, both physically and emotionally. After his many exertions and his fruitless trip, he wanted at that moment to revert to his intrinsic state. He would not want his host to find him that way, though, and so he simply waited.

Isn't that all I ever do these days? he asked himself. *Isn't that almost all I've ever done?* Decades earlier, he had waited for Doctor Mora to recognize him as a life-form and communicate with him. On Terok Nor, he waited for the Bajorans to overthrow the Cardassians. On Deep Space 9, he waited to find his people, and then to be accepted by them, and then for the end of the war. In the Dominion, he waited for the Great Link to mature and understand the injustices in their thinking. He waited for the Vorta and the Jem'Hadar to throw off their shackles and become all that they could become. Odo had taken action in all of those cases—he'd tried hard to make contact with Doctor Mora, he'd worked to undermine the Cardassians, he'd searched for his people, then pushed for peace with them, and finally struggled to show the Founders and the Vorta and the Jem'Hadar better ways. In all those instances, though, he had spent too much time waiting for things to happen.

And since I've been back in the Alpha Quadrant, I've been waiting too. For two years, he'd been leaving Bajor for weeks or months at a time in search of the Hundred or other Changelings. Sixteen months into that effort, he actually did locate another shape-shifter. One of the Hundred, she called herself Moon, and she had been badly injured when Odo found her. Too late to help, he could only wait for her to die.

Of course, I also keep coming back to Bajor, he thought. He attempted to justify that choice to himself, tried to pretend he returned to the Vanadwan Monastery again and again to ease the pain of somebody other than himself, but in truth, he came back for Nerys. She'd been lost and probably dead for two years, yet he continued to wait for her.

Odo didn't really know what to do, other than what he'd been doing. If he could, he mused, he would go back to the beginning, to his own beginning, to when he had been discovered adrift in the Denorios Belt. Living his life over again, he would make other choices than he had, he would do so many things in other ways. Ironically, considering his ability to alter his form at will, he thought he wanted more than anything to be a different person.

Outside, the sound of somebody approaching rose along the path. Odo waited—*Waited!*—to see if the footsteps would lead to the shanty in which he sat. They did.

A lone figure appeared in the doorway. She wore a simple brown robe that hung loosely about her tall physique. A hood covered her head, but within, Odo could see her large golden eyes, fluted around the edges as though melting into her silver, metallic-looking skin.

Odo stood up from the chair. "Raiq," he said. "It's good to see you."

The Ascendant bowed her head in acknowledgment. Though she possessed a naturally musical voice, she said nothing. Unless she had spoken during Odo's latest time away from Bajor, Raiq had not uttered a sound since the wormhole had collapsed with Nerys inside it. She did not seem incapable of talking, merely unwilling. In silence, her grief remained palpable.

Raiq stepped inside. She peered at Odo with a slight cock of her head to one side. He recognized the questioning look.

"In my travels, I found none of my people," he said. "Nor did I find any of yours." Odo had not specifically searched for any of the supposedly missing Ascendants, but he certainly would have told Raiq had he encountered any of her people.

Raiq closed her eyes and lowered her head for a moment. When she looked up again, she pointed to Odo. So often had they played out similar scenarios that he understood her almost as well as if she'd spoken to him. Off and on for two years, Odo had stayed with her at the Vanadwan Monastery whenever he returned to Bajor.

"I've come back so that I can attend the dedication ceremony aboard Deep Space Nine tomorrow," he said. "After that, I don't know. I'll probably spend a few days at the monastery, maybe a week, before heading back out into space again." He cursed himself for his apparent lack of direction.

Raiq nodded. Odo expected another unspoken question, but instead she walked toward him. The movement surprised him, and he tensed. Raiq stopped at once and held up her hands, palms out, demonstrating that she carried neither weapons nor anything else, and suggesting that he had no reason not to remain calm.

Odo relaxed his body, and Raiq slowly finished crossing the room. At the desk, she retrieved the padd resting there. She tapped at its display, then held it out to Odo. He accepted it from her and examined the readout. He saw that she had queued up a message that had been sent to him half a day earlier. He worked the padd to play it.

"This is Lieutenant Ed Radickey aboard the U.S.S. Robinson, *contacting Mister Odo,"* said a male voice. *"Captain Sisko would like to speak with you as soon as you're able. Please contact him aboard the* Robinson." Odo felt his own head incline to one side as he looked up at Raiq.

"If I may," Odo said, "I'd like to use your padd to contact Captain Sisko."

Raiq nodded once, quickly.

"Thank you. I'll be back in just a moment." He crossed the room and went back outside, closing the door behind him. As he operated the padd to open a channel to *Robinson*—he assumed that the ship remained in the Bajoran system and in communications range—he wondered why Captain Sisko needed to speak with him so urgently. He didn't try to delude himself into thinking it would be good news. Whatever the reason, though, he needed to find out.

"Bajor to the *Robinson*," he said once he'd opened a channel. "This is Odo trying to reach Captain Sisko."

Six

Kira ran in the direction of the Orb of the Prophets, though she could no longer see it. She raced ahead anyway, confident that she knew what she must do, that she must reach the Orb. She didn't know why she needed to do so, or even how she would cross the chasm separating her from it, but she envisioned reaching her goal, kneeling down before it, and allowing it to bathe her in its ghostly radiance. She imagined that an Orb experience would follow, and from that she would learn how to proceed. The Prophets would guide her.

The brilliant white glow emanating from the chasm intensified. Not only had the Orb been lost to Kira's sight, but so too had the chasm itself, as well as the cliff faces rising up to either side of her. She didn't stop. She simply fixed her gaze on the ground before her and concentrated on moving forward.

The glare increased. Kira could no longer see the earth on which she ran. Even though she hurried on, even though she could feel the impact of her feet against a solid surface, it appeared as though she moved through a white realm of sheer emptiness.

And still Kira ran.

As she did, she felt her mind . . . detaching . . . from her body. Her point of view seemed to float upward, away from her physical self. She *felt* her legs pumping, her arms swinging, but at the same time she also watched herself from afar.

And still Kira ran.

She thought about stopping, or at least slowing, but all at once it didn't seem as though she any longer knew how to do that. She looked on from above, observing herself in a way she had never experienced—until her mind suddenly dived down, racing toward her body. With a rush of motion and then a sensation of instantaneous deceleration, her awareness slammed back into her corporal existence.

And still . . .

. . . Keev ran.

She held her hands out before her, trying to deflect the leaves and branches through which she moved—although suffering lacerations across her face hardly seemed to matter. Even with the sounds of her crashing through the dense wood, she could hear whoever chased her closing the gap between them. She didn't know how she possibly could have been followed, but at that point she had no recourse but to outrace her pursuer to her destination.

Something sharp pierced Keev's left palm. She pulled her arm toward her body, but only for a moment. She'd caught the end of a tree limb, she thought, and not a revolver shot, but either way, she did not stop running. She did not even examine her hand for blood or for a wound before thrusting her arm back out before her.

Despite her efforts, leaves and branches lashed at Keev's face as she sped through the wood. She didn't care. She only needed to reach—

There! her mind screamed as she spied through all the leaves the familiar tree lying dead across her path. It rose up to at least half her height. When she normally approached it, Keev would leap up onto the trunk, take a step across it, and then jump down on the other side. But—

I'm running out of time, she thought in a panic. She could hear the person chasing her tearing through the wood, closer than before. When Keev reached the tree, she opted not to spring onto it, but to attempt to hurdle it in a single bound. She led with her right foot, and her heel just cleared the bark. She tried to pull her trailing leg up high enough, but the tip of her boot grazed the tree at its apex.

Keev's body jerked to the left and she landed awkwardly. For an instant, she sought to keep her balance, but she came down on the outside of her right foot. Acting on instinct, she let her body collapse to the ground, knowing that if she tried to complete her landing, she would twist her ankle badly, perhaps even break it.

Keev threw her shoulder into the fall. Her upper arm struck soft earth—it had rained the night before—and she rolled, riding her momentum. Her legs came around and she drove her boots into the ground, her hands coming down and acting like pistons, pushing herself back to her feet. Then she ran on.

Just a moment later, she heard two almost simultaneous thuds and then a grunt. Whoever followed her had landed after negotiating the dead tree. Keev understood that she had almost no time left.

Desperate, she sacrificed safety for speed. Keev dropped her arms to her sides and swung them in her natural running motion, pushing herself as fast as she could go. Leaves and branches bombarded her face, and though she ignored the pain, she could no longer survey the ground even just immediately ahead of her. A rock or a depression in the soil, a broken bough, or anything else in her path could bring her down. If that happened, she doubted that she would have a second opportunity to pick herself up and start running again.

Between her gulps of air, Keev heard labored breathing behind her. She considered stopping and making a stand but didn't think she'd have enough time to draw the wooden blade from the sheath strapped to her calf. She wished that she had carried a revolver with her that day. *But then I never would've been able to bluff my way through that Aleiran checkpoint,* she realized.

Keev suddenly burst from the trees and into the small tract that had been cleared by her gild. She saw every face there already turned toward her, along with at least three revolvers. "Ice!" Keev called out, even as she expected to hear the report of weapons fire and to feel her flesh torn apart by multiple slugs. She threw herself to the ground, spinning around so that she landed on her back, facing the way she'd come. Even as she scrambled for her hidden blade, yanking up the right leg of her pants, it amazed her that she hadn't been shot by her compatriots. As she reached to draw her honed hardwood dagger, her pursuer erupted from the same spot where Keev had emerged into the clearing.

The man skidded to a halt as though a steel wall had been dropped in his path. His eyes darted about, presumably taking in the weapons aimed in his direction. Keev unsheathed her blade and cocked her arm.

"I'm not ice! I'm not ice!" the man yelled, throwing his empty hands in the air. Keev wondered if he used those words because he'd heard her only a moment before, but then he added, "I'm sky!"

Keev whipped her arm forward and down, intending to fling her blade at the man who had chased her through the wood. She aimed for his neck, and in her mind's eye, she saw the hilt of her weapon extending from the soft flesh of his throat. At the last instant, though, she held on to her dagger, her hand coming down and striking the ground beside her. It had not been her pursuer's claim of being "sky"—her gild's label for anybody associated with efforts to free the oppressed—and not "ice"—their label for the oppressors; Keev hadn't thrown her blade because it registered that none of her compatriots had fired their revolvers.

For an uncomfortable moment, stillness descended on the clearing. Nobody spoke and nobody moved. Finally, Keev turned her head and gazed at the members of her gild. Several looked back at her, and as though that movement had undammed a river, events began to flow again.

Veralla Sil stood closest to the intruder. The leader of the gild, he stepped forward. One of three people who had brought their revolvers to bear, Veralla lowered his weapon. Keev noted that the other two did not.

Veralla said nothing. Instead, he carefully studied the man who had chased Keev, and so she took the opportunity to do so as well. Her gaze never left him as she climbed back to her feet, the hilt of her dagger still clutched in her hand. She first noticed the intruder's height—not quite that of Veralla, but a head taller than Keev herself. He had short, straight hair, almost black, and though it did not appear perfectly coiffed, she could see that only his sprint through the wood had disturbed its usual neat style. His hands looked clean, his fingernails well manicured. His clothing—light boots, brown pants, and an unbuttoned brown vest worn over a white long-sleeved shirt— seemed an unlikely choice for an outing in the wood. He resembled an office worker more than a freedom fighter, a

slaveholder more than a man who worked to free slaves—
ice more than sky. Keev couldn't tell simply by looking at
him, of course, but he struck her as one of the Aleira rather
than one of the Bajora.

He began to lower his arms, which prompted Veralla
to raise his revolver again. The man reacted by freezing,
but he did not lift his arms back up. "Slowly," Veralla told
him. "And keep your hands away from your clothing." He
nodded and complied with the orders.

Veralla started to walk around the man, scrutiniz-
ing him, but then stopped. "Take two steps forward," he
ordered. As the man did as he'd been bade, the two other
gild members holding revolvers—Jennica Lin, a woman
and the youngest among them, and Renet Losig, a man
and the oldest—stepped back, keeping their distance from
the intruder and their weapons aimed at him.

Keev saw that Veralla had instructed the man to move
in order to provide enough room in the clearing to walk
safely behind him. Veralla did so, visually examining the
man from head to toe. While he did, Keev peered at her
pursuer's face. He had dark eyes and a swarthy complexion. Clean-shaven—in fact, *closely* shaven—he had well-
defined features, including high cheekbones and a fine set
of evenly spaced ridges at the top of his nose. Keev might
have described him as handsome if she hadn't wanted to
plunge her blade into his throat.

Once Veralla had walked a complete circuit around the
man, he turned toward Keev. Without a word, he adjusted
the revolver in his hand, then held it out to her, grip first.
She accepted it, settled it in her own hand—she ignored
the blood smeared across her palm and the accompanying
pain—and trained it on the intruder.

Veralla turned back toward the man. Keev expected

the gild leader to begin asking questions, but instead he remained quiet. Tension filled the clearing. Again without saying anything—hardly unusual for the laconic Veralla—he reached out and patted the man down, starting at his hair and working down to his boots. The man made no move to stop or hinder him in any way. When Veralla finished, he repeated the process from behind the intruder. He conducted his search thoroughly, turning out pockets and leaving no part of the man's anatomy untouched. For his part, the target of Veralla's inspection offered no objections, seeming to understand the seriousness of the situation and his need to cooperate.

"He's clean," Veralla said at last. He moved back in front of the man. "What's your name?" he asked almost casually, as though the two men had met at a social event.

"I'm Altek Dans," the man said. "I'm from Joradell. I'm a doctor."

"A doctor?" Jennica asked, skepticism evident in her tone. "And you were just out for a walk in the deep wood?" She still had not lowered her weapon, though Keev saw that she had shifted it from one hand to the other.

Veralla ignored the interruption. "Why were you chasing my friend?" he asked. Keev noted that Veralla did not use her name. He also did not reveal the purpose of the gild's presence in the wood, although that would have been obvious to anybody who'd spent any time at all in Joradell over the previous few years.

"I was not 'chasing' your friend," Altek said, but then he seemed to think better of his claim. "I mean, I was chasing her, but probably not for the reason you think."

"You have no idea what we think," blustered Jennica. Other voices were grumbling, and Keev glanced over her shoulder at her compatriots. Besides Jennica and Renet, she saw two of the three remaining members of their gild: Cawlder Vinik and Cawlder Losor, husband and wife, a few years younger than Keev, in their middle thirties. She did not spot the final member of their group until she had gazed around the other side of the clearing. In his late twenties, Synder Nogar crouched behind his duffel; he also had his revolver out and aimed at Altek Dans.

"Why were you chasing my friend?" Veralla repeated. Keev returned her attention to the two men in front of her. Though Veralla had asked the question a second time, his even voice had sounded calm and reasonable.

"I was looking for you," Altek admitted. He looked past Veralla at the other members of the gild. When his gaze fell on Keev, she raised the barrel of her revolver, slightly but noticeably. She hadn't intended to do so; it just happened.

Altek looked back at Veralla and went on, "I was looking for all of you. I want to join your efforts. Grenta Sor sent me." The name meant nothing to Keev, but she thought she saw a glimmer of recognition in Veralla's face.

"That still doesn't explain why you were chasing Keev," Jennica said. Keev did not appreciate having her name announced to the intruder, but at that point, they wouldn't be able to release him anyway, so what difference did it make?

Veralla turned and stared directly at Jennica. He quietly said her name. Though he added nothing more, he made his message clear: *I lead this gild and I am conducting this interrogation, so I will be the only one to speak.* In the years that Keev had worked with Veralla, he had never needed to raise his voice or employ excessive verbiage in order to command his troops.

Veralla turned back to Altek. The intruder looked

as though he anticipated another question, but Veralla waited quietly. At last, as though prodded to it, Altek said, "I was sent by Grenta Sor, who told me how to reach your location. I was almost here when I saw movement ahead of me in the wood, off to my left. It was that woman—" He pointed at Keev. "—and it looked like she was headed for your encampment." Altek paused, as though deciding how best to frame what he would say next. "Sir," he finally managed, though he appeared to be near Keev's own age, perhaps five or seven years older than Veralla, "I thought she was the enemy."

Keev found the assertion absurd coming from somebody who had just chased her at a full run. Veralla, though, simply nodded. When he did not say anything, Altek did.

"Look, I thought she was either going to spy on your gild or attack it," he said. "I didn't know what to do. Since you didn't know me, I couldn't just show up here to warn you, and I didn't want to do nothing. It seemed the best course of action to try to subdue her."

Veralla nodded again, but then he asked a question. "How do you know Grenta Sor?"

"We work together at the hospital in Joradell," Altek said. "We're both physicians."

"You are an Aleira then," Veralla said, presenting his words not as a question, but as a statement.

Altek hesitated, but then said, "Yes."

Keev heard a gasp and more grumbling from the others in the clearing. The Aleira held very different beliefs from the Bajora. The Aleira denied not only the divinity of the Prophets, but Their very existence. Of greater significance, they did not subscribe to the equality of all people. In their lands, they had mistreated visiting Bajora for decades, perhaps even for centuries. Within their borders, they subjugated not just the Bajora, but all who were not Aleira. They maintained a two-tiered system in which their people enjoyed all the benefits of society, with the rest forced to provide those benefits. Participation was not a choice.

Five decades prior, a new vein of Aleiran belief had arisen in the Bajoran city of Joradell. It grew slowly at first, with prevalent cultural disapproval of their avaricious, anti-intellectual brand of chauvinism. Still, their numbers increased, and twenty years later, they ultimately seized control of the city. Some of the Bajora and others escaped to freedom, but many had been forced into a life of slavery virtually overnight as the new order had taken power, declaring all non-Aleira as worthy only of either death or use as tools by the state.

"We should kill him," asserted Jennica, always the quickest in their gild to suggest extreme action—and sometimes to take such action. In the present situation, though, Keev thought she agreed with the young firebrand.

Without looking around, Veralla raised one hand and held it open for a moment, a clear signal that he wanted everybody to remain quiet. Jennica said nothing more. After Veralla lowered his arm, he said, "I went to university with Doctor Grenta."

Altek's mouth opened wide in an expression that seemed to mix surprise and relief. "Yes," he proclaimed. "Yes." He looked down, not as if peering at the ground, but as if trying to remember something. He muttered to himself for a moment before gazing back up at Veralla. "You . . . you both attended medical classes, but Sor had an aptitude for anatomy that you lacked."

The statement seemed to Keev an odd response, not

least of all because it sounded like an insult. Veralla did not appear to take it that way, though. Rather, he stepped forward and placed his hands on the intruder's upper arms. "Welcome," he said, and then called back over his shoulder to the rest of the gild, "Stand down."

Keev watched Jennica and Renet lower their revolvers. Synder rose from his place behind his duffel and tucked his weapon into the waistband of his pants. They and the others all started toward Veralla and Altek.

The apparent and sudden resolution did not feel right to Keev. "Wait," she said, so sharply that everybody immediately stopped and peered over at her. "Wait," she said again, lowering her voice. She looked to Veralla. "You believe him, Sil?" She rarely used his given name, but chose to do so in an attempt to underscore the gravity of her concerns.

"I do," Veralla said, holding Keev's gaze. "An old friend has sent Altek to us. An old and *trusted* friend."

The words startled Keev, largely because Veralla spoke of *friends* and *trust* only sparingly. As the gild leader began introducing their people to Altek, Keev looked away. She replayed Veralla's conversation with her pursuer in her mind and decided that, at the end, Veralla must have uttered a prearranged sign to the intruder, who had obviously responded with the appropriate countersign—*Sor had an aptitude for anatomy,* or whatever he'd said. She could think of no other reason that Veralla would so quickly accept a stranger into their group. They already risked their lives every day in their efforts to free individual Bajora from their servitude to the Aleira; placing their faith in the wrong person would put not just their gild at risk, but the entire operation, all the way to Joradell.

"And Kira Nerys, my second-in-command," Veralla said.

Keev snapped her head around to look at Veralla, who held his arm out toward her, apparently introducing her to Altek. "What?" she asked. "What did you say?"

"I said, 'Keev Anora's my second-in-command,'" Veralla told her.

"Oh," Keev said, the word almost inaudible.

"I'm sorry about that," Altek said to her, hiking a thumb back over his shoulder, evidently to indicate their frantic dash through the wood. "I made the wrong choice." He shrugged. "It was bad timing, I guess."

"Bad timing," Keev echoed. She forced up one side of her mouth into what she knew must be a lopsided smile, but she could do no better. She resolved to speak privately with Veralla about their new recruit. The gild leader might have been satisfied with Altek Dans, but Keev wasn't . . . at least not yet.

Seven

Captain Ezri Dax sat behind the desk in her ready room aboard *U.S.S. Aventine.* With her hands wrapped around a steaming mug of *raktajino,* she studied the image of the new Deep Space 9 on her computer interface. She could have viewed it in three-dimensional form utilizing the holographic display built into her desktop, but she wanted to see the starbase in its everyday domain, hanging in space, set against a span of stars.

The overall design of the new station surprised Dax, in that it conjured in her mind the facility that preceded it. Both versions of DS9 possessed a general roundness to their shape, and the three orthogonal rings on the replacement reminded her of the docking ring and the curved docking pylons on the original. Many visible details of the new starbase distinguished it from those of the old, but Dax wondered if anybody else saw what she saw. If so, she wondered if the team who had designed Starfleet's Deep Space 9 had intentionally attempted to evoke the impression of Cardassia's Terok Nor.

Regardless of any superficial similarities, though, Dax could tell simply by looking at the new station that it improved considerably on its predecessor. *How could it* not *be an improvement?* she thought. Terok Nor had been constructed nearly four decades earlier, by the Cardassians—

whose notions of comfort and accommodation none of her hosts had ever understood—and it had been built not as a starbase, but as a plant to process ore.

More than that, though, Dax could see—

An audible alert interrupted the captain's thoughts. "Come in," she called. The doors leading to the bridge parted to reveal her first officer.

"Am I interrupting?" asked Commander Samaritan Bowers as he entered the ready room from the bridge.

"Not at all, Sam," Dax said. Bowers approached her desk, the doors closing behind him. "Have you taken a good look at the new station?" She turned her computer interface around so that Bowers could see its display.

"I saw it on the bridge when we arrived this morning," he said. "But other than that, no, not really."

Dax shook her head. "It's really something."

"Something good or something bad?" Bowers asked. He sat down in one of the two chairs in front of the captain's desk.

"Well," Dax said with a little smile, "it's certainly no Terok Nor."

Bowers chuckled. "So then definitely a good thing." Like Dax, he'd spent several years assigned to the old station.

"I'll say. For one thing, it obviously wasn't designed to process ore."

"It already sounds like a dream posting," Bowers joked.

"Right," Dax agreed. "It's always a positive first step when the place you live wasn't planned as an industrial site."

Bowers leaned an arm on the front of the captain's desktop and peered at the display. "It certainly looks bigger than our old bucket of self-sealing stem bolts."

"It's a lot bigger," Dax said. "I was looking at the specs. They've got three times the crew we had, twice the overall population, plus they can handle scores of ships at once."

"And did you see the park?" Bowers asked.

"I know, a park," Dax said. "And sports fields and a theater and a swimming complex and who knows what else."

"You sound jealous," Bowers said.

"No, not jealous," Dax said. "I'm sure that thing—" She pointed at the image of the starbase on the display. "—can't generate a slipstream corridor and travel at hyperwarp velocities."

"No, but it does have Quark's."

"Is Quark back?" Dax asked. "I hadn't heard."

"That's what I'm told," Bowers said. "And supposedly he's still keeping the place he set up on Bajor while the new station was being built."

"Quark has two establishments?" Dax said. "So he's finally a business magnate?" The news actually delighted her; though Kira and Worf and others hadn't much cared for the Ferengi, she'd always felt quite fond of him.

Bowers laughed. "I'm sure he'd tell you that he's wildly successful, but I'm equally sure he hasn't stopped complaining about how bad business is."

"If he's got two bars," Dax said, "then life is undoubtedly twice as difficult for him now."

Bowers agreed, then asked, "So are you going to go over?"

"To Quark's?" Dax said. "I guess I probably will. I just thought I'd wait to escort President Bacco over, whenever she's ready to go."

"Oh," Bowers said. "That's what I came to tell you: the president left the *Aventine* for the station a few minutes ago."

"Oh," Dax said. As the highest-ranking officer aboard ship, she'd intended to escort President Bacco as a matter of courtesy and respect.

"I just happened to be checking in with her security team when she decided to go," Bowers explained. "I told her I'd contact you, but she said she didn't want to disturb you. She even refused my offer to accompany her."

"A politician who doesn't want special treatment?" Dax said, surprised. "No wonder she got reelected." Not quite a year earlier, Nanietta Bacco had run for another term. She'd faced some vocal opposition, primarily because of Andor's secession from the Federation, but after the defeat of the Borg and her deft handling of the Typhon Pact, she'd ridden a wave of popularity and considerable public approval to a decisive victory. She had even earned Dax's vote.

"So," Bowers asked again, "are you going to go over?" He hitched his head in the general direction of *Aventine*'s stern, to where the ship connected to DS9 via one of the station's airlocks.

Dax sat back in her chair, inhaled deeply, then breathed out in what amounted to a long, slow sigh. "I guess I should get it over with, huh?"

"Julian?" Bowers asked.

"Oh, come on," Dax said. "That's what you were asking, wasn't it, Sam?"

"Well, if memory serves, the last time you two saw each other, you didn't exactly part on the best of terms."

"No, we didn't," Dax said, recalling the last time she'd been alone with Julian, and the tense conversation they'd had over dinner. *Not over dinner,* Dax remembered. *We didn't even make it to our meal.* She could still see in her mind the image of Julian storming out of her quarters, looking back over his shoulder to tell her that he didn't really care whether or not she approved of the choices he'd made in his life. Though her recollection of that argument remained vivid, in some ways it felt as if it had taken place eons ago—or maybe even never taken place at all. "How long ago was that, Sam?"

"It was during our mission to the Breen Confederacy," Bowers said. "That was what? Two years ago?"

Dax nodded, though she could hardly believe it had been that long since she'd had a personal conversation with Julian. It made her feel ashamed. Whatever their differences, they had loved each other, and they certainly should have been able to remain friends. "Two years," she said, but then something occurred to her. "Wait a minute, Sam. Wasn't it just about two years ago that we visited the Venetan Outpost?"

Bowers looked off to one side for a few seconds, then back at the captain. "You're right."

"Our mission to Breen space was *three* years ago," Dax said. It embarrassed her that even more time had passed since her last contact with Julian, doubly so because she hadn't even been able to recall when it had taken place. She stood up and looked across her desk at Bowers. "I've got to go see him, Sam."

"What are you going to say?"

"I don't know," Dax admitted. "But this is no way for adults to behave." She started out from behind her desk, but then the door signal announced another visitor. Her eyebrows rose in a questioning expression.

"If that's Julian," Bowers said, "you should go enter the Lissepian lottery."

Dax offered a close-lipped smile, then said, "Come in." The doors sighed open to reveal a crewman she didn't recognize, and who appeared barely old enough to have even *entered* Starfleet Academy. He stepped inside carrying a padd. "Yes, Crewman?"

"Captain, I'm Barry Herriot," he said, in an accent that Dax thought she recognized as Australian. "I'm a security officer aboard Deep Space Nine. Captain Ro has asked me to invite you to the starbase this evening for a memorial service she's leading. It's specifically to honor the crew who perished when the first station was lost." He held up the padd. "I have all the details for you right here."

Dax walked over to the crewman and took the padd from him. "Thank you, Mister Herriot." She glanced at the display and saw that the service would be held at twenty hundred hours in a place called the Observation Gallery.

"Captain Ro asked me to mention that she's aware that, because you served aboard Deep Space Nine, you knew some of the people who were lost," Herriot said. "She knows that's also the case with several members of your crew. She'd therefore like to extend an invitation to all of them as well, pending your approval, of course."

"Thank you, Mister Herriot," Dax said. "Please thank Captain Ro and tell her that I—" She looked over to Bowers, who nodded. "—and my first officer will attend. I will also pass on her invitation to those other members of my crew."

"Yes, Captain," Herriot said. "Thank you."

"Dismissed," Dax said, and the DS9 crewman retreated the way he'd come. Bowers stood up and walked over to the captain. She handed him the padd.

"I'll let Leishman and Tarses know," he said. *Aventine*'s chief engineer and chief medical officer had both served aboard Deep Space 9 at the same time as Dax and Bowers. "I think there might also be a couple of others who were posted to the station at one time or another. I'll check."

"Thanks, Sam," Dax said. "I'll be on the station. The ship is yours."

They exited her ready room to the bridge, where Bowers paced toward an aft engineering console at which Lieutenant Mikaela Leishman worked. Dax entered a turbolift and specified her destination as the aft hatch. Moments later, she passed the *Aventine* security team standing watch at the ship's wide airlock, then cleared the DS9 sentries guarding the station's lock.

Dax crossed the wide corridor of the starbase's horizontal ring to another turbolift. The feel of the new Deep Space 9 already made an impression on her. The narrow, dimly lighted spaces of its Cardassian forebear had been replaced with broad, bright areas.

"Infirmary," Dax said.

To the captain's surprise, the turbolift did not react by simply accelerating her on her way, but by replying to her audibly. *"Beginning journey to the hospital,"* said the familiar female computer voice in use throughout Starfleet. Dax didn't know if such an announcement accompanied the start of every trip on the station by turbolift, but she suspected that it had been more likely informing her of the designation afforded DS9's medical facility: *hospital*, not *infirmary*.

After a few seconds, the lift started on its way. As the cab glided horizontally along, Dax studied the map of the starbase on the rear bulkhead. She saw that her route had been highlighted in red. The turbolift would take her around the outer ring to a crossover bridge, over to the main body of the station, and directly to the hospital, located on the deck below an area labeled the Plaza, which the captain assumed equated to the old DS9's Promenade.

Dax tapped at the hospital on the map, and the image

expanded to provide an overhead view of the facility. She could see immediately why the designers had eschewed the name *infirmary* for *hospital*: the place occupied nearly a quarter of the circular deck on which it sat. While the diagram lacked specific detail, the facility obviously had a much larger capacity for patients, and Dax guessed that it probably had more than one operating theater, as well as a number of medical laboratories.

When the lift finally eased to a stop, Dax stepped out into another broad corridor. Directly across from her stood the entrance to the hospital, a wide opening with a circular desk set in the center. The words SECTOR GENERAL marched across the front of the desk in Federation Standard. Several security guards stood deeper inside, next to corridors that radiated away from the entrance like the spokes of a wheel.

Dax approached the desk, where a Bajoran man looked up and greeted her by rank. He did not wear a Starfleet uniform. A small sign atop the desk identified him as Damas Hayl. "How may I help you?" he asked.

"I'd like to speak with Doctor Bashir," Dax said.

The man consulted a computer interface. "Doctor Bashir is in his office at the moment," he said, and then he tapped at the display. "You can follow the green lights straight back." He stood up and pointed to the central corridor, where Dax saw a row of small lights embedded in the floor.

"Thank you, Mister Damas." Dax circled the reception desk and headed into the corridor, past the security guard posted there. As she walked, she wondered if Damas would let Julian know of her impending arrival. The receptionist hadn't asked for her name, but despite the traffic at the station—she'd seen several Starfleet vessels docked at the starbase when *Aventine* had arrived, not to mention Klingon, Cardassian, Ferengi, Romulan, and Gorn ships—Dax doubted anybody could find more than one Trill captain at DS9.

When she arrived at Julian's office, Dax touched the door chime immediately, not wanting to give herself any time to reconsider. She received no response, and she wondered if Julian had been warned and had decided to bolt. Just as she reached up to the door signal again, she heard his voice. "Come in," he said, and she could tell from the distracted note in his tone that he'd been busy. It did not surprise her after all the time that had passed that she still seemed to know Julian well.

Dax stepped forward and the doors slid open. As she entered, she saw Julian across from her at his desk, his face turned toward a computer interface. A slew of padds lay before him. Dax didn't say anything, and after a moment, he finally looked up. His mouth fell open at once. "Ezri," he said.

"Hello, Julian," she said warmly. She felt awkward, but not too much so—not more than she'd expected after not having seen him for such a long time. She didn't feel as though she harbored any resentment toward him.

Julian didn't move at first, his surprise at seeing her apparently overwhelming any other reaction he might have. At last, though, he shook off his shock and said her name again. That time, he did so with a smile it pleased Dax to see. He came out from behind his desk and approached her, then stutter-stepped at the last instant, as though he'd had second thoughts about hugging her. Dax moved forward at once and embraced him.

It felt right—not like two lovers finding each other again, but two friends reconnecting. Dax knew that one hug did not resolve whatever issues still lingered between them, but at that moment, it seemed like a fine start. She could not help but smile.

When she stepped back, she regarded Julian with an appraising eye. He looked good—his thick hair and close-cropped beard, his dark coloring, his lithe body—and she told him so, though not in detail. He quickly reciprocated.

"You look good too, Ezri," he said. "I guess starship command agrees with you."

His mention of her position in Starfleet immediately set Dax on edge. Back when she had been assigned to Deep Space 9, her decision to forsake her counselor's duties for a career in command had been a contentious issue between them. Or at least she thought so, though Julian—and his ego—likely would have disagreed. Dax nodded, unable to find words with which she could respond that wouldn't sound petty and send them right back into an argument.

Fortunately, Julian didn't seem to notice her discomfort. More likely, Dax realized, he noticed but chose to ignore it. *The better part of valor, as they say.*

Julian motioned to one of the chairs in front of his desk, and Dax sat down. He took the seat beside her. "I have to apologize," he told her. "I saw that the *Aventine* arrived this morning, and I had every intention of contacting you. I just had so much work to get through on my shift today . . ." He waved a hand toward his desk and the many padds amassed atop it.

"I completely understand, Julian," Dax said. She knew at once that she had overcompensated by using the word *completely*. Until that moment, she hadn't even considered that it had hurt her not to hear from Julian during the few hours that *Aventine* had been docked at the station.

Julian seemed to match her disappointment—in

him, in their absurdly extended situation, in herself—with his own. He slumped back in his chair, only slightly, but enough to convey his frame of mind. "No, I guess I wasn't too busy," he said. "I think I just didn't know what to say."

Dax smiled. "Now that, I *do* completely understand," she said, and then laughed. Julian smiled as well—not a wide smile, but at least one that appeared genuine. "But actually, I think I do know what to say: I'm sorry." She'd said the same thing when she'd seen him three years earlier. She couldn't recall whether he had also apologized to her, but she knew it wouldn't have mattered back then; at the time, neither one of them had been all that remorseful.

"Ezri, you don't have to say that," Julian told her.

"Maybe not for you," Dax said, careful to speak her words gently, "but I certainly need to do so for myself. I behaved badly."

"It wasn't just you," Julian admitted.

"No, I didn't think it was," Dax agreed, again taking pains to sound neither challenging nor reproachful. "But I can only apologize for my behavior. No matter what you did or what I thought you did, I'm responsible for how I acted and reacted. I think there were reasons for some of what I did, some of what I said—"

"You were going through a lot of changes," Julian said, not unkindly. "Ezri Tigan never planned on joining with a symbiont, or on transferring to the command track and becoming captain of a starship. I can't even imagine what all of that must have been like for you."

Dax nodded, thinking back to those uncertain days. "Both of those changes were difficult in ways I hadn't anticipated—that I *couldn't* have anticipated. But even so, it's not an excuse."

"It was more of an excuse than I had," Julian said. "I was leading with my ego."

"Well," Dax said, debating whether or not to say the words that popped into her mind, and then deciding that she would. "It's hard not to lead with an ego as large as a starship." Although she said the words through a smile, Julian reacted as though she'd thrown a punch into his stomach. Dax worried that she had reopened old wounds, but then Julian offered her a smile of his own—a sheepish smile, it pleased her to see.

"I was genetically enhanced," he said lightly. "It wasn't just my physical and mental abilities that increased."

Dax chuckled, grateful that, after all that time, they finally seemed to be making some headway. "Hey, I've got the egos of eight previous hosts, Dax, and Ezri in here," she said, tapping her fingers against her abdomen. They both laughed together, and then Julian reached over and took one of her hands in both of his. Dax nearly pulled away, but then gathered that he meant the gesture more in a fraternal than a romantic way.

"I really am sorry," he said. He sounded so earnest that it reminded Dax of one of the things that had attracted her to him in the first place. As dashing and accomplished a man as he was, as superior because of his genetic enhancements, he still nurtured an innocent little boy inside him. "I know you think I loved Jadzia, and I did, but I also loved you, Ezri. I loved you for you."

Dax patted his hand, which still rested atop her own. "I know you did, Julian." In truth, she'd always had her doubts, and still did, but she also recognized that they no longer mattered. "Listen, I'm sorry about how things ended with us, but I'm not sorry that we were together."

"I treasure those memories," Julian said.

"I do too," Dax said. "And even though I'm sorry for the way I behaved, for how I hurt you, I'm not sorry that we're no longer in a romantic relationship. We were right for each other when we were together, but in the long run . . ." She didn't need to finish her thought.

"You're right, of course," Julian said. "It would be nice, though . . . I mean, I hope that we can still be friends."

Even with everything they'd already said, Dax felt relieved to hear Julian state that explicitly. "That's why I'm here," she said. "I wanted to apologize, and I wanted to see if I could get back somebody in my life who I still truly care about."

"I want that too," Julian said. Dax reached forward and put her arms around him, and he hugged her back. When they parted, Dax stood up from her chair, and Julian followed suit.

"Well, I really do have a lot of work," she said.

"I'd like it if we could see each other while you're here."

"I'd like that too."

"How long are you on the station for?" Julian asked.

"Until the day after tomorrow," Dax said. "After the dedication, we'll be taking President Bacco to Cardassia for some high-level meetings there."

"Not a lot of time," Julian noted.

"No," Dax said. "Will you be going to the memorial service tonight?" Although it would be a somber occasion, she thought that perhaps they could have a drink at Quark's afterward.

"Yes," Julian said. "Sarina and I will be there."

Dax felt her eyebrows rise on her forehead and she forced them back down. "Sarina," she said, and felt foolish for parroting the name. "So you two are still together?"

"We are," Julian said.

"That's wonderful," Dax said. "I'm happy for you." *Did I even know that Sarina was serving on Deep Space Nine?* For some reason, she thought she had known that. *Did I forget it—or did I intentionally put it out of my mind?*

"Thank you," Julian said. If he detected any of the stray thoughts running through her head, he gave no indication.

"I'll check my schedule and figure out a time when we can get together," Dax said, choosing not to mention her idea of meeting at Quark's after the memorial. "We can talk after the service."

"Great," Julian said.

Dax left his office. As she made her way through the corridor and out of the hospital, she had to classify her meeting with Julian as a success. She didn't know if they'd said enough to each other, if they'd each dealt with whatever residual issues they still might have, but at the very least, it seemed like a good start on the road back to friendship. She certainly hoped so.

She also hoped that Julian had found the right woman for himself in Sarina Douglas. Dax wasn't so sure.

Federation President Nanietta Bacco strode down a corridor on Deep Space 9, two of her protection detail leading the way and two following behind her. For a long time after she had initially taken office, she'd found their continual presence around her bothersome, though she'd eventually become inured to it. But all that had changed after the grisly events the previous year on Orion. Although Bacco had come to genuinely accept the necessity of the agents' company, she resumed her earlier preference not to have them around, but for a different reason. Where before she had simply found the incessant attendance of her bodyguards at her side intrusive, she had come to fear for their lives.

It's so tiring, Bacco thought. Of course, from her first day as Federation president nearly six years prior, she'd experienced a more or less uninterrupted state of fatigue. And although she'd enjoyed a sound sleep the night before in her cabin aboard *Aventine,* she still felt exhausted.

But not just *exhausted,* she realized. *I feel like I'm operating on autopilot.*

That had been the case for quite a while—for better than a year, to be sure. Losing Esperanza Piñiero had been an almost unbearable blow. Decades earlier, Bacco had been close friends with Esperanza's parents and so had watched her grow up on Cestus III. When Bacco had later served as governor of that world, the woman she'd once called "Espy"—and who'd in turn called her "Auntie Nan"—had followed a successful career in Starfleet by joining her in the political arena. It had been Esperanza who had convinced her to seek the Federation presidency, who had then acted as her campaign manager, and who'd finally served with distinction in the Palais de la Concorde as her chief of staff.

And now she's gone. The past year had been so personally difficult for Bacco. She had considered ending her run for another term, but somehow, through a combination of her own inertia—a body in motion tends to stay in motion, as she'd learned in school—and the efforts of Ashanté Phiri, her new chief of staff, she'd remained in the race and scored a convincing win. Bacco honestly appreciated the vast, Federation-wide support she received, pleased that what amounted to a referendum on her presidency not only validated her accomplishments in office, but also underlined the enormous contributions Esperanza had made to the people of the UFP—whether or not they knew it.

And if she were here, Esperanza would tell me to stop feeling sorry for myself, Bacco thought. *And when I get back to the* Aventine, *Ashanté* will *tell me that.*

Bacco had left her chief of staff back on the starship that had carried them from Earth to DS9. One of Esperanza's former deputies, Phiri had done an exceptional job shepherding the president through her period of mourning. In recent months, though, she had begun to take a harder line with Bacco, clearly attempting to push her fully through her grief and out the other side.

And she's right to do so, the president thought. Phiri hadn't been entirely successful—Bacco still lamented daily the death of her friend—but the work actually seemed to have gotten easier lately. The president still needed more hours in the day, more days in the week, more weeks in the year to do all that she needed to do to keep the people of the Federation safe and moving forward, and she still always felt weary. Sometimes, Bacco wondered if all her recent achievements had occurred only as the result of her momentum mixed with the hard work of people like Ashanté Phiri.

Nonsense, Bacco told herself, in a voice that sounded suspiciously like Esperanza's. *It's not just momentum; you're actively doing your job.* It had been Bacco's idea to invite the Romulan praetor and the Gorn imperator to the official dedication of Deep Space 9, which she envisioned becoming not merely a celebration of perseverance and resilience in the face of adversity, but also an attempt to demonstrate a principle that Gell Kamemor had once shared with her: that art, intellect, and romance must ultimately triumph over cynicism, ignorance, and brutality. The president had personally asked Praetor Kamemor and Imperator Sozzerozs to attend the ceremony, and then had spent months convincing them to do so.

So I am *doing my job,* Bacco thought. And even though the presidency required so much of her—it required so much of whoever held the position—she realized that it was the moments in between the work that she had come to find the hardest to bear. In those moments—in the occasional quiet of her office, or in the solitude when she lay her head down at night, or even when walking silently down a corridor to a meeting—she would feel her exhaustion completely, rendering her incapable of preventing all her sorrows from filling her.

Up ahead, Bacco saw two more members of her protection detail—they seemed to have multiplied since the incident on Orion. The agents stood beside adjacent doors. Advance scouts, they preceded the president to a destination in order to secure it.

One of the agents walking ahead of Bacco, a woman named Magdalena Ferson, consulted with the advance team. The other security officers with the president took up positions in the corridor on either side of the doors. Ferson, a tall, solidly built woman with red hair, approached Bacco.

"The room has been cleared for you to enter, Madam President," she said.

"Thank you, Agent Ferson." Bacco walked alone through the nearer set of doors. She noted immediately the four portable transport inhibitors set into the corners of the room. Since Orion, Federation Security had redoubled its efforts to keep her safe.

Large ports lined the outer, curved bulkhead of the meeting room. A long conference table stood before them. At the end of the table, facing her, sat a man Bacco recognized, a Starfleet officer with whom she had spoken on several occasions. He stood up when she entered. At the far end of the room, another man stopped his apparent pacing and turned toward her.

Bacco approached the conference table. "Captain Sisko," she said, "it is good to see you again."

"Thank you, Madam President," said the captain. "It's good to see you."

Bacco turned her attention to the other man. He wore brown pants and a matching shirt, an outfit that resembled the uniform of the Bajoran Militia, though the president saw no insignia on it. His face had unusually smooth features and his hair lay slicked straight back on his head. "I trust that you are Mister Odo," Bacco said, taking a few steps toward him.

The man put his hands behind his back. "Just Odo will do, thank you, Madam President." His voice did not hide his displeasure, and Bacco wondered how difficult it had been for Captain Sisko to convince the shape-shifter to attend the meeting.

"I'm sorry, I meant no disrespect," she said, attempting to defuse his obvious annoyance. "On the contrary, I intended the reverse. Is there some other honorific I may employ when addressing you? Perhaps your former title of *constable*?" In preparation for the meeting, Bacco had read all of the reports she could find about Odo—many of them written by Captain Sisko. As a result, she knew of his intelligence and his abilities as a security officer. She therefore entertained no illusions that he did not understand her purpose in making reference to his time serving aboard Deep Space 9; regardless, mentioning Odo's association with Captain Sisko would still evoke that period in the Changeling's mind.

"Just Odo," he repeated.

"Very well, then," Bacco said. "It is a pleasure to meet you, Odo."

Odo nodded curtly. "Madam President," he offered in terse acknowledgment.

Bacco waited before saying anything more. Odo seemed to grow increasingly uncomfortable. He glanced over at Sisko, but the captain wisely said nothing.

"I'm sorry, Madam President," Odo finally said, "but it is unclear why you've asked me here today."

"Why don't we sit," Bacco suggested, "and I'll tell you."

Odo hesitated, which Bacco interpreted as a sign of his uneasiness. He clearly wanted the meeting to end as soon as possible, and he viewed even the simple act of sitting down as an impediment to that. Still, as Bacco moved to take a seat at the head of the table, to Sisko's right, Odo followed. With undisguised reluctance, he sat down across from the captain, to the president's right.

"I've asked to meet with you, Odo, because I have something I wish to tell you," Bacco said. "Something I wish to *offer* you."

Her assertion seemed to annoy Odo. He glanced at the captain again before saying, "Thank you, but there is nothing that I need."

Bacco allowed her eyebrows to dance upward. "Nothing?" she asked, sowing a note of disbelief into her voice. "Don't we all need something?"

"Perhaps humanoids do," Odo said.

"Now, that sounds racist to me," Bacco said. She had hoped to conduct her meeting with the Changeling with as little confrontation as possible, but it seemed clear that Odo did not intend to make it easy for her.

"Madam President, I promise you that Odo is no such

thing," Sisko said at once. "I have known him for sixteen years, and I can tell you that's just not who he is."

"Have I misinterpreted your assertion, Odo?" Bacco asked. "Are you perhaps suggesting that you don't need anything because you can *be* anything?"

"I'm not suggesting anything, other than there is nothing you can offer me that I need," Odo said. "To be completely honest, Madam President, I didn't want to attend this meeting. I'm doing so only because Captain Sisko asked me to." Odo paused, then added, "I am not trying to be disrespectful."

Bacco laughed. "I don't find you disrespectful, Odo," she said. "Believe me, if I was asked to have a meeting with me, I'd want to get out of it too." She had hoped to elicit some sort of amused reaction from the shape-shifter, but he continued to regard her blank faced. *In this case, almost* literally *blank faced,* Bacco thought, at least amusing herself. "I'll be completely honest with you as well, Odo. I asked Captain Sisko to be here only as an enticement to ensure that you would come too." She nodded apologetically toward Sisko, who did not appear particularly surprised or offended by the admission. While not entirely true, Bacco absolutely had used the Changeling's relationship with the captain as an inducement to meet with her. The president also wanted the captain there in order to help her assess both Odo's reactions to what she would tell him, and his motives in making whatever choices he then did.

"I see," Odo said. "Since you have succeeded in getting me here, then perhaps you can tell me what it is you want to tell me."

Bacco leaned forward, resting her forearms on the edge of the conference table. "I have to tell you, Odo, that I find your people fascinating." She intended the statement to be provocative, and it immediately produced the desired effect.

"Captain Sisko told me that you would not ask me about either the Founders or the Dominion," Odo said, bristling.

"And I won't," Bacco said. "But I cannot claim that your people do not interest me, that the state of the Dominion does not interest me—especially in light of the fact that, when Captain Sisko visited you there two years ago, he discovered that the world of the Great Link had been deserted. Of course, we know that the Founders have relocated themselves before, abandoning one planet for another, but other details suggest that something else might have happened. I suspect that you could shed some light on that."

"Is this you not asking me about my people?" Odo said, his temper rising.

"I have asked you nothing," Bacco pointed out, though she had hoped that Odo might be willing to reveal some details about the Founders' situation. "And I expect you to tell me nothing." Bacco leaned back as she plotted how to drive the conversation where she wanted it to go. "Odo, your role in ending the Dominion War is not widely known among the general Federation population. It seems that my predecessor and his administration believed it wiser not to reveal to a war-weary public that hostilities ended partly because you cured the Founders of a disease that would have wiped them out. I only learned of that later myself, and I have to say that I agree with the decision at that time not to reveal those details."

"What is the point of all this?" Odo wanted to know.

"I'm mentioning this to you because I want you to know that I am aware of the major part you played in ending the war," Bacco said. "Captain Sisko and others have spoken on the record and at length about your actions, about your dedication to justice, about your loyalty to your friends. In short, many people affirm that you are a good man."

"I am not a man," Odo said, although his statement seemed delivered more out of reflex than his having taken offense.

"Forgive me for my imprecise language," Bacco said. "My point is that many people have sung your praises, and that I recognize that you have been a staunch ally of the Federation."

"I do not consider myself an 'ally' of the Federation," Odo said.

"You have nevertheless consistently behaved in a manner that demonstrates your trustworthiness and value," Bacco maintained. "Because of that, I have asked you here so that I can speak to you about two things. First, I understand that, when the wormhole collapsed after you were ejected from it into the Alpha Quadrant, you believed yourself stranded, that unless the wormhole had not been destroyed, that unless it reopened, you would not be able to return to the Gamma Quadrant and to your people."

"I did believe that at first," Odo said. "But Federation officials and Starfleet officers met with me to tell me that one of your starships equipped with quantum slipstream drive could carry me back to the Dominion in a relatively short amount of time."

"You declined," Bacco said.

"Yes."

"But I believe that you did not make it clear why you did not wish to return to the Dominion," Bacco said.

"Are you asking my reasons?"

"Certainly not; your reasons are your own," Bacco said, though she very much wanted to understand the choice Odo had made. "A recent event, however, has brought your decision back to mind. It occurred to me—and I am not asking if this was the case—that you might not have wanted a Starfleet vessel to return you home because you did not want any foreign ship to enter Dominion space." Bacco offered a questioning look to Sisko.

"You did make it quite clear," the captain told Odo, "that the Dominion had closed its borders, and you specifically mentioned that included ships and people from the Federation."

"If you are concerned about Starfleet violating those borders when we bring you back home, I can promise you that we would honor your wishes and remain outside the Dominion," Bacco said. "I am told that you have the capability of traveling on your own through space, so one of our starships could deliver you to a location just outside the border."

"Yes, I can travel in space," Odo said, "and you needn't assure me of anything."

"Odo," Captain Sisko interjected, "I think President Bacco is making you an offer."

"That is what I'm doing," Bacco said. "I know that you rejected the offer before, but I wanted you to know, from the highest official in the Federation, that we are both able and willing to take you back to the Dominion on a voyage that would be measured in days, not in months or years." Bacco paused in order to emphasize what she would say next. "In fact, in light of your significant contributions to the Federation, we would be honored to be of such service to you."

"Thank you," Odo said. "I am . . . grateful . . . for your

offer. But I am content right now to remain in the Alpha Quadrant."

"Very well," Bacco said. "Should you change your mind, you may get word to me through Starfleet. I cannot promise that one of our slipstream starships will be available at any given moment, but we would arrange for your journey at the earliest possible time."

"Thank you, Madam President," Odo said. Though Bacco found the Changeling difficult to read, she thought he seemed satisfied.

"Now, as I mentioned, there is a second issue I wanted to discuss with you," Bacco said. "Recently, a Starfleet vessel was conducting a scientific mission in a remote star system. During routine scans of an asteroid belt, they detected readings they could not explain. Closer examination of one of the asteroids showed an unusual substance on its surface. We cannot be sure, but we suspect there's a chance that the substance may be a shape-shifter."

"What?" Odo said. "What do you mean 'may be'?"

"I'm not a scientist," Bacco said. "I can't provide you the particulars of what the *Nova* crew discovered, only their conclusion. Although the . . . I think they called it the 'matrix' of the substance . . . doesn't precisely match yours, it is extremely similar."

"Has it actually shape-shifted?" asked Sisko.

"So far, no," Bacco said. "But I've been informed that when Odo was found floating in the Bajoran system, he was in an unformed state." The president had read a file in which she learned that Odo had begun to alter his shape only after a Bajoran scientist had begun conducting experiments on him.

"That's true," Odo confirmed. "And I didn't change into something for years after that."

"It may be that the *Nova* crew has found an interesting substance and nothing more, not something alive," Bacco said. "Or maybe it is a shape-shifter, perhaps an offshoot of your own species. Or maybe the *Nova* crew missed something and it is a Founder. Given the possibility of the substance's sentience, though, we do not wish to make it endure what you had to, Odo."

"I understand," Odo said. "And I appreciate that."

"Where is the substance now?" Sisko asked.

"It has been taken by the *Nova* crew to a secure scientific facility," Bacco said. At the mention of a scientific facility, Odo's eyes widened and he opened his mouth as though to object. Bacco put up a hand to stop him. "Scientists are observing the substance and doing nothing more. As I said, we have no desire to make this being— if it is a being—suffer the pain and indignity that you did—which is the other reason I'm here. I wanted to know if you would be interested in examining the substance yourself . . . perhaps try to interact with it . . . make contact, if that's possible."

"For what purpose?" Odo asked.

"For no other purpose than to help a fellow life-form, if possible," Bacco said, "And to expand our knowledge of the universe."

Odo did not take much time to consider the president's offer. "I'm interested."

"Excellent," Bacco said. "I will notify Admiral Akaar and have Starfleet route a ship to Deep Space Nine for you. I'm sure we can have a vessel here for you in a couple of days to take you to the science facility."

"Why not just bring the substance here?" Odo asked.

"I've been told that, until our scientists—or you—can identify the precise nature of the substance, they'd prefer to keep it contained," Bacco said. "A precautionary measure."

Odo nodded his understanding.

Bacco stood up. "Well, thank you, gentlemen," she said. "Odo, I'll have Captain Ro assign you quarters until the ship arrives for you." Her business completed, the president headed for the door.

Out in the corridor, her protection detail fell in about her and they started as a group back toward the airlock at which *Aventine* had docked. Bacco hadn't learned anything new about the Founders or the Dominion, but she hadn't expected to; given the necessity of speaking with Odo, though, she'd felt it worthwhile to make the attempt. The president had accomplished what she'd set out to do, though: she'd confirmed Odo's disinterest in returning to the Gamma Quadrant, and she'd enlisted his aid regarding the substance that the *Nova* crew had found.

As she walked along the corridor, Bacco realized that she no longer felt quite so tired.

The doors whisked open before Doctor Julian Bashir, revealing the base of the Observation Gallery. He stepped out of the turbolift with Lieutenant Commander Sarina Douglas by his side. Neither of them had visited that part of the starbase yet, though it had been completed and made accessible to the crew a few days earlier. Bashir had wanted to wait for the memorial Captain Ro had planned, and Sarina had agreed.

"I guess we're not as early as we thought," Bashir said quietly as he and Sarina moved away from the lift. They had decided to arrive well before the service so that they would have time to explore the new space in relative privacy. Other members of the crew had clearly entertained the same idea, though, since quite a few already milled about, all of them—like Bashir and Sarina—in their dress uniforms.

"I think everybody just wanted some time to see this place," Sarina said. "Especially those who were on the station before." She spoke softly, but her voice dropped out almost completely on her final word.

Before, Bashir thought. A single word that said so much. *Before Typhon Pact starships launched an unprovoked attack on the first Deep Space Nine. Before the first station was destroyed. Before a thousand Federation lives had been extinguished in the blink of an eye.*

Bashir and Sarina moved slowly across the expansive deck, which, though filled with members of the crew, otherwise appeared to contain little else. Looking around, the doctor saw that the turbolift they had exited stood in a circular bank of four in the center of the round space. The shafts ended there, climbing up to the Observation Gallery through the vertical spire atop the main sphere and rising no farther.

The doctor had heard that, during the design and construction of the starbase, somebody in the crew had suggested to the captain that the new Deep Space 9 should include a memorial to the old Deep Space 9 and the lives lost in its destruction. Ro agreed. After successfully pitching the idea to Starfleet Command, the captain worked with the starbase's designers—among them, DS9's top two engineers, Miles O'Brien and Nog—to develop a suitable location for it. Once that had been accomplished, Ro had commissioned a Bajoran artist, a woman named Acto Viri, to develop the memorial itself.

Bashir wondered how many other people knew that Kira Nerys had appreciated Acto's art. Kira had been

killed two years earlier in the collapse of the wormhole—
although many Bajorans chose to consider her not dead,
but missing. Years before that, when she commanded
the station, she purchased one of Acto's paintings, *Bajor
at Peace*, and hung it in her office. Later, when she left
Starfleet, she made a gift of the artwork to Ro Laren,
though the painting had been lost with the station. Bashir
felt certain that Ro had chosen the memorial artist as a
means of honoring Kira.

The doctor strolled with Sarina among their crewmates,
moving farther and farther from the turbolifts. When
they neared the perimeter of the space, they both stopped
abruptly. Transparent and angled outward, the exterior
bulkheads offered dramatic views of the starbase. The
Observation Gallery nestled below the upper intersection of
the two vertical rings, and Bashir gazed out at one of those
rings descending in an impressive arc off to his right. When
he looked down, he saw the upper half of the station's main
section, the sphere, and through the transparent hull there,
he beheld the brilliant green of the park.

"Wow," Sarina said simply.

"I think that about covers it," Bashir agreed.

They stood there for a few minutes taking in the spectacular vista, then began walking along the outer bulkhead.
Partway around the circular compartment, they reached a
ramp that rose to the deck above. Set a few meters in from
the outer bulkhead and constructed of an extremely thin
material that had been frosted white, it had no visible sup-
ports. As a result, the crew on the ramp looked as though
they floated in midair.

Bashir and Sarina opted to bypass the ramp so that
they could look out at the starbase from different points.

The doctor noticed that when people spoke, they did so as he and Sarina had, in hushed tones. He thought that the stunning panorama could have inspired such reactions, but suspected that it had more to do with the nature of the place and the upcoming event.

Eventually, Bashir and Sarina arrived at a second ramp, set directly opposite the first. "Do you want to go up?" she asked.

"'Want' might be a bit strong," Bashir said. Even two years after the fact, he found the loss of so many people all at once—so many friends and colleagues, in a catastrophe that need never have happened—difficult to accept. Such losses had been hard enough to deal with during wartime; in peace, it became nearly impossible. While Bashir wanted very much to honor his fallen comrades, he did not want to experience all of the deep emotions that would come with doing so.

"I know what you mean," Sarina said. Still, they started slowly up the ramp together.

The next deck very much resembled the one below, but with some notable distinctions. Because the exterior bulkheads angled outward, the upper deck of the Observation Gallery enclosed slightly more space, but it seemed larger also because the overhead did not hang four or five meters above them, as on the lower deck, but a dozen or more. No turbolifts or other doors served the space; other than by transporter, it could be accessed only via the ramps. And as quiet as the lower deck had been, with people speaking in low voices, the silence on the upper deck went totally unchallenged.

As they had below, Bashir and Sarina approached the outer bulkhead. Once there, Sarina stopped and pointed down toward their feet. Bashir followed her gesture and saw that the half meter or so of the deck that abutted the exterior bulkhead had been layered with a black, marbled stone, and a low, raised rim set it apart. Names had been etched into the stone.

MICHELLE ROBINSON, read the name in front of Bashir, and in smaller letters directly below that, LIEU-TENANT COMMANDER, SECURITY, DEEP SPACE 9.

ELEG RWATT, read the next entry. ENSIGN, ENGINEER-ING, *U.S.S. ROBINSON*. More than thirty of the starship's crew had perished when it had defended the station.

AIDA SELZNER. LIEUTENANT J.G., COMMUNICATIONS, *U.S.S. NILE*. Bashir assumed that the DS9 comm officer had been assigned to the runabout during the evacuation.

JASON SENKOWSKI. LIEUTENANT, ENGINEERING, DEEP SPACE 9.

JANG SI NARAN. LIEUTENANT, SECURITY, DEEP SPACE 9.

Bashir's vision began to blur. He looked up, away from the names, and took in a deep breath through his nose. It amazed him how fresh the wound felt, even after all the time that had passed.

Sarina took his hand and squeezed it, but he couldn't look at her. Bashir knew that if they saw each other's tears threatening, there would be no holding them back. He tightened his hand about hers, then resumed walking.

They continued around the deck. Bashir didn't know about Sarina, but when he peered down at the names inscribed in the dark stone, he allowed his gaze to pass over them, picking out words here and there, but not really reading them. At that moment, together with Sarina and among so many of their crewmates, he couldn't think of all his lost colleagues without breaking down. Occa-sionally, though, some names managed to penetrate his attempts to filter them out: JEANNETTE CHAO. HATRAM NABIR. CATHY LING. LUIS GARCÍA MÁRQUEZ, who had been Kasidy Yates's chief engineer aboard her freighter, *Xhosa*, which had been lost with everyone aboard. Bashir had known them all.

When they had made their way completely around, they turned toward the inner part of the deck. Because he had been looking down as he and Sarina walked along the names of the dead, and because so many of the crew filled the upper deck of the Observation Gallery, Bashir hadn't noticed much else about the space. As they moved toward the center of the deck, though, he saw past all the members of the crew that a massive object stood there. Mounted atop a vertical black pole as though magically balanced, a huge, curved piece of metal looked to Bashir like a lower section that had been ripped from a great globe. Greenish-gray, with a slash of black singed across its surface, its ragged edges conveyed with no words the original Deep Space 9's violent end.

As Bashir and Sarina circled the artifact, they came across three plaques mounted around its base. The first displayed a silhouette of the original station, with a highlighted section indicating the precise location of the hull fragment. Below the image, the sign read:

SECTION OF BULKHEAD FROM
ORIGINAL DEEP SPACE 9
HABITAT RING
CORRIDOR K-17-R

The second sign gave the particulars of the first DS9's construction as an ore-processing facility during the Occupation, its status as a command post by the Cardassian prefect, and its subsequent use by the Federation Starfleet. Though presented in the antiseptic language of museums, the description still managed to impart a sense of both the horrors and triumphs of which the original station had been a part. No matter the neutrality of the words employed, neither the abomination of the Occupation nor the exultation of Bajor's liberation could be minimized.

The final plaque detailed the actual loss of the station. Though stated impartially, the roles in the disaster of the crews of three Typhon Pact starships—a Romulan warbird, a Tzenkethi marauder, and a Breen warship—could not be denied. The account concluded by noting that Bajor and the Federation had opted to construct a new starbase, which would enter into service on the second anniversary of the first station's loss.

Finishing their trip around the monument, Bashir and Sarina passed a small platform—about four meters by two, rising not even a meter above the deck—that had clearly been placed there for the event. They drifted about the space, not speaking or looking at each other, but holding hands very tightly. Around them, people continued to arrive in the Observation Gallery.

As the scheduled time of the memorial service neared, Bashir estimated that several hundred people had gathered. Ro had invited those members of the crew who had served on the old station at the time of its destruction, although not all 263 survivors remained in the Bajoran system, or even in Starfleet. The captain had also asked any civilians who had endured the loss of the station to attend, though after two years, only a small number— fewer than two hundred of the more than five thousand successfully evacuated—had opted to call the new Deep

Space 9 home. Ro had also invited anybody else at the station who had ever been posted to the old DS9, or whose friends or family had been. Consequently, as Bashir gazed around at the people assembled, he saw exclusively faces he had known for years, including many of the current senior staff: Ro Laren and Cenn Desca, John Candlewood and Jefferson Blackmer, Zivan Slaine. He also spotted others he'd known on the old station, but who had moved on: Benjamin Sisko and Kasidy Yates from *Robinson*, and Ezri Dax, Samaritan Bowers, Simon Tarses, Mikaela Leishman, and a few others from *Aventine*. Miles O'Brien and Nog fit into both categories. Bashir also spied Quark lingering on the periphery of the gathering, as though still deciding whether he truly wanted to be there. Treir stood beside him, evidently having made the trip from Bajor for the service. Oddly, Odo stood not far from Quark.

A rustling sound drifted through the Observation Gallery as people began to move, turning toward the center of the deck and the fragment of hull that served as a cenotaph. Bashir and Sarina followed the leads of those around them and shifted to face in the same direction as everyone else. There, beside the memorialized wreckage, Captain Ro Laren rose up out of the crowd, mounting the portable platform. She waited just a moment as people stopped moving and the compartment quieted.

"Welcome to the Observation Gallery, and to the Memorial Deck, of our new starbase," the captain said. She did not speak loudly, but her voice carried easily in the otherwise overwhelming silence. "Thank you for joining me here this evening. I know that this is not easy for any of us, but I am pleased to see so many of you who lived through our shared ordeal."

Bashir recalled the first anniversary of the station's destruction, when Ro had stood before the crew at Bajoran Space Central and said a few words in remembrance. That event had felt different from the one presently unfurling on the new station. A year earlier, the surviving DS9 crew members had not all been assigned to the same location; some had served on Bajor, while others had been posted to the various starships that patrolled the system. Of those who served planetside, many had attended a service held in Ashalla by the Vedek Assembly and presided over by First Minister Asarem and Kai Pralon. Ro's words that day at BSC, though clearly heartfelt, had been brief. Though not the fault of the captain, that observance had lacked cohesiveness and a sense of moment.

"The Memorial Deck was, by the request of Starfleet, designed by a Bajoran artist named Acto Viri," Ro continued. "I am grateful to Ms. Acto for her contribution to us and to those we remember. I invited Ms. Acto to join us for this service, but she politely demurred. From an artist's perspective, she said, this memorial she created must speak for itself, which I certainly think it does. But Ms. Acto also told me that she declined to attend because she did not wish to intrude on the bond that all of us here share. I appreciate both her artistry and her grace."

Bashir thought that in different circumstances, those present would have applauded. Acto Viri merited both recognition and gratitude. Not a single person clapped, though; as best Bashir could tell, nobody even moved.

"We come here tonight to honor our fallen comrades," Ro went on. "They were men and women with whom we worked, with whom we lived, crewmates and neighbors, friends and family. In some very meaningful ways, those of us fortunate enough to continue on are now one family.

We will forever be linked through our common experience, our mutual grief, and our continued existence."

Ro paused, peering out across the people arrayed about her. At one point, her gaze intersected with Bashir's. He felt a shock surge through him, as though his brief connection with the captain had in an instant taken him back to that dreadful day, that dreadful moment, when Deep Space 9 had ceased to be. Bashir froze, and he remained motionless even after the captain's attention had moved past him. He had to force himself to resume breathing.

As Ro continued speaking, the doctor's mind took him backward through two years of his life to the hours when he didn't know if he even wanted to survive. During the evacuation of the station, he had been helping direct civilians to the nearest means of rescue. When the emergency bulkheads thundered closed, they sealed him in a section of one of the crossover bridges linking the Habitat Ring to the Docking Ring.

Just moments later, Deep Space 9 had exploded. The crossover segment broke off from the station, tumbling away into space. The emergency bulkheads held, sealing him in with twelve other people, all of them civilians, two of them children. As the lone member of DS9's crew there, Bashir knew that he needed to take the lead, to keep all of the others calm. But even as he did so, he worried about Sarina's safety. For a long time, he had no idea whether she had lived or died. His dread had been palpable, and if the woman he loved, the woman for whom he had waited his entire life, had perished aboard the station, he'd had no notion at all of what he would do.

As Bashir stood beside his beloved Sarina on the new starbase, he thought about all the people on the original Deep Space 9 who, like him, had lived through its demise, but whose loved ones had not. *How did they get through it?* he wondered. *How would I have gotten through it?*

It occurred to Bashir that in the wake of the destruction of DS9, he had nearly driven himself to a point where he would have found out firsthand: he had begun to doubt Sarina. He questioned her commitment to what he believed to be their common objective of bringing down Section 31, fearing that she actually worked *for* the nefarious covert organization. In the end, though, even with no ironclad evidence of Sarina's intentions—*How could there ever be, with Section 31 involved?*—Bashir made the only choice he could: he chose to love her, and stand by her, and put his full trust in her. To do otherwise would have been almost as devastating to him as if he'd lost her in the station's destruction.

Bashir regarded Sarina. Even at a time and place that had already dredged up so much emotional pain within him, he realized that he felt happy. Bashir knew that he would listen to the words spoken that night, that he would grieve for the people he'd lost and all the others too, but he also knew that it would be all right because he would do so beside Sarina.

"There are no magic words that I can say that will ease the suffering we feel because of the people we've lost," Ro said as Bashir peered back up at the captain. "But there is also no greater honor we can bestow upon our absent comrades than to move on in our lives—not only to move on, but to succeed. And as we do, we will carry our memories of them with us."

Ro looked down and to the side, and a moment later, four of her senior staff—Cenn Desca, Jefferson Blackmer, John Candlewood, and Zivan Slaine—joined her on the platform. All five had been rescued from the station just seconds before it blew apart. "In honor of those we have lost, with the intention of always remembering them, always keeping them in our hearts and minds, we will speak their names aloud, for all of us to hear."

Cenn Desca, the last executive officer of the original Deep Space 9 and the first of the new, stepped forward on the platform. He raised a padd and began to read from it. "Ferdinand Abejo. Açero Kyne. Jerot Afrane." Cenn pronounced each name carefully, perfectly, his mouth moving over the syllables almost as though he had performed such a ritual a thousand times. "Massoud Ahzed. Rey Alfonzo. Alden Allard." His voice neither rose nor fell, and yet it somehow managed to carry emotion within it.

For the first time since Ro had begun the service, Bashir heard something on the Memorial Deck other than the voice of the speaker. People cried. Sometimes it happened with the recitation of a particular name—Sherman Ravid broke into sobs when Lieutenant Commander Candlewood read out "Cathy Ling"—and at other times, the sounds of sorrow seemed to swell from everywhere, like waves breaking on the sand.

Toward the end, once Captain Ro had begun to read the names on her padd, Bashir glanced at Sarina. Though she had not uttered a sound during the service, her eyes were rimmed in red, the curves of her cheeks wet from her tears. His heart both heavy and full, he could only cheer his great fortune that he and Sarina had survived the destruction of Deep Space 9 so that they could continue spending their lives together.

When Sarina gazed up at Bashir, she looked so sad, and yet the side of her mouth ticked up. He felt their connection. He didn't even realize that he'd been crying until Sarina reached up to his face and dried his tears with her fingertips.

It took well over an hour to complete the reading of the names of people who would never again be held by a parent, or a child, or a friend, or a lover.

Eight

The timepiece ticked the afternoon away, its hands sweeping incessantly around its plain face. Keev had pulled it from the pocket of the gray cover-up she wore over her blue dress and looked at it again—*For what? The hundredth time?* She thought it might as well have been a timer wired to an improvised bomb. *Because I'm going to explode soon.* It took all of her willpower not to uncover the trapdoor and crawl back out through the hidden tunnel that ran beneath the dooryard at the back of the house.

I knew he couldn't be trusted, Keev thought as she hunkered in the dirt-floored root cellar of the Ranga House. In the three months since Altek Dans had joined her gild, she'd had the same thought about him on more than one occasion. She recalled how he had introduced himself to her and Veralla and the others, by chasing her through the wood to their encampment. *That should have made everybody skeptical of him.*

In truth, it had. As Altek began working with the gild, providing another operative within the city, Keev spoke with the others about him. From young Jennica to old man Renet, everybody expressed reservations about adding the doctor to their gild. *Everybody except Veralla,* Keev thought in frustration.

In the dim illumination of the small gas lamp in the

corner, she peered around the cellar—more a crawl space, really, since she couldn't stand up fully without hitting her head on the joists that supported the floor above. As small as the house was—little more than a bungalow, it had two small rooms in the front, with an antiquated kitchen and bathroom in the rear—the cellar managed to be even smaller. In addition to its low ceiling, it occupied only the area beneath the kitchen, and the rickety plank steps that led down into it consumed some of that space. Stacks of old crates filled up much of what remained. Some of those wooden boxes contained bunches of root vegetables, while others had been packed with preserves and canned goods. Still others held empty jars.

Pushed up against the whitewashed brick wall opposite the steps and piled atop each other, each of the crates had a purpose. Heaped to overflowing with potatoes and kava roots and *katterpods*, the boxes with the vegetables proved unwieldy when handled. The ones containing preserved foodstuffs in jars and cans weighed a great deal, and those holding empty jars rattled noisily when moved. All that would make a thorough inspection of the basement time-consuming, difficult, and loud. Ideally, the stacked crates would prevent the trapdoor buried under the dirt beneath them from being found; at worst, they would slow a search and announce it to anybody down in the tunnel.

Keev shifted on her haunches and stood up—stood up as much as she could, anyway. She threw her hands up to a support beam, both to prevent herself from slamming her head into it and to lean against it, easing the burden of bending over while on her feet. She'd already stayed in the basement for two hours longer than planned, and later in the day than would be safe. *As though anything we do can be labeled* safe.

Keev looked down and kicked the toe of her shoe into the hardpan, sending a few crumbs of dirt skittering away. She straightened her blue patterned dress, as uncomfortable as always in her Aleiran attire, which she always donned as camouflage whenever she entered Joradell. Of course, if she ever needed her disguise while in the city, then something had gone wrong.

Something is going wrong, Keev thought. *Where is Altek? And why does Veralla trust him?*

Keev and Veralla had known each other—had operated together in the Bajoran gilds around Joradell—for five years. During the first two years, they ran in a gild led by a woman named Salan Ral, but the Aleira killed her in a raid on one of the houses they used as a hideout for escaped Bajora. The fiasco resulted from an undercover action, an Aleiran security officer posing as a fleeing Bajoran slave. The deaths of six members of their gild, including Salan, should have been a high enough price to pay, but an additional cost followed: the Aleiran authorities in Joradell increased security throughout the city, ramping up patrols and conducting random house searches.

The impact on the various gilds had been immediate and severe. Keev's own disbanded, and the others put all their operations on hold until they could determine how best to thwart the new Aleiran security procedures. Figuring that out became more expensive, costing more lives along the way. Ultimately, though, the gilds—reconstituted to smaller, more independent cells—resumed their work. Veralla started his own gild, into which he recruited Keev.

For the nearly three years their gild had operated, they'd been a tight, successful band. Veralla didn't talk much, and never about himself, but he led well. They started out with seven members and lost only one, not to the Aleira, but to an arboreal emerald snake. That happened two years earlier, and Veralla recruited Synder Nogar as a replacement.

Seven members, Keev thought. *Seven members, and two Aleiran contacts within the city. Until Altek made a third contact.* They hadn't needed another Aleiran contact for their gild, not in Keev's opinion, and taking another one on posed tremendous risks. Beyond even the issue of Altek's true allegiance—ever since what had happened to Salan, the gilds feared other Aleiran spies—they should have questioned his competence, his ability to act without further endangering their people or the operation.

But Veralla didn't do that, Keev thought. Veralla trusted Altek, and since everybody trusted Veralla, they all lived with their doubts. Even Keev.

She consulted her timepiece again and couldn't believe how late in the day it had gotten. The sun would set soon, meaning that evening patrols would begin before long. In the summer, in the heat of the afternoon, Aleiran security mostly stayed off the streets, assuming less need for it during daylight hours. As evening approached and the temperature cooled, patrols and searches increased. Keev knew that she should shift the crates—she knew the proper few to move for a quick getaway—dig through the dirt to the trapdoor, and make her way through the tunnel, out beyond Joradell's security perimeter.

If I wait here, I'm putting myself at risk, Keev thought. She carried false identification with her, but it wouldn't stand up to more than a cursory look. If Altek had abandoned his mission, for whatever reason, Keev stood nothing to gain by staying. If something had happened and he merely ran late, he faced a greater prospect of running into a patrol. Whether loyal to the cause or not, he could end up sinking them all.

Keev reached for one of the upper crates. She would haul it and a few others away from the stack so that she could get to the tunnel. After nightfall, out beyond the security perimeter, she could make good her escape.

But this isn't just about me, Keev thought. *It's about the girl.* Then, with some reluctance, she added, *It's even about Altek.*

Keev released her grip on the crate, turned, and headed for the stairway. In the corner, she quickly extinguished the lamp. She then rushed up the steps.

At the top, Keev listened at the door and heard the sounds of somebody working in the kitchen. She pushed the door slowly open and looked in that direction. An elderly but still vital woman placed a large pot on the stove, then turned and saw Keev standing there. The woman's eyes went wide.

"What are you doing here?" she asked Keev.

"He's late."

"I know he's late—*too* late. That's why I expected you to be gone." Ranga Hoon, an Aleira and secretly an abolitionist, owned the house. She picked up a towel from the small kitchen table and wiped her hands. "I was just about to go down to the cellar and get some kava roots and katterpods."

Keev understood that Ranga meant not only that she would retrieve food for her dinner, but that she would also fill in the dirt over the trapdoor and then restack all the crates atop it. Keev always worried that the old woman would be unable to physically manage the boxes, particularly the heavier ones, but that had yet to happen. Ranga promised to let the gild know if the task became

too much for her to handle. Keev didn't know how Veralla would resolve the situation if that happened, but they
certainly couldn't allow their tunnel to be found by the
Aleira. Ranga's house had already been searched several
times during the prior months—always in the mornings
or evenings—so they all understood the continual danger
they faced.

"Have you seen him?" Keev asked.

"No," Ranga said. "But I don't look often. We don't
need anybody noticing me staring out my window at the
street. Not in these days."

Keev nodded. She'd been working with Ranga for two
years, but Ranga had been helping smuggle slaves out of
Joradell far longer than that. As long as she could keep the
entrance to the tunnel hidden, the woman knew how to
avoid getting caught.

"I have to go see," Keev said. She turned and darted
into the front room. The shadows had grown long as the
setting sun angled low through the sheer curtains drawn
over the single window. Furnished with a ratty stuffed
chair and standing lamp in one corner, a pair of mis-
matched wooden seats against the far wall, and an empty
crate standing in as a table, the small space couldn't have
fit anything more. Keev moved to the front wall, to the
window, and pulled the curtain aside so that she could
look down the street.

"You should leave," Ranga said. Keev hadn't heard
her walk the few paces from the kitchen. For a woman of
advanced years, Ranga retained not only her strength, but
also a surprising lightness on her feet. "This is the time
they usually start the house searches."

"I have my papers," Keev said.

"And how long will they convince them for?" Ranga

asked. "With you here, they'll search this place twice as hard, and there's just not all that much to look at before they start moving crates."

"I know," Keev said. "There are already two patrol officers out there." She saw the two uniformed men in the middle of the intersection just down the street, one of them busy checking the documents of a pedestrian.

"Then go," Ranga insisted. "Either he's not coming or he is, and if he is, then he's going to get stopped. Whichever the case, there's nothing you can do to help him."

Keev let the curtain drift back to the window and peered over at Ranga. "You're right."

"Of course I'm right," the old woman said. "Now go on. Get out of here."

Keev nodded, then lifted the curtain and took one last look outside. She immediately saw Altek, and he had the girl—Ahleen—with him. "They're coming," Keev said, her voice falling to a whisper, as though the patrol outside might hear her. But it didn't matter anyway: Altek and the girl had already been stopped.

Ranga said something, but Keev didn't hear her words—didn't *listen* to them. She needed to think, and she needed to do so quickly. Keev had her fraudulent identification with her, and Altek surely had his genuine documentation, but because everything had happened so quickly, they had none for the girl. Late last night, the gild received an urgent message from Altek explaining the girl's story. A twelve-year-old Bajora, Ahleen had worked with her mother as a slave in an Aleiran industrial laundry. In an accident the day before, the mother had fallen into a vat of boiling water. After being recovered and taken to a hospital, she died.

With no other living relatives, Ahleen normally would

have been assigned as the responsibility of some other adult slave—or, at the age of twelve, simply treated like an adult slave herself. One of the nurses at the hospital—an Aleiran nurse—took pity on the girl and cleaned her up, bathing her and finding her fresh clothes to wear. When the gild read Altek's account, they cheered the example of kindness.

According to Altek, it had been a ghastly error. A high-ranking Aleiran official visiting the hospital saw the fresh-faced Ahleen, tall for her age and already developing into a young woman. The official ordered the girl medically examined and then brought to his home. Altek knew that the life Ahleen would endure there would have made slaving in an industrial laundry until her premature death seem idyllic.

Altek had been the doctor charged with conducting the girl's physical exam. He considered falsifying her test results, making her undesirable to the official, but beyond the difficulty of doing so without any of the lab technicians or nurses finding out, he worried about condemning Ahleen to an inescapable fate. Bajora classed as physically deficient were often just killed, particularly those who in some way disappointed a prominent official.

Altek had taken the only action he reasonably felt he could: he prolonged Ahleen's medical tests so that she would have to remain in the hospital overnight. In getting his message to the gild, he made it clear that they would have only the next day to smuggle Ahleen out of the city. Keev volunteered to make the attempt.

"I have to do something," she told Ranga. She couldn't allow the Aleira to consign a twelve-year-old girl either to death or to a fate that could be considered perhaps even more horrible.

"There's nothing you *can* do," Ranga said. "Not without getting yourself killed."

Keev watched as Altek produced his identification for the patrol officers, both of whom looked like all the men in Aleiran security: large and well muscled in their crisp gray uniforms. One of them—with a broader back than his leaner fellow officer—gestured toward Ahleen.

Keev released the curtain from her fingertips and pushed away from the wall. She glanced at the front door for only an instant, knowing that she could not put Ranga—and the tunnel—at risk. Instead, she raced through the kitchen and out the back door. Just three steps took her across what passed for a yard—a patch of dirt sprinkled with pallid stalks of dead grass—to a rotting board fence. She yanked free two slats already hanging loose, then pushed through into the equally small—and empty—yard of the house behind Ranga's.

Without stopping, Keev hurried along the side of the house—she could barely squeeze through the gap between it and the house next door—and out into the street. She immediately spied another patrol in the intersection to her left, and so she moved in the opposite direction, forcing herself to slow to a walk, not wanting to draw attention to herself. She made her way down two short blocks before turning to her right into an alley. When she saw nobody there, she broke into a sprint—a bit awkwardly in the dress she had donned as part of her cover, but at least she wore flat-soled shoes.

Keev exited the alley on the street that Ranga's house fronted and walked quickly in that direction. Up ahead, Altek was patting the jacket he wore and checking its pockets, doubtless searching—or pretending to search—for Ahleen's identification. As Keev passed in front of Ranga's house, drawing within a block of the group, she saw the broad-backed patrol officer turn the doctor toward the wall of a building, forcing his hands up onto its brick facing. Even as Broad Back began running a portable metal detector up and down Altek's body, Keev started to run.

"Dans, Dans," she called out. As the two officers turned toward Keev, Altek's head whipped around in surprise, and she wondered if she'd made a terrible mistake. She remained unconvinced of the doctor's loyalty and his ability, and she was about to test them both. "Dans," she said again as she got closer. She slowed to a walk, making sure to exaggerate her breathing, avoiding the suggestion that she regularly ran.

"Dans," she said again as she arrived before the group. It pleased her to see that the expression of surprise on Altek's face had shifted to one of recognition and relief. It impressed Keev to see Ahleen offer a similar look. "I've been worried, my love," she went on. "You two are so late."

Altek turned from the wall and moved as though to hug her, and Keev stepped forward and opened her arms. One of the officers, the leaner of the two, shifted sideways to block her way. "I'm sorry, ma'am, but you'll have to step back."

"What?" Keev asked, acting confused. Then, as though coming to a realization, she said, "Oh, no, this is my husband and our niece." She flipped her hand through the air before her face, trying to wave away the officer's concern.

Leaner looked doubtful, as did Broad Back behind him. Keev noted, though, that the latter had stopped searching Altek. *Perhaps not the best and brightest in Aleiran security,* she thought, hopeful.

"Do you have your papers, ma'am?" Leaner asked.

"Yes, of course," Keev said. She reached into a pocket

in her cover-up and extracted her fabricated identity documents. "I'm Aven Meru." She handed the papers to Leaner, who gave them only a perfunctory glance before passing them to his partner. Broad Back examined them more carefully. Keev waited, making sure to appear as though she felt impatient and inconvenienced, but not anxious. She knew that her documentation would bear up to some measure of inspection, but if the patrol officers looked beyond the surface and tried to verify her existence within the city, her cover would unravel quickly.

Keev could feel Ahleen's gaze on her. She glanced at the girl and offered her a smile of familiarity. Keev could only hope that Altek had spoken with the girl and that she understood enough not to give them all away.

Broad Back gave Keev's papers back to Leaner, who didn't even look at them again before handing them back to her. She noted that Leaner had the look of a man who didn't particularly care for his job, which she hoped she could turn to her advantage. Broad Back, though, might be more difficult to convince. Past the officers, Keev saw, a couple of pedestrians had queued up so that they could be validated and pass.

"These look all right," Leaner sad. "But your husband has no papers for your niece, so I'm afraid we—"

"What?" Keev said loudly, throwing a mix of both shock and disgust into her voice. She stared past both patrol officers and regarded Altek angrily. "You did this *again*?"

"I . . . I'm sorry, love," Altek said, sounding duly chastened. "It was your brother's fault. He was supposed to come down to the surgical wing today—"

"I don't want to hear your excuses," Keev sniped at him. "You know we can't travel without proper identification—

not with those filthy Bajora here in the city and always try-ing to run." She looked at Leaner and rolled her eyes: *Can you believe I have to put up with this?*

Leaner peered over his shoulder at Altek. The doctor's eyes widened as his shoulders rose in the most minimal of shrugs, perfectly capturing the unspoken frustration of a badgered husband. It delighted Keev to see Leaner flash Altek a sympathetic look in return.

"Officers," Altek said, "I don't suppose you could just allow us through." Uttered with just the right amount of pleading in his tone, he didn't have to actually say, *I've got enough to deal with at home, so please don't make things worse.*

"No," Keev said. She raised her arm and pointed at Altek, but spoke to Leaner. "Don't let him off the hook. He's done this before. He needs to learn that there are ways we do things here in Joradell and ways we don't."

Leaner looked to his partner and shrugged, but Broad Back said, "We really should see the girl's papers."

"Officers—" Altek started again, but Keev interrupted him at once.

"Stop it!" she said, raising her voice and hoping that she read the two patrol officers accurately. "Don't you try to make these men break the rules for *you*. Go back and find my brother and get my niece's papers." As a matter of course, members of the gild agreed on ersatz names to use in such circumstances, but even if Altek had coached Ahleen on her false identity, Keev feared that saying that name aloud could throw the girl and undermine them all.

"If I go get her papers," Altek asked, "will you wait?"

"Of course we'll wait," Keev said before casting an infuriated scoff in the doctor's direction. She looked at Leaner again, lifted her hands palms-up to the sky—*Have you ever heard such an idiotic question?*—then let them slap down against her sides.

Altek looked to the patrol officers. Leaner nodded. The doctor thanked him and started down the street. Keev wondered how far he would go before trying to abscond from the city. She didn't know what had happened to make him so late, but with Ahleen disappearing from the hospital and Altek getting stopped with a girl by a patrol, he'd ended his career in Joradell—ended any chance to continue his *life* there. When he didn't return with papers for Ahleen, he'd likely be reported by the patrol—if Keev left them alive. Even if the officers chose not to report the incident, Altek would have no way of knowing that; he couldn't risk being labeled an abolitionist. At best, they would arrest and imprison him; at worst, they would brand him a traitor to the Aleira and execute him.

"I'm so sorry," Keev told the officers, then looked past them to include the other pair of waiting pedestrians in her apology.

"If you'll just step aside for right now, ma'am," Broad Back said.

Keev smiled and nodded, then put a hand on Ahleen's elbow, leading her a few paces away. She crouched down before the girl. "Everything will be all right," Keev told her.

The girl looked back with bright eyes, and Keev saw years of experience that did not belong on the face of a twelve-year-old—exemplified by a scar in the shape of a crescent high up on her left cheek. Ahleen said nothing. Keev thought that probably for the best, and she reached up and ran her hand lovingly over the girl's black hair; though chopped short, it still complemented Ahleen's beautiful, dark features. It galled her to think of some man calling for this young girl to be brought to him as some sort of plaything. No matter what had happened to delay Altek, Keev could see why he took the risk in attempting to get Ahleen to freedom.

But what am I going to do? Still squatting, Keev brought her hand to her side. A quick move and she could draw her blade from where she'd strapped its sheath to the inside of her opposite thigh. She didn't doubt that she could dispatch both patrol officers, but would prefer not having to do so in front of the girl, who'd just lost her mother. Keev also preferred not to kill, if possible, though she had no difficulty justifying such actions; the patrol officers, though not wholly responsible for the Aleiran enslavement of Bajora, worked to prop up that immoral and unconscionable system.

Whatever I do, I can't wait for long, she thought. When Altek didn't return, the patrol officers would have to deal with Keev and Ahleen, probably calling in other security to assist. She couldn't let that happen; she needed to move the situation along while she had only two men to fight.

The officers finished validating the few people there, who moved on. Keev stood back up, though she placed her hand on Ahleen's shoulder, seeking to reassure her. To the patrol officers, she complained, "He's done this twice before. He just doesn't pay attention."

"Ma'am," Leaner said, "if you'll just wait quietly—"

"It's hard to be quiet when your husband refuses to do things the right way," Keev said. "I mean, he knows what the procedures are. I don't know why he just can't follow them." She could see frustration on the faces of both men for having to listen to her harangue. "I mean, I know that you must see it all the time, but—"

"Aunt Meru," Ahleen suddenly said, "I need to use a bathroom."

Keev didn't know if Altek had instructed the girl in any way, or if she acted on her own, or if she merely spoke the truth, but it certainly seemed helpful to their cause. "I'm sorry, but you saw what just happened," Keev told her. "We have to wait."

"But Auntie," the girl whined, which Keev appreciated hearing.

"Is there anywhere we can go?" she asked Leaner.

"Ma'am," he said, his forbearance dripping from his voice, "we're out on the street."

Keev looked down at Ahleen. "I'm sorry your uncle was so careless," she said. "Let's just hope he doesn't take long to get back." She saw the officers share an exasperated look. Taking a risk, Keev stared at Ahleen and gave a quick flick of her head toward the patrol. She didn't know if the girl would take her meaning, but thought there might be a chance.

"Auntie-e-e," Ahleen immediately wailed. "I have to go-o-o." To Keev's delight, the girl actually started to squirm where she stood.

Looking back at Leaner, Keev said, "Are you sure there's no place?" Again, the officers looked at each other. "You know, I live just a couple of blocks away. One of you could take us there." If Keev could split Leaner and Broad Back up, she'd have an easier time subduing just one of them.

"Ma'am," Leaner began as though about to deny her again, but then he seemed to relent. "Just go."

"Thank you," Keev said, reaching out and squeezing the man's arm, still playing the role she'd assumed. "Thank you. I'm sorry for all the trouble."

"All right, ma'am," Leaner said. "Just make sure your husband doesn't let this happen again."

"Oh, believe me, I will," Keev said, making it sound as though her husband would not enjoy his night at home. She took Ahleen's hand, then started back down the street. She led the girl past Ranga's house, sure that the old woman had watched all that had taken place, and probably still watched, though Keev didn't chance even glancing in that direction. She walked with Ahleen along the next block, and then left into the alley she'd come down earlier. Seeing nobody around, she whispered, "Are you all right?"

The girl nodded, her expression sad but her manner earnest.

"My name is really Keev Anora," she said. "You can call me Anora."

"I'm Resten Ahleen," the girl said. "You can call me Ahleen." She offered her second statement with something of a grin. The small dose of humor caught Keev off guard, but she counted it a good sign for what it suggested about both the girl's intelligence and her emotional state.

"Do you really need the bathroom?" Keev asked.

"No," Ahleen said, her lips sneaking into a whole smile.

Keev smiled back, impressed. She retraced the path she'd taken from Ranga's house. Before exiting the alley, she carefully peered in both directions down the street, checking for any new patrols that might have appeared. Fortunately, none had.

When they arrived at the house behind Ranga's—with another patrol still up ahead—Keev pulled the girl along its side and then through the rotting board fence. Once in Ranga's yard, Keev saw the back door standing open.

"Come on," she said. Her hand still wrapped around the girl's, Keev guided her inside and closed the door behind them.

They found nobody in the kitchen. "Ranga?" Keev called out in a stage whisper. She heard no response, but then she saw the door leading to the basement ajar. She didn't hesitate.

"Ranga?" she called as she and Ahleen thundered down the unsteady steps.

"Here, come on, there's no time to waste," the old woman called from the cellar. She stepped out of the way as Keev and Ahleen hurried past—Ranga didn't even need to duck her head in the low space. Neither did the girl. "I don't know what you said out there, but if they figure out you were lying to them, they're going to come banging on every door, so you need to go."

Keev saw that Ranga had already moved the proper crates and used a spade to dig out the dirt above the trap-door, which had been hauled open. Keev indicated the dark hole, then crouched before the girl. "This tunnel is going to take us out of the city," she said. "Okay?"

Ahleen nodded but didn't say anything.

Keev stretched her leg into the hole, feeling for the ladder there. When she found it, she descended into the darkness until she reached the bottom of the tunnel. She felt for the corner and found the bag of clothes she'd left there, as well as a handheld beacon, which she switched on. "Okay," Keev called back up to the cellar.

"Go on, dearie," she heard Ranga say, and a moment later, Ahleen's foot and leg appeared and began groping for the top rung of the ladder. Keev started back up to help, but then the girl began scrambling down. Keev stepped back until Ahleen stood with her at the end of the tunnel.

Without another word, Ranga slammed the trapdoor closed above them. Ahleen flinched at the noise, and whatever poise she'd shown with the patrol and on the way to the house vanished. Tears formed in her eyes and she suddenly seemed fragile, as though the next loud noise could break her into a thousand pieces.

"Everything's going to be all right," Keev assured her. "We're going to get you out of Joradell."

Above them, Keev heard a thump. *Ranga's covering the trapdoor,* she thought. The girl's lip started to quiver.

Keev took the girl's hands. "Really, it's going to be all right," she told her. And Keev knew that it would be— eventually. *But the girl just lost her mother, and right now she's got nobody else in the world.*

Keev put her arms around Ahleen and hugged her. The girl clamped her own arms around Keev and held on tightly as she began to sob. They stayed that way for a long time, the girl's body quaking as she wept.

When finally Ahleen let go of Keev and pulled back, she asked, "Who are you, Anora?"

"I'm your friend," Keev said.

"Are you really helping me?" The question broke Keev's heart. How could the girl trust anybody after living a life—a child's life—in servitude. She'd at least had her mother, but no longer.

"I'm really helping you," Keev said. "I know it's hard to trust anybody, but you can trust me. Things will get better. And the first thing we're going to do is get you as far away from this place as possible."

"And never come back?" Ahleen asked in a small voice.

Keev felt her features tense. "You *never* have to come back here again," she said. "I promise."

Ahleen looked at her without saying anything for a few moments, as though trying to decide on the truth of what she'd been told. Finally, she nodded.

"Okay, then," Keev said. "Let me change out of this dress and we'll get going."

They reached the other end of the tunnel in the early evening, then waited for night to fall. Under the cover of darkness, with the landscape lighted by slivers of two moons, they made it to the wood. By midnight, they finally reached the gild.

Altek arrived the next morning, his life as a physician in Joradell finished.

Nine

Quark stood behind his gleaming new bar—purchased for a small fortune from a metalwright on Sauria—and gazed out at his customers . . . his *paltry* number of customers. "A brand-new starbase," he said, picking up a clean brandy snifter and wiping it down for the third time. "They told me business would boom. Triple the number of crew as the old station. More than ten thousand civilians. And I've got . . . what?" He peered out over the bar, from the pair of empty poker tables sitting against the far left wall, to the equally empty *dabo* table in the center of the long space, to the *dom-jot* table located along the right-hand wall. Round black tables of varying dimensions filled the large area between the gaming surfaces, though few people sat at any of them. "Three customers," Quark said, answering his own question. "I've got more employees in here right now."

"Just remember that I'm not one of those employees," said Treir, her tall, lithe form draped over the end of the bar.

"That's right," Quark said. "I'm not paying you to be here; I'm paying you to manage my place on Bajor." After the destruction of Deep Space 9, Quark had opened an establishment on the planet, in the town of Aljuli, not far from where Starfleet had set up Bajoran Space Central to help fill in for the lost station. He thought about relocating out of the system, but the Congress of Economic Advisors agreed to pay out on his insurance only if he reestablished the Ferengi Embassy to Bajor. Of course, his transition to the planet had been rendered far more palatable—enjoyable, even—because Ro Laren had taken command of BSC.

To Quark's astonishment, his two years in Aljuli had actually turned out solidly profitable—so much so that when the prospect of launching a bar on the new starbase had arisen, he'd considered declining. Instead, he opted to heed the warning of the Ninety-fifth Rule of Acquisition— *Expand or die*—and to trust in the promise of the Ninth— *Opportunity plus instinct equals profit.* He built a new bar—and embassy—on the new DS9, while leaving Treir to operate his place on Bajor. He couldn't be sure that his business in Aljuli would continue in the black with Starfleet leaving the area, but it well might, since the Bajorans intended to staff and use the BSC facility. He also couldn't guarantee that opening a bar on the new station would prove successful; although he would serve a larger population, he would do so with more competition. Of course, his transition to the starbase would be rendered far more palatable—enjoyable, even—because Ro Laren would be commanding it.

"I know you expected me to be on Bajor tonight," Treir said, "but I was invited to the memorial. I wasn't going to miss it." They'd both come back from the ceremony just a few minutes earlier. Treir paused, then added, "I lost friends."

"I lost customers," Quark said, quietly and without malice. He thought about all the hundreds of names that Laren and some of the crew had read out that evening. Quark recognized most of those names, and could associate faces with them too. Many had been his customers. Some had been his friends.

Quark caught himself and decided to think about other things before his despondence about his dearth of customers slipped into a full-blown melancholy. "If you're here," he asked Treir, "then what's going on in my place in Aljuli? You didn't close for the evening, did you?"

"No, the bar's still open."

"Then who's running it?" Quark wanted to know.

Treir smiled. "Hetik."

"Hetik?" Quark repeated. "*Hetik?* The dabo boy?"

"Trust me, he's no boy," Treir said. She peeled herself from the surface of the bar and sat up straight on her stool to look down at Quark. "Anyway, this isn't the first time I've put him in charge. He's a good manager." She shrugged. "He'd have to be; *I* trained him."

"Marvelous," Quark muttered to himself. He absently wiped down the snifter for the fourth time. "You probably trained him how to embezzle from me."

"What was that?" Treir asked.

Quark looked back over at her. "Nothing," he said.

"Good." Clad in a sleeveless white dress—clingy, thigh length, and low cut—Treir slipped back down and arranged her arms and torso languidly atop the bar. Quark noticed how nicely her green Orion flesh contrasted with the polished silver surface.

Maybe I should let Hetik manage my place on Bajor and bring Treir back here, he thought. Customers would certainly linger—and drink—at the sight of her lounging comfortably against the bar. *That is, if I actually had customers.*

"By the way, you don't have just three customers,"

Treir said, as though reading his thoughts. "There are half a dozen on the second level."

"Half a dozen?" Quark said. "I guess I can just close up now and purchase the moon I've always dreamed of owning."

"Oh, stop complaining," Treir told him. "You've only been open a couple of days."

"A couple of long, empty, profitless days," Quark said.

"You know what they say: 'Satisfaction is *not* guaranteed.'"

"Wait a minute," Quark said. "*You're* quoting the Rules of Acquisition to *me?*"

Treir bared her teeth in a wide smile as intoxicating as any of the liquor behind the bar. "I've been around you long enough that I should know the Rules by now."

"Then how come you don't know the Thirty-third?" Quark asked. *It never hurts to suck up to the boss.*

"Oh, I know it," Treir said. "I just don't subscribe to it."

"Of course you don't," Quark said. He tossed down the cloth and set the snifter back in its place. He came out from behind the bar and crossed past where the smooth-nosed M'Pella waited patiently beside the dabo wheel for anybody who wanted to gamble. Quark felt as though the silence of the wheel, its stillness, mocked him.

He paced to the wide entrance in the half wall that separated his Public House, Café, Gaming Emporium, Holosuite Arcade, and Ferengi Embassy to Bajor from the expansive walkway of the Plaza. Through the bowed transparent bulkhead that extended from above the third level and curved out and then back to the residential level below, Quark could see the broad span of the station's horizontal *x*-ring and, out beyond it, the saucer section of

U.S.S. Robinson. To the right, he could just make out the long-necked, green-hulled form of a Romulan warbird; he read the small native characters on its hull: *I.R.W. Tranome Sar.*

Now where are those crews? he thought. *It's not as though Romulans are celebrated for their restraint.* Quark knew that other starships besides those had arrived at the station during the previous twenty-six hours. He'd taken a stroll earlier—checking out the state of his competition on the Plaza—and noted the other vessels docked at DS9: Ezri Dax's ship, *Aventine*; Chancellor Martok's flagship, *Sword of Kahless*; a Cardassian battle cruiser, *Jorrene*; and an asymmetric Gorn leviathan, *S'persson.*

"So where is everybody?" Quark asked aloud. Down the Plaza to his left, he saw a Starfleet security officer, a Tellarite named Ansarg, whom he'd met only on the prior day. She looked over at him when he spoke, but said nothing.

Quark peered out into space, at *U.S.S. Robinson*, then back at his nearly empty business. He'd seen that some of that ship's crew—including Captain Sisko and his wife—had been invited to the memorial service Laren had held, and he'd expected at least some of them to stop by the bar before returning to their ship. Quark suspected that perhaps the crew—and those of the other vessels—had been embargoed because of the dignitaries visiting the station, though if so, that would probably last only until the various protection details had been permitted to reconnoiter DS9's layout.

I could find out for sure if I could tap in to the starbase's computer, he thought. While Quark liked his new establishment, he did miss the old one—not down on Bajor, but on the original Deep Space 9. After years spent there—

all the way back to when the Cardassians had run it as Terok Nor—he had devised numerous means of gleaning information, including learning procedures and acquiring devices that allowed him to bypass security encoding and access the main computer on a deep level—both when the Guard had run the station and when Starfleet had taken it over.

The day before, Quark had made his first attempt at circumventing the starbase's computing defenses. It earned him nothing more than a visit from DS9's head of security. Lieutenant Commander Blackmer accepted Quark's explanation of having simply made a mistake at his companel, but the security chief also made it clear that he would tolerate such an excuse—or *any* excuse—just the one time.

I'm going to have to be exceedingly careful, Quark thought. He felt confident that he could ultimately gain access to the assets he would need on the starbase, but it would require finesse and time. More than anything, he wanted to avoid drawing the wrath of Ro Laren.

Or that might be the only way to get her attention these days, he thought. Quark had moved to the station from Bajor three months earlier to prepare for his new venture. He tried to make time to see Laren, but her own responsibilities in advance of Deep Space 9 becoming fully operational kept her extremely busy—and even more so recently. Over the previous ten days, Quark had seen her just twice, and one of those times had been at the memorial.

Maybe that explains why none of the starbase crew are here, Quark thought, turning to regard the bar. Hosting a head of state anywhere could bring complications, doubly so on a new facility. Laren faced more than that, though:

multiple chief executives currently quartered at DS9, two of them—Imperator Sozzerozs and Praetor Kamemor—from historically adversarial powers. The crew had been working around the clock to ensure that everything proceeded smoothly up to and through the dedication and the diplomatic visits.

Quark also knew that most of the new civilian residents wouldn't arrive until after that. *So why did I even bother opening so soon?* he asked himself—though he needn't have, since he knew the answer. First of all, any new business venture required time to set up and find its way, and better that happen before being inundated by customers. Second, Laren—*The station commander*—requested that all the proprietors on the Plaza open prior to the dedication. And finally, where high-ranking political officials traveled, high-value information followed. As the Twenty-second Rule stated: *A wise man can hear profit in the wind.* With imperators and chancellors, presidents and praetors present, the hot air on the station would blow at gale force.

Quark started back across the room, but then stopped for a moment to appreciate the place. He loved its sleek, ultramodern look. To the left of the bar, a staircase rose straight up to the rear of the second level, which sat tiered back from the first level, and then to the third level, following the line of DS9's upper hemisphere. An open lift operated, funicular-like, to the right of the bar. The third level stepped back from the second.

Past the stairway on the left, a corridor led to several storerooms, as well as refreshers for the employees and a pair of offices. On the right, beyond the lift, another corridor ran past customer 'freshers back to his holosuite arcade. Also reaching up three levels, the holocomplex featured twice as many units as his place on the old station, all of them larger and with more sophisticated processors.

As if that matters without customers. Quark shook his head as he paced back across the floor and behind the bar. Plenty of items still required his attention in the new establishment, but instead he plucked the snifter off the shelf and began wiping it down again.

"Will you stop moping already," Treir said, once more paring herself from atop the bar. "I understand that you're always concerned about your business interests, but you're only two days into this place, you've got ten thousand new customers coming to live here in just a few days, and you still have a successful operation on Bajor. And I know you know all of that, so what's really bothering you?"

Quark stared at Treir. *She's right,* he thought.

"The memorial was difficult," Treir said quietly. She reached behind the bar and picked up an empty glass, which she held up in front of her. "To absent friends," she said.

The way Treir offered her toast reminded Quark of somebody else who had always wanted to drink to one thing or another—an absent friend. "You shouldn't be sitting there," he told her.

"What?" Treir asked. "What are you talking about?"

Quark set down the glass and rag, then walked over until he stood across the end of the bar from Treir. "Morn should be sitting there," he said.

Treir frowned. "That's not quite what I meant by 'absent friends.'"

"I know," Quark told her, and he did know, but he also didn't want to think anymore that night about the people who hadn't escaped the destruction of the station.

"You haven't heard from Morn at all?" Treir's concern

seemed a matter of friendship, though Quark believed that the two had enjoyed a bit more than that at one point.

"Not for more than a year," Quark said. Morn had evacuated from DS9—had actually done so with Quark, helping to carry a holosuite simulation tester preserving the Vic Fontaine program. After that, Morn ran his shipping business from Bajor for a while, regularly visiting Quark's bar in Aljuli. The local customers loved the big, bald Lurian, frequently crowding around to hear one or another of his long, meandering tales that invariably had everybody around him convulsing with laughter. Morn, of course, appreciated the opportunity to recycle his stories for a new audience, and he clearly adored the attention—almost as much as Quark adored the invariable uptick in sales that came with his presence.

Even so, Quark thought, *I could see he wasn't quite himself.* Despite still acting like the life of the party, Morn had seemed deeply troubled. Quark didn't know if he suffered from survivor's guilt, or post-traumatic stress, or just plain grief. He did attempt to broach the subject with Morn once, to no avail. Not long after that, Morn stopped patronizing the bar.

"You did try to contact him, right?" Treir asked.

"Of course I did," Quark said. "I counted the monthly payment of his tab as a long-term asset." Treir tilted her head and arched an eyebrow in an expression that told him she knew he valued Morn as more than just a financial boon.

"I know he doesn't still owe you money," she said.

"No," Quark said. Within ten days of Morn's last appearance at the bar in Aljuli, a cash payment had arrived by courier, completely satisfying his tab. "But I do keep trying to track him down. I just want to make sure . . ."

Quark shrugged. "I just want to make sure that he's all right."

"I know," Treir said.

A sudden whisper of noise reached Quark's ears, followed by a pounding sound. "Do you hear that?" he asked Treir.

"Look at me," Treir said. "I'm tall and green. *You're* the one with the big ears."

"So I am," Quark agreed. "And these ears just heard a turbolift arrive, and now there are footsteps headed in this direction." He waited a moment, then added, "And voices."

"Whose voices?"

Quark listened. "Chief O'Brien," he finally said. "And that wayward nephew of mine . . . and Doctor Bashir."

"That's it?"

"No, there are at least six people walking . . . seven."

"Are they coming here?"

"I can hear sounds, not thoughts," Quark grumbled, but he waited to see if the voices and footsteps grew quieter, which they would if the group chose to enter the Replimat, or Bella's Confections, or Café Parisienne, or any of the other establishments between that turbolift and Quark's.

"I can hear them now," Treir said. "I think they *are* coming this way."

Seconds later, the group arrived, Doctor Bashir and Chief O'Brien leading the way, chattering with each other as though nothing had changed in years. To Quark's surprise, Lieutenant Commander Douglas and Captain Dax walked side by side following the men, although they did not appear to be chatting. Commander Bowers trailed behind them, along with two of the starbase's security team, Olivia Dellasant and Ventor Bixx. Bashir and

O'Brien peered around until the chief pointed out a large table that would seat all of them. As most of them headed in that direction, the doctor walked over to the bar. Two waiters, Frool and Grimp, started over toward the table.

"Quark," Bashir said. Spoken in the doctor's accent, his name always sounded like the noise some animal would make: *Kwahk*.

"Doctor," Quark said, "it's good to see you." Bashir hadn't been in the bar since it had opened, although they had seen each other several times since Quark had moved back to the station.

"I don't suppose the dartboard has arrived yet?" the doctor asked.

"Not yet," Quark said. Bashir and O'Brien had hung a dartboard in the bar on Bajor that they'd wanted to bring with them to DS9, but the game had become so popular in Aljuli that they'd decided to leave it there. When Quark got to the station, they asked him to order a new one. "I've got a shipment of goods coming in from Alpha Centauri in just a few days, and I expect it to be in there."

"Excellent," Bashir said.

"Hello, Julian," Treir said, standing up from her barstool.

"Treir," Bashir said, almost singing her name. "It's lovely to see you."

She started toward the table where Chief O'Brien had led the others. "I thought you weren't working," Quark said to her.

"I'm not going to take their orders," Treir said, smiling. "I'm going to join them." Then, looking to the doctor for approval, she added, "If that's all right with you, Julian."

"Please," Bashir said. "By all means."

As Treir sauntered across the room, Quark felt annoyed, but only for an instant. He realized that it would make him as happy to take Treir's latinum as anybody else's. In fact, it might make him even *happier*, considering the ridiculous salary she extorted from him.

The doctor watched Treir for a moment as she crossed the room, and then he turned back to Quark. "Any word on Vic?" he asked.

"I'm afraid not," Quark said. "There are some interface issues with the new holosuites."

"Can't you get it fixed?"

"Believe me, Doctor, I'd like to," Quark said. "For one thing, I'd like to be able to use my tester again." Although Quark had eventually found the resources to install a pair of holosuites in his place on Bajor, they hadn't had the capacity to handle Vic's complex simulation matrix. Because of that, he'd chosen to allow the program to continue running in his tester.

"Miles said that you shouldn't use it for any other program while Vic's in there," Bashir said, his tone betraying his concern.

"I know that, Doctor; I've been hearing it for two years," Quark said. "That's why I want to get Vic out of there and into a holosuite. At least in there, he can bring in some customers. The problem is that the Starfleet engineers have been too busy making Deep Space Nine fully operational to help out here, and right now, the few civilian engineers on the starbase are working for other establishments on the Plaza."

"Can't you just hire an engineer from Bajor?"

Quark couldn't keep himself from smiling, and he felt the reassuring sharpness of his teeth against his lips. "Thank you for your business advice, Doctor, but I think

I'll wait until the supply of available engineers on the station increases enough to bring down the cost of my demand."

"Of course," Bashir said. "I understand. It's just that I'm concerned about Vic. He's spent two years by himself."

"He hasn't been by himself," Quark said. "I've told you, the tester has been executing his program all along. It doesn't project the holograms or generate the sounds or any of the other tangible aspects of his matrix, but his whole world is in there and moving forward."

"At least you think it is," Bashir said. "What if something's gone wrong?"

"If something's gone wrong, then something's gone wrong," Quark said matter-of-factly. "Maybe we'll be able to do something about that and maybe not, but as you said, it's been two years. Do you really think a few more days will make a difference?"

The doctor sighed. "No, I suppose not."

"I promise to let you know as soon as I know," Quark said. And he certainly would keep the doctor informed, particularly once he'd migrated Vic's program back to a holosuite, because that would be sure to lure Bashir and his friends to the bar.

"Thank you, Quark." *Kwahk.*

Bashir walked back over to the table. Ezri and Sarina talked, Quark saw, but not to each other, and he wondered about that dynamic. While he studied the group, Ezri looked up and saw him. She immediately excused herself and made her way over to the bar.

"Quark." She reached over and patted his hand. "How are you? I've been told that you're something of a tycoon now—places on both Bajor and Deep Space Nine."

The compliment sent a tingle through Quark's lobes.

"Well, yes, I'm keeping the bar on Bajor that I opened after . . ." He found that he didn't want to explicitly mention the fate of the original station, and so he finished, "After."

"It must be successful, then," Ezri said. "Congratulations."

"Thank you," Quark said, honestly touched by her attention and kind words. "And what about you? How's life aboard the *Aventine*?" He hadn't seen her in three years, since her duties had last brought her ship to the old station.

"I've got nothing to complain about," Ezri said, and then she leaned in and added, sotto voce, "Although that usually doesn't stop me."

"Good thinking," Quark said. "It keeps you in practice for when you really do have complaints—such as having an almost empty bar on a gigantic starbase where six starships are docked." He waved his hand at the room.

Ezri gazed around the space. "I'm sure it'll fill up—if not tonight, then soon."

As she spoke, Quark heard something else beyond her words: the breath of turbolift doors opening—and not the doors of the lift he'd heard a few minutes earlier, but those of the lift closest to the bar. As before, the sounds of numerous feet traipsing on the deck arose, and just seconds later, another group of Starfleet officers appeared from the other direction. He saw Captain Sisko and Kasidy Yates, along with Lieutenant Commander Blackmer, Lieutenant Commander Wheeler Stinson, Lieutenant Aleco Vel, and a Starfleet officer Quark didn't recognize, a Bajoran woman. He realized how much work he still had to do in getting to know the crew.

"See that," Ezri said. "Six more customers."

Six, Quark thought, *plus Ezri's group of seven, plus the nine already in the bar, makes twenty-two.* Twenty-three, if he counted Treir. Not exactly standing room only, but certainly better than nothing.

As two more of his waiters, Broik and Zirk, hurried over to serve Captain Sisko's party, Quark heard the turbolift doors open again. He smiled. Maybe his new bar would succeed after all.

"How are you feeling, Minister?"

Asarem Wadeen allowed herself to fall backward onto the plush sofa. She soughed heavily as she relaxed into the comfortable cushions. It delighted her to see that Captain Ro and her crew had been thoughtful enough to place a vase of fresh nerak blossoms in her guest quarters, atop the low table in front of the sofa. Across from her, they had also rendered the wide port in the outer wall transparent, allowing her a stunning view of the stars through the equally pellucid band around the equator of the starbase's sphere. She could also see the horizontal docking ring and, moored there, the transport that had brought her to DS9. *Coincidence,* she wondered, *or another thoughtful touch?*

It had been a long day, sometimes difficult, but on the whole satisfying. As many decisions as the first minister made on a day-to-day basis, as many arguments as she delivered to the Chamber of Ministers and to the Bajoran populace, as many actions as she took, she was never more aware of the importance and power of her office than when she interacted with people individually and in small gatherings. The memorial service she and Pralon Onala had led in Ashalla earlier had been of a considerably different nature from the one they'd held a year prior, on the one-year anniversary of Deep Space 9's destruction. That first memorial had taken place in Liberty Court, the huge, open-air ellipse not far from the Great Assembly. Bajorans had flocked to the service, not only filling the courtyard, but also spilling out onto the Grand Avenue of Lights. That occasion had been somber, made all the more so by the quiet collective remembrance of so many.

The second memorial had been far more personal. Like most Bajorans, Asarem tended to remember all the ills—present-day and historic—that had befallen her people. But also like most of her fellow citizens, the first minister tended to avoid regularly lamenting those ills, instead choosing to celebrate past achievements and other special occasions. Consequently, rather than hosting another service for the masses, Asarem and the kai had invited to the Great Assembly individuals and families who'd lost loved ones aboard Deep Space 9. More than a thousand people—including some Starfleet officers from Bajoran Space Central before they departed for the new space station—had attended throughout the day, and Asarem and Pralon had spoken with them separately and in small groups. Tears had flowed along with the reminiscences, but overall it had been a positive, cathartic, life-affirming experience. There had even been plenty of smiles, which Asarem had found particularly good to see on the threshold of the opening of the new starbase.

"I'm drained," the first minister told Enkar Sirsy. "It hasn't been an easy day."

"No, ma'am," Enkar said. "But it has been a good one, I think."

"Oh, I agree." Asarem sat up on the sofa, reached behind her head, and removed the tie that held her dark brown hair back from her face. She ran her fingers through the shoulder-length strands, urging them to fall back into their natural shape.

"Can I help with anything, Minister?" Enkar asked.

"No, I don't think so," Asarem said. She glanced over at Enkar, who stood beside the table in the dining area, rummaging through her ubiquitous portfolio, in which she always toted around an inordinate number of padds. She wore a suit that looked as though it had just been pressed. The subtly patterned black jacket and matching skirt complemented her gray blouse, all of which nicely set off her long, straight red hair. "How is it, Sirsy, that at this time of night, after all we've done today, you still look so fresh?"

"Because I didn't have to do the hard work today, ma'am; *you* did."

"You and I both know that's not true," Asarem said. "You worked just as hard as I did—and probably harder." Enkar Sirsy had served in the Bajoran government for most of her adult life, since her early twenties, when the Cardassians had finally withdrawn their occupying forces. In just a few years, she became assistant to the first minister at the time, Shakaar Edon. After Shakaar's unexpected death, Second Minister Asarem ascended to his post, and although she already relied on her own assistant, Altrine Theno, she opted to add Enkar to her staff.

That had proven a serendipitous choice. Although for a long time she held the title of assistant, and then aide, Enkar became much more than that to Asarem: confidant, analyst, speechwriter. Eventually, she worked her way up to the official position of advisor to the first minister, and during the last election, three years earlier, she served as campaign director. Upon winning her second six-year term, Asarem appointed Enkar as her chief of staff, a position she had handled admirably.

"I'm leaving a copy of your schedule for tomorrow, Minister," Enkar said, extracting one of her padds from her portfolio and placing it on the dining table. "The schedule for the entire event is also included, as are the remarks you've prepared."

"Thank you, Sirsy." Asarem reached down and tugged off her shoes, letting them fall to the carpet with first one thump, then another. "What time is the ceremony?"

"It will commence at midday, at thirteen o'clock," she said. "Starfleet security will arrive to escort you to the venue a quarter of an hour before that. Lustrate Vorat has asked to accompany you to the theater. I would follow with one of his aides."

"That'll be fine," she told Enkar. "You know, I'm glad you convinced me to travel to Deep Space Nine tonight. I'd hate to wake up tomorrow and have to make that trip in the morning." She stood up, preparing to go into the bedroom to get out of her suit. She knew that the earth-toned jacket and skirt, with a cream-colored top, looked good on her, but after so many hours in it, it no longer felt good.

Before Asarem could even take a step, though, the door chime called out. She had arrived back on the starbase only a few minutes earlier, and she certainly hadn't planned any meetings for such a late hour. She peered over at her chief of staff, who looked as surprised as Asarem felt.

"I'll see who that is and what they want, ma'am," Enkar said. Leaving her portfolio on the table, she padded over to the doors, which opened before her. She exited into the vestibule, and the doors promptly closed. Asarem waited, knowing that Enkar would speak to the security detail, the outer buffer between the first minister and the outside world. The chief of staff would find out why they had rung through to her quarters.

Enkar returned almost at once. "You have a visitor requesting to speak with you, Minister," she said. "It's the Romulan praetor."

Asarem blinked. "Really?" Both the Romulan praetor and the Gorn imperator had agreed to visit Bajor after the dedication, the first time that individuals in their positions would ever do so. Asarem assumed that she would speak to both leaders during their stays on Deep Space 9, presumably before or after the ceremony, but certainly not almost as soon as she set foot on the starbase.

Maybe the praetor's canceling her trip to Bajor, the first minister thought. *The same way the castellan did.* The notion brought a touch of rancor. While Asarem's two days with Lustrate Vorat on Bajor had gone well enough, their time together had lacked the magnitude that a visit by Castellan Garan would have had. The first minister could only hope that the praetor did not intend to renege on her promise to visit Bajor as well.

"What do you think, Sirsy?" Asarem asked.

"I'm not sure, Minister," the chief of staff said. "I think it could be that the praetor is reconsidering her trip to Bajor after the dedication."

"I had the same thought," Asarem said, disappointed. "Well, if that's why she's here, let's see if I can change her mind."

"Yes, ma'am." Enkar paced quickly to the dining table, where she picked up the padd she'd laid out for the first minister and packed it away again in her portfolio.

"I'll bring this back to you and check in after the praetor leaves."

"Thank you, Sirsy."

"Thank you, Madam First Minister."

Asarem quickly put her shoes back on as her chief of staff exited once more, taking her portfolio with her. A moment later, the Romulan praetor stepped inside. She wore dark blue slacks and a lighter blouse, along with a black, floor-length cape. Asarem recalled that the woman had lived a quarter of the way into her second century, but her ebon hair and toned physique did nothing to confirm that.

"Madam First Minister, thank you for agreeing to see me." She carried herself with an unmistakable sense of dignity. "I am Gell Kamemor, praetor of the Romulan Star Empire."

"I am Asarem Wadeen," the first minister said. She walked over to face Kamemor from a few paces away. "I'm pleased to meet you, Madam Praetor, but I also must admit that I'm nonplussed by the timing of your visit. I only just arrived from Bajor, it's late in the day, and I assumed I would be meeting you tomorrow, at the dedication ceremony."

"Forgive the intrusion," Kamemor said. "I'm aware of your travel and the hour, and that you did not expect me to call on you. If you will indulge me, I would ask only a few moments of your time."

Asarem considered declining the praetor's request, not because she objected to the breach of protocol, but because her day had been quite full—and taxing—already. She counted meeting the Romulan head of state as extremely important, and so she would have preferred doing so when she didn't feel quite so fatigued. Still, she had no desire to initiate her political relationship with Kamemor by refusing a request, particularly one so easily fulfilled.

"Please have a seat," Asarem invited the praetor, motioning to the round table in the compartment's dining area.

"Thank you," Kamemor said.

As Asarem led the praetor to the table, she asked, "May I offer you something to drink?"

"No, thank you," Kamemor said. "I wish to take up no more of your time than is necessary."

"Are you sure? I'm going to have something myself." Asarem walked over to the replicator set into the side wall.

As Kamemor sat down at the table, she said, "Perhaps a cup of tea, then."

Asarem had in mind something else entirely—a nightcap, such as a glass of *kis*—but she wanted to try to put the praetor at ease. "Would you care for it with sweetener?" she asked.

"No, thank you."

Asarem tapped the activation control on the replicator, which chirped in response. "Two cups of hot *deka* tea." On the replicator pad, amid a hum and a haze of sparkling white light, the tea materialized. Asarem picked up the cups and saucers and carried them to the table. She placed one set in front of the praetor, then sat across from her with her own.

"'Deka' tea?" Kamemor said. "Is this a Bajoran variety?"

"It is," Asarem said. "I hope you enjoy it." The first minister lifted her cup and sipped from it, as did the praetor. Looking across the table at the Romulan, Asarem noticed the arresting gray color of her eyes.

"Again, forgive my intrusion," Kamemor said, setting her teacup back down on its saucer. "I've come here tonight because I wanted to speak with you privately and in person, and before we begin discussing any political matters."

"This isn't a diplomatic visit?" Asarem asked, still confused.

"No," the praetor said. "It may have political repercussions, of course, but that is not the reason I'm here."

"You have me intrigued," Asarem said. "And you have my attention."

"First Minister, I know that quite some time has passed since the destruction of the space station that this facility—" The praetor glanced upward and around the compartment, clearly intending to indicate the whole of Deep Space 9. "—has been constructed to replace. I also know, as you must, that a Romulan starship and its crew were a part of that regrettable incident."

"A renegade crew," Asarem said, "if I understand correctly."

"That was the case, yes," Kamemor said. "I'm sure you're also aware that I and my government denounced that crew and its rogue actions."

Asarem nodded. She remembered the praetor's official statement. The first minister knew that it would be thoroughly tactless to reveal her own emotional reaction to Kamemor's declaration, but then—probably owing to the events of the day—she chose to give voice to her thoughts. "I heard your denunciation, Praetor. I found it . . . appropriate . . . but also something less than an expression of remorse."

"That is true," Kamemor said, "and it is the reason I am here to see you tonight." The admission surprised Asarem, and she suddenly wished that she'd ordered the glass of kis. "I wanted to personally apologize to you for what took place in your system, for the loss of life, at the hands of Romulans."

Instead of gratitude, though, the first minister felt something else: anger. She sought to contain the rush of emotion by measuring her words. "I'd like to tell you that I appreciate your sentiments, Praetor," she said, but then found that she did not want to keep herself from telling Kamemor the complete truth. "Your apology also seems to me like an empty gesture."

"My words are not empty," the praetor insisted. "I mean them. I *feel* them. But they are of course only words. They cannot restore the lives that were lost here, nor fully heal the scars left by all of those deaths."

"No. No, they can't," Asarem agreed. "But if you know that, then why are you here?"

"Two reasons have driven me here," Kamemor said. "The first is because this is the fitting thing, the *right* thing, to do. The Romulan participation in the destruction of Deep Space Nine occurred while I led the Empire. It was therefore my responsibility."

Again, Asarem considered not telling Kamemor what she thought, given its impolitic nature. *But she came here to talk about this.* Asarem hesitated, then forged ahead. "There are some who believe that the attack was much more than your responsibility, Praetor," she said. "There are some who think it was your *plan*." She braced herself for the denial surely to come.

Instead, Kamemor nodded.

"You're not rejecting that claim?" Asarem asked, thunderstruck.

"Such a claim is untrue," Kamemor said calmly. "I neither planned the attack nor even knew anything about it until after it had taken place."

"But you don't seem surprised or offended by people who believe otherwise?"

"Should I be?" Kamemor asked. "I think not. The Romulan Empire and the Federation have been opponents for more than two centuries. An attack on a Federation asset by a force that included a Romulan starship *should* engender fear and distrust. How could it *not* do so? Why wouldn't your citizens believe that the praetor intentionally acted against them? Were the roles reversed, wouldn't the Romulan people evaluate President Bacco in the same way?"

Kamemor seemed to the first minister almost too reasonable, as though she sought to hide her true agenda behind a veil of rationality. "Speaking of President Bacco," Asarem said, "shouldn't you be proclaiming all of this to her?"

"I already have," Kamemor said. "We spoke about it not long after the attack."

Asarem shook her head. "I don't mean to be adversarial, Praetor, but if you apologized to the Federation president two years ago, then why are you here *now*?" Asarem brought her teacup down too hard and it clattered against the saucer.

"My apology appears to have angered you," Kamemor said.

"Maybe it has," Asarem allowed. "You say that this is the right thing to do, but why two years after the fact? It seems . . . disingenuous. And why apologize only to me? If you're truly trying to do the right thing, isn't a public apology warranted?"

"I have come to you to say what I have because you lead your people," Kamemor said. "But I do not intend to speak *only* to you. With your permission, during my time on Bajor, I will issue a public apology to your people."

Asarem's eyes widened. She thought for an instant that she had misheard the praetor, but knew that she hadn't. "I . . . I would . . . my people would welcome such a statement of contrition, but . . . I have to ask again: why do this now, after so much time has passed? Frankly, it makes me suspect your motives."

"I do this now because the opportunity has presented itself with my invitation to the dedication, and to Bajor," Kamemor said. "I do it now because President Bacco and I have been attempting to resolve the differences between our worlds, between our peoples, between our alliances. I do it now because you and I are speaking for the first time, and I am hopeful that we can begin our dialogue with a foundation built of trust and respect." The praetor paused, as though deciding whether or not she should say more. At last, she did: "And I do this now because I can."

"What?" Asarem asked. "What does that mean?"

"It means that if I had publicly apologized for the Romulan Star Empire two years ago," Kamemor said, "I might well have been deposed—in one way or another."

The admission floored Asarem. "Are you saying that you didn't offer an official apology so that you could hold on to power?"

"Essentially, yes, though I would phrase it in a different fashion," Kamemor said. "When I rose to power, it was as a victim of circumstance. My people—and in particular our government—suffer from an institutional hubris, a collective chauvinism that I do not share. I drew immediate opposition, and in the wake of the rogue attack in the Bajoran system, I had to tread lightly. There were those who already thought me too weak to serve as praetor because I had known nothing about the attack, and because I argued for peace over war, for détente over brinkmanship. But there were also those who saw where I wanted to take the Empire—to a time of peace and pro-ductivity, of hope and prosperity. I needed to convince or subdue the first group, and cultivate and strengthen the second. A public apology would have been perceived as weakness and would have undercut those aims."

"That sounds like political justification," Asarem noted.

"And so it was," Kamemor said. "But I believed in the justification. If I had been removed from office, my replacement would not have hewed to my vision for the advancement—the maturation—of our society. Indeed, it was quite likely that I would have been supplanted by a hard-line war hawk. That would not have served the Empire well—or the Federation and its allies."

Asarem wondered if the praetor heard the hefty ambi-tion in her own words. "But now you have consolidated your power?" she asked. "Now you are not as vulnerable?"

"My government is changing," Kamemor said. "To the benefit of the Romulan people, and also to the benefit of the people beyond our borders."

"Like the Bajorans."

"Like all of our interstellar neighbors," Kamemor said. "Withholding a public apology from the Federation and the Bajorans immediately after the attack did not bring excessive harm, but issuing one at that time could have crippled the progress of the Romulan government."

"And the progress of which you speak is why you have taken the actions you have?" Asarem asked.

"Why do you do anything as first minister?" Kamemor responded, answering a question with a question.

"To protect and enrich the lives of the Bajoran people," Asarem said without hesitation.

"Of course," Kamemor said. "And war does not do that—even wars that are won. What keeps people safe, and what allows for the enrichment of their lives, is peace. That is why I have been working to change the character of the Romulan leadership—to keep the Empire at peace."

"I agree that those are laudable aims," Asarem said.

"Your agreement is the second reason I have come to see you tonight," Kamemor said. "I hope to establish a rapport with you, with your people, to create a relationship between Ki Baratan and Ashalla, between Romulus and Bajor. For where there is knowledge and understanding, where there is amity, there will be peace."

Kamemor's words reached the first minister in almost a primal way. Asarem had grown up under the yoke of the Occupation, had lost both parents and her only sister to Cardassian savagery. She'd spent more than two-thirds of her life in servitude and, when newly freed, had sought a place in government so that she could actively work to protect her people.

In Asarem's years as second minister to Shakaar's first, she had fought for a strong Bajor. She believed in border control, a widespread intelligence community, and preemption. She trusted in firepower—even if Bajor's most powerful weapons arrived in the hands of Starfleet personnel.

Over time, though, Asarem's views had shifted. She could see the devastation wrought by the Dominion on Cardassia—eight hundred million dead in an attempted genocide—as deserved retribution, but living the life she had, she could also see it as an abomination. Slowly, her way of thinking about the safety of her people evolved. The tens of billions—including many Bajorans—killed during the Borg invasion, and the resolution that ultimately brought an end to hostilities, only reinforced her conclusion that peace achieved exclusively at the emitter end of a phaser would always be a fragile peace.

Asarem understood what the praetor preached, but didn't know if she could truly trust the Romulan leader. She would have to consult with President Bacco, seek out her opinion about Gell Kamemor. But—

But I want to trust her.

Asarem noticed that the praetor's teacup was still almost completely full. "Do you not care for the tea?"

"I suppose that I should be diplomatic and just drink it down," Kamemor said. "But in an attempt to foster trust, I will tell you honestly that, no, I do not like it."

"We all have different tastes," Asarem said with a casual shrug. "There are many types of tea on Bajor, though. Can I interest you in sampling another?"

The praetor rose from her chair. "I did not intend to intrude on so much of your time," she said.

Asarem stood up as well and faced Kamemor across the dining table. "I do not consider your visit an intrusion," the first minister said. "And I always make time for the issues of which you speak." She walked over to the replicator, but then turned back toward the praetor. "Did you know that humans have an idiom: when they don't like something, they say, 'It's not my cup of tea.'"

"Really?" Kamemor said, one eyebrow arching, the sides of her mouth curling up just slightly, but enough to indicate her amusement. "I will have to remember that for my meeting with President Bacco."

"Just don't tell her you heard it from me." Asarem again activated the replicator with a touch, then ordered two cups of *chiraltan* tea. When she carried them over to the table, the praetor sat back down.

The two women talked deep into the night.

• • •

Sisko walked along Deck 8 of *Robinson*, his wife's arm curled comfortably through his. They ambled together contentedly, not saying much in the quiet corridor, the lighting dimmed to reflect the simulated nighttime hours aboard ship. They hadn't intended to stay on Deep Space 9 quite so late, but their conversations with friends, former crewmates, and some of the new station personnel had flowed easily—as had the drinks in Quark's new bar.

Sisko reached over with his free hand and placed it atop Kasidy's forearm, just below the sleeve of the elegant black dress she wore. Her flesh felt warm beneath his touch, and he cherished the sensation. It immediately brought him back to the first time he remembered taking her hand in his own.

It had been aboard her freighter, *Xhosa*, in her small cabin, on another late night. Pushed together by Jake, the two agreed to meet for coffee in the Replimat aboard the original Deep Space 9. The conversation proceeded well enough, but the revelation that Kasidy enjoyed baseball— that she even knew about the sport in the first place—gave them something in common and a good place to start.

At Kasidy's invitation, Sisko had accompanied her to *Xhosa*, where they'd listened to an incoming transmission, a play-by-play account of a baseball game in which her youngest brother had participated. They sat for a couple of hours in her cramped quarters, Kasidy on her bunk, Sisko in a chair beside her companel. They cheered Kornelius Yates through his at bats and plays in the field, and later lamented the Pike City Pioneers' four–three loss to the Cestus Comets on a bases-loaded double in the bottom of the ninth inning.

Afterward, Kasidy had walked Sisko to the hatch of

her ship, where she'd stood before him and looked up with her beautiful eyes. At the time, it had been nearly five years since he'd lost Jennifer, and he hadn't really thought about even the possibility of meeting anyone else. His immediate affection for Kasidy didn't confuse him so much as surprise him. He'd been out of practice in matters of the heart, and as he stood at *Xhosa*'s hatch with Kasidy looking up at him expectantly, he felt awkward and uncertain.

As Sisko had stood merely gazing into Kasidy's eyes, she had given up on him, at least for that moment. She raised her arm between them as though offering to shake hands and said, "All right, then." Sisko laughed, but then reached forward and, for the first time, took Kasidy's hand. He pulled her to him and their lips met, warmly, sweetly, perfectly. They parted smiling, and Sisko walked through the station all the way back to his cabin, forgoing the turbolift so that he could prolong the night and reflect on the evening just past.

Sisko didn't know if he should silently thank the Prophets for maneuvering his life in such a way that it eventually intersected with Kasidy's. He doubted that she would approve of such an idea. More likely, Kasidy would blame them for allowing—or even causing—circumstances to part the couple. In the normal course of his days and nights, Sisko didn't actually think about them much, or—thankfully—dream about them. He did remain grateful, though, that they had finally released him from his service to them and to Bajor.

"You're awfully quiet," Kasidy said, her soft voice appropriate to the dim lighting.

"Just thinking about . . . about the past, I guess."

"The station?" Kasidy asked. Sisko nodded. "Yeah. I was thinking about Brathaw and Pardshay and Luis." The three men had been part of Kasidy's crew aboard *Xhosa*, and all had perished during the final attack on the original DS9.

"I know it's hard," Sisko said. He could still see in his mind the Tzenkethi marauder's tail section slicing through *Xhosa* amidships, as well as the ensuing explosion that had consumed the vessel. Worse, he could still remember the horrible hopelessness and loss and guilt he'd felt, believing that Kasidy and Rebecca had been aboard. "Did you talk to their families today?"

"I sent messages," Kasidy said. "I just told them that I was thinking of them. I sent them your regards too."

"Good." He paused, thinking about the evening. "Captain Ro led a good service, I thought. A fitting service."

"I thought so too," Kasidy said. "I was moved. I think everybody was." She quieted for a moment, then added, "It was also nice to see some of your old crew—Ezri and Julian and Miles and Nog."

Sisko nodded. "It was even nice to see Quark."

"Well, I never had any problems with Quark," Kasidy said.

"Of course not," Sisko said. "You were the station commander's girlfriend and then wife. Quark may be many things, but he's not stupid."

"No, definitely not," Kasidy agreed.

They arrived at their quarters, and Kasidy touched her fingertip to the identification pad. Although *Robinson* remained secure even docked at a starbase, they always left their cabin sealed when Rebecca stayed home without them. Sisko didn't think often about their daughter's abduction, which had occurred more than five years earlier, and he didn't think Kasidy did anymore either, but they had not forgotten it.

The doors parted and they entered their quarters. Sixteen-year-old Alicia Flynn, daughter of one of the ship's schoolteachers, sat on the sofa against the outer bulkhead, her stocking feet up on the low table in front of her. "Hi, Captain and Missus Sisko," she said, looking up from the padd in her lap. Though Kasidy went by the surname *Yates*, Sisko knew that she didn't mind the shorthand people sometimes used. "How was your evening aboard the starbase?" When they'd asked the young woman to stay with Rebecca, they hadn't mentioned the memorial service, since they'd chosen to keep the event from their daughter.

"Hi, Alicia," Kasidy said. "We had a good night, thanks, but we're sorry we're so late."

"Oh, it's fine." Alicia waved away the apology with the insouciance of youth. "When you contacted me from the station, I would've told you if I couldn't stay later. Whether I was here or in our cabin, all I would've been doing is reading anyway." She dropped her feet to the deck and sat up, holding her padd in the air. "I'm slogging my way through *The Stars Within Reach*. We have to read it for history class."

"That's about the founding of the first Alpha Centauri colony, isn't it?" Sisko asked. Alicia nodded. "I've never read that, but I've always meant to."

"It's a wonderful book," Kasidy said. "But isn't it also a bit . . . mature for you, Alicia?"

Alicia stood up and deactivated her padd with a touch. "If by 'mature,' you mean boring, then yes, absolutely."

Kasidy laughed. "Try it again in ten or fifteen years and you'll think differently."

"It might take me that long to finish it," Alicia said. "Anyway, Rebecca's fine. She went to bed at her regular time. I haven't heard a peep out of her since."

"She went to bed without any argument?" Kasidy asked.

"Well, she did convince me to let her read in bed, but when I checked on her ten minutes later, she was already asleep," Alicia said. "I took her book out of her hands and turned out the light without her waking up."

"That girl could sleep through a warp core breach," Sisko said. Since she had started sleeping through the night as an infant, Rebecca had never had any difficulties getting her rest.

Alicia put on her shoes and crossed the cabin toward the doors. "Good night, Missus Sisko. Good night, Captain Sisko."

"Good night," Kasidy said. "Say hello to your parents."

After Alicia had gone, Sisko turned to his wife. "Care for a nightcap?"

"Not tonight, Ben," Kasidy said, putting her hand on the front of his shoulder. "I've got to get an early start tomorrow. I met the Gorn delegation today, but I'd like a little more time with them before the ceremony."

"Okay." Sisko took Kasidy's hand from his shoulder and lifted it to his lips for a quick kiss of her fingertips. "I'll check on Rebecca while you get ready for bed."

Sisko watched Kasidy make her way through the door in the side bulkhead and into their bedroom, then turned and started across the living area. He'd gotten halfway when he suddenly stopped short, startled. Rebecca stood in the doorway to her bedroom. He hadn't even heard the door glide open.

For a beat, he stared at his daughter. She stood there motionless, without saying a word. "Rebecca, honey, are you all right?" Sisko asked. He hurried the rest of the way across the cabin, and as he neared, she held her hands up to him. He whisked her up into his arms. Still small for her age, she reached barely 125 centimeters in height and weighed only 25 kilos. He looked at her adorable face, framed by her straight, dark hair that ran down almost to her shoulders. Sisko thought she looked more like her mother than like him, but Kasidy thought the reverse.

"I'm fine, Daddy," Rebecca said. "How are you?"

"I'm fine too," Sisko said. "Your mother and I are both fine. But it's way past your bedtime. What are you doing up? Did you have to go to the refresher?"

"No. I just wanted to see you."

Sisko carried his daughter forward, past her closet and 'fresher, and into her bedroom. "Well, you're seeing me now. I'm sorry if we woke you up."

"You didn't wake me up," Rebecca said. "I woke up to see you."

Sisko didn't quite follow his daughter's words, but she had a tendency sometimes to abandon logic. *Plus she probably just woke up out of a sound sleep.* He set her down in her bed, and she immediately burrowed into the bedclothes. He waited for her inevitable plea to read to her from the book they'd been making their way through in recent days.

"How was the memorial service?" Rebecca asked.

A jolt rocked Sisko like an electric charge. He felt the muscles of his jaws tighten. "What, honey?" He thought he must have misunderstood her.

"How was the memorial service?" Rebecca repeated.

Sisko sat down on the edge of his daughter's bed, trying to keep his surprise from showing on his face. "It was fine, but where did you hear about that?" he asked. "Did Alicia mention it to you?" Even though Sisko and Kasidy hadn't spoken of the memorial to the young woman, she certainly could have heard about it from someone else aboard ship—despite that few people on *Robinson* had known about it.

"Alicia didn't tell me," Rebecca said. "Nobody told me. I just knew."

Sisko smiled at his daughter in an attempt to mask the dread surfacing inside him. "What do you mean you just knew, honey?" he asked. "You must have heard about it somewhere."

Rebecca regarded him without responding. After a few seconds, she raised her shoulders in an exaggerated shrug. She then yawned. "I'm tired," she said. "Good night, Daddy." She pulled the bedclothes more tightly about her, then rolled over on her side, her back to Sisko.

He thought about pursuing the subject, but he didn't want to upset his daughter—or, if she came in, his wife. *Probably it's nothing,* he told himself. *Of course it's nothing.*

Sisko leaned forward and kissed Rebecca on the side of her face that he could still see. He then rose, turned off the light, and moved back out into the living area, the door to his daughter's bedroom closing behind him. He stopped and raised a hand to rub at his temple.

Am I overreacting? he thought. Rebecca surely must have heard about the memorial from somebody else, even if she didn't remember that herself. *Things like that happen all the time. There's nothing to worry about.*

Mostly, Sisko believed that. He had always been vigilant about watching for any . . . peculiarities . . . in his daughter. He knew what he had experienced in his own life: his communications with the Prophets, his pagh'tem'fars, his visions of himself in another life. He believed all that had happened because of physical events—such as him entering the Bajoran wormhole, or being under the influence of an Orb, or even suffering a plasma shock in a holosuite—but he also questioned whether any portion of those events had resulted from a Prophet inhabiting and controlling the body of his biological mother at the time of his conception and birth. Sisko always wondered if he was, in some sense, part Prophet himself. That, in turn, made him ask the same question of his daughter.

And Rebecca is *different.* Smaller in stature than other human girls her own age, whip smart, often quiet and introspective, and just a bit . . . off . . . from her friends and schoolmates. All of that could have been quite natural, though, having nothing at all to do with the Prophets. *Nothing at all,* Sisko thought, *but—*

But another time had once caught his attention in the same way. It had been a couple of years earlier, on a day when he and Jasmine Tey had been taking Rebecca to school. He could see the incident so clearly in his memory.

His daughter had been skipping along the cobblestoned main avenue of Adarak, on Bajor. She wore a pale blue dress and carried a padd slung across her shoulder. As she traced a serpentine path through the old-fashioned lampposts that lined the outer edges of the pedestrian thoroughfare, he saw the smile on her face and marveled at the joy that such simple movement could bring to a child. Rebecca seemed remarkably happy and well-adjusted.

Up ahead of him, Rebecca's shoe had struck a particularly high cobble and she'd gone sprawling to the ground, her hands out in front of her, her padd clattering on the stones. Sisko raced forward, as did Tey at his side. By the time they crossed the few meters to Rebecca, she had already started to pick herself up and dust herself off. Sisko expected to see tears, if not from the pain of scraped hands and knees, then simply from the surprise of a sudden fall.

But as he crouched to examine his daughter, even before he could ask her if she'd hurt herself, she looked up and declared, "I'm okay."

"Yeah?" Sisko had said, turning her hands up to look at her palms and then examining her knees. He saw that she'd scraped some skin from one shin, but nothing too bad. "Are you sure?"

"I knew I was gonna fall," Rebecca had said. "So I kinda stopped myself."

"What? What do you mean, honey?"

"I'm okay," Rebecca had repeated. "We better go or I'm gonna be late for school." Her padd had fallen to the ground, but its strap still twisted around her arm in the crook of her elbow. She hoisted it back onto her shoulder, then turned without waiting for a response and resumed skipping down the avenue.

Sisko had stood up and looked at Tey. As they started to follow Rebecca, Sisko asked, "Do you know what she meant by that? That she 'knew' she was going to fall, and that she 'stopped' herself?"

Tey had shaken her head. "I don't, not really. Clearly she didn't really stop herself from falling. But Rebecca does make curious pronouncements like that sometimes."

"Like what exactly?" Sisko had asked. Even back then, the idea of Rebecca acting differently from other children, behaving or saying things out of the norm, concerned him.

"She just sometimes says that she knew that something was going to happen," Tey had said. "And sometimes she gives the impression that she knows things you didn't think she could. But children's minds are like sponges: they absorb so much."

"Have you talked with Ms. Yates about this?" Sisko

had asked. As he spoke with Tey, he kept a watchful eye on Rebecca.

"We've spoken about it a couple of times," Tey had said. "I don't really think it's anything other than a quirk of Rebecca's personality, and maybe an advanced observational or intuitional sense."

"You . . . you know our history," Sisko had said. "You know *my* history."

"Yes, sir, I do, Captain Sisko. And you know that I'm not a believer in Bajoran mysticism—in any kind of mysticism. What I believe in is helping to take care of your wonderful little girl. If she ever did or said anything that concerned me, or that would concern you or Ms. Yates, I wouldn't keep it to myself."

"Thank you," Sisko had said. "I know that, and I appreciate it." Down the avenue, he saw Rebecca approaching a side lane, into which a stream of children poured. She started to turn the corner with them, headed in the direction of her school. Sisko hurried ahead, not wanting to lose sight of her. Tey followed.

Rebecca had disappeared around the corner. Sisko felt as though a knife had been thrust into his gut. He knew that he would reach the lane and turn into it—and his daughter would have vanished. A cold sweat broke out on his skin. He turned the corner, already gulping air into his lungs to yell out Rebecca's name.

But she'd been standing right there, just a couple of steps into the lane, looking at him. Waiting for him. As she had just a few moments earlier, she said, "I'm okay."

Sisko had bent down on one knee and pulled Rebecca to him, hugging her tightly. "Honey, you can't do that," he told her. "You can't run away so that whoever's with you can't see you. Okay?" He pulled back and held her at arm's length, looking into her deep, dark eyes—eyes, it suddenly struck him, that seemed far too . . . *knowing* . . . for her age.

But then Rebecca had rolled those eyes and all at once had appeared seven years of age and no older. "Oh, Dad," she said. Those sounded like words out of a child's mouth too, and Sisko smiled. His desperate concern for his daughter felt foolish. As a parent, he wanted, he *needed*, to watch out for her safety, of course, but he couldn't let the shadows of his own experiences cloud his judgment.

As Sisko stood in the middle of his family's quarters aboard *Robinson*, he asked himself again if he was doing that, impressing the nature of his own sometimes unusual past on his daughter. He thought about it, and answered himself aloud: "I probably am overreacting." He considered speaking with Kasidy about it, but feared worrying her unnecessarily. He felt certain that if she had any concerns about Rebecca, she would have voiced them.

Sisko glanced over his shoulder at his daughter's closed bedroom door without really seeing it. Two days later, he would note the new message that Rebecca had already written on the glowpane hanging on her door, but he wouldn't connect it to anything that had happened or that he'd thought on the night of the memorial.

"It's nothing," he told himself about his foolish concern. "Nothing at all." He then headed into the bedroom he shared with Kasidy.

Rebecca's glowpane read: *Nothing is still something.*

Ten

Keev Anora swung her handheld beacon from side to side in front of her, illuminating the walls and floor of the cave. Beside her, Altek Dans did the same. The ambient temperature, which had dropped continuously since they'd started back from the far entrance, seemed finally to have stabilized. That, coupled with the muscles in Keev's legs revealing that, at least in some places, they had begun to climb, told her that they had passed the halfway mark of their return journey.

Keev and Altek hiked through the cave system, their boots thudding heavily against the dirt and stone over which they trod. They did not speak, although Altek had occasionally tried to begin a conversation. Each time, Keev had shut him down, claiming the need to concentrate so that she could find and read the coded markers that delineated their route.

That claim had been true, at least in part. The extensive cave system beneath the Merzang Mountains grew more complex the deeper it reached into the range. Their path varied from narrow slits through which they had to edge sideways, to even narrower ledges bordering precipitous drops, to low crawlways that sent them onto their bellies, to huge open chambers off of which led numerous other passages. As far as anyone in any of the gilds knew, only one course through the labyrinthine subterranean network had ever been found that allowed travel from one side of the mountains to the other. A one-way journey that began before dawn would end past midday, and along the way, a hundred or more choices had to be made. A single wrong turn could multiply the possibilities of getting lost by an order of magnitude. Through the years, more than one gild member who'd entered the caverns had never returned to the open air. They risked it, though, because it bypassed the trip around the mountains, reducing the travel time to the distant Bajoran city of Shavalla by weeks.

Keev and Altek had left their gild's encampment in the middle of the night to ensure that they would reach the cave entrance before even the first hints of sunrise robbed them of the cover of darkness. They brought with them four Bajora the gild had helped flee their enslavement in Joradell. The twelve-year-old Resten Ahleen had been among them.

Everybody in Keev's gild had wanted to move Ahleen from their encampment, through the caves, to true freedom, as soon as possible. Life in the wood, always on the run and under the threat of imminent attack, humbled the heartiest of adults; children did not belong. On top of that, the burden of protecting Ahleen in such circumstances weakened their ability to defend themselves, whether by flight or with weapons. More than all of those considerations, though, the members of the gild simply wanted the girl to begin her new life.

But that hadn't been possible. When Keev successfully smuggled Ahleen out of Joradell, the girl arrived at the gild's encampment malnourished, poorly rested, and—worst of all—the victim of physical abuse. Her rescue might have saved her from sexual exploitation, but scars and still-healing wounds scored her back from where she had been lashed. She could not possibly have made the journey through the mountain caves in her condition.

Additionally, although she had somehow gathered the wherewithal to participate in her escape from Joradell, her spirit had been shattered. She had run from tyranny, but she could not run from her own grief. When she had lost her mother, the girl had lost all that mattered to her in the world.

For two months, the gild had cared for Ahleen. As she ate and slept and spent her days free from violence, she grew stronger, in both body and spirit. While no one could replace her mother, she did bond with Keev, as well as with Altek, no doubt because they had been directly responsible for her delivery from daily torment.

Eventually, just after the rescue of three adult slaves, Ahleen had been deemed ready for the arduous trek through the caves. After beginning in darkness, they reached the entrance with dawn still ahead of them. Keev and Altek uncovered the hidden cave entrance, then, once all of them had entered, carefully concealed it again.

With Keev leading the way, they had made steady progress beneath the mountains. They arrived on the other side of the range, at the far end of the caves, after the sun had reached its zenith for the day. A group from Shavalla greeted them there, ready to lead the freed slaves to liberty.

Ahleen, though, had been unwilling to part from Keev and Altek. Although she had managed the trip through the caves with few problems, and despite that she'd known what awaited her on the other side, still she clung to the two people who had set her free. It had taken time and a promise from Keev to visit her in Shavalla to convince the girl to say good-bye.

I shouldn't have given my word, Keev thought as she tramped through a long, narrowing cave. *I shouldn't have promised to visit Ahleen, because she's had enough disappointments in her young life already.*

The walls closed in as Keev and Altek moved forward, until they no longer had sufficient room to walk side by side. She quickly jogged a step ahead of him—just as she'd done many times prior to that—leaving him to follow her. He did so without comment.

A few steps later, in the light of her beacon, the passage cleaved in two, into a pair of tapering openings. Keev recognized the divide—she had long ago lost count of how often she had traversed the underground route. She recalled that they needed to take the right-hand branch, but the procedures that Veralla had put in place for their gild didn't allow her to rely on memory alone.

"Stop," Keev said over her shoulder, and Altek did as instructed. She looked forward and estimated her distance from the divide, then turned around. "You need to take a few steps back."

"It's the right fork," Altek said, pointing over her shoulder.

"I know it's the right fork," Keev said. "Now take three steps back."

"No wonder this trip takes so long," Altek groused, but he did as he'd been instructed and moved backward.

"Stop complaining," Keev said, more harshly than she'd intended. Altek hadn't carped at all until that point.

Keev stepped forward, into the space Altek had vacated. She swept the beam of her beacon along the bases of the cave walls, searching. At last, she saw two stones wedged into a fold in the rock, and she looked a distance on either side of them until she saw the third stone, which she bent and examined. She saw on its surface a carved mark that specified the route they needed to take.

Keev stood up and, without looking at Altek, said, "It's the right fork."

As she turned away from him and started forward again, he murmured, "I wish I'd said that."

Keev whirled on him, causing Altek to stop short. "Hey," she growled at him, shoving her palm into the middle of his chest, "I'm leading this mission. We have procedures—" She pointed in the direction of the stone markers. "—to prevent us from getting lost and dying in here, but if you want to go on alone, I won't stop you."

Altek regarded her with an expression of surprise, but then his features changed. In the reflected light of their beacons, which sent shadows upward on his face, Keev watched his muscles harden and his brow furrow, his ego plainly asserting itself. She waited for him to fire back at her, but then he seemed to rein in his anger. "Sorry," he finally said. "I'll follow you."

Keev felt foolish. Crossing beneath the mountains, always grueling, had been made less so by Altek's participation, especially when they'd escorted the four former slaves. She had no real reason to snap at him.

With a curt nod, Keev resumed their trip. She followed the right-hand branch of the cave, up to the point where the walls tapered to just a couple of hand widths apart. She unclasped the harness in which she carried her water bottle, which hung at her waist. Though she'd refilled the container at the far entrance, she'd already drunk more than half of its replenished contents.

Sidling up to the narrow opening, Keev tossed her water bottle and its harness through it. They rattled along the ground where they landed. The harness remained connected to her belt by a cord, ensuring that she would not lose it off an unseen ledge or down a hidden fissure. She then lobbed her beacon, also tied to her belt, after the water bottle. Finally, she removed her jacket and threw it forward as well.

Without having to be told, Altek held his beacon on Keev so that she could see. She dipped her hand in a pouch on her belt and collected some fine powder on her fingertips, which she rubbed on her hands and then up and down the front of her clothing. She then wedged herself into the opening and began easing her way through it.

Keev could feel the coldness of the rock against her. She moved by degrees, shifting her feet in small increments. She turned her head sideways, squeezing her body through the tight opening.

She made it halfway through before she became stuck, a protrusion of rock hard against the center of her chest. It felt as though it pressed against her, as though trying to crush her. She'd experienced such tight spaces frequently on her trips through the caves, and so she knew how to maneuver herself through them. No matter what she tried, though, she could not move forward.

Keev saw Altek facing her, but could not see his face in the shadows behind his beacon. She yelled in frustration, a formless, guttural cry that echoed around them. She pushed and pulled with all her might, struggling to make it through the opening.

At last, she grew still. What had begun as mere frustration and anger graduated to fear. Keev did not suffer from claustrophobia, but the real possibility that she could be trapped there in the cave scared her. The hard surface of the rock felt both unforgiving and final.

"Anora?" Altek said quietly, for the first time ever

using her given name. He moved closer to her, but smartly kept some distance between them. She did not need to be crowded by him. "Anora, it's all right."

She said nothing. She took as much of a breath as she could—the cave walls compressing her chest—and then tried once more to make her way through the narrow space. Keev didn't budge.

"Anora, it's Ahleen, isn't it?" Altek asked.

"What?" Keev said. The question seemed completely out of place.

"You're troubled by leaving the girl," he said. "And you're mad at yourself for making a vow to her that you're not sure you can keep."

Keev sagged, despite being lodged in stone. "I don't know what you're talking about," she said—but of course she did know, and so did he.

"It doesn't matter what you told her today," Altek said. "It doesn't even matter if you never see her again. You *saved* her. You gave Ahleen back a life that had been stolen from her." He paused, as though in thought, and then added, "No, you didn't give her life back. You gave her a life she's never had. You—"

"Stop," Keev said. The cold stone beside her mouth grew clammy beneath her warm breath. "Just stop."

"I'm sorry," Altek said. He closed the distance between them, drawing in close to her. "How can I help you get through?"

"You can't," Keev said, although she realized that he probably already had. Thinking for even a moment about something other than her physical predicament, she had already lost some of the tension in her body. "Just . . . give me a moment. I need to relax." Keev tried to clear her head. She closed her eyes and envisioned a serene scene, away from Joradell, away from the gild and the wood, away from the caves. She visualized walking down the streets of Shavalla, free from care.

In her imagination, she entered an old building, tramped down a decrepit, poorly lit hallway, and found herself standing before a closed door. She hadn't tried to paint that picture in her mind, but she saw it anyway, as though she no longer controlled her own thoughts. Yet somehow it didn't trouble her.

The door swung inward, revealing a man with a warm, dark face and close-cropped black hair. A look of recognition lighted his features. *Nerys,* he said, clearly mistaking her for somebody else—except that the name for some reason resonated with Keev. *You're all right.*

"Of course, I'm all right," Keev said aloud, and her eyelids winked open. She still stood in a cave beneath the Merzang Mountains, lodged in a narrow passage. She saw Altek peering at her, wearing a concerned expression. Keev nodded at him, then began to shift her body. She twisted and shimmied, concentrating on keeping her body loose. Her torso moved forward, got stuck again, then finally pushed free into the wider passage beyond. She let out a long, relieved sigh.

"Good job," Altek called. "Are you all right?"

Of course, I'm all right, Keev thought. "I'm fine," she told Altek. She retrieved her jacket and donned it once more, her perspiration already growing cold on her skin. She took a drink from her water bottle, then replaced it, along with her beacon, on her belt. She then returned to the small space she'd just squeezed through and looked past it at Altek. "Are you ready to come through?" she asked him.

"I am."

Keev reached through the stone slit, and Altek handed

her his water bottle, jacket, and finally his beacon. She kept the latter shining in his direction so that he could see his surroundings. Keev stepped back when she saw his hand and arm come through the opening. Though taller and heavier than Keev, Altek took a much shorter time to negotiate the passage than she had, the different heights of the various parts of his body helping him to avoid becoming trapped in the same way that she had.

Once Keev had given Altek his supplies back, they continued their journey. The cave widened, enabling them to walk beside each other. They resumed their silence.

The temperature around them started to increase, to the point where both Keev and Altek removed their jackets. The cave floor rose, ascending toward the entrance. With less than an hour left to go, Keev said, "I shouldn't have lied to Ahleen."

She could feel Altek regard her. When he didn't say anything, she turned her head to face him. "Was it a lie?" he asked her when they made eye contact.

"Of course it was."

"Really?" Altek asked. He did not sound argumentative, but curious. "Do you think you'll *never* go to Shavalla?"

"Well, not *never*," Keev said, "but certainly not right now." She looked back down at the ground ahead of them, the dirt-and-stone surface rolling out beneath the beams of their beacons.

"I didn't hear you say anything about visiting Ahleen 'right now.'"

"It doesn't matter," Keev said. "You know what that little girl believes. She thinks I'll be there to see her in just a few days."

"Maybe," Altek granted. "But she'll also have a lot of

other things going on. She may not even remember what you said, and even if she does, she'll understand, either now or later."

Keev shook her head. "I don't feel good about it."

"Well, you should," Altek said forcefully. "You said what you had to say, did what you had to do, to get Ahleen to the next stage of her life—to the point where she'll actually have a real life. And you saved her in the first place."

"*We* saved her," Keev said, more out of reflex than for any other reason.

"Yes, *we* did," Altek agreed. "And yet you still don't trust me."

Keev did not reply. How could she? She wore her skepticism—about everything, including Altek—like a badge of honor.

"I understood it at first," Altek continued. "We didn't exactly meet under the friendliest of circumstances. But it's been five months now. I think I've proven my loyalty to the cause and to the members of our gild. I think I've also proven my value."

Again, Keev did not reply.

"I assume you're not saying anything because you don't want to deny your distrust, but we both know it's true," Altek said. "After all this time, after all I've done with the gild . . . it doesn't make sense not to trust me anymore. I gave up a very comfortable life in Joradell for this."

Keev seized on his last assertion. "It says something that you could be comfortable living in a city that enslaved people."

Altek stopped. Keev did so as well. "I meant that I occupied a respected position in Joradell, that I owned a nice home and enjoyed a measure of wealth. Obviously, that wasn't more important to me than the inexcusable injustice, the immorality of slavery. I relinquished my own personal comfort to fight for the greater good."

"Not at first," Keev argued. "At first, you kept your *comfortable* life." After initially making contact with the gild, Altek had retained his position in the city.

"I did that so I could provide a resource to the gild within Joradell," he said. In so doing, he had helped in freeing numerous Bajoran slaves. "You know that."

"You only left the city when it seemed like you had no choice." Keev's voice had risen, and it resounded to her from the cave walls.

"When it 'seemed' like I had no choice?" Altek said. "I saw the condition that Ahleen was in when they brought her into the hospital, and later, how the local prefect looked at her. I risked lying to keep her overnight for more medical tests so I could get a message to the gild, and then even though I was detained at the hospital the next day until after the patrols had begun, I tried to get Ahleen out anyway."

"And what would you have done if I hadn't shown up?" Keev asked.

"Believe me, I didn't expect to see you," Altek said. "I hoped we would manage to get through the city without getting stopped by a patrol, but if we did get stopped, I had my own plan."

"And what was your plan? Would you have killed those officers?" Keev asked, her disbelief evident even to her own ears.

"If I had to," Altek said quietly.

"Really?"

"You're not the only one with a wooden blade to avoid the Aleiran metal detectors."

The assertion surprised Keev. She considered asking

to see Altek's phantom weapon, but she supposed that if she did, it would still prove nothing. Careful to keep an even tone, she said, "I'm just saying that your joining our gild could be a ruse specifically designed to build up our trust in you." She paused, then added, "We've been fooled before."

"I understand," Altek said. "But you have to understand that it's been five months, and I didn't just join the gild. I left Joradell, I've helped get escaped slaves to Shavalla, I've treated the members of the gild for illness and injury. At this point, I know all of you, I know the places you set up camp in the wood, I know about the caves and how you get the escaped Bajora to freedom. If I were an Aleiran agent, you'd all be dead or in prison by now."

"Or enslaved," Keev said.

"Yes, or enslaved," Altek said.

They stood quietly for a few moments, and then Keev began walking again. Altek fell in beside her. "So where do we go from here?" he wanted to know.

Keev shook her head. "Why does Veralla trust you so much?" she asked. "Why did he trust you the instant you arrived in our encampment?"

"He didn't trust me the instant I arrived," Altek avowed. "I'm not even sure he trusts me now."

"He obviously trusts you now," Keev said. "And he has from the very beginning."

"No," Altek insisted. "He didn't trust *me*; he trusted Grenta Sor." Keev recalled the name. Altek had used it essentially as an introduction after he'd run into the encampment.

"And who is Grenta Sor?" Keev asked. Immediately after Altek had arrived, she'd asked Veralla about the name. She thought that it might be a code of some sort that Altek had received from somebody, either willingly or by means of coercion. Veralla had deflected the question without answering it.

"Grenta Sor is a physician," Altek said. "We worked together at the hospital in Joradell." He paused, then said, "She's also Veralla's sister."

Keev stopped in her tracks, shocked. "What?" She hadn't known that Veralla even had siblings—or any living family at all, for that matter.

"Grenta Sor is Veralla's sister," Altek repeated.

Without warning, a loud noise filled the cave around them and the ground began to tremble. "What—?" Keev began, but then the shaking earth knocked her from her feet. Her beacon slipped from her grasp, sending distorted shadows capering wildly across the cave walls. Altek crashed to the ground beside her. Dirt and small pieces of stone rained down on them from the roof of the cave.

Keev scrambled back up, then helped Altek stand. She grabbed her beacon and shined it ahead, then tapped Altek on the elbow. "Come on," she said. Keev ran, and Altek followed.

Another explosion shook the cave. It sounded louder and closer, not from farther along in the caves, but from within the rock above them. Keev steadied herself with a hand against the side wall, but she kept moving. So did Altek.

They rounded a corner together, and their beacons illuminated a long, straight passage before them. Keev recognized it and knew that it wouldn't take them more than half an hour or so to reach the cave entrance. They ran on, but as they did, Keev saw a flash in the distance. Once they'd gotten closer, she discerned that a circular section of the cave roof had begun to glow, a great red flaw in the surface of the rock. It grew brighter and brighter as they approached it, as though building to a critical mass of color. "Hurry," Keev called to Altek, and she realized that a loud hum had begun to infuse the cave. The sense of an impending explosion could not have been greater.

We have to get past it, Keev thought desperately. They could run in the other direction, retrace their steps to the far entrance of the cave system, but if the roof collapsed, they would be cut off from the gild unless they spent weeks circumnavigating the mountains—if cave-ins didn't trap them inside before they could even get out. *No, we need to get past that spot and out on the gild side.*

They raced through the straight tunnel. The light from their beacons wavered rapidly along the cave surfaces as they pumped their arms. Keev could only hope that they could make it safely past the flaming red portion of the roof.

They reached the location at a dead run. The third boom came from directly above them. Then the roof of the cave came crashing down.

Eleven

In the 'fresher, Chief Engineer Miles O'Brien studied himself in the full-length mirror. He didn't really care for Starfleet's dress whites—they accentuated the health of his appetite a little too much—but at least he didn't find them as uncomfortable as previous styles. He quickly affixed to his left breast the commendations he'd earned from the Starfleet Corps of Engineers, then headed out into the living area of his quarters.

Crossing to the companel, he checked the time—both on the station and in Ashalla. "Come on, Keiko," he said, hoping that he would hear from his wife in the few minutes before he had to leave. Anxious, he moved over to the replicator and tapped its activation pad. "Coffee, Kona blend, double strong, double sweet," he ordered, then grabbed up the tall white mug that materialized. He took a moment to savor the heady aroma, then sipped noisily at the steaming brew.

O'Brien chuckled. "If Keiko were here, she'd tell me to drink my coffee like a human, not like a Klingon." He missed his wife. Two years earlier, after he'd been assigned to help design and construct the new Deep Space 9 as its chief engineer, Keiko and Molly and Yoshi had at first remained on Cardassia, where the family had made a home for almost seven years.

They had initially relocated to Cardassia not long after the Dominion War, as part of the Federation's endeavors to help rebuild the Union. While Keiko led an agrarian renewal project operated by the Interstellar Agricultural Aid Commission, a private organization that worked closely with the UFP, O'Brien left his professorship at Starfleet Academy and transferred to the SCE. Keiko's original commitment had been for two years, but everybody in the family had quickly become very comfortable in their new home, and two years had stretched to four, and then to six.

O'Brien hadn't been looking to leave Cardassia or the Corps of Engineers—although he'd traveled offworld on a number of assignments with the SCE—but Starfleet had transferred him to the Bajoran system after the destruction of the old DS9. O'Brien relocated first, allowing him and Keiko time to decide how best to deal with his new posting. In the interim, the proximity of Bajor and Cardassia permitted quick trips between the two, mitigating the family's separation.

Two months later, Keiko had found an opportunity with the University of Ashalla on Bajor. She led a year-long botanical analysis of flora collected during a research project into the jungles of Ver'laht, then re-upped for a second year. After so much time in the field on Cardassia, Keiko had enjoyed returning to the lab, and so she'd spoken to Captain Ro about prospects for work on the new starbase. With Starfleet preparing to launch a major exploratory initiative out beyond Bajor, and with a bevy of advanced scientific facilities being installed on Deep Space 9, the station had numerous civilian openings. Keiko accepted a position as chief botanist, though her term would not begin for another two months, after she'd completed her second year at the university. O'Brien looked forward to living full-time with his wife and children again.

He set his mug down on the dining table beside the replicator, then peered upward. "O'Brien to T'Lune."

"T'Lune here." During his absence from alpha shift that day, O'Brien had assigned one of his staff to crew the main engineering console in the Hub. *"Go ahead, Chief."*

"I'm just checking in," O'Brien said. "How are things looking?"

"All primary systems are up and running," T'Lune reported. *"We had a minor power fluctuation in one of the backup reactors during standard testing this morning. I shut it down and have a team working on it."*

"What about the other backups?" O'Brien asked. Eight mark-XIII fusion reactors powered Deep Space 9, with another quartet providing redundancy. Standard procedure included regular testing of the four backups.

"We executed tests," T'Lune said. *"Results were optimal."*

"Any idea yet of the problem?" O'Brien asked.

"Preliminary indications are a materials defect in one of the induction tubes," T'Lune said, *"but we haven't yet completed our analysis."* O'Brien liked T'Lune and thought her a solid engineer, but the Vulcan always wanted to run one more diagnostic, perform one more test.

"All right," he said. "I'll probably be up to the Hub late this afternoon, depending on how long the ceremony goes."

"Understood, Chief," T'Lune said.

Before O'Brien could sign off, another voice spoke up. *"Chief? This is Ensign Becerra."* Becerra, O'Brien knew, had taken over at the communications station for Lieutenant Viss, who, like the rest of Ro's senior staff, would be attending the dedication. *"You've got an incoming transmission from Bajor."*

"Great," O'Brien said. "I'll take it in my quarters. O'Brien out."

By the time he made it back to the companel, a flashing indicator signaled the arriving message. He touched a control surface, and Keiko's image appeared on the screen. She'd recently cut her black hair into a short, spiky style that made her look a decade younger than her fifty-two years. Through the window behind her, he could see people walking along a tree-covered quadrangle, telling O'Brien that his wife had made it back to her office. *"Miles,"* she said from where she sat at her desk. *"My, don't you look dapper?"*

O'Brien glanced down at his stark white dress uniform. "I look like a nurse working a quarantine unit."

"But a very handsome nurse," Keiko said with a smile. *"At a very fashionable quarantine unit, I'm sure."*

Miles laughed, a sound that came out somewhere between a chuckle and a grunt. "So how did it go?" he asked his wife. "Did they *ooh* and *aah* over your presentation?"

"They did," Keiko said, visibly excited. *"I think we really made the case to continue the research."*

"That's wonderful," O'Brien said. The University of Ashalla lacked the resources to continue the analysis of the Ver'laht samples that Keiko and her team had performed, and so they'd asked to present their findings to the Federation Department of Science in the hopes of securing the necessary personnel and equipment. "I knew you could do it."

"I don't think it was me as much as the number and variation of the new species that were found," Keiko said, with

more than a small amount of modesty. *"But whatever the case, it looks like there's a really good chance that the research will continue."*

"Congratulations," O'Brien said. "Does this mean I might get you and the kids up here sooner?"

"Afraid not," Keiko said. *"The university will be lucky if they can get an answer by the time I leave, so they need me to stay for these last two months."*

"Well, at least you're only a transport ride away."

"And I'll be up with Molly and Yoshi in just a few days," Keiko said.

"I can't wait to show you the new place," O'Brien said. "There are so many more things to do than on the old station, and there are going to be so many more people."

"And it's not forty years old and designed to process ore," Keiko said, *"so you shouldn't have to spend twenty-six hours a day maintaining it."*

"I can't lie," O'Brien said. "Once I joined the Corps of Engineers, it took me no time to get accustomed to using Starfleet technology again. And this place is state of the art."

"Just make sure that the science labs are—"

The door chime sounded, interrupting Keiko. O'Brien checked the time again.

"That's Nog," he said, then called for him to come in. "I need to get going." The doors opened and the Ferengi engineer entered. "Hi, Nog. I'm just talking to Keiko."

Nog walked over to the companel. "Hello, Keiko."

"Hi, Nog," Keiko said with a wave. *"Look at you."*

As O'Brien had done earlier, Nog peered down at the dress uniform he wore. "I look like a snowdrift with ears," he said.

"Well, I think you look very elegant," Keiko told him.

"Thanks. It'll be a miracle if I can keep it clean the entire afternoon," Nog said. "So how are you?"

"I'm great. Just looking forward to seeing my husband and that brand-new starbase of yours in a few days."

"Fantastic," Nog said. "Make sure he takes you flying in the park."

"What?" Keiko said. *"I'm not sure I heard you right."*

"You'll see," O'Brien said. Then, fixing Nog with an admonishing glare, he added, "It was supposed to be a surprise."

"It will be, since I have no idea what Nog's talking about," Keiko said. *"Anyway, let's talk later. I want to hear all about the dedication ceremony."*

"All right," O'Brien said. "Congratulations on your presentation."

"Thanks. I love you."

"I love you too." Keiko's image vanished from the screen, replaced by the Starfleet logo. O'Brien deactivated the companel. "I guess we should be on our way," he told Nog, who agreed.

The two men headed out onto the greensward surrounding the residential level at the equator of the sphere. They bypassed the turbolift and made their way to the nearest stairway, which took them up to the Plaza. They walked to the theater, joining the throng of DS9 personnel also attending the ceremony. Captain Ro had left a command crew in the Hub, as well as security teams at the occupied docking ports and around the rest of the starbase, but otherwise, she had invited most of the twenty-five hundred crew members aboard to the dedication, as well as the couple of hundred civilians who had already taken up residence on the station, a few journalists, and several members of the *Aventine* and *Robinson* crews.

O'Brien saw that perhaps half of the theater's three thousand seats had already filled up. He and Nog started down a sloping aisle in the direction of the stage. Partway along, O'Brien heard somebody call out his given name. He followed the voice and saw Julian sitting beside Sarina Douglas. The doctor waved, and so O'Brien and Nog took the seats next to the couple.

After exchanging greetings, the group quieted. O'Brien gazed around the theater, which he hadn't been inside since it had been completed. It had been decorated in a modern style, in blue and silver tones. A set of enormous curtains hung closed across the stage; Starfleet blue, they were adorned in the center with a silver silhouette of Deep Space 9.

"I wish Keiko were here for this," O'Brien said. The lights had not yet gone down, but he spoke quietly, not wanting to be impolite to those around him. "I know the Boslics hosted that summit on their homeworld a couple of years ago, but this has got to be the most interstellar heads of state ever at an event held in Federation space."

Sarina leaned forward and looked past Julian at O'Brien. "What about the Federation Council?" she asked. "It convenes representatives from more than a hundred and fifty worlds."

"But not heads of state," O'Brien pointed out.

"What about at the founding of the Federation?" Julian asked. "Eighteen worlds, represented by—"

"I'm not talking about worlds," O'Brien said. "I'm talking about empires and unions and hegemonies."

"Don't forget alliances," Nog said, doubtless speaking of his Ferengi origins.

"And alliances," O'Brien said.

"Well, it is an impressive assemblage of power,"

Julian conceded. "Nog, have you gotten to see your father yet?"

"For a little while last night," Nog said. "I visited him and Leeta and my little sister aboard their ship."

"*Half* sister," Julian corrected.

"What?" Nog asked.

"Bena's your *half* sister," Julian said.

"How could I possibly have *half* a sister?" Nog asked, clearly incredulous.

"Rom is your father," Julian explained, "and he's also Bena's father—"

"Right," Nog interrupted. "So Bena's my sister."

"But you two have different mothers," Julian forged ahead, "so you're *half* siblings."

"How can anybody have *half* a sibling?" Nog insisted, but O'Brien thought from the spark in his eye that he must be giving the doctor a hard time for his own amusement. "Hew-mons," Nog said, rolling his eyes. When Julian turned to look at Sarina, the Ferengi gave O'Brien a wink.

Over the next few minutes, the theater filled almost to capacity. With so many Starfleet personnel clad in their white dress uniforms, O'Brien thought that Nog had it right: it looked as though it had snowed inside the auditorium. At thirteen hundred hours precisely—Nog held up a padd and showed O'Brien the time—the doors at the back of the house closed. The murmur of hushed conversation faded, and a few seconds later, so did the overhead lighting, leaving only the stage illuminated. The regal strains of the "Anthem of the United Federation of Planets" began, and the audience rose almost as one.

During the instrumental song, the curtains parted and withdrew into the wings, revealing a backdrop that featured a view of the new Deep Space 9 taken from space, from "above" the starbase. The Hub, at the intersection of the two vertical rings, drew O'Brien's attention first, which then led him to examine the transparent bulkhead surrounding the Observation Gallery just below it. The wide horizontal *x*-ring curved around the main sphere, helping to highlight the residential level and the Plaza at the equator. The clear, semicircular bulkhead set above the Plaza dominated the scene, though, revealing the great, green expanse of the station's park.

A metal podium stood at the front center of the stage, the Starfleet emblem emblazoned in blue on it. As the anthem neared its conclusion, a lone figure strode onto the stage from the right. She stopped behind the podium.

When the music ended, the audience returned to their seats. Captain Ro looked out into the theater and said, "Honored guests, Starfleet personnel, and residents, thank you all for coming this afternoon." An audio pickup captured her words and delivered them not only to the people present, O'Brien knew, but also to the members of the crew still on duty throughout the station. "Welcome," Ro went on, "to the new Deep Space Nine."

Once more, everybody in the auditorium stood. O'Brien began to clap, but not alone. The audience delivered a thunderous ovation.

Nan Bacco stood in the wings of the theater, just offstage, as her fellow political leaders prepared to march out to address the crew of the grand new Starfleet facility that she had come to help dedicate. Her chief of staff, Ashanté Phiri, had urged the president to watch the proceedings on a viewscreen, from a room behind the scenes, until her time came to speak. The head of Bacco's protection detail, Magdalena Ferson, offered the same counsel.

The president had refused. She recalled that nineteenth-century statesman Otto von Bismarck once famously declared that politics is the art of the *possible*, a maxim that highlighted the difficulties of achieving anything significant within that arena. And yet on the new Deep Space 9, former and current enemies had come together in the spirit of goodwill: Cardassians in an alliance with Bajor. Klingons similarly aligned with humans. The Ferengi joining forces with anybody.

The leaders of the Gorn Hegemony and the Romulan Star Empire had come too—allied with each other, but not with any of the other powers present. *Not yet, anyway,* Bacco thought, ever hopeful. Despite all that had happened between the Federation and the Typhon Pact over the prior few years, the president had actually had meaningful, even substantive, conversations with both Sozzerozs and Gell Kamemor. For friendships to form, though, they had to begin somewhere—something had to make friendship *possible,* and the participation of the Gorn and the Romulans in the dedication ceremony marked another step on that diplomatic journey.

No, I wasn't about to sequester myself away from all this, Bacco thought. She wanted to watch the speeches live, wanted to hear the words as they were spoken and not after they'd been transmitted to her secondhand. She wanted to *feel* the reaction of the audience.

After Ro Laren's introduction—the captain exited through the wings and surreptitiously took a seat in the front row of the auditorium—the grand nagus of the Ferengi Alliance took the stage, the podium automatically adjusting to his smaller height. He related the story of the years he'd spent on the first Deep Space 9. Bacco didn't know until Rom revealed it, but he had lived on the station under Cardassian rule as long as he had during the Federation's tenure there. He raised his son, Nog, on Terok Nor and DS9, from the time the boy had been ten until he became the first Ferengi ever to join Starfleet. In what the president considered an amazing happenstance, Lieutenant Commander Nog had been instrumental in helping plan and build the new starbase, and he presently served as its assistant chief engineer.

Although he spoke in a looping, halting cadence, it seemed to Bacco that the grand nagus tied the new station to the old in a meaningful way. "There is, uh, real value in overcoming obstacles and moving forward, uh, especially in challenging times," Rom said. "The people of Bajor and, uh, the Federation suffered a terrible blow when the original Deep Space Nine was destroyed and all those lives were lost. But they have, uh, persevered to build this new station, reaching beyond the, uh, adversity of the past to the, uh, hope of the future. I think that's an example of considerable worth."

And who better to talk about value *and* worth *than a Ferengi,* Bacco thought—especially with all of the reforms the grand nagus had introduced into his society in the nearly ten years he'd been in office. Rom lacked poise and a smooth delivery, but his words connected with the Federation president. Defeats great and small happened all the time, the nagus seemed to say, but the measure of an individual, of a civilization, came not in the defeat itself, but in how they responded to it. The nagus left the stage to a warm reaction from the audience.

Filling in for Castellan Rakena Garan, Lustrate Enevek Vorat followed Rom at the podium. Bacco believed that of all the participants in the event, Vorat faced the most difficult task—even more so than Praetor Kamemor, despite that a Romulan starship had been involved in the final attack on the original DS9. Though not the head of the Cardassian government, but its second highest official, the lustrate still represented a society that had oppressed the Bajorans for half a century, whose construction and operation of Terok Nor had long stood as an emblem of occupation and slavery. For him or any Cardassian to refer to that space station in any way in front of Bajorans seemed problematic at best, and potentially a political minefield.

The president didn't know if Vorat delivered the same address that Castellan Garan had intended to give, but without seeming as though he intended to do so, he elegantly avoided the trap of invoking Terok Nor, even inadvertently, as a symbol of the Occupation. He spoke instead of the power of forgiveness, pointing out that the leaders of two Typhon Pact nations had been welcomed to the new starbase even after the crews of Typhon Pact starships—rogue though they had been—had destroyed the first Deep Space 9. The lustrate did not need to explicitly point out that a Cardassian had been invited to express those sentiments on a Federation space station in the Bajoran system, yet another act of absolution. Emphasizing the delicate nature of his comments, Vorat spoke for only a short time—notable, Bacco thought, considering how much Cardassians loved to orate, seemingly on any subject, at any time.

It disappointed the president that Castellan Garan had been unable to stay on Deep Space 9 for the ceremony or to visit Bajor. Although Cardassia had entered the Khitomer Accords almost three years earlier, and Bajor had been a member planet of the Federation for nine, the relationship between the two worlds remained fragile. Bacco believed that a sitting castellan visiting Ashalla as a guest of a sitting first minister could go a long way in fortifying that connection.

Garan had sent the president a transmission aboard *Aventine*, informing her of the change in plans. The castellan did not say so outright, but Bacco read the subtext in her words and realized that Garan faced political trouble at home. The advent of Cardassia First, yet another pro-Cardassian, anti-the-rest-of-the-galaxy faction, imperiled not only the castellan's upcoming bid for reelection, but also the Union's membership in the Khitomer Accords. Fortunately, the president had already dispatched Captain Picard and *Enterprise* to Cardassia to assist in treaty negotiations relating to Starfleet personnel left stationed there after the Dominion War. Picard would read the situation and react accordingly, while Bacco, once she had finished with the DS9 dedication, would board *Aventine* and travel to Cardassia herself.

Praetor Kamemor spoke after Lustrate Vorat, focusing on the generous spirit embodied by the Federation's gesture in inviting the Romulan Star Empire to take part in the ceremony. Klingon Chancellor Martok predictably championed the view of the original Deep Space 9 as a citadel from which magnificent battles had been launched and glorious victories won. Gorn Imperator Sozzerozs hissed his way through a speech that proclaimed admiration for the fierce determination that Bajor and the Federation had shown in not permitting others to dictate their paths, instead making their own choices and letting nothing stand in their way.

On his way from the stage, amid a round of generous applause, Sozzerozs stopped beside the president. He peered at her with his silver, faceted eyes, then back at the podium where he had just spoken. When he looked at her again, he said, in the sibilance of his native tongue, "Double." Bacco laughed aloud, grateful that the audience's clapping would hide her reaction. She certainly had not expected the Gorn leader to make a reference to baseball, a sport that few humans even knew about, and that puzzled most of the ones who did.

"Not at all, Imperator," Bacco said. "I think you hit a home run." Sozzerozs laughed in return, though it sounded to the president more like a rasping snake warning away another animal.

The final orator before Bacco, First Minister Asarem Wadeen walked out to the loudest applause of the afternoon—understandable, since a fair percentage of the Deep Space 9 crew hailed from Bajor. When the clapping ultimately subsided, Asarem gazed out over the assemblage and spoke in a bright, high voice that exposed her gifts as a political leader. "To all of our invited guests, to the crew and residents of this wondrous starbase, to the men and women who envisioned, championed, designed, and constructed this new Deep Space Nine, thank you.

"As I weighted just what I wanted to say to all of you here today," the first minister continued, "so many thoughts rose in my mind. I tried to focus, I made notes, but when I searched for coherence, I could find only one truth about how this day and how this event have impacted me. I am overwhelmed."

Bacco wondered if Asarem meant that, or if she had simply sought out some rhetorical flair.

"I am overwhelmed by the memory of the first space station that floated in space in this location, and that prior to that had hung in orbit over Bajor," Asarem went on. "That facility was built not to be a starbase—and most certainly not to be an *open* starbase—but as a place to process ore. Ore that had been quarried from the ground by an oppressed people . . . an enslaved people. Ore covered not only with the remnants of the soil from which it came, but with the blood that had seeped from the hands of those who'd mined it."

The president noted that Asarem had studiously avoided using the name *Terok Nor* or mentioning the Cardassians.

"I am overwhelmed that the people forced to dredge up and process that ore—*my* people—fought and clawed and eventually threw off their shackles, an act of strength and bravery that stands against any other in the galaxy.

"I am overwhelmed that even as the people of Bajor rose tall in their newfound freedom, they demonstrated still greater strength by being willing to ask for aid.

"I am overwhelmed that the United Federation of Planets provided us that aid, that they partnered with us, and in so doing, helped turn a dark symbol of our long oppression into a beacon of enlightenment and hope."

Again, Asarem did not name either Terok Nor or the Cardassians.

"I am overwhelmed that the destruction of that re-invented symbol, and the taking of so many precious lives, did not deter the people of Bajor or the Federation from moving forward . . . did not prevent us from exercising our compassion and forgiveness . . . did not stop us from demonstrating our fortitude by avowing that in defeat, we would find victory, not in the destruction of others, but in the reclamation of ourselves.

"I am overwhelmed that President Bacco—" The president listened with such rapt attention that when she heard her name, it startled her. "—and Chancellor Martok and Grand Nagus Rom have come here to exhibit their support for Bajor. I am overwhelmed that Castellan Garan came here to do the same, and, although circumstances pulled her away from this event, that Lustrate Vorat arrived in her stead to represent Cardassia.

"I am overwhelmed that in addition to the presence of allies, we are here with people we have historically regarded as enemies. But as the castellan and the lustrate have shown, a foe one day can become a friend the next. I am overwhelmed to see Praetor Kamemor and Imperator Sozzerozs here, and I relish the reality that where we once met on the field of battle, we now meet in peace, and I cling to the hope that we can sustain that beyond today and far into the future.

"And in addition to all of that, I am overwhelmed by this spectacular starbase—by the physical nature of it, with its great park and this beautiful theater, with its soon to be busy Plaza and its splendid residences, with its capacious spaces for people and cargo. But I am also overwhelmed by the intangibles of this new Deep Space Nine—by its ambition and intention, to replace what came before with something better, to open its doors wide to weary travelers, and to create a new symbol of our joyous present and our hopeful future.

"I am overwhelmed . . . and I am grateful to all the people who have contributed to make me feel that way." Asarem took a step back from the podium. "Thank you."

As the first minister strode toward the wings, the applause did not begin slowly and build; it started at full volume and crashed down on the stage like an avalanche of sound. Though she could not see the audience from her vantage, Bacco could tell that every person in the auditorium had risen to their feet as they brought their hands together in appreciation of Asarem Wadeen and the remarks she had made.

"Ashanté?" Bacco said, but already her chief of staff had moved to stand in front of her. Phiri looked at her from close range, then took two steps back and inspected her appearance once more. The president couldn't prevent herself from peering down at the outfit she wore—a simple, sophisticated, pale-blue dress—and then gazing over at her chief of staff for approval. *Not that Phiri could tell me at this point that I should have worn something else.*

"You look good, ma'am," pronounced Phiri. "Very presidential."

Bacco laughed. The appraisal had become a private joke. No matter the circumstances or how Bacco looked, felt, or sounded, her chief of staff would, if she felt it necessary, lighten the mood by asserting that the president was indeed "very presidential."

"Thank you, Ashanté." *Boy,* Bacco thought, *Esperanza taught her well.* The memory of her late friend caused a moment of sadness, but the president pushed it away. *Esperanza also taught* me *well.*

When the first minister reached the wings, Bacco told her, "Next time, we compare speeches ahead of time." Asarem looked at her with a perplexed expression, and the president explained her meaning by way of a question: "How am I supposed to make an impression after that?"

The first minister smiled—a home-field–advantage sort of a smile, Bacco thought. "Good luck," Asarem said. The president knew that, although exceedingly important to Starfleet and the Federation, Deep Space 9 in many ways meant even more to the people of Bajor. It would not bother her at all to be upstaged by the first minister.

"Thank you," Bacco said. She stepped to the edge of the wings. She waited just a moment, until the ovation for

Asarem had begun to fade, then walked out onto the stage and strode toward the podium.

The clapping grew in vigor as the president appeared, and she looked out into the auditorium. Because of the lights shining on her, Bacco could make out only the general, shadowy mass of the audience. When she reached the podium, she took her place behind it, placed her hands up on either side of its surface, and waited.

When the applause ended, Bacco opened her mouth to speak. *To our honored guests,* she thought, but before she said anything, she saw a flash of yellow-red light near the back of the auditorium. For a fraction of a second, it occurred to her that somebody had taken a holophoto of her, but then she staggered backward and couldn't figure out why. Even in the darkness shrouding the audience, the president could tell that many of them had turned their heads to look behind them, as though to condemn the holophotographer for interrupting the proceedings.

But then a loud report resounded in the theater, and Bacco realized that it was the *second* such noise she'd heard. She staggered back again, and then felt annoyed with herself for doing so. The podium stood a couple of meters in front of her, she saw, and suddenly she couldn't remember how she had planned to begin her speech.

Confused, Bacco peered down at herself, just as she had a few moments prior with Phiri. It surprised the president to see flaws in her lovely dress: two crimson florets bloomed on her bodice, and she tried to figure out how she hadn't seen them earlier. Suddenly, though, she realized that she could no longer stand, that her legs were going to give out and that she would fall down right there in the middle of the stage.

President Bacco heard a third report, and then everything went black.

Dust

Twelve

The blackness faded, replaced only by a gauzy shade of gray. Without opening her eyes and without moving—it scared her to imagine what she would discover if she tried to move—she attempted to take stock of herself. She lay on her right side. She didn't feel cold. Her breathing didn't seem strained or shallow, but slow and regular. Her head ached, but no pains troubled her anywhere else on her body.

Satisfied—and hopeful—she flexed her muscles, one part of her body at a time: left arm . . . left hand . . . right arm . . . right hand . . . left leg . . . left foot— She stopped, concerned, and tensed her left foot again. It met with resistance.

Something's wrong with my foot, she thought.

"Keev?" a voice whispered, though she could not tell from which direction. Even that soft sound had sent back echoes from the cave walls.

Is that Altek? she wondered. She didn't know who else it could be, but then she hadn't anticipated explosions in the cave, either. She remembered the reverberating booms, and running with Altek, and wanting to make it past the glowing red spot on the roof of the cave. She even remembered the third boom—seemingly directly above them—and all the earth and stone falling around them.

Keev squinted her eyes open. She saw a run of bright

light across her field of vision, and beyond it, nothing but an impenetrable darkness. She waited, allowing her eyes time to adjust, but it didn't help; she could still see nothing but the streak of light.

"Keev?" A bit louder, the voice revealed itself as Altek's.

"I'm here," she said, though it sounded more like croaking than actual words. She swallowed, and her mouth tasted dry—more than dry: it tasted like dirt. "I'm here," she said again, a little more clearly.

Keev saw movement in the form of shadows capering about her, and then the bar of light shifted. Altek appeared, down on his haunches, a beacon shining toward him from its place on the cave floor. Dirt blanketed his clothes and darkened his face, but he looked uninjured. "Are you all right?" he asked. "How do you feel?"

"Like I've just been in a cave-in," Keev said. Her tongue felt as though she had licked the ground. She pushed herself up off of her side, but then she felt a sharp pain slice through her foot. She winced and immediately stopped moving.

"Hold on, hold on," Altek said, dropping to his hands and knees and moving toward her. She felt his hand on her upper arm, through a jacket, which she realized had been draped over her. "Just lie there for a moment so we can make sure you're all right."

"I need—" Keev started, but then she coughed over the dry, gritty feeling in her mouth and throat. Lowering her voice to a whisper, she said, "I need water."

Altek's hand withdrew from her arm and moved down to her waist. She felt him tug at her water bottle and free it from its harness. She heard him twist the cap off, and then he held the mouth of the bottle up to her lips.

"I need to spit after I drink," Keev told him.

"Okay." He shifted out of her way, then picked up the beacon and shined it on the cave wall in front of her. "Here's your water." He brought the bottle back up to her lips and tilted it up.

Keev felt the smoothness of the liquid, still cool from its insulated container. She filled her mouth and closed her lips, then sloshed the water around. She felt the grit of the dirt as it floated free, and she visualized stirring up a swamp. She leaned forward and spat toward the wall.

"Better?" Altek asked.

"Yes," Keev said. She wiped her mouth with her left hand, then reached toward Altek. "May I?" she asked. He handed her the water bottle, and she drank down two long pulls, emptying it. "What happened? How long was I unconscious?"

"You were out for about half an hour," Altek told her. "I tried to wake you at first. I also examined your head. You've got a knot on the left side, directly above your ear, and a gash. I applied pressure to it, so it's no longer bleeding."

"What about the rest of me?"

"I used the beacon to check for any visible injuries," Altek said. "I didn't see any blood or any bones breaking through your skin anywhere."

Keev nodded, thinking that all of that sounded good. A wave of exhaustion suddenly broke over her, though, and she wanted to lie back down. As she moved to do so, Altek helped her ease herself toward the ground. She expected to feel the hard, coarse floor of the cave against the side of her face, but instead found a soft mound there, obviously a rolled-up jacket that Altek had placed beneath her head. "I just need to rest a minute," she said, then asked again, "What happened?"

"Do you remember the explosions?" Altek asked.

"Yes."

"Those—or at least the last one—clearly caused the roof of the cave to collapse."

"Are we trapped?" Keev asked. "Do we have to go back?" With the way she felt, Keev did not look forward to having to backtrack to the far entrance.

"We don't have to go back," Altek said. "We made it past where the roof caved in. We're on the Joradell side of it. But . . . we might be trapped."

"What?" Keev said. "What does that mean?"

Altek directed the beam of the beacon down her body. "Your leg appears to be pinned," he said. Keev followed the light and saw her shin disappear beneath a wall of rubble that she lost sight of in the darkness above the beacon's reach.

"How far up does it go?" Keev pointed at the heap of fallen rock.

"Up to the roof of the cave." Altek shined the light there to show her. "It looks impassable."

Keev shook her head. She didn't want to think about the repercussions of that. If the gild had to move escaped slaves to Shavalla without access to the passage beneath the Merzang Mountains, it would take weeks longer and of course would require that much more time to return to the gild. The extended trip would expose them to greater natural dangers, as well as to detection by the Aleira.

"How does your leg feel?" Altek asked. He seemed reluctant to pose the question.

Keev studied the place where her shin disappeared beneath the mass of stone. She tried to move her leg. Once again, she felt a stabbing pain and grimaced. "It hurts when I try to move it," she told Altek. She imagined her shinbone fractured and piercing through her torn flesh. The image made her shiver, and she pushed it away.

"I removed some of the rocks that were covering your leg," Altek said, "but there's a large one there that I couldn't move easily, and I didn't want to risk crushing your foot by trying. I did reach in through an open space and felt around as much as possible; when I pulled my hand back out, there was no blood on it."

No blood, Keev thought. That sounded like a poor excuse for good news, but she'd take it. "Can you move the large rock at all?" she asked.

"I might be able to, if I lie down and get my arms below it."

"Try," Keev said. "If you can lift it at all, I'll try to pull my leg out."

Altek nodded. He propped the beacon atop a rock so that it shined along the lower part of Keev's body and the pile of stone. He then went around Keev and stretched out prone, his head toward the roof collapse. He dug his elbows into the ground, set his hands beneath the edge of the large rock, and pushed against it.

Nothing happened.

Altek glanced back at her, then rolled over onto his back. He repositioned his arms beneath the rock and reached up to it again. "Okay, here we go," he said, and Keev saw his body tense as he tried again to free her. As moments ticked away, Altek issued a throaty cry.

And still nothing happened.

"Try it with your legs," Keev suggested.

Altek nodded. "I can," he said, sitting up and facing her. "I'm just concerned I won't be able to control how the rock will shift if I move it. I don't want it coming down and compressing your leg."

"If you can't move that rock, then I'm not going to be able to use my leg anyway," Keev said.

"I can go get help," Altek told her. She thought she heard a note of desperation in his tone.

Keev considered allowing Altek to leave so he could bring back assistance. *If he comes back at all,* she thought, realizing that he could just leave her there to die from dehydration. She recognized the illogic of her paranoia: Altek could simply have left her trapped while she'd been unconscious. Of course, he couldn't be sure that her leg had been stuck; for all he knew, she could have awoken and pulled herself free.

If he wanted me dead, he could have dropped a rock onto my head, Keev thought, *and then told everybody in the gild that I died in the cave-in.* No, she really needed to stop distrusting him. He'd demonstrated his loyalty more than once, and while she supposed he still might be an Aleiran spy trying to earn their trust, that possibility seemed less and less probable.

Still, Keev did not like the idea of staying in the cave by herself. "Half an hour or so to the cave entrance?" she asked.

"If there's not another cave-in farther along," Altek pointed out.

"Right," Keev said. "But if there's not, then half an hour to the entrance, a few hours to the gild, then a few hours back here."

"That's not that long," Altek said, clearly reading her concern. "I'll leave my water bottle; it's still about a third full." He pulled the container out of its harness and set it down beside her.

"No, that's not that long, but . . ." She thought about the situation, about what had occurred, and tried to make sense of it. "What happened here?" she asked. "Those booming noises before the roof collapsed didn't sound natural. They sounded like explosive charges going off."

"I agree," Altek said. "And there was a part of the cave roof that was glowing red, like it had been superheated."

"Yes, I saw that too," Keev said. "So who was doing it? Not our gild . . . surely not any of the gilds."

"No," Altek agreed. "It must have been the Aleira."

"Doing what, though?" Keev asked. "Trying to kill us?"

"If they knew we were here, then why go to so much trouble?" Altek asked. "And why resort to a method that didn't guarantee our deaths? They could have just waited outside the entrance and, when we emerged, gunned us down."

Keev nodded; Altek's reasoning made sense. "But then what were they doing? Mining?"

Altek took a moment to respond, apparently considering her question. "I think maybe so," he finally said.

"If there's a chance that the Aleira are somewhere in the mountains right now," Keev said, "then I don't want to stay here, even for just a matter of hours." She could easily envision a squad of Aleira finding her, freeing her, and then carrying her into Joradell only to take that freedom away.

"All right," Altek said. "Let me try using my legs." For a third time, he positioned himself beside the wall of broken stone that had swallowed Keev's foot. He placed the soles of his boots against the edge of the large rock, then searched for handholds in the floor of the cave. Once he'd found some and grabbed on to them, he asked, "Are you ready?"

Keev nodded but said nothing. She watched Altek's arms and legs tense. He gritted his teeth, and the cords in his neck tightened.

The rock shifted, not even a hand's width. She tried to pull her leg from beneath it, felt the sharp pain again, but also felt her foot move toward her. A fist-size stone farther up in the rubble came crashing down and struck her just below the knee. She cried out, and when she did, she saw Altek relax his muscles, probably easing off out of concern for her. "Don't stop," she told him. "My foot's moving."

Altek resumed his efforts. The rock moved again, farther, and Keev pulled her foot toward her even more. Altek began to groan with his exertion. "Keep going," Keev said.

Suddenly, Altek's legs thrust forward, pushing the rock upward for a moment. Other pieces of debris began to spill down, striking both Altek's legs and Keev's. She dug the heel of her free foot into a ridge in the cave floor and pushed with all her might. In a flash of movement, her trapped foot came free. She quickly scrambled away, as did Altek beside her. The large rock dropped back down.

A stone rolled into the beacon and sent it flying. Light careened around the cave and then seemed to get swallowed up, leaving Keev and Altek in darkness. They huddled together amid the sound of falling rocks.

After a few moments, silence reasserted itself as the loosened debris settled. Keev became aware that she could see, that the beacon still functioned wherever it had been thrown, its beam mostly buried but emitting enough light to allow her adjusted eyes to cut through the shadows.

Directly in front of her, she saw Altek's face—and to her surprise, especially considering the circumstances, she noticed how handsome he was. For a moment, she could tell that he saw her too, and they looked into each other's eyes. "Are you all right?" she asked him.

"Yeah," he said. "Probably a few bruises from the rocks coming down, but it doesn't feel like anything too bad."

He leaned in toward her and, for a disconcerting instant, she thought he might kiss her. Instead, he reached past her, dug around, and cleared off the beacon. "Let's take a look at your foot."

Keev hadn't even been thinking about her foot, but when she did, she realized it hurt badly. Altek shined the light on it. A triangle of jagged stone stuck out of the top of her boot. "Does that hurt?" Altek asked.

"Yes."

"I should take it out," Altek said. "But let me take a look at your leg first." He moved in that direction, planted the beacon on the ground, and used both hands to feel along her shin. "Anything?" he asked her.

"It all feels fine," she said. "I mean, I've got some aches, but nothing unbearable."

"All right. I'm going to remove this, then." Altek motioned toward the triangular piece of stone. Keev closed her eyes and braced herself. When Altek took hold of the stone, pain shot through her as though the nerve endings in her foot had been set afire. In the next moment, though, he pulled it free, and the pain immediately faded to a dull ache.

Keev opened her eyes to see Altek hold the stone up in the beam of the beacon. She saw the light reflect off its point in a way that suggested it was wet. "There's blood on here," Altek said. "I think it punctured your foot."

"It feels like that," Keev said.

"I need to treat it. I'll be as gentle as I can." Altek untied her boot, his movements slow and careful. She flinched twice, but reassured him each time that he should keep going. Eventually, he removed her boot, and then her sock. Streaks of blood painted her flesh from the top of her foot down to her heel. Altek bent in close and examined her. "Definitely a puncture wound," he told her. "It doesn't look too deep, but I'm going to have to wash it out and wrap it." He looked up at her with an apologetic expression. "I'm afraid it's going to hurt."

"I want to get out of here," Keev said. "Do what you have to do."

Altek used the rest of his water to clean out her wound, then cut a strip from the lining of his jacket to swathe it. Keev cried out more than once, but each time urged Altek to continue his ministrations.

When he'd done as much as he could in their situation, he helped her try to put her boot back on her foot. She left her sock off and the boot untied, and she finally managed it. Altek helped her up, and she found that she could stand and walk well enough.

"Are you sure you're okay to travel?" he asked her.

"I don't want to stay here," Keev said. "We don't know if there are Aleira around, or even if they might start blasting again."

Together, they resumed their journey through the cave.

Thirteen

The instant Ro heard the report, she thought that something had fallen at the back of the theater—something large—and she worried that something had gone wrong with the new starbase. But before she could even turn her head to find out what had happened, she saw President Bacco lurch backward. At first, Ro thought that the president had simply reacted to the thunderous noise, and indeed, when a second roar filled the theater, Bacco reeled again.

Even as the captain sensed the people around her turning toward the source of the two great bangs, she stood up in the front row of the auditorium and took a step forward. By the time the third report rang out, a figure had raced from the wings and onto the stage—a woman Ro recognized as Agent Ferson, the head of the president's protection detail. Amid the sound of voices rising around her and the rush of movement, Ro dashed forward and leaped onto the stage. Somewhere behind her, she heard the shriek of a phaser.

Several paces behind the podium, President Bacco collapsed—not as though her knees had given way, but like so much dead weight. Ro arrived at Bacco's fallen form at the same time as Ferson. The captain saw two holes in the bodice of the president's dress. The red of

Bacco's blood radiated out from each like the rays of some dark sun.

As Ferson dropped to her knees and reached for the president's wrist, the captain slapped at her combadge, which warbled in response. "Ro to Sector General," she said. "Emergency medical support to the theater stage." Without waiting for a response, she tapped her combadge a second time. "Ro to Lieutenant Aleco." She peered out from the stage, and in the glow of the houselights, which had been activated, she saw security officers converging toward the rear of the auditorium, weapons drawn.

"Aleco here, Captain," said a male voice. Because of the dedication ceremony, the lieutenant had taken over at tactical during alpha shift.

"Lieutenant, go to red alert; this is *not* a drill," Ro said, ticking off in her mind everything she needed to do. "Raise the shields, lock all hatches closed, and secure the mooring clamps. I want no one leaving or entering the station, even to and from Starfleet vessels, and I want all ships to remain in place. And shut down all communications until further notice." She paused, considering what other immediate steps she should take, and already she heard the blare of the red alert klaxons calling the crew to general quarters. "Raise the thoron shield too," she concluded. She wanted the starbase sealed up as tightly as possible.

"Yes, Captain," Aleco said.

"Ro out." She looked down at Ferson, who had the tips of two fingers against the president's wrist.

"I've got a pulse," the agent said. "Weak, but it's there." Ferson wore a stony visage of professionalism, but the captain could see more than one emotion in her eyes: fear, desperation, guilt. It made Ro think that nothing could be done, but then Doctor Boudreaux arrived on the run;

he'd doubtless been at the ceremony. The captain heard other footsteps hurrying toward them from behind, but she watched the doctor as he got to his knees and felt along Bacco's neck.

"What happened?" Boudreaux asked. "Shot? With a projectile weapon?" Ro thought he spoke as much to himself as to anybody else, but Ferson replied.

"It looks like it," she said in a voice that sounded impossibly unemotional.

The doctor used his thumbs and forefingers to open both of the president's eyes at once. He leaned in and examined them, then seemed to see something else. He moved around to inspect Bacco's head. Only then did Ro see the pool of blood beneath the president's hair.

Doctor Bashir appeared and raced to the other side of Bacco's body, where he dropped to one knee. He studied the president's inert form, then looked to his fellow doctor, who punched his combadge with the side of his fist. "Boudreaux to Sector General," he said. "Emergency medical transport." He glanced at Bashir, and then at Ro, and finally at Ferson. Only the captain shook her head; the other two nodded.

"Keep me informed," Ro said, and then she backed away a step from the horrible tableau: the two doctors and the protection officer kneeling over the motionless body of the fallen Federation president.

"Sector General, Etana here," came the response over Boudreaux's combadge. *"Emergency transport on your order."*

"Four to beam in from my location," Boudreaux said. "Go." Blue-white streaks of light spilled down at once around the quartet, and all four began to fade in a bramble of whirling motes.

Even before they finished dematerializing, Ro turned toward the front of the stage—and toward chaos erupting on Deep Space 9. *No, not chaos,* she thought, even as she saw masses of her crew streaming through the theater's exits on their way to their battle stations. They didn't move in a panic—neither did the few civilians and journalists among them—but in an orderly fashion. Already more than half the auditorium had emptied, though only scant minutes had passed since the first shot.

A crowd that included Captain Sisko and Captain Dax looked toward Ro, half of them on the stage and half in front of it. Her first officer, Cenn Desca, stood beside her. All but four of the people she saw wore Starfleet uniforms, and a quick glance told her that, other than Cenn, all the members of her crew there belonged to security; the call to general quarters would have sent them to specific posts unless they detected a location of greater need, which clearly they had. Ro also saw another member of President Bacco's protection detail; the captain surmised that the others had headed to the hospital, while the one had been left behind to monitor the situation. Chancellor Martok had also come out onto the stage, two of the *Yan-Isleth*—the Brotherhood of the Sword, who guarded the Klingon leader—at his side.

"Captain—" Martok began, but Ro cut him off with a raised hand. She pointed to Sarina Douglas, the highest-ranking security officer she saw and who stood directly in front of her.

"Lieutenant Commander, I want the theater sealed and security posted at every entrance. I also want teams around each of the visiting dignitaries," Ro ordered. "A minimum of four guards for each. If they haven't gone already—" She glanced up at the chancellor. "—take them into the backstage facilities and lock them down. One dignitary to a room, with all the security and aides they have with them in the theater." She turned to Cenn. "Go with them, Colonel. I'll need you to keep everybody calm."

"Yes, sir," Cenn said.

"Captain," Martok said, "my men and I—"

"Are invited guests here, Chancellor," Ro said, interrupting the Klingon leader again. "That means you're my responsibility. I need you and your men locked down and safe until I can determine the situation." She fixed him with her most serious, most challenging look, which, under the circumstances, cost her virtually no effort.

"Very well, Captain," the chancellor said, and he and his guards started toward the wings with Cenn and the security personnel, leaving Sisko and Dax standing with Ro.

"You've locked down the station?" Sisko asked.

"Yes, until we find whoever's done this," Ro said.

"So how can we help?" Dax wanted to know. "I've got twelve of my crew here." She gestured toward the auditorium, where Ro saw those members of the *Aventine* crew clustered together.

"And I've got seven," Sisko said. "Plus my wife and daughter."

Ro nodded. She knew that the journalists and resident civilians on the starbase had been drilled in emergency procedures for their own safety, which typically meant taking the shortest route to their quarters or another designated, non-Starfleet location; resident guests would typically be instructed to take cover in the nearest appropriate place. "For the moment," Ro said, addressing Dax, "I'd like you to take Captain Sisko's family and the crews of both ships into backstage rooms here. I'll assign security to you." Dax looked to Captain Sisko, the most senior of the three officers. He nodded, and Dax immediately stepped away and activated her combadge.

"And what about me?" Sisko asked.

"Talk to your family first," Ro said, "but then I need your help. I've put a—" Ro's combadge chirped.

"Blackmer to Captain Ro," said the voice of the starbase's security chief. She could hear the strain in his voice.

Ro hit her combadge. "Ro here," she said. "Go ahead."

"Captain," Blackmer said, *"we've captured the shooter."*

Bashir materialized with Boudreaux and Ferson in the emergency transporter bay in Sector General. The stillbreathing but badly damaged body of Nanietta Bacco lay before them. Nurses Etana Kol, Edgardo Juarez, and Kabo waited in front of the platform. Behind them, an array of medical equipment stood at the ready.

Etana and Juarez immediately jumped up onto the platform and held out medical tricorders to the two doctors. As Bashir accepted a device from Juarez, he saw the nurse glance down at the president. He clearly recognized her at once; his mouth fell open in an expression that mixed surprise and horror.

Bashir held up the tricorder, which Juarez had already opened and activated. As Boudreaux examined the president's head, Bashir worked over her torso. He scanned the holes in her chest and identified two blunt-tipped projectiles still inside her body. One appeared to have fractured one of Bacco's ribs and ricocheted down and to the left, lodging in the paraspinal muscle tissue surrounding the thoracic spine. He detected damage to a facet joint and the vertebra below it, suggesting possible partial paralysis for the president.

If she even survives, Bashir thought. At that point, paralysis seemed like one of the better potential prognoses.

The other projectile, Bashir saw, had injured Bacco's right ventricle. She suffered from pericardial effusion—the escape of blood into the membranous sac enclosing the heart. He considered performing a pericardiocentesis to aspirate the fluid, but a thoracotomy would allow him to attempt to repair the heart. "Nurse Kabo, prepare for transport to a surgical bay," he ordered, and she quickly turned to operate a control panel. "Pascal, what have you—"

The look on his colleague's face stopped Bashir cold. Boudreaux held out his tricorder for him to read. Bashir saw a gruesome picture: a third projectile had penetrated Bacco's skull just inside her hairline. Much of her brain had essentially exploded. Even if he could repair her heart—even if he replaced it entirely—there was nothing of Nanietta Bacco left to save.

Bashir gazed back down at the president as though in a dream—as though in a *nightmare*. He saw that she had stopped breathing, not that it even mattered. Bashir slumped down on the transporter platform.

President Nanietta Bacco was dead.

Fourteen

Keev lay on her sleeping roll, the last embers of the night's fire fading before her. The faces of her gild's members—not Synder and not old man Renet, but all the others—floated in the darkness that had fallen around the once hearty campfire. Earlier, they had shared their evening meal, a veritable feast compared to their typical fare. Cawlder Losor and Cawlder Vinik had trapped an adult *hara* cat that morning, allowing them a supper of *grolanda* stew, with *mapa* bread and the last of the treat that Veralla had brought back with him on his last run into Joradell, *moba* fruit.

For a change, their repast had been quiet, conversation—and, as had been the case in recent days, argument—forsaken for the rare pleasure of a full meal. Even with sated appetites, though, the peace hadn't lasted much longer than the few remaining pieces of moba fruit. Soon after the pulp had been chewed from the last rind, Jennica had re-ignited the disagreement that had been plaguing the gild for the previous few weeks.

"It's not working," the young woman had declared, and everybody had known precisely what she'd meant. A group discussion had evolved—and sometimes devolved—from there.

It had been nearly two months since the explosions and

cave-in that had come close to burying Keev and Altek. Reconnaissance by the gild—but for Keev, who required a couple of weeks for her foot to heal—revealed a small Aleiran exploratory operation in the Merzang Mountains, conducting tests for potential mining sites. Fortunately, despite the roof collapse they had caused, the Aleira hadn't yet detected the caverns beneath the range. That meant that if the gild could clear the rubble and reinforce that section of the cave, they could resume using it to move escaped slaves to freedom.

If we can clear the Aleira out of the mountains, Keev thought. Veralla had decided after Keev and Altek's close call that the gild would not attempt to dig out the block- age in the caverns—would not reenter them at all—as long as the operation above them continued. He deemed it too dangerous, and while he would listen to other points of view, no one had so far swayed him to relent. Veralla could not deny that the members of his gild already took risks in working to liberate enslaved Bajora, but he insisted that they minimize those risks.

To that end, they had chosen another course of action: they had begun sabotaging the work camp of the Aleira, though they took pains not to do so in any obvious way. Had the gild simply destroyed equipment or eliminated personnel, Aleiran security would have descended on the area en masse, making it impossible for Veralla and his troops to continue their mission—even if they man- aged to avoid capture. Instead, they started penetrating the operation under the cover of night, performing minor acts meant to mimic nature. They set small, undetect- able charges to detonate in the ground beneath the heavy equipment the Aleira employed; they pumped water into the ground to soften it; and they caught burrowing animals in the wood and released them at the work site. They randomly loosened fittings, and they broke panels and hoses in ways that made it appear that mountain creatures had done the damage.

Not everybody agreed about the worth of Veralla's plan to drive out the Aleira. Some, such as Jennica, urged a full assault on the operation, arguing that destroying the equipment and killing the handful of workers at the site would draw no more attention than the gild's liberation of Bajoran slaves already did; security squads from Joradell already patrolled the surrounding regions, searching out the gilds. Others, such as Cawlder Vinik, contended that, despite the possibility of additional collapses, they should take the chance of clearing away the debris from the cave and reinforcing its walls and roof.

So when Jennica had declared, "It's not working," after supper, Keev—and everybody else, as it turned out—had understood what she'd meant. They argued the points they'd already made, trying to find some new way of persuading Veralla to their perspective. Frustrations abounded, surely a by-product of their inability to effectively continue their work after the cave-in. Voices rose and emotions flared, but Keev knew that everybody wanted the same thing: to return to freeing as many Bajoran slaves from Joradell as possible.

As the fire had died, so too had the conversation. Veralla eventually suggested that they get some sleep, and while there had been murmured agreement all around, only Keev and Jennica had lain down. Neither slept, though, continuing to regard their fellow gild members across the last few glowing cinders.

Keev did not even realize she had closed her eyes until she heard Veralla speak. Into the silence of the wood—

which was not really a silence at all, but an olio of sounds that lacked only voices—he said, "There's another choice we haven't yet considered." He talked, as he almost always did, in measured tones.

"Not go around the mountains," Cawlder Losor said. "Forgetting about all the added dangers, it would reduce our effectiveness dramatically."

"No," Veralla said. "We could go around the mountains, but we all see what that does to our timelines." Not long after the cave-in, Synder Nogar had returned from Joradell with two more escaped Bajora. They spent a few days in the wood, but doing so longer than that would have endangered everybody, depleting the gild's supplies and hindering their ability to relocate their camp quickly, which they did at irregular but short intervals. Keeping twelve-year-old Resten Ahleen with them for as long as they had—out of necessity for her well-being—had been a burden on them. With the route beneath the mountains blocked and the Aleiran mining exploration ongoing, Veralla had little choice but to order the freed Bajora taken overland around the mountains. Synder and Renet Losig volunteered for the duty to lead the former slaves to the road to Shavalla. They had yet to return.

"What we can do is move farther down the range," Veralla said. "We can try to find another cave, or maybe even a pass through the mountains."

"But we can't be sure another cave exists," Cawlder Losor pointed out. "And even if it does, it could take years to map it and find a way through—if it even goes all the way through the mountain."

Keev propped herself up on her elbow. "At the same time, we have no idea if a useful pass exists, but even if one does, traveling exposed like that would increase the possibilities of being spotted by the Aleira." It occurred to her that Veralla already knew what she had just said, and what Cawlder Losor had said. Keev wondered if he had brought up the prospect of displacing the gild to a completely new area not to rally the others to such a plan, but to guide them back to his first strategy. Veralla led the group and they would follow him no matter his decision, but she knew that, in matters as significant as relocation, he preferred to draw a consensus.

"We'd also be increasing our distance from Joradell," Cawlder Vinik said. "That would be positive in some ways, but it would also increase our travel times and complicate our logistics."

"It wouldn't necessarily solve our problems long-term anyway," Jennica added, "since there's no guarantee that the Aleira won't start up mining operations near wherever we go. And if they have success here, you can bet they'll want to expand."

Keev saw the opening that Veralla clearly sought, and she took advantage of it for him. "That sounds like a good reason for us to convince the Aleira that attempting to mine in this area is a bad idea. If we can force them to abandon the site now because it's unsuitable, we can be certain they won't return."

"Veralla," Jennica said, "if we just—"

Veralla shot to his feet in the darkness and turned. Keev saw the moonlight glint off the revolver suddenly in his hand, as though he'd been holding it all night—which she knew he hadn't. He stood motionless, as though waiting, as though he'd heard something in the wood, out beyond the small clearing.

Keev followed Veralla's lead, finding her revolver in her bedroll and standing up. The others scrambled to do the same. She strained to hear what Veralla obviously heard and caught the rustle of leaves the moment before a shadowy figure stumbled into their camp.

"Don't fire," said a weary voice. "It's Renet Losig." He slipped to his knees, and then to his hands, and finally down onto his side.

Jennica started over to the old man, but Veralla stopped her with a hand on her arm. She'd been in the gild long enough that she should have known better. "Wait," Veralla said, just loudly enough for everybody in the clearing to hear.

Renet should have known better too, Keev thought. He hadn't called out before he got to the encampment, nor had he used any of the key phrases that would have told the members of his gild that he had arrived on his own, or under duress, or with others following. *And where is Synder?* Keev wondered.

After several moments in which everybody listened for the sounds of others approaching, Veralla turned to Jennica. "Please restart the fire," he said. He then turned on a beacon—Keev could only marvel at how he'd managed to get it to his hand so smoothly and without her noticing. He shined the beam on the fallen form of Renet.

The old man looked terrible. His clothing bore the scars of a difficult journey: loose, muddy, and torn. He trembled where he lay, as though the cool of the night had somehow gotten inside of him.

Veralla went to him, his hand up and holding the others where they stood—except for Jennica, who tended the coals and tried to coax a new piece of wood to catch flame. The gild leader paced cautiously over to Renet, squatted down, and examined him. Finally, in the penumbra of his beacon, he said, "All right," and he waved everybody over—everybody but Altek, whom Veralla asked to stand guard. The rest of the group holstered their revolvers.

Carefully, they wrapped Renet in a blanket and brought him over to sit before the renewed fire. They gave him water and cleaned him up. Altek cooked up some of the leftover hara meat for him.

Though plainly still exhausted, the water and food did revive Renet a bit. Veralla must have seen that, because he asked, "Losig, are you all right?" Rarely did Veralla— rarely did any of them—refer to their comrades by their given names.

Renet looked at Veralla, and Keev thought that the old man might weep. She interpreted the deep emotion as a product of whatever he'd been through, as well as his apparent salvation. "I'm alive," Renet said, his voice a rasp. "I'm alive, and that's a start."

"It is," Veralla agreed, and he tapped a hand gently on the old man's knee. "It is a start." Renet seemed to want to smile, but his effort fell far short of convincing. Veralla waited a few beats, and then asked, "Can you tell us what happened?"

Renet looked away from Veralla—he looked into the fire, away from everybody. "Nogar's dead," he finally said.

Nobody gasped. At that point, they all must have been expecting the news. Keev certainly had been. That still didn't stop her heart from hurting when Renet confirmed the brutal fact.

"A *krelo* bear got him," the old man continued. The large brown animals typically didn't travel that near the Merzang Mountains, but Keev had heard of a number of incidents with them through the years. "Nogar saved me." Tears filled Renet's eyes. Keev pitied him for what he must have seen.

Veralla nodded. Keev wanted to hear about the encounter, wanted to ease Renet's burden by sharing it with him, wanted to honor the sacrifice that her fellow gild member—her *friend*—had made, but she knew that the question would likely have to wait. In the next moment, Veralla asked, "What about the freed Bajora?"

The question seemed to bring Renet back, as though he welcomed the focus on the man and the woman he and Synder had been tasked with delivering to the road to Shavalla. "We made it through," he said. "Twenty-two days. We had no real problems . . . the man sprained his ankle, but not until late in the trip."

Twenty-two days, Keev thought. Renet and Synder had departed more than fifty days earlier, meaning that the trip back had not only been obviously grueling for the old man, but also far longer than the trip out.

"What happened?" Jennica blurted out, as though she could no longer contain her youthful curiosity. "How did you get through?"

I can't blame her curiosity on her age, Keev thought. *I want to know too.*

Renet peered across the flames at the young woman. "It . . ." he started, but again, tears filled his eyes. He looked down at his hands, which he twisted together anxiously. "It was awful," he said. "Poor Nogar, he . . ."

"It's all right," Veralla said in a soothing voice. "Why don't you get some sleep? You must be exhausted."

Keev agreed. It must have been impossible for Renet to get much sleep with one eye open to watch out for more krelo bears. *Not to mention having to travel alone all the way around the mountains and through the wood.*

Renet nodded gratefully, and he let Veralla help him over to a bedroll. When the gild leader stood up again

and moved back to the fire, Cawlder Vinik said, "Do you
think—" Veralla interrupted by holding up a single finger.

"We'll palaver in the morning," he said. "We don't
need to make any decisions about anything tonight."

As the other members of the gild took to their sleeping
rolls, Veralla buried the fire. In the last flickering light of
the flames, Keev read the expression on his face. If there
had been any question about the course of action that
the gild must take next, the death of Synder Nogar had
answered it.

Beneath the light of three moons, the clusters of heavy
machinery glowed as though their filthy daytime
appearance had somehow been purified. The same could
not be said of the great iron drill that some of the
machinery drove, and that hung in a crosstie derrick
as though daring gravity to take hold. The moonlight
washed the unevenly angled wood of the gantry white,
but at best it could only smooth the pitted contours of
the screw-shaped apparatus suspended like a threat above
the ground.

Nearby stood two shacks that appeared hastily constructed, and past those, a ramshackle privy. Of all the
structures in the work camp, only the three wide, sheet-
metal cylinders that collected rainwater gave any impression of endurance. So deep into the night that B'hava'el
would rise in less time than it had already been gone, the
mountaintop lay still.

Keev broke that calm when she streaked from a coppice and toward the rightmost of the three tanks, curls of
narrow hose encircling one of her shoulders. She reached
the cistern on the opposite side of the windowless shacks,
out of sight of any workers who might happen to walk out

to the privy. She threw down the coil of hose, tucking one end into the waistband of her pants. Where two of the metal panels that formed the water tank met in an edge joint, Keev began to climb. She wore thick gloves to allow her solid handholds along the raised seam, and the large bolts that bound the metal together provided her sufficient footing for her ascent.

When she had climbed high enough, Keev peered across the top of the tank, which had been covered by a metal grille. She pulled the end of the hose from her waistband and threaded it through the grille, feeding it down until she heard it plop through the surface of the water. She then lowered herself back to the ground, not wanting to jump for fear of leaving boot prints in the soil, and thus potential evidence that any troubles at the work site had been caused not by the local conditions, but by saboteurs.

Keev looked over to the machinery beside the derrick and drill, searching for the figure she expected to see there. In the waxy cover given by Derna, Endalla, and Baraddo—*Baraddo, also known as the Prodigal,* as one grade-school teacher used to make Keev's class recite—she at first saw nobody. Then a hand waved, and she darted across the open space, pulling the other end of the hose with her, to where Altek squatted.

When she arrived, Altek pointed to the corner of the machinery closest to the derrick, where they had concentrated their efforts over the past weeks. He crawled in that direction, then pointed around the corner, something he had never done in the time that they'd been systematically trespassing at the work camp. Keev moved forward until she crouched beside him.

She stuck her head past the machinery and gazed over at the derrick, the great drill hanging within it. Not knowing what to look for, she turned to Altek, who gestured toward the ground. It took only a moment for Keev to see what he obviously wanted her to see: a series of metal weights had been affixed to the far legs of the derrick. She hoped that meant that all of their efforts there had finally begun to have tangible results.

Drawing back from the corner of the machinery, Keev watched as Altek pulled up a tuft of grass. She pulled a beacon from her pocket and used it to look down. The hole that Altek had dug out with a manual auger reached down five or six arm lengths.

Keev glanced up at him for agreement and received it in the form of a nod. She immediately brought the end of the hose to her lips and inhaled deeply several times, creating negative pressure within the long tube. She then fed the hose into the hole and waited with an ear beside the opening. When Keev heard the trickle of water, she flashed her beacon into the hole. The water level rose more quickly than at any time in the weeks they'd been visiting the work site.

Keev handed the beacon to Altek, who shifted over to take a look in the opening. He nodded emphatically, clearly as pleased as she felt. The rapid rise of the water level in the hole suggested that the soil around it absorbed the liquid at a slower rate than it had been doing, and therefore that the gild had succeeded in saturating the ground there. Keev took back her beacon and pocketed it. She waited until the water rose almost to the top, then raced back along the length of hose and pulled it free from the tank. She grabbed its end and began wrapping it in big loops over her shoulder. Water spilled from the end, soaking her clothing, but she ignored the sensation as she walked back toward Altek while reeling in the hose.

Back beside the machinery, Keev saw that Altek held a charge in his hand. He had concealed the hole that she'd filled with water, and he'd exposed a second one. He looked at her questioningly and she nodded. He activated the charge, dropped it in the hole, and covered it back up. Together, they raced for the tree line.

When they entered the coppice, they ducked down behind the trunk of a tree. Keev gazed back at the work camp, though she knew she would neither see, hear, nor feel the small explosion that Altek had initiated. Beside her, he dug into his jacket pocket. He unraveled a thin white cord, placed one fitted end into his ear, and held a small cone at the other end against the ground.

They waited for only a few seconds before Altek removed the earpiece and began winding the wire around his hand. "It detonated," he whispered. He put his listening device back in his pocket, and then the two of them headed through the trees, on their way back down the mountain.

They had gone only a few steps when a low-pitched sound rose up, sounding to Keev like the wild call of a wounded animal. She and Altek both stopped, then ran back to the edge of the work site. At first, Keev saw nothing unusual or out of place, but then she noticed that the machinery where they had just worked canted to one side. She also saw movement by the derrick—

No, not *by* the derrick: the derrick itself moved, leaning to one side. The machinery atop the ground that they had just sabotaged connected directly to the drill, and Keev saw that the drill listed as well. Clearly, the gild's weeks of work had succeeded in weakening the ground and—

A loud crack shot through the camp. The derrick

lurched farther to one side, and the drill followed. As though deciding whether or not to fall, the entire assembly teetered.

The door of the shack flew open and a man wearing long underwear appeared. He looked outside just as the derrick and drill toppled to the ground with what Keev considered a satisfying crash. Then she turned to Altek and said, "We need to go."

It took them hours to get back to the gild, but when they did, they brought the good news with them.

Fifteen

Blackmer stood at the back of the auditorium, listening to the visiting heads of state talk about Deep Space 9, both past and present. He considered taking a seat—the theater hadn't quite filled up completely—but it always made him uncomfortable to sit down at such events, even when not on duty. He liked to think that he'd been trained too well for that, but he understood that, in reality, his anxiety had developed during his first posting out of the Academy. At a reception for a visiting admiral on Starbase 189, he'd been chatting up another young ensign when a door opened and a Quist sped inside, terrifying everybody and nearly igniting a war with the previously unknown species.

What a way to make first contact, Blackmer thought, able to smile about the incident so many years later. At the time, though, the shock of seeing something so thoroughly unexpected like that, of being faced with an unfamiliar life-form that caused such fear and revulsion, had driven him to rethink his priorities. Although he hadn't been on duty during the reception on Starbase 189, the overall security breach had bothered him so much that he'd resolved to take more care at similar events, even as a guest.

Captain Ro had invited the entire senior staff to attend

the dedication ceremony, and they'd all agreed—including Blackmer. Later, though, he spoke with the captain and let her know that he'd prefer to sit at the back of the theater where he could, while enjoying the occasion, at least keep an eye on things. Ro paused a moment, perhaps questioning the security chief's appeal, but Blackmer's relationship with her had improved significantly since his first months under her command—he'd earned her trust and respect—and she granted his request.

Except I can't even sit, he thought. *Maybe because I just got off duty.* Ten minutes before the start of the ceremony, he had completed a circuit of the theater, from the lobby to the stage, from the control booth to the wings, from the refreshers to the dressing rooms. Half an hour prior to that, he'd received a report from Lieutenant Commander Douglas—who had become his top deputy in security during the past year—after she'd done a preliminary inspection of the venue.

Blackmer tried to concentrate on the speeches, knowing he had no real cause for concern. Not only had he and Douglas swept the theater themselves, but his staff had the theater—and the entire starbase—well secured. Having half a dozen heads of state aboard certainly raised the pressure, but those officials also traveled with their own protection details, which helped mitigate the burden.

As the ceremony proceeded, Blackmer found the comments of the grand nagus the most personal, touching on Rom's own years on the old station and how he'd raised his son there. Lustrate Vorat, Praetor Kamemor, and Impetator Sozzerozs all spoke of virtues—forgiveness and generosity and determination—while Chancellor Martok's speech sounded . . . well, the most Klingon. First Minister Asarem followed all of those remarks with the most rousing address, bringing the audience to its feet. Had he not already been standing, Blackmer would have risen as well.

President Bacco stepped out onto the stage after the first minister. Blackmer had voted for Bacco in the last election, believing that she'd distinguished herself during her years in office as a solid leader and an exceptional diplomat and negotiator, particularly with respect to the Typhon Pact. She had avoided war without having to resort to appeasement, and her stance on—

A shot tore through the theater, a noise Blackmer had not heard often, but that he recognized at once. It sounded as though it had come from the center of the auditorium. He saw the president reel backward on the stage, and he knew that she'd been hit.

Blackmer drew his phaser and ran down the sloped aisle, peering into the middle of the audience. Just as he registered many people turning and looking toward the back of the theater, a second shot bellowed from somewhere behind him. He glanced at the president and saw her struck again, then turned and scanned the rear of the auditorium for the shooter. He heard a third shot at the same time he spied a flash of light—the spark of a firearm in action, he realized—in an opening high up on the back wall. Blackmer's arm moved as of its own accord, bringing his phaser up, and he fired. The reddish-yellow beam streaked through the window, but too late: the security chief saw it strike the overhead inside the theater's control booth, missing the shooter.

But at least it might slow them down.

Two members of his staff, Cardok and Hava, appeared at Blackmer's side. The security chief pointed to the three openings that looked out over the auditorium and stage from the control booth, which should have been empty during the ceremony; only the curtains and house lights were in operation, and they were controlled from offstage.

"The shooter's there," Blackmer told Cardok and Hava. "If you see movement, fire. I'm going up." As the officers acknowledged his order, Blackmer raced back up the aisle. The house lights came on just as he pushed through the swinging doors and out into the lobby. He looked left and right, and on each side saw the two security officers he'd posted beside the access points to the second level. Each of his people clutched a phaser.

"Sir?" Ansarg called out.

"Stay there," Blackmer yelled, pointing to his left, to where the Tellarite and her partner stood guard before the turbolift that led up to the next level. "Allow no one in or out." The security chief sprinted in the opposite direction, toward the stairway. "Follow me, phasers up," he told the two officers there, Shul and ch'Larn.

Blackmer took the steps two at a time, first to a landing, and then right, up to the long corridor that stretched between the top of the staircase and the turbolift. Beneath the urgent call of the red alert klaxon, which had begun to blare, he heard the footfalls of his people behind him. Blackmer stopped on the uppermost step, halting Shul and ch'Larn with a gesture. He took a quick look around the corner.

The corridor was empty. Three sets of doors stood closed along its length, all on the same wall. The two on either end of the corridor led to refreshers, Blackmer knew—he'd searched them himself when inspecting the theater—while the middle set opened into the control booth.

He tapped his combadge. "Blackmer to Walenista."

"Walenista here. Go ahead, Commander." Blackmer had assigned the lieutenant to the Hub during the ceremony.

"Patrycja, scan the control booth in the theater," Blackmer said. "Is there anybody there?"

"Scanning," Walenista said. *"I'm not reading anyone inside."*

"There's somebody there," Blackmer said. "I saw them. They're armed with a projectile weapon. Attempt a generic transport of anybody inside into the stockade."

A moment passed. *"Sir, I can't establish a transporter lock."*

Of course not. "All available security to the theater," Blackmer ordered. "Out." He glanced back over his shoulder. "Cover me." Without waiting for a response, but trusting his people, Blackmer ran down the corridor, pulling up alongside the control booth doors. He touched the OPEN control, but the feedback signal told him that it had been locked—which he'd done himself prior to the ceremony, although clearly somebody had gotten inside the booth anyway.

Blackmer keyed in his security override, leaving his fingertip on the pad to allow the system to confirm his identity. He then activated his combadge again. "Blackmer to Cardok," he said.

"Cardok here."

"I'm going into the control booth," Blackmer said. "Don't fire."

"Yes, sir."

"Out." Blackmer touched the OPEN control again. The doors parted, but nothing else happened. "This is Lieutenant Commander Jefferson Blackmer," he called. "You are surrounded. You can also hear the red alert, which means that all avenues of escape from this starbase have been closed to you."

Blackmer received no response. He listened attentively, but he heard no sounds within the booth. With an abundance of caution, he bent low and quickly ducked his head past the side of the doorway to look inside. When he pulled back, he processed what he'd seen: one person in the darkened compartment, lying on the deck, a firearm by their side but not in their grasp.

Blackmer whirled from the wall and into the doorway, his phaser up before him and aimed at the person on the deck inside. The figure didn't move. Three bright rectangles marched across the deck, thrown there by the lights in the theater through the openings in the front of the booth.

Taking a step inside, Blackmer looked to either side of the doorway, but he saw nobody else. "Computer, lights," he said. The overhead panels came on at once. Blackmer peered around at the control panels used to operate lighting and sound and other functions within the theater. Nothing appeared out of place but the woman lying on the deck before him, and the firearm by her open right hand.

The sound of running feet alerted Blackmer that Shul and ch'Larn had followed to back him up. He didn't look around, but kept his gaze on the woman. She lay on her back, her face turned away from him. Her chest rose and fell with her breathing. She had long, straight red hair.

Carefully, Blackmer approached the woman. When he drew close enough, he used his foot to move the weapon out of her reach. He began to bend down when the woman stirred.

Blackmer backed up a step as she pushed herself up to a sitting position. She shook her head as though clearing it, and her hair fell away from her face. Blackmer aimed his phaser in her direction. "Don't move," he ordered. The woman looked up at him, and her eyes widened.

The security chief tapped his combadge. "Blackmer to

Captain Ro," he said. He fought to keep his voice level as he wondered if the president had survived the attack.

"Ro here. Go ahead."

"Captain, we've captured the shooter," Blackmer said. "It's Enkar Sirsy, the first minister's chief of staff."

Ben Sisko walked up the aisle of the theater alongside Captain Ro. He had just spoken with Kasidy, who'd wanted him to stay with her and Rebecca—she hadn't said so outright, but he could read the feeling in her eyes. He'd wanted that as well. But they both understood that he had a duty to assist Ro, and Kasidy focused on the two other actions she needed to take at the moment: to keep their daughter safe, and to begin dealing with the emotional impact of what they'd all just witnessed.

I just hope President Bacco survives, Sisko thought. She'd been a good leader for the Federation, but he felt something more personal than that: nobody deserved to have their life stolen from them, whether president or pauper.

"Why would Enkar Sirsy do this?" Sisko asked as he and Ro pushed through the doors at the top of the aisle and entered the lobby.

"This way." Ro pointed left, and they headed in that direction. Then, responding to his question, she said, "I don't know. I've known Sirsy and dealt with her a long time. I *liked* her. I never could have predicted this."

"I couldn't either," Sisko said. He had first met Enkar more than a dozen years earlier, when she'd served as an assistant to Shakaar Edon after he'd been elected first minister of Bajor. Sisko had interacted with her only on a professional basis, and so he couldn't claim to truly know her, but he'd always found her skilled in her job and pleasant to work with. The notion of her attempting to assassinate the president of the Federation seemed inexplicable.

A pair of security officers stood watch outside a turbolift, and they parted as Sisko and Ro approached. "Allow no one else through," Ro ordered. The two captains entered the lift, and as they turned to face front, Sisko saw another set of guards taking up a position on the other side of the lobby, at the base of a stairway.

The turbolift ascended quickly, discharging Sisko and Ro on the second level of the theater. The long corridor ended at the top of a stairway, doubtless the same one Sisko had just seen in the lobby. Two more security officers stood halfway down the corridor, outside an open door that clearly led to the theater's control booth, the location from which Lieutenant Commander Blackmer had contacted Ro.

Sisko and Ro had just started down the corridor when her combadge chirped. *"Sector General to Captain Ro."* Sisko recognized the voice of Doctor Bashir.

Ro stopped walking at once. "Ro here," she said. "What can you tell me, Doctor?"

"I need to see you in the hospital right away, Captain," Bashir said, the evenness in his tone doing little to hide the urgency in his words.

Sisko's heart sank. He read the doctor's unwillingness to elaborate on President Bacco's condition as an indication that she had not survived. Just the thought made Sisko feel hopeless.

"I'm on my way, Doctor," Ro said. "Out."

Ro continued walking toward the open doorway, and Sisko went with her. The security officers backed away to allow them past. Inside the control booth, Lieutenant Commander Blackmer stood with his phaser in his hand and what looked like a projectile firearm on the deck between his feet. Across from him, Enkar Sirsy slouched on a chair, her hair hanging down in her face. She looked up as Sisko and Ro entered.

"Captain," she said, quickly standing up. Sisko saw that her wrists had been bound. Blackmer stepped forward and told her to sit back down. Enkar did as instructed, but she peered up at Ro beseechingly. "Captain, I don't know what's happening. I don't even know how I got here, but Commander Blackmer has arrested me."

Sisko saw Ro glance over at the security chief, who stared back as though his features had been set in stone. *I feel what he feels: sadness, anger, betrayal, loss.* Sisko wondered how he and Kasidy could possibly explain to their daughter what had happened. *Hell, I can't even explain it to myself.*

Ro looked back over at Enkar, but when she spoke, she directed her words to Blackmer. "Take her to the stockade and hold her under the highest security," she said. "Inform her of her rights under Starfleet regulations, Bajoran law, and Federation law."

"Aye, sir."

Ro stepped away from Enkar and over to the security chief. "No one gets to see her without my authorization."

"Understood."

"Captain," Enkar said, "I—"

Ro wheeled on the Bajoran woman with such speed that Sisko thought for a moment that the captain intended to strike her. Instead, she again spoke to Blackmer while facing Enkar. "Use the transporter," she said. "I don't want her anywhere on our starbase but in a cell." If Ro had spat on her, it would not have surprised Sisko.

Ro stared at Enkar, who did not look away.

"Captain," Sisko said gently, wanting to avoid any potential trouble.

Ro shook her head in disgust, then walked out of the control booth. Sisko followed her out, and so did the security chief.

"Captain," Blackmer said, and he waited for Ro to turn back toward him. "Captain, we were unable to scan Enkar or beam her out of the booth before. She may be carrying a sensor block or a transporter inhibitor, or there might be one hidden in the compartment or somewhere nearby. We've performed cursory searches of both the prisoner and the booth, but we haven't been able to locate anything yet."

"Did you ask Enkar about it?" Sisko wanted to know. As upset as Ro clearly was, he didn't think she'd mind him asking the question. He could have pulled rank anyway, if he needed to, but he wanted to respect her command of the starbase.

"She denies knowing anything about it," Blackmer said.

Ro took a deep breath, then let it out quickly. "Attempt to transport her from the corridor or the lobby," she said. "If that doesn't work, then walk her to a turbolift and take her to the stockade that way. Cordon off your route and place security all along the way. I don't want to take any chances."

"Aye, sir."

Ro looked down, then took a step closer to Blackmer. "Jeff, I know you know this, but I have to say it," she told him, her voice low. "I need you to be painstaking in your investigation: clean sensor logs, documented chain of custody for all the evidence, nothing compromised."

"I understand, Captain," Blackmer said. "Believe me, I want her to go away for the rest of her miserable life."

"Easy, Mister Blackmer," Sisko said quietly. "Conduct your inquiry before we sentence anyone to life in prison." He understood the rage plainly coursing through the security chief, and through Ro too—Sisko felt it himself. Blackmer probably also fought against guilt, given his position. But they would not find justice by indulging their heightened emotions.

"Yes, sir," Blackmer said. Then, of Ro, he asked, "Is there anything else, Captain?"

"Just keep me informed," Ro said. When she turned back toward the turbolift, Sisko again walked by her side. They rode down to the lobby of the theater, then strode out onto the Plaza. They entered another turbolift, which Ro ordered to take them to Sector General. They traveled in silence for a few moments, Ro staring at her feet. Then, without looked up, she asked, "How did this happen?"

Sisko shook his head. "I don't know. But I do know that you and your crew will do everything possible to find out. And right now, you also have the crews of the *Robinson* and the *Aventine* at your service."

"But this station was designed to be a *fortress*," Ro said, almost as though pleading for her words to be true at the same time that she condemned them.

"And it probably is a fortress against enemies," Sisko said. "Just not against people we think are friends."

When Ro finally looked over at Sisko, he could see the pain on her face, the tremendous strain she felt. "How could she do this?" Ro asked, clearly meaning Enkar Sirsy. "Why?"

"I don't know," Sisko said honestly.

"Do you think . . ." Ro began, but then she stopped, as though searching for the thread of her thoughts. At the same time, the turbolift eased to a halt. "Computer, hold," she said before the doors opened. "Captain, could this have anything to do with the Cardassians?"

"What?" Sisko said. The question surprised him. "Why would you ask that?"

"Something Castellan Garan mentioned when she told me she had to return home," Ro said. "She was supposed to attend the dedication, but there's a group called Cardassia First making trouble in the Union."

"I've heard about them," Sisko said. "They have an ultranationalist agenda."

"I mention them just because they're not happy about the Cardassian Union joining the Khitomer Accords—and essentially allying with Bajor," Ro explained. "But they're not the only ones who are unhappy."

"No?" Sisko didn't know if Ro spoke of her own sentiments.

"There are still Bajorans who don't think that we should be in an alliance that includes the Cardassians," Ro said. "More than a few."

"But Bajor has been helping to rebuild Cardassia for almost a decade," Sisko said. "First Minister Asarem has supported those efforts wholeheartedly, and she won reelection with more than two-thirds of the vote."

"Those aren't the Bajorans I'm talking about."

"So you think Enkar Sirsy hates the Cardassians so much that she couldn't endure the Federation, and therefore Bajor, being in the same alliance with them?" Sisko asked, trying to parse Ro's reasoning. "And so she blamed President Bacco for that? Not Lustrate Vorat? Or even the first minister?"

"I don't know," Ro said. "I'm just . . . I'm trying to make sense out of this."

"We may learn the reasons Enkar did this," Sisko told Ro, "but I doubt it will ever make sense to us."

"Yeah. I'm sure you're right," Ro said, and then, "Computer, resume." The turbolift doors glided open.

Sisko and Ro crossed a wide corridor to the starbase's hospital. A man in civilian attire sat at a circular desk in the entrance, and a number of security officers guarded corridors leading into the medical complex. Another security officer, a human man, stood in front of the desk, and he addressed Ro.

"Captain," he said, "Doctor Bashir is waiting for you in the emergency medical transporter room."

"Thank you, Jack," Ro said, and she pointed toward the corridor just left of center. She and Sisko circled the reception desk and walked in that direction. They made their way down the entire length of the corridor, to where two more security guards stood watch outside the doors at the end. They stepped aside for Sisko and Ro to enter.

To Sisko, the compartment looked like a combination sickbay and transporter room. Doctor Bashir stood directly ahead, speaking with the other doctor Sisko had seen in the theater. Just past them stood three nurses—a human, a Bajoran, and a Bolian; all three looked as though they'd been crying. To the right, members of the president's protection detail waited silently. They maintained a stoic exterior, but Sisko knew that could only be a front.

To the left, a body lay on the transporter platform, a sheet draped over it. Even though he had expected it, Sisko felt as though the wind had been knocked out of him.

"I'm sorry," Bashir said, stepping forward. The color had drained from his face. "President Bacco was shot twice in the chest and once through the skull. Her body technically survived for a few moments after she sustained those wounds, but the brain injury killed her."

Sisko and Ro both gazed over at the transporter platform, at the corpse of the woman who had so ably led the Federation for nearly six years. "Thank you, Doctor Bashir," Ro said, her voice flat. "And you, Doctor Boudreaux. You both acted quickly. You did everything you could." She took another deep breath, but she exhaled slowly, as though preparing herself for what lay ahead.

Or maybe just trying to deal right now with what's happened, Sisko thought.

"Transport President Bacco's body to the autopsy suite for postmortem examination," Ro said. "Collect any evidence you can. I want the room sealed—"

One member of the presidential protection detail paced over to face Ro. "Captain," she said, "we still have a duty to President Bacco."

Ro nodded. "Yes, Agent Ferson, of course. Two of your group may observe, if Doctor Bashir has no medical objection."

"No," Bashir said. "We can make room for two agents."

"Thank you," Ferson said.

Addressing Bashir again, Ro said, "I want the room sealed and under constant guard as long as the . . . as long as the body . . . is on Deep Space Nine. I also want absolutely no discussion of this outside of the people in this room until the entire crew is informed."

"Understood, Captain," Bashir said.

"Agreed," Ferson said.

Ro peered over at Sisko, then told Bashir, "Doctor, I need an empty room."

Bashir thought for a moment. "When you leave here,

the second door on the left is a surgeon's prep room. It's empty."

"Thank you," Ro said, and motioned to Sisko. She led the way out of the emergency medical transporter compartment and into the surgeon's prep room. In the spare facility, Sisko recognized a row of sleek devices as sonic disinfecting units. "Captain, the loss of President Bacco—" Ro's voice broke. Just hearing her on the verge of tears threatened to unleash a similar flood in Sisko. Ro closed her eyes a moment, and then continued. "This loss will obviously devastate the people of the Federation. I can't let the news leave the station until I've been able to inform the Federation Council."

"Agreed," Sisko said. "The people shouldn't hear rumors, only information from our central government. They'll disseminate it in the best, most efficient way they can."

"And probably only once they have the president pro tem in place," Ro said. By law, any vacancy in the office of the president mandated that the Federation Council fill the position of the president pro tempore. The chosen official would have the responsibilities and powers of the president for a period not to exceed sixty days—raised from thirty days after Ra'ch B'ullhy's term in 2379— during which time he or she must call for a special election so that the people of the Federation could select a new leader.

"Probably so," Sisko agreed. He remembered what had happened after President Zife had stepped down near the end of his second term. "I suggest contacting Admiral Akaar. He'll request an emergency, closed session of the Council and inform them that way."

"I want to get word to San Francisco as soon as possible, then," Ro said. Starfleet Headquarters called the Earth city home and housed the commander in chief's office.

"You can contact Comm Station Eta Three," Sisko said. "They'll be able to boost a signal and line up starships along the way to Earth for a real-time conversation."

"I've locked down the station, though, and that includes a communications blackout," Ro said. "I'd rather not lift that, even for something this important. I want to contain the news of what's happened, and also prevent Enkar and any possible conspirators from being able to contact anybody not on Deep Space Nine."

"And so you want me to contact Admiral Akaar from the *Robinson*," Sisko said.

"I'd appreciate it, Captain. Deep Space Nine is my responsibility, but you're the ranking officer here. I think the news should come from you."

"And as the commander of Deep Space Nine," Sisko said, "you need to remain here."

"I do," Ro said. "I don't want to leave the starbase for even a second until we can be absolutely sure that we have all the perpetrators of this monstrous act in custody."

"I understand, and I'm perfectly willing to contact the admiral," Sisko said. "But you're going to have another problem on your hands. Once they learn about President Bacco, all of the political leaders on the starbase are going to want to leave immediately."

"I know," Ro said. "Their protection details will certainly argue that they're not safe on the starbase."

"The leaders will also want to distance themselves from the assassination as quickly as they can," Sisko said. Employing the word *assassination* for the first time felt surreal to him. *Not just surreal, but* un*real.* "That'll probably be particularly true of the Gorn imperator and the Romulan praetor, who'll be concerned about their people being blamed for the crime."

"You're right," Ro said. "That just means we have to make sure we've arrested the right culprit or culprits as soon as possible."

"All right," Sisko said. "So if you've locked down the station, how do I get to the *Robinson*?"

"I'll escort you to the hatch," Ro said. "I hope you understand that your crew and your wife and daughter will need to remain on Deep Space Nine for right now."

"I do," Sisko said. "But I'll want to return to the station to be with Kasidy and Rebecca."

"How long will it take you to contact Admiral Akaar?"

"That depends on how long it takes for Eta Three to set up the real-time connection," Sisko said.

"When you're ready to come back to the starbase, enable the *Robinson*'s navigational beacon," Ro suggested. "I'll have my crew watch for it, then I'll meet you ten minutes later at the hatch."

Sisko agreed, and Ro thanked him for his assistance. They left the surgeon's prep room together and headed toward *Robinson*. Once aboard, Sisko would have a conversation with Starfleet's commander in chief that he absolutely did not want to have.

L. J. Akaar awoke to an unwelcome sound, but not one unfamiliar to him: the high-pitched squawk that roused him immediately from sleep signaled an incoming transmission designated highest priority. Starfleet's commander in chief bounded from bed, his massive form shaking the floor of his Cow Hollow villa. "Signal off," he barked, his deep, resonant voice still gravelly from his slumber. The piercing tone ceased.

On his way across the room, Akaar grabbed his black robe from where he'd draped it across an easy chair and threw the garment on. He reached the sitting area of his bedroom almost at a run. "Companel on," he said, standing before the device. He noted the time: zero three thirty-seven hours.

The screen of the companel winked to life displaying the Starfleet Headquarters emblem. "Admiral Leonard James Akaar, security clearance theta-omicron six-nine-two-nine-three L-E-N four," he said, reciting that month's identification cipher, which, combined with his voiceprint, would allow him access to coded Starfleet channels. The display blinked again, and the image of the petite, long-haired Commander Talin Aslanyan appeared. Akaar could see through the transparent wall behind her that she sat in her secure office within the primary communications center at Starfleet. "Go ahead, Commander."

"Admiral Akaar," Aslanyan said, dispensing with formalities, *"we are receiving a red one transmission from Captain Benjamin Sisko aboard the* U.S.S. Robinson, *priority one."* The signal that had pulled the admiral from sleep had indicated the importance of the incoming message, and *priority one* confirmed that. The designation *red one*, though, gave him greater cause for concern; it indicated that Captain Sisko had enjoined some combination of comm stations, starbases, and starships between Deep Space 9 and Earth to ensure that he could speak with Akaar in real time. Only the most serious situations warranted such measures.

"Route it to me here," Akaar ordered. He did not need to tell Commander Aslanyan to scramble the transmission; such high-priority messages demanded encryption from source to destination.

"*Routing the transmission to your home, Admiral,*" Aslanyan said.

"Akaar out." He waited for only a second before the image of the commander vanished, replaced by that of Captain Sisko—who looked grave. "Captain," Akaar said.

"*Admiral,*" Sisko said. "*I'm contacting you from the* Robinson. *We're presently docked at Deep Space Nine.*" Through the port over the captain's shoulder, Akaar thought he could actually make out a rounded section of the starbase hull. "*We're here for the dedication ceremony.*"

So are Dax and the Aventine, Akaar thought. *Along with President Bacco and more politicians than anybody should ever be subjected to at one time.* Akaar maintained a close working relationship with the Federation president—and a personal respect and fondness for her—but he'd joked with her recently that she'd shown more courage in convening half a dozen other heads of state with her on DS9 than he had when he'd commanded *Wyoming* during the last Federation-Tzenkethi war. "I'm aware of the *Robinson*'s movements," he told the captain.

"*The dedication ceremony was held a few hours ago,*" Sisko said. Akaar could tell from the increasing tension in the captain's features that he neared the purpose of his message. "*While President Bacco was speaking, she was shot with a projectile weapon.*"

Damn! Akaar could only hope that the Federation president hadn't been hurt too badly and that she hadn't been attacked by some element in either the Gorn or Romulan delegations. Bacco had invited the imperator and the praetor to the dedication for the express purpose of furthering détente, not to provide a catalyst for an act of war.

"What is the president's condition?" Akaar asked. Even if they didn't have to contend with a new threat to the fragile peace they'd established with the Typhon Pact, the admiral knew that *Aventine* had been scheduled to ferry Bacco to Cardassia from Deep Space 9 for important talks—and to show solidarity with Castellan Garan in the face of some anti-Federation sentiment within the Union. If the president required any significant recovery time, the chief of Starfleet operations would need to adjust starship assignments, and the Federation Council would likely want to send another representative to Cardassia.

"Admiral," Sisko said, *"I'm afraid that President Bacco is dead."*

All at once, Akaar's pulse pumped loudly in his ears, as though his heart might beat right out of his chest. *"What?!"* He took a step backward, away from the companel, as though Sisko had assaulted him with his words. Akaar's foot struck the front of an easy chair. He did not even attempt to keep his balance, but allowed himself to fold into the piece of furniture.

Nan, he thought. *Dead.*

Akaar couldn't believe it—didn't *want* to believe it. He and President Bacco had always worked well together, even when they hadn't agreed. *Perhaps especially when we didn't agree.* That ability had always impressed him about her. And although they didn't attend the theater together or sit across a three-dimensional chessboard from each other— when had either of them had the time?—Akaar still felt that they had something more than a professional relationship. A friendship, to be sure, but he actually thought of her in some ways as a mother figure to him—a feeling he'd never shared with anybody, and which seemed ridiculous, considering that he was a quarter of a century her senior.

Akaar had been close to his own mother—she'd been a heroic individual in his eyes—and her death had left an emptiness in his life. And while nobody else could ever fill that void, Nanietta Bacco had helped make it smaller.

The admiral realized that his attention had wandered from Captain Sisko, who had stopped speaking. If the captain had said anything after delivering his unwelcome news, Akaar hadn't heard it. At that moment, he didn't want to hear anything else—he didn't want to move or even really think, but he knew that he suddenly had a great deal to accomplish in a very short amount of time.

Climbing back to his feet, Akaar said, "Captain, tell me precisely what happened."

"I was present in Deep Space Nine's theater at the time, but I was a witness only to the effect, not the cause," Sisko said. *"Captain Ro has taken a Bajoran national into custody. The available evidence, which appears to be strong, indicates that she acted alone, firing on President Bacco from the control booth at the back of the theater."* For a long time, Akaar had held a low opinion of Ro Laren, and he'd even voted against reinstating her in Starfleet when Bajor had been admitted to the Federation. In the years since, however, it had pleased him to be proven wrong about her. *"Captain Ro has locked down the starbase and is continuing to investigate. She's also implemented a communications blackout to ensure that news of what happened doesn't leak out from Deep Space Nine, but comes directly from the Federation government. The blackout is also why I'm contacting you from the* Robinson."

Akaar took in all of the information and processed it as he determined his next courses of action. "What about the heads of state?" he asked.

"At the moment, they're locked down too," Sisko said.

"Captain Ro has them guarded by their own protection details, as well as by Deep Space Nine security."

That won't stand for long, Akaar thought. If neither the Gorn nor the Romulan contingents had anything to do with the assassination—and he certainly hoped they hadn't—the Federation would face a thorny diplomatic situation by restricting their movements, particularly at a time when they could legitimately argue that they feared for their own safety. Akaar would need to talk with Ro about that, but first he'd have to provide her a reason to end the communications blackout.

Another thought occurred to Akaar. "You said a Bajoran did this?"

"That seems to be the case," Sisko said. *"It was First Minister Asarem's chief of staff."*

None of that made much sense to Akaar. *But when do such crimes ever make sense to rational people?* The involvement of a member of the first minister's own staff, though, would add another complication, but he had to set that aside for the moment. The Federation had been robbed of its leader, and that could not be permitted to endure for any length of time.

"Captain, I will notify you aboard the *Robinson* as soon as the news has been released to the public," Akaar said. "At that time, you will have Captain Ro contact me. For now, keep the direct line of real-time communication open between *Robinson* and Earth, on my authority."

"Yes, sir."

"Is there anything else?"

"No, Admiral," Sisko said. *"Except that I'm very sorry."*

Akaar could see the captain fighting back his emotions. He knew how Sisko felt—how all the people of the Federation would once they learned the news. "I'm sorry too, Captain," the admiral said quietly. He paused, until all that he had to do could wait no more. "Akaar out."

The Starfleet Headquarters insignia once more showed on the companel. "Admiral Akaar to Commander Aslanyan." The image of the communications officer reappeared.

"Commander Aslanyan here," she said. *"How can I assist you, Admiral?"*

"Connect me with Jas Abrik," Akaar said. "Priority one." Abrik, a former Starfleet admiral, had served as the Federation security advisor since President Bacco took office six years earlier. "Employ our highest encryption protocol. While I'm speaking with him, make arrangements for me to be beamed to Starfleet Headquarters, and then directly to the Palais." The personal transporter installed in the admiral's home had a limited range, allowing him to transport to safety during an emergency, but it would not reach all the way to the Palais de la Concorde in Paris. Moreover, transport into both Starfleet Headquarters and the Palais required secure procedures.

"Right away, Admiral," Aslanyan said.

Akaar would inform Abrik of what had happened. The security advisor would request an immediate closed-door meeting with the Federation Council, which they would grant, and Abrik and Akaar would brief them on events. The councillors would then be obligated to select one among their number to serve as president pro tempore. After that, the Council would announce both President Bacco's death and the swearing in of the president pro tem.

They'll go with Agreho, Akaar thought. *Or Ishan—* although, under the circumstances, that could prove problematic, he realized. Given the amount of influence they wielded within the Federation Council and the force of their personalities, those two seemed the likeliest selections.

As Akaar waited for the communications officer to connect him with Jas Abrik, he again checked the time: zero three forty-eight hours. *Eleven minutes ago, as far as I knew, the galaxy was a different place,* he thought. *A better place.*

Sixteen

Keev set her gloved hands behind the large chunk of rock and hauled back, straining against its weight. She felt perspiration forming on her skin. As she struggled to move the irregularly shaped block, she let out a frustrated cry, which echoed loudly in the close quarters of the cavern.

Despite the hard labor of digging through the rubble of the tunnel collapse, it felt good to be working toward resuming the mission of the gild. It had been two months since their sabotage of the exploratory mining operation had succeeded in taking down the derrick, the drill, and the drive. The Aleira had remained on site the following day, examining the damage and presumably attempting to determine its cause. Over time, the gild had wisely weakened other portions of the work site, and so soft soil abounded. The Aleira had departed the next day, and they'd returned just once since then, lugging away the salvageable machinery. Finally, ten days after their last appearance, Veralla had given the go-ahead to begin excavating the cave.

Since Renet had come back from the tragic journey he'd taken with poor Synder Nogar, the gild had freed no more slaves from Joradell. Synder's death had been difficult for them, but they had been fortunate not to lose

Renet or either of the escaped Bajora whom the two men had delivered to freedom via their long trip around the mountains. Veralla made the decision—fully supported by every member of the gild—to wait until they had cleared their path through the caverns to resume transporting newly unbound slaves.

With one more effort, Keev pulled at the mass of stone. It tilted toward her, and she nimbly sidestepped it as it tumbled down onto the wide piece of thick bark she'd set on the ground. As she took a moment to catch her breath, she regarded the mound of earth and rock that still obstructed the cave. It reached from wall to wall and from floor to roof—or at least to the space where the roof once had been. They didn't know how far back the blockage reached, but they had to that point removed a great deal of rubble. Using improvised sledges made from large sheets of strong, rugged bark they'd sliced from huge trees, they towed the debris they collected back along the tunnel, offloading it bit by bit along the sides.

They had accomplished more than that, though. Keev turned and regarded the structural reinforcement that had been installed in the cave. For forty paces or so, columns lined the walls, standing perhaps six or seven paces apart. Support beams reached from the top of one column to the next, and joists sat atop those beams across the width of the tunnel.

In the stark white light thrown by beacons set at different locations within the cave, Keev smiled. It pleased her—it pleased everybody in the gild—to have made so much progress toward restoring them to their purpose. They worked hard each day, by twos and fours, to dig out from the cave-in. The wearing manual labor left them all exhausted, but also satisfied.

But Keev also smiled to cover her unease. Once the members of the gild had begun clearing away the rubble, Veralla had insisted that they needed to protect themselves against the weakened structure of the cavern. While the others worked at digging through the debris, he set himself the task of securing resources to buttress the cave walls and roof. Every few days, he made several trips with a couple of the gild members—usually the Cawlders, but sometimes Jennica and Renet—to bring back columns, beams, and joists.

Keev herself had helped carry the building materials into the cavern. Under Veralla's supervision, she and the others placed the columns along the recovered lengths of the tunnel, hoisted the support beams atop them, set the joists in place atop those. They bound everything together with tools that Veralla provided and explained how to use, and that Keev did not recognize or even understand. Almost revolver-like in shape, the devices emitted colored beams of light, with one surface showing strings of ever-changing letters and numbers.

When she'd questioned Veralla about the nature of the tools, he would say only that they were required for their purposes, and clearly they helped them accomplish their goals. When she asked about the origin of the tools, he would claim only that he acquired them because of their need for them. Keev mentioned her curiosity to the others, but other than Altek, nobody seemed especially interested. It apparently sated her fellow gild members to know that everything Veralla supplied worked as he said it would. They trusted him completely.

And I trust him completely too, Keev thought. She had known him and worked with him for years, and his leadership had rarely steered the gild wrong. *And he's always been reticent.* His reserved nature, which often gave the appearance of secretiveness, did not mark a change in his behavior, but kept consistent with the character she had always known him to have.

The strange tools, though, marked only one peculiarity in their fortification of the cave. The columns and support beams and joists all appeared to be composed of ordinary materials—wood, she thought—but she could not tell with certainty, which seemed odd. When binding the different components together, they sometimes, for a fraction of an instant, seemed to be made of something else entirely, though Keev could not exactly say what—something like soft glass, filled with liquid and light.

And sometimes while she worked in the cave, she would see movement in her peripheral vision. She would turn and think she saw the reinforcing structure rendered translucent, with blue and white streamers wavering within—but only for the span of a heartbeat. She wondered if anybody else experienced the phenomenon. Keev hadn't mentioned her—*What? Hallucinations? Visions?*—to anybody, but she thought she might tell Altek.

She turned away from the support framework, then looked quickly back. She saw nothing out of the ordinary, even for a brief time. It seemed that Keev could not force her perceptions.

She shrugged off her concerns. *Except they're not really concerns, are they?* she asked herself. *I don't really feel uneasy.* No, Keev felt captivated by her peculiar, transient observations.

She stepped over to the nearest column and rested her hand against it. The surface looked like wood, and it felt hard and rough. Keev began to drop her hand and turn away, and in that moment, she saw as though through a glass, darkly, and where her fingertip touched the surface of the column, circles of light spread outward from it, like ripples in a pond.

But when she looked back, the column was just a column.

Keev moved to her makeshift sledge, the smooth side of the bark against the ground. She picked up the rope affixed to its two front corners, set her feet, and pulled backward. The stone came forward a short way. Keev reset her feet and pulled again. Once more, the sledge moved, but the bark must have rubbed against something abrasive on the ground because it suddenly stopped. Not expecting that, Keev lost her grip on the rope, overbalanced, and tumbled backward. She cried out, more in surprise than in pain, though she felt a twinge as her head snapped toward the ground.

"Anora!" Altek called from farther down the cave. She saw him from her inverted position. He dropped his own bark-and-rope sledge and raced forward, the beam of his beacon jumping as he did so. When he reached her, he kneeled down and placed a comforting hand on her shoulder. "Are you all right?"

"I'm fine, I'm fine," Keev said. "I only wounded my pride." As she sat up, she felt an ache in the side of her neck. "Oh," she said, reaching up to rub her injury.

"You don't sound all right," Altek said. "Let me see."

"I'm sure it's nothing," Keev said, still rubbing. "I just twisted my neck when I fell."

"Let me see," Altek repeated. Keev pulled her hand away, and he raised his beacon to shine it in the slope between her head and her shoulder. He reached with his other hand and tugged the loose fabric of her blouse away from her neck. "It looks like it's starting to swell," he said, leaning in. She could feel the heat of his breath on her flesh. "You'll probably have a knot there and a pretty good bruise for a few days."

"Serves me right for daydreaming while I work," Keev said.

Altek seemed to take too much time examining her shoulder, and she worried for a moment that he might have seen something more serious there than a simple bump. But then he leaned forward and touched his lips to her flesh. They felt soft and hot against her, a gentle intensity. She closed her eyes and visualized him kissing her like that, seeing him kneeling beside her on the floor of the cave, his mouth nestled in the crook of her neck.

Altek pulled back suddenly. Keev turned her head and looked at him. "I . . . I'm sorry," he said. "I just . . . I . . ." He looked as though he believed she would rebuke him for his transgression.

Instead, she leaned forward and pressed her lips to his.

Seventeen

Ro awoke well before Deep Space 9's simulated dawn—except that she hadn't slept, not really. Maybe an hour or two in total, dozing on and off, but mostly she succeeded only in wringing her bedclothes into knots—which also amounted to a fair description of how her stomach felt: in knots. *However long I slept,* Ro thought, *I sure as hell didn't* rest.

The weight of the previous day's events hadn't lessened, and she didn't see how it could anytime soon. She'd had direct contact with only a handful of DS9's twenty-five hundred crew members after the assassination, and with almost none of the few hundred civilians aboard, but those she had interacted with had all displayed signs of confusion and anger and grief. *And I'm sure I showed those same emotions, because that's how I felt too,* Ro thought. *That's still* how I feel.

Even Quark had been affected. Although he usually behaved as though events held meaning for him only insofar as they impacted his business, Ro knew better. Quark's brusque exterior and the time and energy he spent pursuing the acquisition of wealth hid a softer, kinder man. It certainly satisfied him—in some way that Ro couldn't quite understand—to project the image of himself as an avaricious Ferengi businessman, but he did other things that virtually nobody knew about—things that not only didn't profit him, but that actually cost him latinum. Quark hadn't even told her about the contributions he'd made to help a number of children orphaned by the destruction of Deep Space 9—not just on Bajor, but on several other worlds as well; Ro had found out incidentally, when she'd contacted the families of those lost. She had never mentioned it to Quark, but neither had she forgotten it.

After the assassination, and after Ro's announcement to the entire starbase, Quark had stopped by her quarters. He came by very late, though not long after she entered her cabin, and she suspected that he'd been calling on her every few minutes throughout the night until she finally arrived. When she opened the door, he peered up at her with an expression of such concern that she almost broke down right then.

Ro had invited Quark inside—just for a few minutes, she'd said—and they'd sat together on the sofa in her living area. He asked about her, about how she felt regarding what had happened, about how she intended to make it through the next few days and beyond. She had no more answers for him than she did for herself, and she eventually told him that she preferred not to talk about any of it. Quark put his arms around her and held her, occasionally stroking her hair.

Ro had actually fallen asleep beside him, briefly, and when she'd woken up, she'd thought that she'd be able to get something close to a night's rest. Quark offered to stay with her, but she declined. He made no argument, other than to remind her that she could contact him at any time if she needed anything at all.

At the door, just before he'd left, Quark had looked up at her with a tight jaw and tears in his eyes. "I liked her," he said. "I mean, she was a good leader. She kept the Federation out of a war with the Typhon Pact, and she got the right people in the right places to stop the Borg from overrunning the entire quadrant." He paused, and Ro thought that he would say no more, but then he added, "The Fortyfourth Rule of Acquisition declares that you should never confuse wisdom with luck. In the case of President Bacco's leadership, I don't think it was luck." Quark then bid her good night with a kiss on the cheek.

When the door to her quarters had closed after him, Ro had started for her bedroom. On the way, she noticed a plush green bag on the console table in the entryway. She picked it up and loosened its drawstring to find several packets of *jumja* tea and two sleeves of *milaberry* biscuits—both Ro's favorite, and the latter being what she considered comfort food. She had no idea how Quark had placed them there without her knowing, but his thoughtfulness touched her.

Ro hadn't enjoyed any of the tea or biscuits, though, because she'd feared doing so might have prevented her from sleeping. *I should've drunk all the tea and eaten all the biscuits, for all the sleep I got.* She knew that she should probably stay in bed at least another hour, to rest as much as she could before what would plainly be another brutal day.

But she couldn't. Ro extracted her feet from among the twisted bedcovers, rose, and padded into the refresher. She stood over the washbasin and stared at herself in the mirror, not pleased with the appearance of the face that stared back at her—with its red-rimmed eyes and dark circles—but not surprised by it.

Ro removed the blue shorts and half shirt in which she slept—*Or tried to sleep*—and adjusted the controls of her shower. Feeling as though she needed more than to simply get clean, she substituted hot water for sonic waves. She stepped beneath the hard spray and let it beat down on her. After just a few seconds, she increased the temperature of the water.

At that point in time, three-quarters of a day after the assassination, Ro realized that much of the quadrant had probably learned of the tragic events. Only a few hours after Captain Sisko had first spoken with Admiral Akaar, the commander in chief had contacted *Robinson,* ordering Ro, through Sisko, to end DS9's communications blackout. Akaar had then opened a secure channel directly to the starbase.

According to the admiral, the Federation Council had appointed Ishan Anjar as president pro tem. The Council then publicly announced the news of President Bacco's death and the selection of her interim replacement. Finally, they began preparations for an impending special election to choose her permanent successor.

Ishan, Ro knew, had taken over from Krim Aldos as Bajor's representative on the Federation Council less than a year earlier. *An interesting choice,* she thought, *considering that the evidence pointed to a Bajoran as the president's assassin.* She supposed that the move might have been intended as a signal to the first minister and the people of Bajor that the Federation—or at least its government— did not hold an entire world responsible for the actions of one individual. *Or maybe it's just the force of Ishan's will.* Ro remembered hearing a rumor—completely unsubstantiated—that Bajor's most recent councillor had maneuvered his predecessor out of his way.

Ro had no time to think about politics, though. As she grabbed soap and a washcloth, she began to consider the day ahead. With the news of the assassination made public by the Federation Council, the captain had agreed with Akaar on dropping the communications blackout, but the starbase remained on lockdown. The only person who'd been permitted to enter or exit DS9 had been Captain Sisko, for the purpose of communicating with Admiral Akaar, but that didn't mean that others didn't want to depart.

After Ro had made her own starbase-wide announcement of the president's death, she had been contacted by every single visiting head of state. She had her first officer relocate all of them from the rooms backstage in the theater to their guest quarters—still under guard by her crew, as well as their own protection details—and then she went to speak in person with each of them. They all professed their sorrow at the loss of Nanietta Bacco, as well as their distress about the course of events, but they also each requested—and in the case of the Cardassian, Klingon, and Gorn dignitaries, *demanded*—that they be permitted to leave Deep Space 9 and return home. Chancellor Martok offered the most vociferous petition; in a long conversation with Ro, he ranged from wanting to board his starship and blast away from DS9 whether or not the Starfleet crew released the docking clamps, to wanting to be allowed to march down to the stockade and exact vengeance on Enkar Sirsy with his own hands.

Captain Sisko had warned Ro that the political officials would want to leave at once, as had Admiral Akaar. The commander in chief's caution, however, also came with a directive from the Federation Council: she had two days, three at the most, before she had to allow the heads of state and their delegations to depart the starbase—and they counted the day of the assassination as the first day. Nobody, including Ro, suspected that any of the other dignitaries or their people had anything to do with Enkar Sirsy's crime, but she needed to confirm that while they all remained within her grasp.

And don't forget that ten thousand civilians are due to arrive on Deep Space Nine in a few days, Ro reminded herself. Though a small consolation, she understood that the current situation on the starbase could have been a great deal more complicated had all of those residents already been in place. Knowing how many things she had to accomplish that day, she decided that she would assign her first officer to deal with the looming arrival of the residential population. Cenn would have to develop a new schedule and slow the process down, at least in the near term.

As though in a dream, Ro gradually realized that she felt pain. She looked down at her left forearm and saw small amounts of red mixed in with the white lather from the soap. She quickly rinsed her arm, then pulled it out of the spray and watched as more of her blood seeped from the abrasions she had scraped into her own skin. *Trying to scrub away your guilt, Laren?* she asked herself cynically. *It wasn't good enough that Deep Space Nine blew up on your watch; now you let the leader of trillions die.*

A surge of energy curled her hand into a fist and she ached to hit something. She wanted to throw a punch into the glass enclosure of her shower, or into the less-forgiving bulkhead. She wanted to see something break, even if it turned out to be her own fingers. But she couldn't. As a captain with as grave a responsibility to discharge as she'd ever had, she needed to be a leader to her crew—*the* leader to her crew.

Tamping down her emotions, Ro rinsed her arm again, then shut off the shower. She dried herself off, dabbing gingerly at her wounded arm, and walked through her bedroom into the living area of her quarters. She wished she could order the replicator to produce a dermal regenerator, but they hadn't been programmed or enabled to produce devices. Instead, she asked for a simple bandage, which she then wrapped around her forearm to the top of her wrist.

Ro started back into her bedroom, but stopped when she saw the jumja tea packets on the console table. She considered having some, but realized that, given her fitful night, she needed something a great deal stronger. She returned to the replicator and ordered a mug of raktajino.

Back in her bedroom, Ro donned a fresh uniform. She finished the raktajino, then went back into the 'fresher to examine herself in the mirror. She still looked as though she hadn't slept well—she suspected that a lot of her crew would look that way—but she appeared improved from when first she'd crawled out of bed.

"You need to be a strong leader today," she told her mirror image. "Your crew needs you." She always tried to be the best captain she could be, and she hoped that she'd so far succeeded during the current crisis. She thought she had, but her address to her crew had been hard. She hadn't known what to say or how to say it, but almost her entire crew had been witness to an attempt on the life of the Federation president; they had both a right and a need to know whether or not Bacco had survived.

After exiting the hospital and escorting Captain Sisko to *Robinson*, Ro had gone to the Hub, where she'd thanked her officers there for their professionalism in securing Deep Space 9 as well and as quickly as they had. She then went to her office, called in Cenn—more to lean on than for any other reason—and then she'd engaged the intra-starbase comm channel.

"This is Captain Ro," she'd begun, "to the crew, residents, and guests of Deep Space Nine. As you all must know by now, and as most of you observed yourselves, during the dedication ceremony today, President Bacco was the victim of an attack on her life. She was struck three times by shots fired from a projectile weapon."

Ro had looked over at Cenn for his support, knowing that the most difficult part had arrived. He nodded once, slowly, and by that simple act communicated his solidarity with her.

"Doctors Bashir and Boudreaux attended the president at once," Ro had continued, "examining her wounds and determining her medical needs. They transported with her to the hospital, hoping to administer lifesaving measures. It is my sad responsibility to report that the president's wounds were too grave to be treated successfully. At fourteen-oh-eight hours starbase time, President Nanietta Bacco was pronounced dead."

Ro's voice had begun to break on the final word, and she took a moment to breathe in deeply to collect her emotions. Cenn walked over and put a hand on her shoulder. That connection, that support, helped.

"An individual has been taken into custody for the perpetration of this monstrous act," Ro had gone on. "The investigation continues and evidence is still being gathered, and Deep Space Nine will remain locked down until those efforts have been completed." She did not reveal the deadline imposed by the Federation Council on releasing the visiting dignitaries to their vessels.

"I know that this incomprehensible act and its repercussions are difficult to deal with," she had continued. "Nanietta Bacco was a strong and popular president. She will be missed, but the Federation must and will endure. Bajor's own representative on the Federation Council,

Ishan Anjar, has been appointed president pro tempore, a position in which he will serve for no longer than sixty days, until a special election can be held. In the meantime, Starfleet needs you to perform your regular duties as best you can. *I* need you to do that. You are a fine crew, and we will get through this together."

The captain had looked again at Cenn, who nodded to her, clearly endorsing what she'd said. "Ro out," she finished, ending the announcement. She then asked a question of her first officer: "How do we go forward from here?"

"I don't know," Cenn had said. "I think we have to do what we Bajorans have been doing for a very long time: we just carry on."

At the time, Ro hadn't thought much of that answer, which had seemed to her like no answer at all. But as she stood looking at herself in the mirror that morning, she wondered if Cenn had been right after all: they could only place one foot in front of the next, marching from today into tomorrow. Eventually it would grow easier.

But probably not for a while, Ro thought. She realized that she needed to add yet another task to the list of her responsibilities that day. She should speak with Lieutenant Commander Matthias about the counseling needs of the crew. Ro's staff aboard the old station had included three counselors—Lieutenants Valeska Knezo and Hamish Collins had served under Matthias—and Starfleet had assigned a fourth—Ensign Valinar—during the crew's time at Bajoran Space Central. With the increase in the number serving aboard the new starbase, Bashir had added a fifth, Ensign Delinia Phlox, to the medical staff. In light of the upsetting events, though, Ro wanted to check with Matthias to see if she thought they should request additional counselors from Starfleet to serve temporarily on DS9.

Deeming her appearance acceptable, Ro left the refresher. She checked the time and saw it was just past zero six hundred hours, still almost two hours before she officially needed to report for her alpha-shift duty. Of course, starbase commanders could never truly consider themselves off duty unless they left their facility entirely. And in the current circumstances, Ro might not have enough hours in the day to do all she needed to do anyway.

So, despite the early hour, Ro Laren left her quarters to begin her workday. She entered the nearest turbolift and ordered it to take her to the very center of Deep Space 9.

In just a few moments, she arrived at the stockade complex.

Eighteen

Keev approached the gild encampment through the wood with a spring in her step. Altek walked beside her after they'd spent another laborious day clearing the rubble of the cave-in. The Cawlders had assisted them until late in the afternoon, but Keev and Altek had chosen to continue on into the evening. Days earlier, they had all felt the vaguest breath of air moving in the tunnel, an indication that they neared the end of the debris. Because of that tantalizing indication that their goal of opening up the cave might be in reach, Keev wanted to work as much as possible to get there. It had been months—far too long—since they'd been able to rescue any more Bajora from Joradell.

When Keev and Altek neared the gild camp, though, too many voices drifted from up ahead of them. *Not just too many voices,* Keev thought. *Unfamiliar voices.* She stopped, grabbing hold of Altek's arm to bring him to a halt too. She put a finger to her lips, then cupped her hand around her ear and listened. Altek did the same.

Keev heard a man's voice that she did not recognize . . . and a woman's . . . and a second woman's. She held up her other hand and counted off the strangers with her fingers: three . . . four . . . five. She balled her hand into a fist, then resumed counting: six . . . seven. She waited, but heard no more unknown voices.

"I hear Jennica," Altek said quietly, leaning in close to Keev. "And Cawlder Vinik." Keev listened specifically for those voices, and after a few moments she heard them too.

But I don't hear Veralla, she thought, then realized that she could stand next to him for hours and not hear him say a word.

"They don't sound to me like they're under duress," Altek said.

Keev listened for several moments more, then agreed. "All right," she said. "Let's go." She let her hand fall to her side, to the reassuring feel of the revolver beneath her jacket, at her hip.

They reached the camp quickly and called out the phrases that told the other gild members their identities and that they traveled alone. When they entered the clearing, Keev saw the faces to which all the new voices belonged: three women and four men, all of them in tattered garments that conveyed their status as slaves—clearly *former* slaves—of the Aleira. Their ages appeared to range from early thirties to late fifties.

Cawlder Losor came over and greeted Keev and Altek, then introduced them around. Like virtually all the Bajora they aided, each of the seven runaways offered voluble thanks. Keev and Altek visited with them while Renet prepared plates for the pair, who had worked past supper. The energy with which Keev had hiked back to the camp from the cave dissipated, and she resisted mentioning what had so pleased her and Altek earlier that evening.

Later, after the visible influences of B'hava'el on the sky had faded and the moons had risen, Keev waited until Veralla moved away from the campfire—gild members and fleeing slaves surrounding it—and over to where he kept his duffel. As he bent to retrieve something from it, she casually eased herself in his direction, to the outer reaches of the fire's glow, attempting to draw no notice to herself. She approached him quietly and from behind, but that didn't prevent him from knowing that she had followed him.

Without turning from where he rummaged in his duffel, Veralla said, "Yes, Keev, what can I do for you? You've wanted to speak with me all night." Not for the first time, she marveled at both the keenness of his senses and the force of his perceptiveness.

"I was surprised to see escaped slaves here again," Keev said. "And so many of them. The way is not yet clear."

"But it soon will be," Veralla said, almost as though he had stood beside Keev in the cave that evening. He closed his bag, then stood and turned to face her. As far as she could tell, he'd placed nothing inside it, nor removed anything from it. She understood that he had walked over there specifically so that she would have an opportunity to speak with him privately.

"Yes," Keev said. "Altek and I broke through the rubble earlier." She did not mention that after Altek had pulled away the stone that revealed a passage through the rubble, she had stepped into his arms. "It'll still take a day or two to finish clearing the way and reinforcing the cave, but we're almost there." She paused, then asked, "How did you know?"

Veralla offered a rare smile, though with only one side of his mouth, and with just the slightest curl moving his lips upward. "I have no magical powers, Anora," he said. "Everybody working in the cave has mentioned feeling a draft in the caverns, a sure sign that enough debris had been removed to allow the flow of air."

"Of course," Keev said, feeling a bit sheepish for her immoderate admiration of the gild leader.

"You did not speak of breaking through the rubble in front of the others," Veralla said.

"I resisted," Keev said. "I didn't know what your plans for these people were, so I didn't want to say anything."

Veralla nodded. "You were worried that some of them might be Aleiran spies."

"I *always* worry about that."

Veralla regarded her for a few silent moments. "They are all escaped slaves, none of them spies," he finally said. "The plan is to finish clearing the cave and then deliver five of the runaways to the road to Shavalla."

"Five?" Keev asked.

"The other two will become gild members."

"Oh," Keev said, surprised. Escaped slaves often enough wanted to contribute to the effort of freeing more Bajora, but seldom did Veralla allow it. Most of the time, newly freed slaves required rest and recuperation, from physical, mental, and emotional wounds.

Veralla took a step forward, so that they stood with almost no distance between them. The shadow of Keev's head eclipsed half his face, while the other half wavered in orange hues beneath the glow thrown by the fire. "You have served very well," he told her. "You have had a great hand in our success. Now, though, it is time for you to move on."

"What?" Keev thought she must not have understood him properly.

"It is time for you to go to Shavalla. It is time for you to go back home."

"I . . . I don't understand," Keev said. "If I've done something wrong—" She suddenly realized that Veralla must know about her and Altek, and that he clearly did not approve. "If this is about Altek . . ." She let her thought hang in the small space between them.

"It is not about Altek, and it is not about you doing anything wrong," Veralla reassured her. "You have done everything not only right, but well. That's why I have one last mission for you."

Keev stalked a few strides away. Not wanting the others to hear their conversation, though, she paced back over to Veralla. "What if I don't want a *last* mission?" she asked angrily. Then, thinking more about his choice of words, she said, "Wait. Do you mean . . . do you mean that I won't be coming back from this mission?"

As deadly serious as Veralla usually appeared, his features took on an even more severe aspect. "You have willingly risked your life for years in the service of freeing your fellow Bajora—and even some Aleira—from oppression. I would not ask you to embark on a mission that would likely end in your death."

Keev thought about that—about *all* of that, including her commitment to a cause she had never regretted joining. "I'm not saying I won't do it," she told Veralla.

"I'm not asking you to risk your life, Keev," he reiterated. "At least, no more than usual—and actually, probably quite a bit *less* than usual."

"I don't know what you're telling me."

"I'm telling you that we need something done, something important, and I trust you more than anybody else to accomplish it." Veralla stepped past Keev and addressed the others. "We're going for a short walk," he called. Faces turned toward them, but nobody questioned Veralla. "We won't be long."

Veralla walked to the edge of the clearing farthest from

the campfire, withdrew a beacon from his jacket pocket, and entered the wood. Keev followed dutifully—and with a degree of curiosity. She had no idea what Veralla wanted her to do—though she would argue with him again if he insisted that she abandon the gild.

They walked for several minutes, farther from the encampment than Keev had expected. Veralla finally stopped in a space that looked no different than any other around them, an area in which she saw nothing—no tree, no rock, no object or formation of any kind—that might have acted as a landmark. Still, she did not doubt that Veralla had brought her where he intended; his sense of direction always impressed her, and had, on occasion, astounded her.

Veralla set his beacon down to illuminate the area, then lowered himself to his knees and brushed fallen leaves and twigs from the ground in front of him. He opened his jacket, reached inside, and extracted a small spade, doubled in two. He unfolded the handle and began digging. Before too long, the spade struck something solid. Keev watched him work his way around a midsize wooden container until he had freed it from the earth. After setting aside the spade, he peered up at Keev. "Would you please help me with this?"

Keev kneeled on the opposite side of the newly dug hole, and together they lifted the container and set it on the ground. It felt substantial to Keev. *No, not the container,* she thought. *Whatever's in it.* It seemed heavy to her, though somehow also . . . motive . . . as though it allowed her and Veralla—or helped them—to move it.

"What is this?" she asked.

"It is your mission," Veralla said. "When we rescued the seven Bajora from Joradell, we also recovered this. I need you to deliver this all the way to Shavalla."

"And then stay there?"

Veralla sighed. "I would have you return to your life," he said. "But it is your choice."

Keev regarded the container. It appeared plain, though she saw some exotic markings carved into it. "What about Altek?" she asked. "Will he be the one coming with me?"

"I need you to make this journey on your own."

"What?" Of all Veralla had said to her that evening, that seemed the oddest. "We *always* travel in groups of two or more."

"I know," Veralla said. "It's a good policy—but not this time. This time, I need you to do this by yourself."

"Why?" Keev wanted to know.

"I cannot tell you." Keev could only stare at Veralla across the empty hole in the ground. "I cannot tell you because I do not know."

"That doesn't make any sense."

"It will," Veralla promised her. "And I can also tell you that when it does make sense to you and you deliver it to Shavalla, Altek Dans will follow you. He and the Cawlders will take the five freed slaves through the caverns and out the other side of the mountains. Only the Cawlders will return to the gild."

It suddenly sounded to Keev as though Veralla wanted her and Altek to leave, to travel to Shavalla, so that they could share a normal, safe life together. "Does Altek know about this?" Keev asked.

"Not yet," Veralla said. "But when he does, he will follow you."

Keev chose not to respond to that assertion, but she believed it true—and it made her happy.

She pointed to the container. "What is this?" she asked.

Veralla reached out as though to rest his hand atop it,

but he pulled back before doing so. "This," he told her, "is a Tear of the Prophets."

Keev gaped at the container in disbelief. "I thought—" she started, but then had to stop and swallow. "I thought the Tears were only legends."

"Not all legends are untrue," Veralla said. "I want you to take this to the temple in Shavalla."

Keev regarded the plain container and thought how incongruous it was that an object of such magnificence and power, of such importance, should be carried in such an ordinary vessel. Even as she examined the unadorned box, she could feel the pull of the object within. She did not doubt Veralla.

Unable to stop herself, Keev reached toward the container. When her fingertips touched it, she felt the uneven surface of the rough-hewn wood. Her hand also began to tingle . . . or she imagined that it did. She could not tell. It seemed almost as though she had reached out of one reality and into another, and yet sensed them both.

"You may open the ark," Veralla said. "You may look upon this Tear of the Prophets and see what you will see. Then you can decide if you will do as I've asked."

"I don't know," Keev said, unsure if she wanted to gaze upon such an object. *If I'm found unworthy—* But even before she could finish her thought, before she could frame her fear, she reached with both hands for the ark. She didn't know how she would open it, but then two of its sides came apart beneath her touch, dividing along a corner.

The brilliance that emanated from within the ark swirled around her. She saw a distinctive shape inside, rounded at the ends and narrower through the middle. It did not rest within the ark, but floated and rotated slowly, its surface not smooth but sharply ragged, as though composed of glass shards. It radiated an ethereal green glow, and as she beheld it, it flared and engulfed her.

At first, her body seemed to float, but then she lost all sense of her position, location, and even orientation. By degrees, Keev became aware of her own heartbeat, slow and steady, like the rhythmic pounding of a drum. Abruptly, a series of images sped across her mind: a standing man; a figure pulling white rock from a pile of rubble; a woman wearing a red headdress; and a girl. It took a moment for Keev's thoughts to catch up to her visualizations, but then she realized that she knew all the faces she saw, even as she grasped that the people represented something beyond themselves: the Prophets.

Keev suddenly stood in a clearing in the wood, in one of the many encampments she had set up over the years with her fellow gild members. She saw their duffels and bedrolls, and a small fire bordered by stones. The sun shined down from its midday zenith.

"Our hand has returned," said Veralla Sil from across the clearing.

Keev turned to look at him. Instead, she found herself looking through a narrow tunnel to a pile of earth and broken stone. As she watched, the debris began to tumble down from the top, more and more, until she could see past it and deeper into the caverns.

"Our hand has opened," said Altek Dans.

"Yes," Keev said, thinking, *I am the hand—and I have opened.*

She heard movement in the cave behind her, and she spun to see inside the Temple of the Bajora in Shavalla.

Candles lent their quivering spark to the round, high-walled space. More than halfway across the room, a table stood against the lone straight wall. A figure bent over the pages of a large tome there.

"Our hand rises where the roads meet," said Denoray Lunas, the spiritual leader of the Bajoran faith. Keev recognized the short, stout woman from pictures, but she had also in her youth once met Denoray, at the time a simple cleric. "There is where our message guides our hand."

"Yes," Keev said. "Guide me. Please guide me. How many roads meet?" She sensed movement beside her, and she turned her head to see Veralla in the clearing.

"Three roads," he said. "All roads meet."

"Some cross," said Altek in the cave.

"Some intersect," said Denoray in the temple.

Veralla crossed in front of Keev, stopped, and turned to face her in the clearing. "Some end."

"Which road ends?" Keev asked, believing that she needed to know the answer to a question she did not even understand.

"Many roads end," Denoray told her from the table in the temple. "The road of the Sisko ends."

The Sisko? Keev thought, unfamiliar with the term, but then another word, a name, bloomed in her mind: *Benjamin*. She said it aloud.

"Yes," said a small voice behind Keev. She turned, knowing she would not see the temple, and she did not. Instead, she stood in another room, a large stone hearth on one wall, and across from it, great windows offering views of a beautiful valley. A little girl peered up at her with confident eyes—the girl, Resten Ahleen, that Keev and Altek had rescued from Joradell, but several years younger, and without the crescent-shaped scar on her cheek. "The Sisko's road ends."

The girl walked in small steps past Keev, from the room in Benjamin's home to the battlements of a great fortress. "The Sisko's road—my father's road—ends," Ahleen repeated. "It leads here no more."

Keev leaned forward to peer down past the parapet, and she saw only a pair of shod feet. She followed the line of the body above them to see Veralla again, back in the clearing. "Time is a continuum," he said, "and the Sisko has altered his."

"He has departed the road that intersects with sorrow," Altek said, back in the caverns beneath the Merzang Mountains.

"He has departed the road that ends here," Ahleen said from atop the fortress wall.

"His road leads away," Denoray said in the temple, no longer at the table, but standing beside Keev. "He must be told."

"Is that the message that will guide me?" Keev asked.

"The message already guides you," Veralla said. "It brought you here."

"Three roads," Altek said. "Three peoples."

"The fortress must not fall," said Ahleen.

Keev closed here eyes, trying to commit to memory everything she had been told. None of it made sense to her, and yet somehow it did. It all seemed so familiar. She had never been there—*To the Celestial Temple!*—and yet she had been. She had been a closed hand sent back into the world to learn how to open.

And I did, Keev thought. She didn't know when, or how, but she knew that she had. She was sure of it.

When she opened her eyes, she stood before the long table in the temple. Denoray Lunas gazed across the pages of the ancient volume before her, then looked up at Keev.

"Follow the path," she said. "When you know where it ends, you will know how to begin."

Keev blinked, and when her eyelids opened, she saw Veralla closing the ark in front of her. She remained perched on her knees before it.

"Are you all right, Anora?" he asked. When Keev glanced at him, his eyes held a mixture of awe and fear. She gathered that he envied her whatever experience she'd just had, but that he worried that it had somehow harmed her. It hadn't. "Did the Tear of Destiny affect you?"

"The Tear of *Destiny*?" Keev said.

"Yes," Veralla told her. "So the ancient markings on the ark claim."

Keev nodded slowly, not quite understanding, but confident that she would. Veralla asked again if she was all right.

"I'm well," Keev said. "I'm very well." She pushed herself up and got to her feet. "And I'm taking the Tear to Shavalla."

Nineteen

Blackmer sat at a desk in one of the offices in the stockade complex, his eyes bleary and his head beginning to pound. He looked again over all the information he had in front of him. It all fit together, but something nagged at him.

"Jeff?"

Blackmer looked up to see Captain Ro standing in the doorless entry. "Captain," he said, startled to see her precisely at that moment, but not surprised that Ro had risen well before the start of alpha shift. "You're up early."

"And either you are too," Ro said, entering the office, "or you've been up all night. I hope it's not the latter."

"Well . . . not *all* night," Blackmer said, trying to mitigate the truth of his exhaustion, to which the captain would clearly object. "I went to my quarters at about oh two hundred."

"And how long did you stay there?" Ro asked.

"Just long enough to realize that I couldn't keep my eyes closed or shut off my brain," Blackmer said. He had actually lain down in bed, and maybe he had even dozed for a few minutes, but by zero four hundred hours, he'd returned to the stockade.

"I don't like hearing that, Jeff," the captain said. "I need you today."

"I'll be fine," Blackmer contended.

"You'll be fine if I order you to your quarters for some sleep," Ro said.

"You can do that, but you'd better have Doctor Bashir bring me some sort of medication, because right now, it doesn't feel like I'm ever going to sleep again."

Ro looked at him with sympathy, but she remained firm. "Believe me, I know the feeling," she said. "But we have to get this investigation done right, and we have to get it done *soon*."

Blackmer felt his brow furrow. "Soon? Why soon?"

"Because we can't keep the station locked down forever," Ro said. "Especially not with imperators and praetors in our midst."

"Oh. Right." *I should have thought of that,* Blackmer told himself. In fact, he had thought of it earlier, but it had slipped his mind. "Well, don't worry about me; I still have some power in my reactors. And Lieutenant Commander Douglas will be here at oh eight hundred."

"Jeff," Ro said. She stopped, took one of the chairs in front of the desk, and leaned in toward him. "Jeff, you've got an hour, and then it's off to your quarters for at least four hours. That's an order. And if you need Doctor Bashir to administer a soporific, then that'll be an order too."

Despite his claim a moment earlier, Blackmer didn't have the energy to argue. *Which should tell me that she's right,* he thought. "Well, fortunately, Captain, we may have just about everything we need already."

"What?" Ro asked. "Has she confessed?" The captain obviously referred to Enkar Sirsy, but Blackmer understood using a pronoun to identify her; he didn't like uttering her name either.

"No, she's maintaining her innocence," Blackmer

said. "Or at least that she remembers nothing about what happened."

"If she doesn't remember what happened," Ro asked, "then how can she be sure she didn't do it?"

"That was my question," Blackmer said.

"How long did you interrogate her?" Ro wanted to know.

"A couple of hours, total, in three separate conversations."

"Has the JAG office sent anybody down to talk with her?" Ro asked.

"Commander Desjardins came down himself," Blackmer said. Gregory Desjardins had arrived just ten days earlier, relocating the judge advocate general's office for the Bajor Sector to Deep Space 9. He did not fall within the starbase's chain of command. "He explained all of Enkar's rights, including his recommendation that, because of the extraordinary circumstance of the lockdown, she should accept preliminary representation by a member of the JAG office."

"And she did and then refused to answer any more questions," Ro concluded.

"No," Blackmer said. "I mean, she said she would accept a JAG attorney—Commander Desjardins took on the job himself—but she was still willing to talk with me and answer all my questions."

"By saying she didn't remember anything," Ro said, obviously frustrated.

"Whether that's relevant or not is up to somebody else to decide," Blackmer said. "For all I know, she might have had some sort of psychotic break and is telling the truth, although Doctor Bashir examined her and pronounced her perfectly healthy. Whether or not she genuinely doesn't remember what happened, though, it doesn't change the evidence."

"And what evidence do we have?" Ro asked. "Anything new since last night?"

"A number of things, actually." Blackmer turned to the computer interface on the desk and tapped a control surface to transfer the set of files he'd been studying to a padd. The interface beeped, and a moment later, one of the padds lying beside it chirped in response. Blackmer picked up the device and handed it to Ro. "If you look at the first file, you'll see that we have a rough time line of her whereabouts before and during the dedication. Sensors place her in the quarters assigned to the first minister at twelve thirty hours yesterday, which was the last time Minister Asarem saw her. Sensors also show her returning to her own cabin, but shortly after that, she drops off the grid."

"Didn't the first minister notice her chief of staff's absence?" Ro asked. A day earlier, when faced with the claim that Enkar Sirsy had assassinated the president of the Federation, Asarem Wadeen had rejected it outright. The minister had known and worked with Enkar for a decade and a half, and they'd had a very close professional relationship for ten of those years.

"Minister Asarem and Lustrate Vorat chose to walk to the dedication together, accompanied by their protection details, of course," Blackmer said. "Enkar was supposed to arrive later, along with Onar Throk, one of Castellan Garan's aides who stayed behind to assist the lustrate. When she didn't appear at his quarters as scheduled, he tried to contact her, and then he went to her cabin, but she didn't seem to be there. He shrugged it off and went to the dedication himself."

"And by that time, she'd already fallen off the sensor grid?" Ro asked.

"It would appear so," Blackmer said. "Meaning the next question is: how did she get into the control booth?"

"It couldn't have been by transporter if sensors couldn't read her," Ro said.

"Not necessarily," Blackmer said. "If she was transported from her cabin, she would have vanished from the sensor grid there, but if she materialized with a sensor block in the booth, she never would have reappeared. That would also explain why I couldn't beam her out of there after the fact. Once we took her from the booth, we were able to beam her directly into the stockade."

"So that's what you think happened?" Ro said. "That she transported from her quarters to the booth?"

"It seems most likely," Blackmer said. "I'm an eyewitness to her presence there after the assassination, and Doctor Bashir's examination has placed her there at the time of it."

"What? How?"

"He detected significant amounts of chemical residue on Enkar's hands and clothing," Blackmer said. "That's the second file." He waited as the captain accessed the data.

"Barium, antimony, and lead," she read from the padd.

"Elements associated with combustion in the firing of the projectile weapon with which she was found," Blackmer said. "And Lieutenant Commander Candlewood performed a ballistic analysis on the three projectiles removed from the president's body. He confirms that they were fired by that weapon."

Ro sat back in her chair. "That's all pretty compelling," she said. "If only she'd used a modern weapon."

"She obviously knew not to," Blackmer said. "It's not

as though we hid our general security setup from our visitors." A dampening field on the station prevented the discharge of any energy weapons not specifically assigned to starbase personnel, and such weapons functioned only when wielded by their registered users. "The doctor also found nothing physically out of the ordinary with Enkar. There was no indication that she had been drugged. And there's more," Blackmer continued. "I wondered how anybody could have transported from one point on the station to another without a security alert being triggered. Our own transporters weren't used, and any beam originating outside the station would have raised an alarm. All of which seems to indicate the use of a portable unit. But that takes energy, and no power sources capable of driving a portable transporter have been detected on Deep Space Nine."

"Could she have tapped into the starbase's power grid?" Ro asked.

"That was my thought," Blackmer said. "So I had Lieutenant Commander Nog sweep the sensor logs looking for any anomalies. His results are in the third file."

Ro tapped the padd and read what appeared in the display. "Ten separate power drains? *Ten?*"

"Yes," Blackmer said, "but each small enough to be within normal fluctuations for the power grid. But you can see that they all occurred at roughly the same time and would have provided more than enough power to use a portable transporter to beam a person to the control booth."

Ro continued to study the data on the padd for a few more seconds, and then she set it down on the desk. "This is fine work, Jeff," she said. "This is incontrovertible."

"It is, but . . ." He didn't finish his thought, but he

brought his hands together, wrapping the fingers of one around the fist of the other.

"Something's troubling you," Ro said. "The portable transporter."

"Yes," he said. "Where is it? That, and the sensor block in the control booth. We haven't been able to find either piece of equipment."

"Could they have self-destructed?"

"Possibly," Blackmer said. "But we've reviewed the sensor logs, and we don't see anything like that."

"The readings could have been blocked," Ro pointed out.

"Yeah, maybe," Blackmer agreed. "But if the plan was to destroy evidence, then why leave the weapon? And why didn't she transport out of the booth?"

"If there was a sensor block in the control booth, how could she beam away?" Ro said. "And maybe she wanted to be caught."

"And now is having second thoughts, so she's claiming not to remember anything," Blackmer said. "It doesn't sound quite right to me. I'd feel a lot more confident about all the evidence we've collected if we could find the portable transporter." In the middle of a frown, he yawned widely.

"Jeff, you need to get some sleep," Ro said. "Who's your lead on delta shift today?"

"Lieutenant ch'Larn," Blackmer said. Lieutenant junior grade Shanradeskel ch'Larn—known as Deskel—had been a member of the DS9 crew on the original station, and he'd been one of only eleven Andorians aboard who had not resigned their commissions after their world seceded from the Federation. "He's leading a search team in Enkar's guest quarters right now."

"All right." Ro stood up. "I'll go consult with Deskel. In the meantime, you have your orders, Lieutenant Commander Blackmer: sleep."

"I'll try, Captain."

"At the very least, you need to rest," Ro told him.

"Yes, sir." He rose from his chair, and they walked out to the turbolift together.

Blackmer went to his quarters and crawled into bed, where he slept far better than he expected. Five hours later, when he checked in with Sarina Douglas, he learned that their efforts had paid off: his security staff had found the portable transporter device, hidden behind a bulkhead in Enkar Sirsy's guest cabin.

Twenty

K eev woke up that morning in darkness, as she usually did, but even earlier. She shared a cold meal with
Veralla and Altek while all the others—gild members
and escaped slaves—slept. At her request, nobody besides
Altek had been told that she would be leaving on her own,
possibly for good. It had been three days since Veralla had
asked her to bring the Tear of the Prophets—the Tear of
Destiny—to Shavalla, and in that time, the gild had finished clearing the tunnel and shoring up its walls and roof.
Keev would deliver the Tear to the Bajoran city, but she
remained undecided about staying there permanently. She
hadn't discussed it with Altek at any length, but when he
arrived in Shavalla, clearly they would make their decision
together.

"Are you ready?" Veralla asked her. The three of them
had walked out into the wood and unearthed the Tear of
Destiny in its ark.

"Yes," Keev said. She carried water, a beacon, and a
revolver at her waist, and a small duffel slung over her
shoulder that contained tools and small explosives. She
had concern that the Tear would not fit through some
of the tighter areas within the caverns, and so she had
brought the means to expand those just enough to allow
her to carry it through.

"I know you don't care for sentiment in situations like this," Veralla said, "but I want to tell you that you are a kind, compassionate, brave woman, and it has been my privilege to work with you in our gild."

"Veralla—" she began, but he held up a hand.

"I know how you feel," he told her. "Just . . . be well." And to Keev's surprise, he leaned in and kissed her on the cheek. He then turned to Altek. "Take as much time as you need," he said, and he walked off into the darkness toward their camp. Altek watched him go before turning back to face Keev.

"I still don't understand why we can't go together," he said.

"I don't really understand it either," Keev said, "but I trust Veralla. If this is what he wants us to do, it must be for the best."

Altek nodded, though he looked unconvinced. "Please be careful."

"I will be," Keev promised. "I want you to be careful too."

"I will be," Altek assured her. "And I'll be right behind you."

"You'd better be," Keev said. "If you're not in Shavalla within a day of when I arrive, I'm coming back after you."

Altek smiled. "I like the idea of you coming after me."

Keev returned his smile. "I bet you do." She stepped forward until her body pressed against his. She looked up into his eyes, and they kissed.

When they parted, Keev retrieved the ark and started off into the wood, in the direction of the mountains and the caverns underneath. She glanced back over her shoulder, but the dense undergrowth quickly stole Altek from her sight. Still, she heard him say one last thing to her, not loudly, not calling after her, but in his normal speaking voice.

"I love you, Anora," he said.

"I love you, Dans," she replied.

Keev couldn't tell whether or not he heard her.

Half an hour into the cave, Keev saw a bluish glow in the distance, up around a curve in the tunnel. It did not surprise her to see it, nor did it concern her. *After my experience with the Tear of Destiny,* she thought, *I'm not sure what would surprise me.*

Keev continued on until she rounded the bend into the long, narrow portion of the caverns in which the cave-in had occurred. Up ahead, where the gild had removed the rubble and added columns and beams and joists for safety, the blue glow intensified. As though in reply, a greenish emanation began to leak from the joints in the ark she carried.

The Tear of Destiny, Keev thought. *I will walk the path that the Prophets have set out for me.*

Keev narrowed her eyes against the glare, but it did not overwhelm her in the same way that the Tear had when first she'd seen it. She strode forward, confident, unconcerned, even excited. As she drew closer, she saw that the columns the gild had installed had become translucent, their surfaces in motion like a pond beneath a spring rain. Concentric circles stippled their surface, enlarging until they faded away.

Stopping just before the first columns, Keev saw that the support beams and joists had lost their appearance of solidity. White and blue streamers of light danced within their forms, swimming in gentle arcs, dazzling her with their complexity and beauty. Keev did not know what lay ahead, but she wanted to find out.

As she walked forward, the blue and white illuminated shapes surrounded her. Keev could feel her legs moving, carrying her along in the cave, but she had the sensation of flying out in space, high above her world. *This must be what the Celestial Temple is truly like.*

Keev passed one pair of columns after another, losing count of them as she moved forward. She wondered if Veralla knew this would happen. She didn't think he did, not specifically, but he must have had some notion that Keev had been meant to make such a journey.

When she reached the last pair of columns that marked the reinforced section of the cave, Keev could not see past them. The blue-white glow surrounding her clouded her view, and yet she knew that she had come to the end of that section of the tunnel. In a way, she didn't want to continue ahead—not out of fear or any concern about the unknown, but because she already felt as though she'd come home.

But this is not my destiny, she thought. *The Celestial Temple or whatever this might be is not my destiny—at least not right now.*

Keev took one step forward, and by the time she'd brought her back foot even with her first, the enveloping light had vanished. The cave walls and roof had vanished. Instead, she stood inside a building, in a hallway, only a bare bulb hanging on a wire providing a dim reprieve from darkness. A door stood closed before her. She knew that she had been in the hall before, although she couldn't remember the circumstances.

The green glow of the Tear no longer leaked from the ark in Keev's arms. She looked down at the plain container, and she saw clothing that she didn't recognize. She wore a dark red jacket and matching skirt over a white blouse. Somehow, though, the outfit felt right.

Keev bent down and set the ark on the floor. When she stood up, she took a deep breath and thought, *Destiny.* Then she raised her hand and knocked on the door.

Keev waited. She heard voices on the other side of the door—a man and a woman, it sounded like. Then she heard footsteps and a series of locks being unlatched. The doorknob turned, and then—

The doors separated and slid apart. A tall, dark man stood there, clad in what looked like a uniform, mostly black, but with gray shoulders and a crimson collar. The Emissary of the Prophets.

"Hello, Benjamin," Kira said. She experienced a moment where she felt so dizzy that she thought she might pass out. She closed her eyes and tilted her head down, trying to regain her balance. When she opened her eyes, she saw that she wore the traditional brown robe that vedeks often favored.

"Nerys," Benjamin said, and Kira thought, *Anora, my name is Anora.* "You're all right."

"Of course, I'm all right," Kay Eaton said. She felt herself wrinkle her nose at her friend Benny. He stood there in a muddy green shirt and dark gray slacks. "You didn't think a little accident would keep me down for long, did you?" Eaton recalled the collision that had sprung a leak in her boat . . . but she also remembered the collapse of the Celestial Temple . . . and a cave-in.

"I . . ." Benny started, but he looked confused.

"Cat got your tongue, Benny?" Eaton asked. "This oughta loosen it." She held up a bottle of red wine she didn't even recall she'd been carrying. *Wasn't I carrying something else? Something larger and more important?* She couldn't remember, but she entered the apartment, and Benny closed the door after her.

Once she had walked deep into the room, Kira faced Benjamin across the desk in his ready room aboard *Robinson*. She set down the elegant curved bottle of springwine and waited for Benjamin to turn toward her. When he did, he said, "Nerys?"

"It's time to celebrate, Benjamin," Kira said. That seemed perfectly appropriate to her.

"That you're alive?" Benjamin asked.

"We don't need to celebrate that I'm alive," Kira told him. "We need to celebrate that *you* are."

"I've got glasses," said a voice to Kira's left, and she saw Kasidy Yates walking over from the replicator. She held three fragile-looking flutes in her hands, which she set down beside the springwine.

"I . . . I don't understand," Benny said.

Eaton pulled the cork from the bottle and poured the deep-red liquor into three water glasses. She handed one to Cassie and then one to Benny. She took the third glass for herself and held it aloft before her. "To family," she said, and then she held her glass out, first toward Cassie, then toward Benny. "To mother, father—" She motioned toward where Becky slept on the couch. "—and daughter." Eaton sipped from her glass, as did Cassie, and finally Benny did too.

"We're a mother and father and daughter," Benjamin said, "but we can't be a family." He spoke the words as though they impaled him.

"Yes, you can," Kira said, completely sure of herself. *The Prophets told me Themselves.* "You can be a family."

"Nerys," Benjamin said. He placed his flute of springwine down on his desk. "You know how much I want that to be true, but you also know the Prophets' warning to me."

"I do know," Kira said. "You told them that you wanted

to spend your life with Kasidy, and They told you that if you did, you would know nothing but sorrow."

Beside Benjamin, Kasidy closed her eyes. She wore her pain like an open wound. "As much as I want to," Benjamin said, "there's nothing I can do."

Kira smiled. "But you already have done something," she said. "You haven't spent your life with Kasidy."

Kasidy opened her eyes. "What are you saying, Nerys?"

"I'm saying that nearly eight years ago, the Prophets told Benjamin that if he spent his life with you, he would know nothing but sorrow," Kira explained. "But he defied their warning, and, eventually, the prophecy began to fulfill itself: Benjamin began to know nothing but sorrow. But then he stopped spending his life with you, so there's no longer anything to be concerned about. You can be together."

"What?" Benjamin said. "If I go back to Kasidy, we'll be right back where we started."

"No, you won't be," Kira insisted. "There's an old saying: you can't step twice into the same river."

"What does that mean?" Kasidy wanted to know.

"It means that as a river flows, it changes," Kira said. "When you enter it for the first time, it's in a certain state. Every drop of water in a particular place, exerting a particular force on the drop next to it. But just by entering the river, you change it. If you leave it and enter it a second time, the drops of water have moved, their forces have changed, and it's not the same river."

"And time is a river?" Benjamin said. He sounded desperate to believe what she told him.

"The Prophets say that it's a continuum," Kira said.

"You've spoken to the Prophets?" Kasidy asked. "Did they save you?"

"They've spoken to me," Kira said. She set her glass down on Benjamin's desk. "Benjamin, they want you to know that you can enter your continuum again."

Benjamin's lips spread into a broad smile. "I'm going to transport down to Bajor," he said. "I'm going to consult an Orb. I'll—"

"Benjamin," Kira said, casting her gaze downward. She knew that she had to tell him all of it.

"What?" Kasidy asked, clearly frightened by whatever Kira might say next. "What is it?"

"Benjamin, you have fulfilled your destiny," Kira said, looking back up at him. "At least, with the Prophets."

"They're done with Ben?" Kasidy asked, excitement rising in her voice.

Kira continued to peer at Sisko, but she didn't say anything. She didn't have to. She knew that he understood precisely what she meant. She thought that maybe he'd understood it for a long time. He'd accomplished all the tasks the Prophets had set him. They therefore had no further need to communicate with him, to be a part of his life.

Benjamin didn't say anything, and Kira watched his face cycle through a scale of emotions: anger, fear, relief, joy, and perhaps finally acceptance. "You're sure, Nerys?" he asked. "About all of it? The Prophets are done with me, but I can safely go back to Kasidy?"

"I'm sure of it," Kira said.

Sisko looked at Kasidy. "Then we *can* celebrate," he told her. "If you'll have me."

Cassie held up her glass of red wine. "To family," she said.

"To family," Eaton echoed, tapping her glass against Cassie's with a clink.

Benny reached forward and touched his own glass against the other two. "To family," he said. He lifted the wine to his lips, closed his eyes, and drank. He looked as though he partook of ambrosia.

And in a real way, Keev thought, *he did.*

At the end of the evening, Kay Eaton said good night to her friends Benny and Cassie. Kira Nerys turned away from a man who had once been her commanding officer, who had become a religious icon to her, and who continued to be a wonderful friend. As Eaton opened the door to the hall, she glanced back. Kira said good-bye again to Benjamin and Kasidy, then exited *Robinson*'s ready room.

In the hall, Keev heard the latch click closed behind her. She turned to look at the door, but she saw only the wall of the cave, bathed a stark white in the light of the beacon she had attached to her arm. *I guess it's time to move on,* she thought.

Keev bent and retrieved the ark containing the Tear of Destiny. She gazed back through the tunnel, back the way she had come, and saw the rugged timbers the gild had used to secure their passage through the area of the cave-in. The light of her beacon didn't even reach the columns farthest away from her.

Then Keev Anora continued her journey to Shavalla.

Twenty-one

Ro stood at the rounded rectangular port in her office, hands behind her back, and gazed out at the stars. She hadn't slept well the previous night, the third in a row since the assassination of President Bacco, but at least she'd finally gotten some measure of rest. When she had woken up that morning, though, the memory of the terrible events of three days prior immediately fell over her like a pall. She proceeded through the day feeling as though she hauled around a tremendous burden, unable to shake the dread pervading her mind. She wondered how long it would take for life to feel normal again.

Has my life ever *felt normal?* she asked herself.

Ro adjusted her eyes and focused on her reflection in the port. "Nice try," she said aloud, chastising herself. She liked to think of herself as tough, having lived through so many trying times, and also as different, having frequently had difficulties fitting in and making friends. But the Federation contained more than nine trillion individuals—and that didn't count all the people in the Klingon Empire and the Cardassian Union and the Ferengi Alliance and all the others—so how tough and how different could she really be? Trying to tell herself that she didn't feel normal—whatever that might be—because she never felt normal missed the point: the president's death troubled her greatly, impacting her in a way that unsettled her and would likely continue to do so for some time. Perhaps the sooner she could fully accept that, the sooner she could heal.

I need to make an appointment with Phillipa, she thought. Until Ro had arrived on the original Deep Space 9, she hadn't had much use for counselors—at least not for herself. Somewhere along the way, though, she'd had a casual conversation with Phillipa Matthias over tea in the Replimat. Ro couldn't recall precisely when that had been, but she thought maybe it had been during the period after Bajor had joined the Federation and she'd needed to choose whether or not to apply for reentry into Starfleet. She liked the counselor personally and found her easy to talk to, but she thought nothing more about her until everything that had taken place with Taran'atar.

Taran'atar, Ro thought, remembering the fearsome presence of the Jem'Hadar elder. When Odo had returned to the Dominion after the war, he'd sent Taran'atar to Deep Space 9 as an observer, hoping both to cement a lasting peace between the Alpha and Gamma Quadrants, and to bring a new perspective to a member of a species specifically bred as soldiers. Ro had gotten to know him, and had grown to consider him a friend.

And then he had brutally attacked her, damaging her spine and facing her with the possibility of permanent paralysis. Ro found it hard enough dealing with the physical trauma and the threat of her potentially life-altering wounds, but the betrayal of trust cut her even more deeply. Although she later learned that Taran'atar had been forced to his violent deeds, and even though he made the only amends he really could, Ro could not seem to get over the emotional pain that the entire incident had caused her, and so she had sought out Counselor Matthias.

That was what? Ro thought. *Seven or eight years ago?* It seemed impossible to her that she'd stayed in the same place for so long, after living a largely itinerant existence, and she thought that the counselor had helped make that happen. Phillipa had taught Ro how to look inward without tearing herself apart, had allowed her to grow more comfortable within her own skin, had let her see that happiness was not something that happened only to other people, but was a *choice* she could make for herself.

Speaking with Counselor Matthias had benefited Ro in so many ways, had helped her endure so much—from Taran'atar's treachery, return, and subsequent death, all the way through the destruction of Deep Space 9 and the loss of all those still aboard the station. She doubted that she could have served successfully as Captain Vaughn's first officer without the benefit of Phillipa's counsel through the years. *And I sure as hell never would have been capable of rising to the rank of captain and the position of starbase commander.*

Ro dropped her gaze and looked down upon the curve of Deep Space 9's sphere and the horizontal ring arcing around it. After the glut of spacecraft in previous days, the station looked not nearly as crowded. Earlier that day, Ro had taken DS9 off lockdown, allowing the visiting delegations to depart, and nearly all of them—Cardassian, Klingon, Gorn, and Romulan—had done so at once, and the first minister and her party—save for one member, of course—would likely be returning home within the next day or two. Asarem had already addressed her people, via the Bajoran comnet, about President Bacco's assassination.

Enkar Sirsy remained in custody in the stockade. Her

guilt had appeared obvious when she'd been caught with a weapon immediately after the assassination, and the continuing investigation the next day had turned up only evidence reinforcing her culpability. Although it had not been easy with all the heads of state aboard, Ro had kept the lockdown in place for that third day, wanting to make absolutely sure that her security and medical staffs were completely convinced of Enkar Sirsy's identity as the lone assassin. One small detail still troubled Blackmer—he hadn't yet been able to locate a sensor block in the theater's control booth—but the overwhelming consensus of Ro's staff—as well as that of the JAG office—remained that Enkar had perpetrated the crime, and that she had acted alone. Finally, the captain had little choice but to throw wide Deep Space 9's hatches and allow the dignitaries to head home.

The first minister's chief of staff no longer proclaimed her innocence, though she also refused to admit her guilt. She continued to maintain that she had no memory of the incident. Enkar waited for the attorney she'd chosen to arrive from Bajor, as well as a Federation judge so that she could be arraigned. Ro could only hope that the trial would take place on Bajor, or somewhere else entirely, rather than on DS9.

She also hoped that the president's body would soon be removed from the station. It remained in the morgue, awaiting the arrival of a Starfleet vessel to retrieve it. Captain Dax had been scheduled to escort President Bacco to Cardassia after the dedication ceremony, but Starfleet Command was in the process of reassigning ships in the wake of the assassination. At the moment, Ro didn't know which starship would travel to Deep Space 9 so that its crew could recover the body, or when it would arrive.

Ro peered along the horizontal ring, where she saw two ships still docked: *Aventine* and *Robinson*. Lieutenant Commander Stinson had taken *Defiant* out on routine patrol, though she suspected that he—and probably the members of the crew he'd taken with him—had simply wanted to get off the starbase. That day, the general mood on DS9 had settled into a pervasive numbness. Ro wished she knew how best to combat that. She hoped that the influx of ten thousand new residents—which Cenn had pushed back and would take place beginning three days hence—would help restore a sense of normalcy to her crew—and to herself.

Captain Dax had informed Ro that *Aventine* would be departing the starbase in the morning, while Captain Sisko awaited confirmation of his existing orders, which would see *Robinson* embark on an extended exploratory mission out beyond the Bajoran system. After the death of President Bacco, Starfleet Command had put such assignments on hold until they could determine whether its matériel might be required elsewhere.

Other than those ships and the first minister's transport, the only vessel still moored at Deep Space 9—though Ro couldn't see it from her office—was *Wealth*, the Ferengi starship that had brought the grand nagus there. The captain had hoped to spend some time with Quark's brother and his family after the dedication ceremony, but circumstances had prevented that from happening. With Rom also leaving the next morning, Ro supposed that such a visit would have to wait.

Turning from the port, Ro stepped over to the replicator, intending to order a glass of *pooncheenee*, a Bajoran fruit juice usually served at breakfast, but then she thought that perhaps she wanted something a bit stronger than that. She knew that the time closed in on midnight and that she should probably go to her quarters and try to get some sleep, but the idea of a quick stop at Quark's appealed to her. Given the mood on the starbase, she'd likely be in there by herself, but a quiet drink—

The door signal chimed, sounding twice, indicating that somebody had come to her office via the corridor, rather than through the Hub. Ro turned from the replicator and said, "Come in." The door panels parted and withdrew into the bulkhead, revealing Asarem Wadeen. Two members of her protective detail stood behind her, and Ro knew that, even though she couldn't see them, two of DS9's own security team also attended her.

"First Minister," Ro said, surprised by the visit—and also wary of it. She had not lost sight of the fact that she had arrested Asarem's chief of staff for the murder of the Federation president. "Please come in."

Asarem entered the office by herself, and the doors whisked closed behind her. The first minister wore a puce, calf-length dress, with a chocolate-colored bolero jacket. She looked elegant and professional, though signs of strain showed on her face. "I trust I'm not interrupting," she said.

"Not at all," Ro said. "Please, have a seat." She waved in the direction of her sofa. Asarem walked over and sat down. "I was just thinking of getting myself a glass of juice. May I offer you something?"

"No, thank you, Captain," Asarem said. "I won't be staying long. In fact, one of the reasons I've come is to let you know that I'm leaving for Bajor."

Ro crossed the compartment and took a seat at the other end of the sofa. "Thank you for informing me, Minister," she said. "Obviously, I wish we could have hosted you here in better circumstances."

Asarem nodded. "I also came here to thank you for your handling of this situation. I know it couldn't have been easy."

"It wasn't easy only because of what caused the need for our arrest of Enkar Sirsy," Ro said. "Honestly, there were no political considerations for me. Enkar was captured almost in the act of the crime, and the evidence against her is exceedingly strong."

The first minister looked down into her lap, where she folded her hands together. When she looked back up, the expression on her face displayed determination. "Notwithstanding all of that evidence, I stand by my chief of staff."

Ro didn't quite know how to respond. Since Enkar had been taken into custody, Asarem had mentioned more than once that she had trouble believing that a woman she'd known for fifteen years, a woman with whom she had worked in close proximity for a decade, could have committed the heinous crime of which she'd been accused. Ro had listened to those plaints, but she had not addressed them. It seemed clear, though, that Asarem wanted her to say something.

"Minister, I can certainly understand why all of this bothers you," Ro said, trying to find her way to a diplomatic reply. "I've known Enkar Sirsy for almost ten years myself, and I never would have predicted her doing anything even remotely like this. I can't explain it. I can only have my crew collect and analyze all the available evidence."

"I understand that, Captain," Asarem said. "Please understand me, though: I am not complaining to you that somebody I know and like is not guilty *because* I know and like her, or because her guilt could cause me considerable political strife. I am telling you that Enkar Sirsy could not have assassinated President Bacco so that you will not lose sight of the need to find out who actually did so."

"We have not stopped searching for additional evidence, or analyzing the evidence we've already collected," Ro said. "I can assure you that we all want to learn the truth and to ensure that President Bacco's assassin faces justice, and holding an innocent person responsible would satisfy neither of those aims. If anything casts the slightest doubt on Enkar's guilt, it will be brought to light."

"The next time you speak with your chief of security," Asarem said, "you will learn that I have questioned one small piece of evidence already." The statement surprised Ro, both because of the first minister's claim, and because she hadn't heard anything from Blackmer. "I asked to read the statement that your security chief made about him finding Sirsy. He declared that she was lying on the floor and possibly unconscious when he first saw her."

"That is my understanding," Ro said cautiously, not wanting to contribute to any sort of misunderstanding that had arisen.

"Lieutenant Commander Blackmer also asserted that the weapon used to . . . used against the president lay on the floor beside Sirsy's right hand," Asarem went on. "But Sirsy is left-handed."

The first minister's contention reminded Ro of a plot point she might have read in a mystery novel. "I will check on those details," she told Asarem. "I believe what you say, but even if it's true, I'm afraid that it is hardly irrefutable proof of Enkar's innocence. Assuming that she is guilty but invented her story of not remembering what happened, she could well have placed the weapon beside her right hand specifically in an attempt to sow doubt."

"I grant you that the possible inconsistency I've identified is a slight detail," Asarem said. "I mention it only to suggest to you that all may not be as it seems to be." She stood up and started toward the door, and Ro followed. "I urge you not to abandon your search for the truth, Captain. Thank you for your time."

"Thank you, First Minister."

Asarem exited, and the captain watched her go. Even after the door closed, Ro stood there, trying to evaluate her brief conversation with the first minister. She had always read Asarem as genuine, although most certainly a politician. Ro couldn't tell if the first minister had been looking for some sort of political cover by saying what she had, or if she meant to coerce—or even threaten—the captain.

Or maybe she just really believes in her chief of staff's innocence, she thought.

Alone in her office, Ro shook her head. "You know what?" she said aloud. "I do need a drink."

She left her office, headed for Quark's.

Lieutenant Commander Nog peeked inside the cabin, stealing one last look at his half sister as she lay sleeping in her bed. When Bena had been born, he'd thought her combination of Ferengi and Bajoran characteristics an unfortunate mix: the outsize shape of her head and her wide nose, joined with rhinal ridges and a patch of brown hair, along with ears too small by one standard and too large by the other. Just shy of her ninth birthday, though, she had become a darling little girl. Her hair had grown long and full, and she wore it down over her ears. Nog thought that her wide Ferengi nose with Bajoran folds lent her an exotic look. Of course, he might have been a bit biased.

Nog stepped back and let the door ease soundlessly

closed. He walked back to the center of the living area of his father's quarters aboard *Wealth*. "She's so adorable," he said.

Rom looked up from where he sat beside Leeta on the sofa. "I know," he said. "She takes after her mother."

"Oh," Leeta said, reaching over to place a hand atop Rom's chest. She had her shoes off and her legs curled up beneath her. "Nobody could be cuter than you."

"She's got Leeta's brain too," Rom said. "Bena knows all the Rules of Acquisition, and she can name every single grand nagus, all the way back to Gint, in order." He beamed with a father's pride.

"And she can list every single kai, all the way up to Pralon Onala," Leeta added.

Nog smiled around his mouthful of sharp, misaligned teeth—an act that felt very good after the past few days on DS9. The murder of the Federation president had been horrible by itself, but it still made Nog shudder to think that, just moments earlier, his father had stood exactly where Bacco had when she'd been killed. He thanked the Great Exchequer that Rom had not been a victim himself.

Not wanting to dwell on what had happened, he told his father and Leeta, "I think you two might already have mentioned all that about Bena." Lately, every single message that Nog received from them included a catalogue of his sister's most recent feats. "You two probably expect her to become the grand nagus *and* the kai."

Leeta looked abashed, pulling her head into her shoulders, and she turned toward Rom.

"She could do it," he said. "If she wanted to, I'm sure she could do both jobs."

Nog just shook his head, while Leeta laughed. "You really are the proud papa, aren't you?" she said.

"Absolutely I am." Rom actually puffed out his chest. "My son was the first Ferengi in Starfleet, so why couldn't my daughter be the first Bajoran nagus and the first Ferengi kai?"

Leeta sat up, still smiling. "No reason whatsoever," she said. She stood and walked over to Nog. "I hate to have to say good-bye, but I'm really tired." She opened her arms and hugged him.

"That's all right," Nog said. "It was so good to see you, even if . . ." He had no interest in finishing his sentence and mentioning the assassination, and so he didn't. "Have a good trip back to Ferenginar."

Rom rose from the sofa as well. "Uh, I was thinking about going to say good-bye to Quark."

"Your brother just left here an hour ago," Leeta said. "We already said our farewells."

"I know," Rom said, "but I don't get to see him very often these days."

"I'll go with you," Nog chimed in, and Rom looked pleadingly at Leeta.

"Oh, all right," she said, and then she pointed at Nog. "Don't you let your father stay out too late; he hasn't gotten very much sleep the last few nights."

None of us has, Nog thought but didn't say.

As Leeta crossed the living area toward their bedroom, Nog and Rom headed out of the cabin and toward the hatch that would take them to Deep Space 9. The nagal bodyguards—a pair of muscle-bound bruisers from Clarus IV—followed behind them. When the group reached the starbase, two Starfleet security officers joined them as well. They all boarded a turbolift, which Nog directed to take them to Quark's.

"Obviously this trip didn't turn out like you planned," Nog told his father.

"Not like any of us planned," Rom agreed.

"But I'm still glad that I got to see you, Father."

"I'm glad I got to see you too," Rom said. "This is really quite a starbase you've designed and built."

"Well, I didn't do it by myself."

"No, of course not," Rom said. "But you're a good engineer. I can tell that there's a lot of you in this place."

"Thank you, Father." Rom's pride gratified Nog more than he could say.

"So . . . how is my brother doing?" Rom asked. "Really?"

"I think he's doing quite well these days, actually," Nog said.

"Really? I know he tells me that when he sends me messages on Ferenginar, but there have been so few people in the bar since we got here. And my brother did nothing but complain."

"Oh, you know Uncle Quark," Nog said as the turbo-lift slowed to a stop. "If he earned all the latinum in the quadrant, he'd complain that he had no place to keep it."

Rom chuckled as the doors opened. "That *does* sound like my brother." He and Nog stepped out into the atrium and headed toward the outer circle of the Plaza.

"The place he opened on Bajor has done really well, and even though he's moved to Deep Space Nine, he's still going to keep it," Nog said. "And the reason that the bar here has been mostly empty is that the crew were so busy getting the station ready for full operation, and then after what happened . . ." Again, Nog chose not to mention the obvious. "Once all the new civilian residents arrive and we open for business, Uncle Quark's will be packed, I'm sure."

"I hope so," Rom said. "For his sake."

"Don't worry about him," Nog said. "He'll be—" As they reached the wide main walkway of the Plaza and turned left toward Quark's, Nog stopped talking. "Do you hear that, Father?"

"I do," Rom said. "Voices . . . coming from Quark's."

"I thought the place might be empty tonight, but I guess not."

As they neared the bar, Nog realized that, although the place might not be empty, the customers spoke in quiet tones. Rather than the raucous environment Quark preferred to promote, and that typically produced greater profits, it sounded more like the hushed conversations heard in the presence of liquidators from the Ferengi Commerce Authority. That seemed understandable, considering the mood on the starbase.

"I hear Chief O'Brien," Rom said as they continued toward the bar.

"I do too," Nog said, listening. He tried to distinguish other voices. "I also hear Doctor Bashir . . . and Captain Ro."

As they reached the bar, Nog saw a handful of people scattered throughout the first level, with the largest contingent seated around a sizable table near the center. Chief O'Brien, Doctor Bashir, and Captain Ro all sat there, as did Captain Dax and even Captain Sisko. "Look," Rom said, gesturing toward one end of the bar. "I thought he was on Bajor."

Nog peered over to where his father pointed. "As far as I know, he mostly is," he said. "But Uncle Quark said he's been in a couple of times in the last few days. He was waiting for a Starfleet vessel to arrive, but after what happened, there've been a lot of changes in ship assignments."

"After all the bickering they used to do," Rom said, "they look like old friends."

Nog regarded Quark's relaxed pose, one elbow up on the bar and talking out of one side of his mouth to Odo. "Uncle always said that the constable loved him."

Nog and Rom entered the bar, leaving the nagal bodyguards and the Starfleet security officers to ensure their safety at a remove. As his father walked over toward Quark, Nog stopped at the table with his current and past crewmates. "Would it be all right if my father and I joined you?" he asked.

To a person, they all said yes.

Twenty-two

The trek through the caverns had never gone smoother or faster for Keev Anora. She hadn't needed to employ tools or explosives in any confined locations, as she'd expected to have to do; somehow, the ark containing the Tear of Destiny managed to clear each tight space, and even she seemed to move herself more easily through those same areas. In what felt like half the time it normally required, Keev reached the final stretch of the cave that would take her out the other side of the Merzang Mountains.

When she saw daylight up ahead, excitement overwhelmed her, and she began to run. The beam of her beacon swung wildly across the cave walls as she ran, its light becoming more and more difficult to discern as the tunnel grew brighter. She held the ark firmly in her arms, one side rapping against her chest as she dashed forward.

Keev exited the cave at a sprint, but then she stopped at once, nearly losing her balance and tumbling to the ground. She had not emerged on the road to Shavalla. Beneath clear blue skies, she saw no road, but a rolling, sun-bathed grassland. Trees of various shapes and sizes dotted the landscape, interspersed with low-lying foliage. Flowers of various hues lent color to the verdant setting.

Keev looked back at the entrance to the cave. She did

not see that either. Instead, she saw a coarse, rocky plain marching away from her, with sheer cliffs rising up on either side. Above, blue sky disappeared from view behind a roiling mass of unbroken gray clouds. Flashes of lightning illuminated the scene in staccato bursts.

Between the two dichotomous vistas, a wide chasm split the land, extending from one ridged rock face to the other. At its center, a series of columns rose at intervals between the two sides of the canyon, and support beams lay across them, while still more beams formed a deck. The structure bridged the wide gap and glowed from within, blue and white streamers of movement flowing through them.

Did I do that? Kira asked herself. *Did I* build *that?*

She didn't know, but a wisp of memory occurred to her, an image of herself carrying beams, setting them in place, scanning them, calibrating them. *But not across a chasm,* Kira thought. *Through a tunnel.*

She turned again, away from the canyon. She thought that she'd been carrying something, but her empty hands came together in the open air before her. Up ahead, though, she saw her destination, remembered striking out toward it when she'd been on the other side of the chasm.

An Orb of the Prophets.

The sparkling hourglass shape hovered just above the grass. It spun slowly in space, emitting an otherworldly green-white glow. *I have to go to it,* Kira thought. *I have to learn what it has to tell me.*

She started forward. As she drew nearer, she expected the ground to shatter, for brilliant white light to engulf her. None of that happened.

Finally, after a journey she didn't know if she could explain, Kira stood before the hallowed artifact. She waited for what would happen next, neither anxious nor fearful. She trusted in the Prophets.

Suddenly, the green radiance of the Orb reached out toward Kira. It swirled around her for an instant, then seemed to coalesce in the center of her body. The light flared a dazzling white.

And then she was gone.

Twenty-three

Lieutenant Commander Sarina Douglas read through the latest pass she'd made at the duty roster. Since she finally knew for sure that they'd begin the arrival process for Deep Space 9's ten thousand new residents in two days, she needed to firm up the assignments of security personnel. She and Blackmer had been working on putting it together over the prior week or so, but the assassination had changed everything.

Fortunately, things have calmed down, she thought, although she couldn't claim that things had returned to normal. Still, with each day that passed, members of the crew seemed to lose some of the glaze that appeared in just about everybody's eyes. *And it'll help even more if we can get the assassin off the station.*

The thought of Enkar Sirsy triggered Douglas to look up from where she sat at a desk in one of the offices in the stockade complex. A viewscreen on the bulkhead displayed an image of the assassin's cell. The first minister's red-haired chief of staff sat in the center of her bunk, her knees drawn up to her chest and her arms wrapped around her legs. She rocked forward and back, not much, just a few centimeters, but she kept moving. She'd begun doing that the day before, perhaps after her initial captivity had convinced her that she might never taste freedom again.

Earlier, Douglas had escorted Enkar's attorney in to see her after he'd arrived from Bajor—representation evidently arranged by Asarem Wadeen's office. Douglas respected the first minister, but her staunch defense of her chief of staff in the face of such overwhelming evidence bewildered the security officer. Such support seemed both unwarranted and politically dangerous.

The attorney—an older man with graying hair and a long face—had met with Enkar all morning. Later that afternoon, lawyer and client would stand before a Federation judge who had also arrived that day from Bajor. Douglas hoped that the arraignment would result in a change to Enkar's imprisonment, relocating her to a facility on Bajor or elsewhere in the Federation. After she had shot and killed President Bacco, her presence on Deep Space 9 felt like an open wound.

Douglas peered back down at the padd on which she worked, reading again through the names and assignments of the security staff. She had just discovered that she had accidentally detailed Crewman Ravid to consecutive shifts on the second day of the residential arrivals when a shrill whistle filled the air. The alarm differed from the starbase-wide red alert klaxon, signaling an emergency situation within the stockade complex. Through the open doorway of the office—none of the compartments within the stockade contained doors—she heard running footsteps: security personnel emerging from the other offices. Two officers—Cardok and Ansarg—had been charged that shift with keeping Enkar under constant surveillance. The stockade contained no other prisoners.

Douglas glanced at the viewscreen. Enkar Sirsy lay on the deck in the middle of her cell. Douglas tossed her padd onto the desk—it slid across it and clattered onto the deck—and bolted through the doorway.

She arrived outside Enkar's cell just behind Cardok and Ansarg. They all observed the accused assassin through the force field. Flat on her back on the deck, Enkar convulsed. Spittle ran from her mouth and down the side of her face.

"Phasers," Douglas told Cardok and Ansarg. "Stand back and give me cover." The security officers acknowledged their orders, drew their weapons, and fell back to the opposite side of the corridor. Douglas lay a fingertip flat on the panel set into the bulkhead beside the opening to the cell. After her fingerprint was scanned and recognized, she keyed in her security code. Finally, she lowered the force field, which automatically locked down the entire stockade complex.

Douglas pulled her own phaser, never more pleased that her weapon would fire only with her hand around the grip. She rushed inside the cell, alert for any sign of deception, any move to harm her or take her hostage. She saw none. Enkar's body continued to shake, seemingly out of control. Douglas dropped to her knees and looked into the prisoner's eyes; they appeared glassy and unfocused.

She immediately reached for her combadge, but then something else caught her attention. She bent low and examined a patch of skin near the nape of Enkar's neck. It glowed a bright red. Douglas realized that she could smell the grisly scent of burning flesh. She slammed her fingers onto her combadge, which chirruped in response.

"Douglas to Sector General," she said. "Emergency medical transport from the stockade."

"Sector General, Bashir," came Julian's immediate reply. *"I'm initiating security protocols."* Standard pro-

cedure in such a situation required that the transporter shield around the cell in the stockade be lowered, and then another erected around the emergency medical transporter compartment once beaming had been completed. Force fields would also be raised. *"Emergency transport on your order."*

"Two to beam in from my location," Douglas said. "Energize."

Blue-white motes of light danced in her eyes as the transporter effect enveloped her and Enkar.

As Nurse Krissten Richter administered the benzodiazepine he'd prescribed for Enkar, Bashir leaned in over the operating table. He studied the readings that projected above his patient's unconscious form, the seizures that had racked her body only seconds earlier easing. "I'm seeing trace amounts of diburnium and tricobalt," he told Richter and Nurse Juarez, who also stood by to assist. The doctor knew that even such small quantities of those transuranic elements were likely responsible for Enkar's condition.

Bashir edged up toward his patient's head. He focused on the ruddy patch of flesh that Sarina had pointed out, where a small section had charred black. The readings jumped dramatically and, for a Bajoran body, inexplicably. "Something's been implanted under her skin," he said. "Computer, visual scan of patient's neck, left posterior."

Within the run of medical data projecting above Enkar's body, a window opened displaying an image of the left rear part of her neck. As the scan pushed into her body, Bashir saw the normal structure interrupted by cauterized tissue. Below that, a foreign object appeared, a small square of material that did not belong.

Bashir turned to Juarez. "Laser scalpel," the doctor said.

Ro sat behind her desk, examining the image displayed on the large viewscreen hanging on the bulkhead across from her. She saw a magnified view of the object Doctor Bashir had surgically removed from Enkar Sirsy's neck. It looked like nothing more than a nondescript square of synthetic resin, but for one corner, which had been singed into a jagged edge.

"It has several purposes, both medical and technological," explained Lieutenant Commander John Candlewood, a computer specialist and the starbase's primary science officer. He sat with Doctor Bashir in the chairs in front of Ro's desk. Commander Blackmer and Lieutenant Commander Douglas stood off to the side. "For one thing," Candlewood said, "it produces a scrambling field to deflect sensors."

"It has its own cloaking device?" Ro said.

"Essentially, yes," said the science officer. "At least in terms of sensor scans. But it can also be used to prevent transport of the subject into which it's implanted."

"Which is why we couldn't beam Enkar out of the theater's control booth into the stockade," Blackmer noted.

"But you *did* transport her to the stockade," Ro said.

"After we removed her from the control booth," Blackmer said.

"The device is sophisticated enough to be programmable," Candlewood said. "I've managed to dump the instruction set. The device can be configured to disallow transport from a specific location."

"Can you tell if it was set up to prevent transport from the control booth?" Ro asked.

"Yes, because it contains a record of executed instructions," Candlewood said. "Once Enkar had been transported into the control booth, that triggered the transporter inhibitor for as long as she remained there."

"Meaning she had no easy avenue of escape," Ro said.

"If she even knew what was happening," Bashir said. "If she was even conscious."

"What?" Ro asked.

"In addition to preventing itself from being scanned and creating a transporter block," Candlewood explained, "the device can emit electromagnetic waves capable of inducing unconsciousness."

"Are you telling me . . . has Enkar been telling the truth?" Ro asked. "She really doesn't remember what happened?" The captain's mind swam with the implications. Had Enkar Sirsy been an unwilling dupe? According to Doctor Bashir, she remained unconscious in Sector General, her recovery from being poisoned likely but uncertain. Even if she survived, though, it seemed improbable that the first minister's chief of staff would or could provide any assistance with the investigation. If she had acted intentionally, she'd already demonstrated that she would not confess her crimes; if she had not acted of her own volition, then she hadn't even been aware of her role in the assassination.

"According to the device's memory, it emitted the electromagnetic waves twenty minutes prior to the start of the dedication," Candlewood said, "and stopped only just before Lieutenant Commander Blackmer entered the control booth."

"Meaning that she was probably unconscious at the time President Bacco was killed," Bashir said.

"But then how can she have committed the crime?"

Ro asked. "And how could the emission of the waves have been timed to stop so perfectly, when the length of the speeches through the ceremony would have been an unknown beforehand?" Even as Ro asked the question, though, she realized the answer.

"Somebody was with her," Blackmer said. "Somebody transported into the control booth with her, used her hands to fire the weapon in order to implicate her, shut down the waves keeping her unconscious, then transported out before I got there."

"We reexamined the readings of the power drains used to feed the portable transporter we found," Douglas said, stepping forward and setting a padd on Ro's desk. "We knew it provided more than enough power to beam Enkar into the control booth. Calculations show it was enough to perform three transports: two people into the booth, and one out."

"We wouldn't have known about any of this if the device hadn't malfunctioned," Candlewood said. "Some of the instruction set and memory were damaged, so I can't tell whether it was supposed to remain hidden but leaked, or whether a self-destruct process went awry."

Ro felt sick to her stomach. She had locked down Deep Space 9—had kept it locked down even in the face of opposition from the visiting heads of state—specifically to ensure that anybody involved in the assassination could not leave the starbase. All of a sudden, it seemed as though whoever had killed President Bacco was probably gone. *Unless*—

"Do we have any indication at all who might have done this?" Ro asked.

Candlewood and Bashir exchanged a knowing glance, as did Blackmer and Douglas. When the doctor looked back over at Ro, he said, "We do have some evidence. There is a microscopic quantity of cellular material— other than Enkar Sirsy's—on the device, an amount you'd expect from somebody handling it."

"Enough cellular material to identify the person who handled it?" Ro asked.

"Not the individual, no, but I can tell you the species," Bashir said. "It's Tzenkethi."

Epilogue

Adrift in Shadows

Captain Ro Laren peered down from the bluff that perched above Deep Space 9's extensive park. Her first officer, Cenn Desca, stood beside her. Above, stars shined down through the transparent bulkhead. Below, much of the crew had congregated across the green expanse, just as they had ten days earlier, when Ro had decided to celebrate the opening of the park and the impending dedication of the starbase.

They had never completed the dedication ceremony, and because of the assassination, DS9's transition to full operational status had occurred without any additional fanfare. In one more day, the influx of ten thousand civilian residents would begin. That meant Ro had only one last opportunity to readily assemble and address a large segment of her crew. Later, the presence of so many people aboard, as well as the arrival and departure of numerous ships, the processing of cargo, the maintenance and repair of Starfleet vessels, along with the implementation of other starbase functions, would render such gatherings problematic.

"Tomorrow, the real work of this starbase begins," Ro said, the words picked up by her communicator and transmitted through the park's audio system to those below. "Tomorrow, we will begin welcoming thousands of new residents, we will open our cargo hatches to freighters, we will open our repair bays to Starfleet vessels, we will open facilities like this park for the rest and recreation of crews throughout Starfleet and the rest of the sector. Tomorrow, Deep Space Nine will become busy, and it will never stop being busy.

"And yet this crew has already been through so much," Ro continued. "For those few of you who served on the original station, it has been two years of dealing with and overcoming disaster, while at the same time working toward the day we could all stand on a new Deep Space Nine. For all of us, we have experienced another disaster, one that will stay with us for some time to come. President Bacco's assassination marks a low point in Federation history. It is an event that wounds us collectively as a people, but it also impacts us on a personal, emotional level."

Ro did not address the possible involvement of the Tzenkethi in the assassination. She had communicated that information to Starfleet Command, and for the moment, at least, it had been designated as classified. Ro could only hope that it would not lead to confrontation and war with the Tzenkethi Coalition and their allies in the Typhon Pact.

"Over the course of the past five days, I have had to deal with my own grief," Ro went on. "It is a process, and I'm sure it will continue for the foreseeable future. But even as I deal with these difficult emotions, I keep asking myself questions: How do I move on from here? How do I go forward when I'm in so much pain? How do *we* go forward?"

Ro glanced at Cenn, acknowledging the words she would say that had originated with him. "I think there's only one answer, and that is simply to keep moving, to keep living. It might not always be easy, but that's what makes it even more vital never to stop, never to stay in place and allow the past to capture us in its unchanging reality. We don't need to ignore what's happened—nor could we—but the only thing we can change, the only thing we can shape, is our future.

"Yesterday was hard," Ro said, "but we can strive to make today better, and to improve tomorrow still more. In that spirit, in recognition of the past, in support of the present, and in hope for the future, I am dedicating this space—our beautiful, green, open space—as Nanietta Bacco Park."

The applause began at once—not a boisterous ovation, but steady clapping that seemed to convey the crew's approval. She turned to Cenn, who had brought his own hands together, and he nodded to her. The moment felt . . . if not good, then at least right.

Ro turned and headed down the slope toward the trees that hid the bulkhead surrounding the park. She and Cenn had made it halfway there when a collective gasp rose behind them. Ro turned toward the noise and immediately saw movement overhead, through the transparent bulkhead.

In a great whirling gyre of blue and white light, the Bajoran wormhole had spun open.

Ro's jaw dropped as she gazed upon the magnificent display. She marveled at the timing of the event. Never before had the wormhole seemed so vital to her, so important. Its reappearance felt as though it represented the hope for the future of which she'd just spoken.

Ro's combadge twittered. *"Slaine to Captain Ro,"* said the tactical officer. She had volunteered to miss the gathering in the park and crew her station in the Hub.

Ro tapped her combadge. "This is Ro. Go ahead."

"Captain, the wormhole has just opened," Slaine said.

"I can see that, Zivan," Ro said with a smile. "It looks beautiful."

"Captain," Slaine said, a note of urgency creeping into her voice, *"there's something emerging from it."*

Ro's smile evaporated. "A ship?"

"No, sir. It appears too small."

"Is there any danger to the starbase?" Ro asked, dreading the tactical officer's response.

"No, it doesn't seem so," Slaine said, at least allaying the captain's immediate concerns.

"Raise the shields," Ro said. "Call the entire senior staff to the Hub. I'm on my way there."

She and Cenn ran for the exit, and beyond it, the turbolift.

Ro stepped with Cenn out of the turbolift and into the Hub. She didn't head for her command chair but instead took the steps down into the Well, to the situation table. "What have we got?" she asked, peering over at Dalin Slaine. Ro saw that Blackmer had already arrived in the Hub, as had Chief O'Brien.

"Captain, I'm having trouble making sense of these scans," Slaine said. "I'm getting unusual energy readings, and . . . there seems to be a life-form aboard."

"I thought you said it wasn't a ship," Ro said. "Let's see it."

Slaine worked her console, and a three-dimensional image appeared above the sit table. Shaped like an hourglass, it glowed a strange green color. Ro recognized it at once as an Orb of the Prophets.

"Captain," O'Brien spoke up. "I know this. Once before,

when Captain Sisko first found the wormhole, he was in a runabout with the station's science officer, Jadzia Dax. The wormhole aliens used one of those—" He pointed to the holographic display above the sit table. "—to send her back to the station."

Ro knew immediately who the Orb carried—the only person it could be: Kira Nerys. She bounded up the steps and toward the doors that led to the Hub's transporter room. "Chief, Jeff, you're with me," she said.

The captain entered the small, four-pad transporter room at a jog. O'Brien and Blackmer followed behind her. "Jeff, draw your phaser, just in case," Ro said. "Chief, give me a level-one containment field and bring it aboard."

"Aye, sir," O'Brien said, moving to the freestanding control console. He quickly operated the panel, and a burst of blue around the perimeter of the transporter platform signaled the initiation of the containment field. "Lowering shields and locking on."

Bright white streaks formed in the air above one of the pads. Pinpoints of light joined the beams, until it all materialized into an object. Ro took a step forward, gazing at the Orb floating before her. "What—" she started to say, but then the compartment filled with a flash of white light. When it faded an instant later, green swirls circled a figure who had suddenly appeared in place of the Orb.

As the green light faded, Ro glanced over her shoulder at O'Brien. He looked back at her quizzically and shrugged. Ro turned back to the platform. "Who are you?" she asked.

"My name," the man said, "is Altek Dans."

Kira existed in a realm she could not characterize. Time did not seem to elapse—or perhaps it all elapsed at once:

past, present, and future blending together the way colors did, into a perfect white. She waited to discover what new path the Prophets had laid out for her. Somehow, she knew that she was leaving the Celestial Temple.

All of a sudden, a flash of white light surrounded her for an instant, then released her. She saw coils of green luminescence twisting around her, and then those too faded. She looked around. She seemed to be on a transporter platform of some sort, in what appeared to be a cargo bay. She didn't recognize—

Kira's gaze came to rest on a figure standing across the compartment from her. She blinked, thinking that she might have mistaken his identity, but when her eyelids rose, he still stood there—he stood there alive, even though he had died years earlier. *But it's him*, Kira thought. Not a double, not a mirror-universe version, not a reanimated corpse, not an illusion or phantasm of any kind. She knew it was him.

"Taran'atar," she said.

Acknowledgments

I always feel it most appropriate to begin by acknowledging the people without whom a particular novel would never even have existed. In the case of *Revelation and Dust,* that means Margaret Clark and Ed Schlesinger. Seeking to publish a *Star Trek* "event" in 2013, they approached me and several other writers with an idea for a five-book series that we would ultimately entitle *The Fall.* For the trust they demonstrated in me, for the opportunity they afforded me, and for their professionalism from beginning to end, I thank Margaret and Ed. I am fortunate indeed to have such skilled editors in my corner.

It has been a great boon—and quite humbling—to be included in a lineup that features exceptionally good writers: Una McCormack, David Mack, James Swallow, and Dayton Ward. The process of working with such fine novelists could not have been more satisfying. Each of them brought great creativity and ability to our project, and the works they have produced are of the highest caliber. They also all proved to be wonderful collaborators, selflessly doing everything they could to ensure that the details of our individual stories meshed to produce five single novels that, when taken together, form a cohesive, overarching story. I thank each of them.

I am also grateful for the cover art depicting the new

Deep Space 9. My entreaties to my editors that we should offer readers a visual rendering of the new starbase did not fall on deaf ears. On the contrary, they enlisted the efforts of Academy Award and Emmy Award winner Doug Drexler to create the cover art, and Doug in turn called upon fellow artists and modelers Andrew J. Probert and Douglas Graves to construct a digital version of the station. I am indebted to all three men for their head-turning efforts.

As is sometimes the case when penning a *Star Trek* work, I found myself reaching for details of the literary *Trek* universe not quite at my fingertips. On several occasions, I turned to Keith R. A. DeCandido with questions, and he graciously provided me the answers I needed. Thanks, Keith.

On a personal level, thanks to Kirsten Beyer and her wonderful family for their friendship. Well known to *Star Trek* readers for her popular *Voyager* novels, Kirsten is a talented writer and a good friend. I've enjoyed our many conversations over lunch—sharing stories and perspectives on the whole process of committing a *Trek* novel to paper—as well as our family dinners.

Over the course of the past year, I have been privileged to witness the inspiring journey taken by Lauren Ragan. Showing determination, courage, compassion, strength, and growth, all in remarkable measure, she provides a stirring example of what it means to take charge of your life. It has been a pleasure to spend time with Lauren; her son, Haydon Bartels; and her parents, Diane Ragan and David Ragan.

Meanwhile, Colleen Ragan continues to be a compelling figure in my world. Bright, warm, funny, and loving, she is a force of nature. Colleen considers herself the

Qveen of All She Surveys, and I count myself as one of her fortunate subjects.

Patriarch of the clan, Walter Ragan also plays an important role in my life. A good man and a good friend, he always leads by example. I could not ask for a more honest, loving, and supportive father figure.

Thanks as well to Anita Smith, a stalwart supporter year after year. Kind, hardworking but quick to joke and laugh, and so loving, she has for decades been half of one of the most inspiring couples I have ever known. We have enjoyed many adventures together, and I look forward to many more.

I also want to thank Jennifer George, my sister, who each and every day makes me the proudest of brothers. "CJ" has accomplished so much in so many different ways: academically, professionally, athletically, artistically, and personally. My little sister has grown into a woman easy to love and admire.

I am likewise grateful to have Patricia Walenista in my life—and for more reasons than the simple fact of my existence. She has given me so much through the years—some of it by example, some of it by intention, some of it directly. She has helped me lead the happy life that I do. I could not have done any of it without her.

Finally, thanks to Karen Ragan-George, a constant source of laughter and joy, of honor and love. She is bright enough to be the sun in my days, and inspiring enough to be the stars in my night. If I owe the universe anything at all, it is for the rhythms of existence that first brought Karen into my life; after that, I owe everything to Karen herself.

About the Author

You have reached the end of *Revelation and Dust,* but David R. George III will be back . . . in the lost era!

You can contact David at facebook.com/DRGIII, and you can follow him on Twitter @DavidRGeorgeIII.